In the House of My Pilgrimage

CROSSWAY BOOKS BY JULIA SHUKEN

Day of the East Wind
In the House of My Pilgrimage

In the House of My Pilgrimage

Julia Shuken

CROSSWAY BOOKS • WHEATON, ILLINOIS
A DIVISION OF GOOD NEWS PUBLISHERS

In the House of My Pilgrimage

Copyright © 1995 by Julia Shuken

Published by Crossway Books
　　　　　a division of Good News Publishers
　　　　　1300 Crescent Street
　　　　　Wheaton, Illinois　60187

Editor: Lila Bishop

Cover illustration: Chris Ellison

Art Direction/Design: Mark Schramm

First printing 1995

Printed in the United States of America

Scripture references are taken from the *New King James Version* copyright © 1982, Thomas Nelson, Inc., Publishers and from the *New American Standard Bible* © 1960, 1962, 1963, 1968, 1971, 1972, 1973, 1975, 1977, by The Lockman Foundation. Used by permission.

Excerpts from Molokan songs were taken from *The Molokan Heritage Collection: "Origins of Molokan Singing,"* volume 4, by Linda Rothe-O'Brien. © 1989 Highgate Road Social Science Research Station, Inc., Berkeley, CA. Used by permission.

With the exception of recognized historical figures, the characters are fictional, and any resemblance to actual persons, living or dead, is purely coincidental.

Library of Congress Cataloging-in-Publication Data
Shuken, Julia.
　　In the house of my pilgrimage / Julia Shuken.
　　　　p.　　cm.
　　　1. Russian Americans—California—History—Fiction.
2. Molokans—California—History—Fiction.　I. Title.
PS3569.H764I5 1995　　　813'.54—dc20　　　　　　94-43703
ISBN 0-89107-839-8

03		02		01		00		99		98		97		96		95
15	14	13	12	11	10	9	8	7	6	5	4	3	2	1

To my parents,
John and Julia Carey,
whose sheltering love
has been a "house of pilgrimage"
for me and for many others

Thy statutes
have been my songs
in the house of my pilgrimage.

PSALM 119:54

Contents

I

The House of Pilgrimage

Fenya traced the chiseled designs on the birchwood box with cherishing fingers. Tonight she would open it, and her life would be changed forever. The carved border captured twining birch leaves, sunflowers with gridded centers, and fan-tailed birds in a prancing geometry. These same designs garnished post and lintel of the thatched *izba* she had shared with her family in Russia. She thought of her father's skilled hand shaping the minute designs that precisely duplicated the carved borders of their three front windows. And the dear ones behind those windows—what of them? Where were they now? How were they? Especially now. Especially after what had happened to Natasha. Her mind sprang back from the thought. *No! I will not think about Natasha! Not tonight.*

"Let me see you!" Aksinia Bogdanoff's full figure blocked the doorway, and the toasted, fruity aroma of freshly baked *nachinki* wafted in with her. Her glossy red and black dress was restrained by a white apron, but nothing could restrain the merriment in her brown eyes. "A beauty!" she pronounced. "Your betrothed will raise his hands in praise when he sees you!"

Fenya lifted her face, smiling as her friend ladled out comfort like hot soup.

"This is how we'll do it," Aksinia began. "Ivan and I will act as your parents; Ilya and Elena Valoff will stand for Piotr. And Ilya has asked a young couple who just arrived from Semyonovka to act as matchmakers. Although, of course, the match has already been made! You'll see. It'll be so much like the old ways that you won't remember you're in Los Angeles! And Bunya will offer prayers, too," she added as the old granny stumbled in with her short, uncertain steps. Bunya's cloudy eyes were steadfast, as though her frail body were being pulled along by that sure expression rather than by her faltering limbs.

"Everyone is acting like someone else, almost like a play," Fenya ventured, fighting the homesickness that welled up in her.

"It's no play, dearie," Bunya assured her. "God has chosen to give you over to love."

"She'll not be single long—that's what I told myself when I first saw you at Natasha's betrothal," Aksinia said. "I was right! Now you're to be a bride."

Natasha! Please don't remind me, Fenya begged silently. *Natasha—broken, cast aside, all this last winter sleeping beneath the snow.* Fenya ached with the thought of it. *I cannot put it away from me. How can I bring anyone joy—especially Piotr who must have joy?*

Bunya stooped toward the window. "They're here!"

Fenya caught a glimpse of Piotr, tall and broad-shouldered in a starched *kosovorotka*, striding between old Ilya Valoff and his wife. Then a young man she didn't recognize mounted the steps, snatching a sheepskin cap from his curly head and crushing it in his fingers. A willowy young woman followed him to the porch. *This must be the couple from Semyonovka,* Fenya surmised. Piotr's kinsman Maxim Merlukov and his stately wife, Lukeria, were next, and, last of all, the huge, bearlike form of a young Molokan friend, Gerassim. As was fitting, Fenya stayed in the bedroom, but her heart somersaulted between gladness and pain. The proceedings were brisk and businesslike, half the voices strange to her. *Like a play—everyone with their part.* She missed her father's diffident voice, her mother's stern words and caressing eyes. She smoothed out her skirt. It was the blue and yellow print she had worn to her sister Natasha's wedding.

"*Kladka.*" The bride price. An unfamiliar voice had spoken the word. She was overwhelmed by a feeling of unworthiness. She knew that Piotr had wrested this American money from harsh circumstances, hoping to rescue his family in Russia. But the Voloshins had been crushed in the chaos of revolution, and Piotr's labor would be given to the Bogdanoffs as bride price for Fenya.

They'll call me any minute. She clutched the wooden box adorned with her father's artistry. She shook her head so that her braid fell straight down to her hips. It was so fair that it looked almost white next to the butter yellow in her skirt.

"Fenya," Aksinia called.

Fenya stepped into the crowded room with its electric light beaming on an embroidered tablecloth. When she looked up, all she could see was Piotr's eyes. *No one has eyes like him.* The hardness that life had brought him had sent the harsh planes slanting down from his high cheekbones. The straight, firm mouth clamped down on all that was unspoken. But she knew what the wide-set eyes were saying. *Dushok, my love, my little one.*

"Ah, look! We've kept her waiting too long; she's half-asleep!"

Piotr started and handed a sack of dollars to Aksinia, who in turn gave it to Fenya. Fenya bowed low to her betrothed, weighing the bride price in her hand. She raised her eyes to Piotr's—*I know what this cost you*—and gave the money back to Aksinia, repaying her, as agreed, for the price of Fenya's passage to America.

Granny Bogdanoff chuckled softly to herself. Then Fenya opened her carved box and drew out a long silk scarf. Piotr bowed, and she slipped the scarf over his neck, her fingers lingering on the colors as they awoke to the glow of the electric light.

The moment drew out on Aksinia's sigh.

"Well, dear ones, the promise is given, the hope lies before you! Come and partake with us. We'll feast the betrothed!"

The meat-filled pastries, lamb, and *lapsha* could have graced any table in Russia, but some of the traditions had slipped away. The matchmakers made no mention of *pridanoe*, the dowry—completely impossible in Fenya's case—and the conversation veered away from the young couple's new life together. *No one, including us, knows what it will be like!* But there was no shortage of talk.

With Easter just past, the Molokans were recounting how their various employers had responded when the Russians had left their jobs to observe Passover week with the traditional daily services. Fenya noticed that the new couple from Semyonovka listened closely. The young man, Makar, was thick-set with an open face and brown curly hair. His wife, Hanya, stretched out her long neck like a hunting swan, her mild eyes blinking as she scooped up each fact about her new home.

"They fired Gerassim on the spot," Ilya Valoff reported, "but what do you think? As soon as the week was out, they hired him right back! But Gerassim's a bear." They all looked at the huge young man as if to verify this. "They can load him up like a freight train and watch him run. At a lumberyard a man like that is worth ten! A good worker is honored even in king's palaces."

Another man, an elder from Delizan, was less sure. "Plenty of the brethren are out of work. It's a persecution just like in Mother Russia. We play by their rules, or we lose everything."

"No, no. Not all are that way," Ilya objected. "Where I work, at the sack factory, a few of us took the week off. We turned deaf ears to the boss's complaints. 'God's ways come first with us,' we told him! 'You'll see what the consequences are,' he said. He was pretty hot! But later a couple of Molokans came up to him and said, 'Well, your honor, we didn't take time off. We put your interests first, so how about a promotion?' Well, the owner turned out to be a Jew. Instead of laying off the churchgoing Molokans, he fired the others. 'If you weren't faithful to your God, why would I think you'd be faithful to me just for a dollar?' That's what he said! So the faithful brethren are still stitching burlap; the others are looking for work."

"We're used to hard work," Makar put in. "But here each man works for himself, his family—not for the tsars and masters."

"There are always masters," Piotr put in quietly. "In America a man's time and muscle are a—a commodity—to be sold like wheat."

"Ah, but at least we get the price of it, right?"

Ilya glanced at the young man's eager face and thoughtfully smeared *smetana* on a crusty *piroshka*. "God provides for each according to his need," he said, and his blunt features seemed to retreat into the snow-bright fluff of his beard.

"We're new here—only a week," Makar said. "Paradise, we were told! Flowering plants all year around, hardly any winter. Work for every man who wants it."

"That's all true," Gerassim said with his bitter smile. "You'll see how true it is! You'll see how sweet our place of refuge is! You start work with us next week, don't you?"

"That's so."

"Well, you'll find out soon enough. Piotr can tell you. How's paradise now that you've forsaken the land and taken up hard labor, Piotr? I thought you'd be plowing the whole of Montebello into bean fields for your rich cousin. But you'll find it's easier for the plowman than for the horse. In the lumberyards they work us like animals . . ."

Piotr shook his head ruefully. "I keep wadding cotton and all sorts of stuff under my shirt, but still my shoulders are so cut up that a shrug sends the blood flowing down my back."

"It gets easier. You'll get used to it. Your shoulders will scar over and toughen up. I've lost enough skin to make a pair of gloves. But it won't be a pretty sight for your young bride." Gerassim's voice grew agitated, and his clear eyes blinked with childlike yearning.

"So," Ilya said turning to Maxim, "you're to lose Piotr's labor!"

Maxim flushed with anger. "He's not a medal. I don't need him round my neck."

Piotr glanced up quickly, but Ilya was unperturbed. "His duty is to his wife-to-be now. It's not easy making a life in the city."

"It didn't take him long to forget the groans of those he left behind," Maxim cut in. "His parents and sisters Nadya and Dausha—the little one only five years old—yet he's left them to the mercy of terrorists and killers—"

"We all know what's been happening in Russia. No need to remind us." The affable old man was getting angry. "We feel every blow that falls on the brethren, but what can we do? They are there; we're here. If you're so concerned, you can give to help bring some families over. But we can't bring those we can't find. . . ."

"A fool can see that." Maxim shrugged.

"The devil's clever, but God doesn't love him."

Fenya looked at Aksinia helplessly. Maxim's words lodged in her heart like a heavy stone; Piotr was bent over the steaming plate, fighting whatever Maxim had stirred up.

Aksinia gave her husband Ivan a pointed look, and he cleared his throat uneasily. "Let's forget the day of sorrow, as the song says, and be glad for our brother who has found a wife."

"God be praised," Aksinia added. "Such a worker! We would have been lost without her—all those weeks on the boat and here with the children. And she's found work in the city, too. She'll be a helpmeet for any man."

"Work?" Piotr swallowed his surprise.

"I didn't know myself until today," Fenya explained. "Phoebe Wentworth found me a job. I'll be working for her family—in Hollywood."

"Hollywood." Piotr savored the word. "It has a nice sound to it. What will you do?"

"I'm to be a woman. Phoebe says they need a woman to come in three times a week. Washing, scrubbing, ironing. Easy work!"

"So you're to be a maidservant. Not bad." Fenya could see that Piotr was pleased. Safe indoor work was considered a real boon.

"Who is this Phoebe?" Lukeria Merlukov asked suspiciously.

"She's the kindergarten teacher, and she goes about helping different people in the city—Russians, Mexicans, Chinese—"

"An almsgiver. We don't need the help of a pork-eating American."

"We do," Aksinia said firmly. "This Phoebe is a good woman. Just like a *zemstvo* worker."

"I know all about *zemstvo* teachers." Lukeria was bored and fixed Fenya with a superior look, but Fenya didn't care. Piotr wore a proud and hopeful expression, and that was all that mattered. *Besides*, Fenya thought, nash or nynash, *Phoebe Wentworth is worth two of Lukeria Merlukov.*

"Stop your women's prattling," Ivan sputtered. "We aren't here to gab about scrubbing and ironing."

"That's right," cried Makar. "Enough talking. We came here to rejoice!" He threw back his head, and song began pouring out of him:

> "*Whither do you fly, little cloud, on the wings of the wind,*
> *Over the earth—or do you carry a sign of love*
> *To water the land of Paradise?*'"

Fenya saw that Hanya had taken up the song with a voice so strong and lovely that it seemed to be shaped by her beautiful white neck. Piotr's tenor joined in:

> "'. . . I have the dew of nature
> You have given the dew from heaven, and I have water
> Taken from water.
> The wind in the air has
> Carried me from the sea and the holy mountain. . . .'"

Fenya let herself be caught up in the song; a teeming gladness swelled and broke within her. *We are sojourners.* She leaned toward Piotr, her shoulder fast against his shoulder, her voice twined with his voice. *We are sojourners but not alone.* "'Whither do you fly, little cloud . . . ,'" she sang.

It was Saturday, but the Utah Street schoolyard was whirling with colorful circles of children—Russian and American and Mexican. Fenya saw that Phoebe Wentworth was already there, her glance wavering between the children and the street. She sprang forward impetuously as soon as she caught sight of Fenya, waving at her with one of the notebooks she seemed always to have in hand.

Fenya guessed that Phoebe was a slim, strong girl, although the odd bunchiness of her clothes made it hard to tell. Peculiar gatherings and tuckings in her white blouse as well as the frilled jabot camouflaged her figure. The contrast between the rather coarse stuff of her clothing and her fresh, scrubbed complexion gave her the look of something silky and beautiful about to burst from a crusted pod or cocoon. Her hat was set at its usual careless angle, and her cotton slip showed above brown boots that, Fenya noted, were suited to walking, unlike the heeled, pointed kind so often seen on the streets.

But in spite of her steadfast friendliness, there was something flickering about Phoebe Wentworth. Her smile would beam out, then get caught on some fleeting hesitation and fade. Her warm friendliness was the same; she'd get tangled in her own easy, affectionate ways and then become suddenly awkward and shy. She had beautiful hazel eyes, but their light was snatched away by occasional blank reflections from her spectacles.

"Hello," she called out. "Guess what! We've got a ride out to the house! We just have to walk over to Hamburger's Department Store. My sister will meet us there with a buggy."

"Buggy?"

"Carriage? No. Cart?" Phoebe supplied, searching Fenya's face for recognition and straightening her hat as she tripped over the curb.

"Cart."

"At any rate, we'll ride. That way you can meet the family one at a time. It'll be easier that way."

But it wasn't easier. The shopping district was crammed with horses and carriages that looked a little like *droshkys* but were apparently called buggies. The sidewalks thronged with people. As they approached Hamburger's Department Store, the crowd grew thick and tense. White placards bearing angry black letters tossed above heads. *A demonstration.* Fenya had never seen one, but hadn't Piotr told her about mobs, strikes, and violence in Tiflis, in Baku? Fear seized her. Phoebe plunged into the chaos and then briefly reappeared to grab her arm.

"What a nuisance! Now how are we going to find Cory?"

"What is it?"

"A nuisance!" Phoebe grumbled. Fenya looked at her searchingly. Then the American girl caught her hand with one of her quick gestures. "You're afraid! No. No. It's not like that, Fenya. I keep forgetting—forgetting what it must have been like for you. Don't worry. It's not like that here, really. It's not. Just hold on to me."

Fenya grabbed a handful of leg-o-mutton sleeve, and they threaded through the crowd. Men waved workers' caps and dented derbies as they clamored and hissed at a speaker who tried to conjure them with waving arms. Policemen in long, fitted coats and bobbies' caps wielded billy clubs at the store entrance. But it was only for show, Fenya could tell. A Mexican sold tamales from a cart, and an occasional demonstrator would forget his rage long enough to refuel it with a spicy mouthful. She noticed that many in the crowd wore shiny round brooches printed with slogans. Some had tiny flasks of clear liquid attached. White placards flashed, the shop windows glared, the little flasks twinkled in the sun.

Something was trying to break through. Fenya clenched her fists, trying to hold it down—to keep it from slitting her defenses and forcing her to think the unthinkable. *I have a secret life,* she realized. What was written there left a dark underside to everything she did. She still could not grasp what had happened to her sister. When the thought of Natasha's defilement—her ugly death—intruded, Fenya fought it back with revulsion.

She bowed before the surge of rage, and suddenly Russia's agony rose before her. She saw her lovely sister Natasha breaking under the weight of it. Many waters rose, glassy and threatening—then a voice like the waters, "You who number my wanderings; will You not put my tears in Your bottle?" The infinite tide turned finite, something that could be contained by the greater—tears counted out like pearls.

"What a nuisance," Phoebe repeated. "Oh, there's Cory! Right at the entrance—wouldn't you know it."

The young woman near the revolving glass doors was cool, poised, and porcelain-smooth, the black braiding on her fitted blue suit outlining a perfect Gibson-girl figure. Her skirt swayed slightly in the breeze from the revolving glass doors, but she was otherwise unruffled. Her hat brim was tilted to reveal a pale gold puff of hair and a fair complexion.

As Fenya and Phoebe squeezed though an opening in the mob, a blond young man shouldered in front of them and began berating the cool beauty. "My brother Charlie," Phoebe explained to Fenya.

"What kind of an idiot are you?" he muttered to Cory. "What a day to go shopping! I told you we were boycotting."

"I'm not."

"Fine. But couldn't you pick some other time? You stroll out into the middle of a demonstration with your hands full of merchandise bought from these bloodsuckers. Don't you realize this could get rather ugly?"

"Ugly?" she asked and raised her eyebrows questioningly. "There's a cotillion tonight, and I needed gloves. The world doesn't revolve around you and your socialist schemes."

Her eyes had lighted on Phoebe. "You see, Phoebe, he's on his high horse again." Her gaze traveled downward. "Your slip is show-ing." While Phoebe blushed and squirmed until the dusty edging of white below her skirt disappeared, Cory took in Fenya. "So this is our new cleaning woman."

Fenya met the girl's stare unflinchingly, standing straight in her best printed cotton. Her patent leather shoes were dusty from the walk, but her kerchief was crisp with starch. She supposed she looked good enough to scrub floors.

"So this is the Russian girl." Charlie Wentworth forgot his sister and studied Fenya. "The great test case of history. Russia—"

"Forget it, Charlie. She's no socialist—otherwise she wouldn't be here. She'd be back in Russia making history," Phoebe intervened.

"Gorky's here. In New York."

"Yes. Making history. And money. The stuff of revolution!"

Charlie laughed good-naturedly. "Of course. There are always those practical needs—as our good sister Cory can tell us." He made a sudden snatch at Cory's shopping bag. She squealed, and a policeman materialized.

"He botherin' you, miss?"

"Yes. He tried to take this."

"You come along, sir."

"Wait!" Phoebe tried to push between Charlie and his captor. "He's our brother!"

"He your brother, miss?"

"No." Cory presented her perfect profile.

Charlie caught the man's quizzical look. "That's right," he said. "She's not my sister. Let's go."

Cory shrugged as they stepped into the carriage. "They'll book him and let him go."

"Let's just wait and see what happens."

"No. I need to get back. Who knows how long they'll keep him."

Phoebe gave an exasperated pull to the reins. "You two!"

But as far as Fenya could tell, this arrest was not the disaster it would have been in Russia.

"Why," she asked suddenly, "do the people wear . . . water?"

Phoebe's initial bafflement eased into a warm smile. "Water! I see. Look, you see these buttons? They say, 'I'm for Owens River Water.' It means that they want the city to build a channel to bring water from far in the north."

"The people want to farm?"

"Well, yes. To farm and to build the city bigger. So more people can come here."

Fenya glanced around. "There are enough now. *Da?*"

"Land will go way up," Cory cut in. "Papa's investment in the San Fernando Valley will be worth a fortune."

But Fenya was thinking of the land going up—swelling into the San Gabriel Mountains that loomed blue on the horizon as the carriage left the city and passed into tree-lined suburbs.

The Wentworth house was much like a home of the gentry in Russia. A long, white-columned porch shaded a glossy white door with brass fittings. The gravel path to the carriage house was lined with slender trees displaying waxy white flowers; the back garden area was neatly broken into sections of roses, dahlias, and lawn.

"Evangeline, our cook, isn't here right now. You'll meet her tomorrow," Phoebe explained as they walked through the big kitchen into a utility room. "Here's where we do laundry. There's the ironing board and the mangle. Now this way. These floors here are polished every day, and all the parlor furniture is dusted."

They crossed the parquet floors into a room filled with plush tapestry and gleaming mahogany tables. Beaded lamps sought out the furtive blues and maroons in a carpet very much like the ones the Armenians sold in Russia. Every table and chest was covered with items of china and brass and silver—just like a shop. Cory settled into one of the upholstered chairs. Phoebe shrugged.

"Dusting won't be easy in here," she began. "So much clutter."

"Not everyone can live like a nun," Cory said defensively.

The older girl ignored her. Fenya noticed that behind the flashing lenses, Phoebe's eyes were tired. Fenya looked around her curiously, wondering what was so hard. *Dusting* she understood. When speaking of baked goods, it meant sprinkling flour on. When speaking of furniture, it meant cleaning the dirt off.

Another surprise waited for her at the top of the curving stairway. "This is Charlie's room. This one is Cory's."

First door to the left—Charlie; second to the left—Cory, Fenya instructed herself. Cory's room was ruffled and airy with lace and pastel florals and lovely linens. *Lots of ironing.*

"And your room?" Fenya had already determined that Phoebe's room would get special attention.

"Oh, I don't live here." She smiled at Fenya's expression, and Fenya quickly grasped that there was no shame in it. "I live in the city. In the inner city. Mary Julia Workman thinks it's better that way. Easier to help those who need it."

"Like us."

"Well, you're helping *us* now! At any rate, I'll show you my room in the city sometime. It's not pretty like this. More austere—and cramped. I'm an austere sort of person. And cramped, too, I suppose," she added in an undertone.

When they went downstairs, Charlie Wentworth and another young man were grouped around the piano with Cory. Charlie's long fingers stroked a bright clatter of notes from the ivory keys, his gold hair curling on either side of his high forehead. The other American was fair-skinned and black-haired with the dark blue, heavily lashed eyes of an Irishman. The music scattered fascination around the room, and Cory sang out a few bars in a weak, pretty voice. Fenya could not quite catch the words—something about love. Phoebe looked more tired than ever. The brisk, nervous tune stayed with Fenya, popping up in her mind as she cleaned and ironed. It didn't make her think of love but of the cluttered rooms, Cory's precise features and vague words, and Phoebe Wentworth's weary eyes.

Later she explained it all to Aksinia and Bunya. "Strange music will snatch away your soul," Bunya declared.

"No, Maminka, her soul is stitched fast to her body. The piano is a toy for the gentry, that's all," Aksinia assured her.

"Ah, but these foreign janglings will stay in your mind like little imps. You'll see how hard it is to get rid of them!"

The old lady is full of odd ideas, Fenya thought, but it was true that the American tunes kept burbling up in her like a spicy aftertaste.

"You'll see what will come of it. You see how this young man is full of Satan's promptings. Take from this one—give to that one. God knows what He's doing. He knows who should be rich and who poor. These socialists are wolves pretending to be sheep! It will lead to killing—as it has in Russia. And, besides, it's a sin for a young woman to live away from her family before she marries."

"But I live away from my family," Fenya put in.

"Yes, dearie, but God called you to refuge—you had no choice. And you had your father's permission."

"We're your family now." Aksinia wrapped Fenya in one of her huge, soft hugs, but Fenya wasn't ready to give up yet.

"Phoebe thinks that God has called her to the city to do a work."

"Good. She can work in the city when the work in her family is done."

"I don't think her family believes in her work."

"That's what I'm saying, dearie. They don't believe. That's the trouble." The old lady creaked to a wavering stance, shaking out her apron as though the crumbs were pestering bugs.

Aksinia sighed. "It's all so complicated! Like a web of lace made by a blind woman. Who can untangle it?"

Bunya's milky gaze drifted over her. Then she began telling a story—completely unrelated as far as Fenya could tell. Aksinia's two-year-old twins, ever alert, toddled over.

"It's about a fowler and some birds," Bunya told them, and they tugged at her until she sat down again. "The hunter netted a great many birds of different kinds—all at one time in one net. But the birds were so large and strong that they lifted the net and flew off with it. The hunter had begun to chase it when a peasant saw him.

"'What are you doing? Do you think you can catch those birds on foot?'

"'If there were only one bird in the net, I couldn't,' said the fowler, 'but these I'll catch!'

"When evening came, all the birds began to pull in different directions, each flying for its own nest—one toward the forest, another toward the field, a third toward the meadowlands. Before long they all fell to earth in the net, and the fowler snatched them up!

"So, dearie, that's your Wentworths. That's your Americans!"

Fenya shook her head. "But who's the fowler?"

"That's it!" The old bunya nodded. "Who's the fowler?"

PIOTR HAD DETERMINED that when he and Fenya began their new life together, it would be in their own place. Many Molokans lived with three or even four families in a house. *Not for us—it's difficult enough as it is*, he thought.

As soon as he collected his first week's wages, he made a thorough search of all the cheap housing in Los Angeles's eighth ward. But even a small apartment cost more than he could scrape together. The landlady of a tiny candy box of a place couldn't repress her smile when he told her what he could afford. The back of his neck had prickled with shame. As a last resort, he strolled over to the railroad tracks that lined the river. Wooden workmen's shacks cluttered the alleyway like crates flung from the retreating flat cars of the Southern Pacific.

Piotr narrowed his eyes speculatively. It was hard to imagine Fenya here—a girl shaped for field and forest. But then he remembered how impossible it was for them. Every time he saw her at Ivan and Aksinia Bogdanoffs', she was surrounded by people—babies, old ladies, young wives. They never had a moment alone. It was hard on their youthful longings but good for their English. They had taken to speaking the foreigner's tongue. Most of the older Russians knew only a few words, certainly not enough to catch what two sweethearts said to each other.

The young wives always seemed to be there, dispensing coy smiles and sly nudgings whenever he came looking for his betrothed. He burned with the thought of it and resolutely approached the fat landlord with his swag of a belly. The man thrust a thumb into his suspenders and pulled himself up the steps of a clap-trap structure. *I've seen rough wood bathhouses put together with more care,* Piotr thought. The steps screeched like a crone as he followed the landlord into a pair of tiny, dim rooms. Slits of light from gaps in the joinery gave almost as much light as the grease-filmed window. Piotr had seen plenty of Russian *izbas* just as small and just as dirty. But the whole flimsy, temporary nature of the thing seemed peculiarly American. *What a hurry they're in, these folk! It's as though they don't need a lodging for the present because they're already lunging toward the future.* Both space and time moved very fast in 1906 Los Angeles.

The landlord jerked a thumb toward the privy. Then he went to the kitchen sink and yanked at the faucet. Piotr started as it knocked and howled before spitting out a rust-flecked spume of water.

"Eight dollars a week," yelled his host, slapping his hand to indicate money.

"I understand."

"How much you got?"

"I can pay six."

"Naw. Sorry, sonny. I can get eight bucks for this place."

Piotr's heart sank. This staggering collection of sticks was his last hope!

"My wife can earn something," he offered.

"You married?" The American stared in surprise.

"Will be next month."

"Oh, yeah?"

"Yeah indeed, God willing."

"I'm sure He won't mind." The pudgy features smoothed over indulgently, then contracted into a frown. "But this ain't no place to bring a lady."

"Oh, Fenya's no lady."

"What! We'll have none of that!"

"What are you saying? My wife—my betrothed—she's a good peasant girl, a good worker."

"A peasant, a good worker, eh? Sounds romantic. Well, sonny, bring her along. You pay your six dollars, and maybe the little lady can put in a few bits. And you can go ahead and move in anytime. You can see it's deserted."

Piotr counted out the bills, and the American took them with a delicate flick of his fat fingers; then he grabbed Piotr's right hand and began pumping it up and down. But Piotr's shoulder was still gouged and bleeding from his first week's work hauling lumber. He winced and bent over in pain.

"No need to bow. I'm no Chinee! Come on, sonny, put some muscle into it. We got a deal."

All the loose boards of Piotr's new slap-dash home broke into applause as the 4:05 Saturday freight clattered in.

PIOTR SHOOK OFF HIS DREAMS and twisted his head toward the window, which was trembling violently with the rumble of a train. For a startled minute, he thought it was covered with hoarfrost—but, no, it was just soot against the fog coming up from the river. He got up and looked out. Steel rasped steel mercilessly; blind windows winked in an endless procession. The sudden estranged moan seemed to escape from his own lungs. A man-shaped shadow crossed the alleyway, and with it a subtle malevolence seemed to rise from the earth. It told him that everything that had come to him in his dreams was true, had happened just so, and that his own journey was bound to end in the same chaos and bloodshed. Those who were not forgotten came to him at night and reminded him of all that he had escaped.

The train gathered speed and hurled itself into the darkness. Flying cinders and grinding wheels spun out his memories of another time, another train. Russia! Black and white. Snow and branches and flying rooks and the drab troop train rattling away from strife-torn Baku to a sleepy village about to blink and stir and awake to a living nightmare. Peasants, the frail and the vigorous, married and gave in marriage, rejoiced at birthings, wept as the beloved slipped from life into the black earth. The Molokans. And there was a song for every tear, for every laugh. How he remembered the singing! Voices, old and young, holding history at bay. For a time.

Piotr dressed quickly and went out. The street lamps faded, and the sky turned the color of a bruise. The porch stoop squawked. *You don't belong here.* The shack had no stove and no hot water, so he walked down to Joe's Cafe where the black proprietor sold strong coffee and rolls. The man's shiny face cracked into his usual welcoming grin. The roll was tasty, and the coffee and warm smile made Piotr feel better.

The Molokans had never seen black men before and called them Arabs. Ilya Valoff said that they had the reputation of running the best small restaurants in Los Angeles: "And only fifty years ago, the Arabee were the property of other men—just like us before the Freedom!" Ilya took this as a sign of hope.

Piotr made his way to the corner streetcar stop. The car stopped at Utah Street, but the conductor always hollered "Whiskers Boulevard" and snickered at the long-bearded Molokans en route to their jobs in San Pedro. By the time Piotr reached the harbor lumberyard, he learned that the earth had shifted during the night. Los Angeles had trembled mildly, but San Francisco had heaved with violent shakings and then burst into apocalyptic flames.

In the lumberyard the Molokans huddled in a group digesting these new catastrophes until the whistle blew. Piotr hefted a beam and straightened to follow the man in front of him. Sawdust and wood chips of cedar, redwood, and pine scented the damp morning. Ships from the north brought in the stacks of beams, posts, and planks that would build the city of the south. Piotr bent under his load, flexing his torso and arms to alleviate the pressure on his flayed shoulder. He heaved the beam onto a pile and turned, squeezing his eyelids against the dust. When he opened them, Makar Kashergan was standing there, looking around with his eager, childlike eyes.

"Look at this," he said. "Where's it all from?"

"Forests. To the north. Oregon, Washington, even Canada."

"Ah, forests! Do you know how long it's been since I've seen a forest?"

Piotr saw that the foreman was eyeing them suspiciously, but

Makar began waving his arms. "Forests are the gardens of God! They're not planted by man's doing but by the wind—God's holy breath!"

"Better load up," Piotr warned him. "The boss'll catch us."

Makar's expressive face clouded, and he quickly pounced on a strapped bundle of planks.

"Better go easy at first. You'll feel that at the end of the day!"

Makar only showed his teeth in a smile, and Piotr shook his head.

The sun came out, bright and hot, and began to shrivel the shadows at the edges of sheds, warehouses, wood stacks. Piotr followed a line of shadow that kept getting closer and closer to the buildings—*like an ox in a furrow*, he thought. By late afternoon, he was bent double. The sun smote the back of his neck and beat on the earth, sending reverberating waves of heat to strike him in the face. He thought of the cool snow of the Caucasus, the hollow rushing of streams in ravines, the comradeship of friends. And he thought of Fenya.

Later when the hot pulse of labor was snuffed in the cool of the day, Gerassim came up to him.

"The trains are crammed with people running from San Francisco! The city is on fire—all the folk from San Francisco are rushing to Los Angeles; and car loads of Angelinos are packing up to go back east. Fear is driving them like a cowman's stick!"

"The earthquake," Piotr echoed. "We barely felt it here." He shrugged; tremors were not unusual in the Caucasus. Apparently California had the same kind of geological jitters.

"But wait, the best is this. Many of our brethren from San Francisco are with the refugees. They've had it with the place of refuge. They're going back!"

"Back?"

"Back. To Russia."

"Russia." Piotr felt that he was breathing out his soul in the roll and hiss of the word. "What is there for us in Russia?"

"The old life. The old ways. Don't you miss them?"

"They aren't there anymore. Not for me."

"That's true." The gray eyes turned awkward. "You've been uprooted, Piotr Gavrilovich!" But when Makar Kashergan came up, Gerassim looked the young man up and down in his old gibing way. Makar's curly brown beard was matted with grime; his eyes were blinded with sweat; his *kosovorotka* —embroidered for his first day of work with a young wife's fanciful touch—was blotched at the shoulders with the familiar rusty stain.

"So, Makar, how's paradise?"

The young Molokan crumpled like paper in an angry fist. He slumped onto a stack of beams and covered his face with his hands. "I don't understand," he said in a voice Piotr would never forget. "I don't understand!"

"Why hammer him with your own bitterness?" Piotr gave vent to his fury, and Gerassim's face distorted with chagrin. Then with a wild look, he blundered away. But Piotr could think of nothing to comfort Makar.

LATER AS HE STRODE UP Vignes Street toward the Bogdanoff house, Piotr remembered that he hadn't yet told Fenya about the shack. *A place of our own!* He felt better already. Not much of a place, but Fenya wasn't used to much. His steps quickened as he spotted her waiting for him beneath the jacaranda tree. In the early evening the tree was blue with bloom under the stars, and a brilliant moon sent flecks like little blue flames sifting through the branches.

"Good news," he told Fenya in English. The English tongue had become a shelter for them—a private world where prying eyes could not enter. Piotr, who had learned the new alphabet at night school, scoured cast-off newspapers for uniquely American phrases that would help them in their new life. And Fenya had always managed to scavenge a few new words in her rounds with Ivan Bogdanoff's produce cart.

"Good news," he repeated, drawing her to the far side of the jacaranda. The boughs stirred and sent down hushed murmurs.

"We'll have a home," he offered. "I found a place for us. A shack—but we'll be together—and alone. Except for the passengers on the Southern Pacific."

"A home!" Her face lit up, and she reached for him, but then drew back as two elderly women appeared. Their kerchiefed heads clicked together as they spied the young couple.

Piotr sighed. "It's not much. I wanted so much more for you."

"But, Piotr, it'll be just us. Think of it! We'll fix it up."

"It'll take some fixing," he ventured.

Fenya lowered her eyes, and her forehead rounded stubbornly under the kerchief. "We'll fix it," she repeated. "We'll make a home." Then she began telling him about her day at the Wentworths. Piotr listened carefully to the details about their life. He was particularly interested in the protest at Hamburger's Department Store.

"Was it a strike?"

"No. The people inside were still working. Phoebe said that it was called a *nuisance*."

This was a new word, but Piotr had read enough to know that most protests in the city could be traced back to the unions that were eager to get a foothold in Los Angeles.

"A *nuisance*." Piotr pondered the new word. "Whatever they call it, it's the unions. They want to get into the city, and the *Times* publisher, General Harrison Otis, wants just as much to keep them out." Otis's vociferous fury against the socialists, as he called them, was a fascinating language study for the young Russian.

"This is the bitter thing about our life here," he said. "Everything depends upon our hourly labor, and that depends upon laws and business and unions—so many capricious things that we don't understand. It's better to depend upon the land."

"There is no land here except for the rich."

"There is, but we'll have to find it."

II

A Bowl of Salt

Piotr thought he knew what a scab was. His own had healed and thickened to whitish weals that buffered his nerves from the brunt and scrape of the heavy timber he shouldered in San Pedro. In September while singing psalms in the Stimson-Lafayette School building with the brethren, he found that *scab*, in the contrary and inexplicable way of the English tongue, meant something else. Of course, no one expected to be smeared with this putrid crust of a word, so when the strangers edged into the Sunday night meeting, the elders rose and bowed respectfully as usual.

Piotr studied them uneasily. A tense little knot amidst the bearded Russians, the five Americans bobbed in their seats like gamecocks. Glances full of restrained anger flew from one to the other until their belligerence broke into action. They strode to the front, elbowing aside the elder, and the psalm died away. With stolid patience the Molokans waited to hear what the intruders would say. Two of the newcomers spoke Russian, and they interpreted for the spokesman. He informed them in ringing tones that the longshoremen had declared a strike in the lumberyards and that the Molokans were wrongdoers in accepting work from the capitalist exploiters. *A familiar dirge. I've heard it all before*, Piotr thought.

"In your own motherland," the agitator intoned, "your people have risen against the criminals that have used the common people, yet you yourselves break a strike—taking jobs away from union workers." The Molokans digested this in passive silence that goaded the speaker to more fiery rhetoric. "Have you no conscience? In English we have a word for people like you. *Scabs*." Piotr could hardly believe his ears. Even the union interpreter, abashed, paused before he could bring himself to translate. "*Scabs.*"

The Russians, like a single organism, shifted and seemed to breathe differently. The word dropped into silence.

Then there was a whispering in the back. Another American visitor tugged at Piotr's sleeve. He was a young man with black hair swept back from a high forehead. "Don't listen to them," he muttered in English. "The unions want to tie up Los Angeles like they did San Francisco. You needn't stand for it."

"Hey, we didn't invite you. Get out!" the union interpreter demanded. Two brawny union toughs glared at the upstart.

"A reporter." One of them scowled. "Throw him out."

But the Molokan elder raised his eyebrows and thrust out his beard. He was a man of such sturdy and forceful meekness that, although he had stepped aside for the intruders, no one doubted that he was still in charge.

"In the house of prayer all are welcome. If the door opens for the American friend to go out, it will be open wide enough for the strangers to go out as well."

The congregation stood quietly—three hundred men and women, eighty-three of them strong laborers in the lumberyards of San Pedro. The agitators subsided. Then they started afresh with a harangue that lasted for two hours. Piotr listened carefully both to the English speaker and the slightly distorted version from the Russian interpreter. He understood strikes, and he understood the demands of oppressed peoples. But from a Molokan point of view, he knew that these men would make no sense. The lumberyard paid them $2.85 a day—plenty enough by peasant standards. If the Americans refused to work for that amount, the Russians would be more than happy to. "Let the workman be content with his wages," the Bible said. And that was the Molokan view.

He noticed that the venerable elder was not attending closely to what the unionists said but instead was looking into their faces. When he judged the time ripe by some standard of his own that had nothing to do with the flow of rhetoric, he stood and called the meeting to a close.

"We have broken no law of God or of man. Be at peace. And Christ go with you," he said to the unbidden guests. His gentleness unnerved them.

"Law! The laws of this country protect the evil. Our task is to insist on justice—not to buckle under laws that serve the rich."

"We serve neither rich nor poor, but the Lord God. We are aliens in a land where the laws are strange and change from time to time. We fled from a land where the tsars and masters are the law. There is only one way whereby we can find our course. *'Thy statutes are my songs in the house of my pilgrimage!'* We are pilgrims on the face of the earth. We come from danger and turmoil. We follow the law of Christ, and this country—America—by its law, gives us the freedom to do that." A spasm of approval rippled through the Molokans.

The interpreter's lip curled. "Singing won't help you if you defy justice. We're demanding that not a single Russian return to work in San Pedro. Anyone who does will pay the consequences, and no law will save you. Remember that! If you go back to work, you go at your own peril!"

"If we were always afraid of the wolves, we would never go to the forest," said the old Molokan calmly, as though explaining something obvious to a young child. Then he dismissed the meeting.

The young American behind Piotr nudged him. "What did he say?"

"If we were always afraid of the wolves, we would never go to the forest," Piotr translated.

"Wolves! Ha! That's swell!" He grabbed a pencil from behind his ear and scribbled on a note pad.

Piotr watched him enviously. "You're a reporter?"

"Right. Mick Mulvaney." He tapped the pencil against his teeth thoughtfully. "And you?"

"Piotr. Piotr Gavrilovich Voloshin."

"Gootamecha, Piotr. I tell ya, Mr. Chandler will be beside himself with joy at the way you boys stood up to those thugs."

"Beside himself?"

Mick's eyes crinkled in a silent laugh. "It means . . . it means . . . good grief! You're forcing me to think. It's a strain at this hour!"

"Beside himself—so full of joy that it would take two of him to hold it?" Piotr suggested.

"Good try. Only *joy* is probably not the right word for what it would take two of Otis Chandler to hold. *Glee*, maybe. Hand-rubbing, cigar-chomping, unholy glee."

Piotr shook his head in confusion. He was up against the wall he slammed into in any conversation that went beyond practicalities. But he wanted it to continue. This young man—not much older than himself—was writing for a great newspaper. Intrigued, he hovered at the street corner.

"So . . ." Mick was still trailing his story. "Whaddaya think? You suppose these Russians will hold out against the strikers? The old, er, elder seemed to think you'll stick it out to a man."

"We will," Piotr said simply.

"How do you know? These unionists can make it pretty hot for you."

Piotr shrugged. "When we must work, we work. Hot or not."

"So you'd say work is important to you?"

"We work as Christ worked. We consider that laboring with our hands is the best way. That's how Christ labored, scarring His hands at the workman's bench until the day of that greater scarring against wood."

Piotr felt the tug of a connection as Mick stared at him out of dark blue eyes.

The American grasped the thought, then deflected it. "So. The dignity of manual labor. But for you, if you had any choice in the world, what would you do for a living?"

Strange question! In Russia no one asked it. If your father was a peasant, you were a peasant, and you farmed the land. Here you took whatever job you could find. But to young men like Mick Mulvaney, America was a land of wild, churning options. Nothing was set in stone, and they were always opening doors and letting the weather in.

"No, seriously," the reporter persisted, "what would you do?"

"Work the land. My own land."

Mick was silent. Again Piotr sensed the tug of connection.

"Land," Mick said at last. "That's something we Irish can understand. But not an easy dream to realize here in California."

Piotr nodded. "It seems that the land is for the rich."

"It takes money, all right. When they broke the news on the Owens River project, the price of land in the San Fernando Valley went up 500 percent! The insiders who bought it up in advance made a killing—the crooks. And put it right out of the reach of ordinary folks like us." Piotr warmed to the "like us." "But California's a big state. Land in the Imperial Valley and in the San Joaquin Valley is still affordable."

"Not for someone making $2.85 a day!"

"You want to know how to make money, I'll tell you. The water department is hiring five thousand men to start the work on this new aqueduct. If you don't mind backbreaking work in a desert where it's 120 degrees in the summer and freezing in the winter, you could scrape up enough to get a small farm."

"You mean people move there? With families?"

"Well, no. They'll set up work camps. Like military barracks. No wives, no children, but a chance to make a good chunk of money."

Piotr shook his head. "Not for me. I'm getting married."

"Oh! Well, I don't blame you. No man wants to leave his bride for the badlands of Inyo County! But those are the stories in Los Angeles. The water and the unions. And I plan to be on hand if something breaks on either. See ya."

Piotr paused, musing about breaking water and unions. "Okay. Maybe I'll see you again. . . ."

"You can bet on it. If there's some trouble after your shift tomorrow, you can expect to see me nosing around."

"Swell," Piotr said.

BUT NOTHING ABOUT MONDAY was newsworthy, though Piotr kept his eye out for union agitators. He and Makar worked an hour overtime unloading a huge shipment of pine that would be used in a new Pasadena hotel. As they rounded the corner from the alley coming up from the harbor, Makar grabbed him by the arm and nodded toward a man slumped beside a warehouse. "Just a drunk." But Piotr hurried forward as he recognized Mick Mulvaney. The young newsman was painfully inching himself up against the sheet metal siding, muttering all the while.

"Ah—Piotr, my chum of one day! Wait a minute while I pry myself off the ground. You're wonderin'—no need to ask. A visit from our union friends. We had words, yes, we did. And they kindly left me with some reminders of their philosophy. As you can see." He delicately fingered the swollen lump on his cheekbone. "Don't mind my palaver. It's just my way of convincing myself I'm alive."

Mick was bruised and rumpled but not seriously hurt. Piotr bolstered him on one side and Makar on the other, and they limped off to the office. At the sight of Mick, the clerk shoved his pencil into his ginger sideburns. "Wait. I'll get water."

Mick drank half of it and dipped his handkerchief into the rest, dabbing at his discolored features with all the grace of a confirmed dandy. "I'm sure I'm a sight to behold," he said.

The clerk began cranking up the telephone, and Mick's hand shot out and stopped him. "Forget it. I don't need the police."

"You're not fit to get home on your own," the clerk argued.

"I'm fit. Just wait. By the end of the week, there'll be a court order that'll hamstring these jokers. We'll let our city servants get involved when they've got a good bit of legislation to clobber these thugs with. Meanwhile, if you don't mind, you can call a friend of mine—the only friend I've got who has both a telephone and a buggy. He'll be interested, I'm sure. Charlie Wentworth."

"Wentworth!" Piotr pricked up his ears. "My fiancée works for a Wentworth family. In Hollywood."

"Whaddayaknow! Must be the same."

"Phoebe Wentworth. That's the one Fenya knows best."

"Figures. The charming Phoebe." Mulvaney sighed gustily. "She sees the foreigner, she sees the needy, she sees just about everything except me. And herself. She looks like she dresses without looking in a mirror. It's one of her chief attractions."

Piotr was baffled. Did Mick really like this Phoebe, or was he being disrespectful? "Fenya says she's a wonderful girl," he said.

"Yes, she is that," Mick assented with a flicker in his blue eyes.

"And her brother?"

"Ah, Charlie. Now that's another story. Charlie has convinced himself that he's a socialist. Of course, in all fairness, I'm well aware that he wouldn't be chums with a son of Irish immigrants if he didn't have these leanings. He does it out of boredom and to annoy his father. In fact, the whole family is motivated mainly by boredom."

"Phoebe, too?"

"No. Not Phoebe. Phoebe is hurt somewhere deep inside, and it makes her feel better if she's mopping up someone else's tears."

"What hurt her?" Piotr started thinking of Fenya.

"I wish I knew."

They exchanged a glance—another fragile, fleeting connection. Piotr knew why Fenya was wounded inside, but he didn't know what to do about it. "I wish I knew," he echoed.

Then a fair-haired man wearing shoddy clothes and expensive shoes sauntered in. The electric bulb glinted off his glasses as he leaned over to give Mick a good, long stare.

"Don't miss anything, Charlie," Mick joked. "Your union buddies have transformed me into a real work of art."

"I think you'll live to smear the work of justice with Chandler's rag for another day," Charlie replied.

"I hope so. I do hope so."

"Well, come on then. We'll fix you up."

"Is Phoebe home? I'm finally in a condition to attract her attention."

"Sorry. She's holed up in her city flat doing lesson plans for the new school year. You'll have to make do with Cory's ministrations."

Mick sighed heavily. "Wait. I'll introduce you to my rescuers. This is Piotr Gavrilovich Voloshin and—" He lifted his brows in a query.

"Makar Kashergan," Piotr supplied.

Charlie stuck out a hand and regarded them with interest. "Russians! Were you there during the recent revolution?"

"I was not there," Piotr said. *Not there in the day of trouble. Not there for my family.*

But his flat tone failed to extinguish Charlie's interest. "Tell me what you know. I'd really like to hear about the movement there."

Piotr shrugged. "Russia needs an answer, but the socialists don't have it."

"Why? Why are you so sure?"

Mick groaned. "Not now, Charlie. He can tell you his story sometime when I'm not writhing in pain."

"Yes, well, I suppose we'll go if you can stagger out to the buggy."

"Right. Let's go. And Piotr, Makar—thanks. You saved my skin."

"We are happy for your skin," Piotr said politely. "See ya."

PIOTR'S EXTRA WORK HOURS left little time to prepare a home for his bride. Besides, he had little idea of how to make the two-room shack more liveable. He did manage to find an iron bedstead in a second-hand shop. He sanded down the chipped black enamel and painted it a beautiful red. It gleamed like a new toy and stank like a chemical factory. Piotr had to sleep on the kitchen floor near the window. But the project gave him an immense satisfaction, and the red bed preyed on his mind as he carried lumber and filled him with a bursting anticipation as the day of his wedding drew near.

Because neither Piotr nor Fenya had parents in America, he assumed that much of the traditional fuss would fall by the wayside. But within two weeks of the ceremony, he found that instead of being nobody's children, he and Fenya were everybody's children. Unseen powers moving beneath the surface designated the Valoffs' house near Utah Street as the "groom's house" and the Bogdanoff home on Vignes as the "bride's house." White-kerchiefed heads converged in secret and a collective motherliness drew Piotr and Fenya into a lavish circle of concern. Granite-ware pots and wooden spoons appeared; the young couple was captured in the house where Makar and Hanya lived and regaled with carved soup bowls and embroidered tea towels. A few enameled plates rimmed with blue and garnished with a lovely emblem that said "St. Louis Stamping Co." appeared. Old women became agitated and rummaged through chests, weighing precious items carried thousands of miles for just such a time. They became desperate to give something away. Fenya's corner at the Bogdanoffs' was heaped with linens, an iron skillet, a brass teapot designed to fit in the top of a samovar that was ten thousand miles away. Fenya and Piotr were filled with an abashed gratitude. They held up useful items and nodded appreciatively. They exchanged glances as they became beneficiaries of some cherished item saved for a dead son or a faraway daughter married to a *muzhik* back in Russia.

Aksinia's women visitors couldn't stop themselves from peeking in to take stock of the "trousseau's" progress with repressed glee. Aksinia herself smothered the couple in quilts and pillows.

"We'll need the quilts," Fenya remarked, "since the houses have no stoves. We won't be cold in the winter."

Piotr grinned at her. He didn't expect that his red bed would ever be cold.

Four days before the wedding, he came home to find his shack transformed. From top to bottom, the two rooms had been scrubbed with lye and whitewashed. Ilya Valoff was still inside scraping daubs of putty from a sparkling new pane of glass in the front room. To the end of his life, the smell of damp putty would stir up springing arrows of gladness in Piotr.

"Just enough light to finish!" he exclaimed when Piotr came in. "Looks like home, eh? You kids will get a good start." His putty knife chased a stray blob into a corner. "Better be careful. Elena won't be too pleased if I mess up her curtains."

Dazed, Piotr looked around. The newly glazed windows were draped with crisp, white tea towels embroidered with stiff-tailed birds and symmetrical sunflowers. The bed, which had lost its pungent odor, was resplendent with patchwork in black and red and blue overlaid with lacy stitched patterns in white, like snowflakes. This was tastefully draped over a white cloth edged with a red geometric design. Stacked orange crates covered with linen stood beside the bed. Just inside the door was a galvanized tin barrel full of water with towels hung on pegs above it. In the tiny kitchen, a scarred but sturdy wooden chest was set up next to the sink. A gas cooktop was positioned on a piece of sheet metal. The ancient brass teakettle sat on one of the two burners.

"That's from Elena and me," Ilya explained. "I know your thoughts haven't harkened to kitchen needs." He winked slyly at the bold, red bed. "But you'll find there are other things to life. It's a blessing to come in from work and guzzle hot tea. That's how I do it."

He took the kettle and filled it from the complaining tap. "For our guests," he explained. Sure enough, within moments the shack was jumping with a crowd of Molokans of all ages. Elena's outstretched arms offered *piroshkiya* and sweet pastries. Three samovars were set to piping near the porch stoop. Fenya came in with Aksinia, who added another little pillow, white with a red embroidered cockerel on it, to the bedstead. Fenya looked confused. She was holding a wooden dish with salt in it. She held onto it as though it were keeping her from flying away. Noise and laughter filled the two small rooms and spilled into the railway yard.

The landlord appeared with his bulldog face and pink rolls of fat cushioning his round skull in the back. He was carrying some kind of square board. The Molokans fell silent, but he quickly reassured them. "Hey, don't let me keep you from your party. Just came by with a gift for the happy couple." He trundled into the kitchen and changed the board into a small table with wooden legs and a woven top. "It's a poker table, but it's the right size."

Fenya smiled and put her bowl of salt in the center. Elena and Aksinia soon had the surface covered with Russian delicacies. The American looked from Elena's outstretched hands to Aksinia's beaming benevolence. He twiddled his fat fingers and accepted a plump *nachinki* from Hanya.

"You've done pretty well for yourself, my boy," he muttered to Piotr. "Such women! They don't make them like that here." He winked at Piotr and waddled out, but not before accepting a *piroshka* from Elena.

Makar came in with several young men, and they began singing psalms. Piotr had struggled with the idea of living with Fenya in that place. Somehow he couldn't imagine their life there. But now the songs of his people filled the shanty with something new, something that hallowed and cushioned their God-breathed love. The stove was sparkling and ready for the spurt of a match; the bed was resplendent and waiting. Piotr went back to sleeping on the kitchen floor.

THE LAND IN LOS ANGELES—that is, the bearing land—was cumbered with squat buildings, skewered with telephone poles, and strapped with railway and streetcar tracks. In the eighth ward, clapboard bungalows straddled the hard-baked clay and held it down along with shaggy tentacles of bermuda grass. But for Piotr the unwieldy trappings and strange soil faded away in a ringing joy. Today on this morning of crisp September sunshine, he would take Fenya Kostrikin as his bride.

Beside him were his brothers, fellow travelers, pilgrims striding with him from the groom's house near Utah Street across the bridge to the bride's house on Vignes Street. Makar, his *druzhko*, glanced sideways at him, a smile struggling with solemnity in his curly brown beard. Gerassim lagged, then lurched ahead, his huge shadow tossing light and dark like unsettled weather.

The men crossed the bridge and closed ranks. The striated river bottom was dry and wheat-colored, like streams of golden grain. Street-corner stares prodded them into a closer configuration. Pranksters, friends of the Bogdanoffs, had set up mock barriers in the street, just as if they were celebrating on a village lane. A blue-clad policeman barked out something about obstructing traffic, but then he touched his helmet with a grin as young Matvei Kalpakov took him aside and explained. The officer puffed out his chest and motioned a plodding buggy away from the procession with a sweep of his white-gloved hand. A bicyclist in white trousers and a straw boater hat wobbled off the road and turned to wave. A cluster of parasols tilted to reveal a knot of pastel women. They parted, and a ruffled little girl flew out and tucked a nosegay into Piotr's hand.

Laughing, he enclosed it in one big fist. He used the other to help Gerassim and Makar push away the jumble of benches and branches set up in the street while the gathering crowd cheered and the policeman tooted fiercely on his whistle.

The Molokan brethren began singing. The blue sky drew up their song and sent it down in a silver seed of meaning. The breath of their lungs, pressed through the modulating throat, shaped notes, warm and human with blood, that smote on Piotr's back. How like other Molokan processions it all was. He could almost see the village street, the loved ones behind him, bearing him up. Could he turn and recognize faces from long ago?

The familiar psalm-borne thoughts surrounded him. How long he had traveled and how barren and labored the way! For months, years, he had pushed himself toward a destination that had no hold on his mind. He could not envision it! Weeks of heaving sea and then the United States—a dock and a docket and a doctor's white coat. California, an elusive paradise. Los Angeles, a mirage at the end of a slick railway track.

But now, surrounded by his brethren, he saw clearly his journey's end, and it was a beloved face. They turned the corner onto Vignes Street, and his mind's vision spilled into his heart. There she was in the doorway, white lace framing her lovely irregular features. The solemn love in her eyes condensed into a deep, deep blue that drew him up the steps.

Aksinia greeted them with bread and a bowl of salt. Prayers of the elders filled the Bogdanoffs' small living room. Then they set off again in an intent throng, Hanya in her matron-of-honor dress, young men matching stride for stride. Elders with their beards spread out or tossed like wing-flare flanked the young people like vigilant angels. Little girls in colored kerchiefs and boys in crisp *kosovorotkas* trailed like angels of another sort.

The procession wound through the streets of Los Angeles, crossed streetcar lines, flowed around city traffic. A stalled cart was islanded in a stream of peasants. Long-stemmed palms raised their rounded tops stiffly against the telephone lines like musical notes. And to Piotr it seemed that the Molokans drew in these foreign notes and conjured them into Russian song. Fenya walked beside him, and every place on the strangers' street that he placed his foot was home.

They marched to the Stimson-Lafayette School building where the binding words were spoken. A concourse of consent arose from the assembly. Piotr sensed his people around him as a complete, intact world, a *mir* in the old Russian sense. And above, a greater firmament that smiled on this union.

It was a strange ceremony—full of resonant familiarity and hollow lapses. Prescribed phrases of Molokan custom and the music of psalms and the love message of the Gospel—all were as they always had been. But the parents' blessing was spoken over their bent heads by someone else. Then a stirring, a shifting, and Fenya was facing him, looking at him with solemn awe—and he could see the sweet, womanly change overshadow her.

Together they spoke the binding words: "We servants of the living God swear before almighty God and before His holy Gospels and before His holy Church that according to the order of the law of God we wish to live in legal marriage, with the blessing and agreement of our parents and by our own will. . . . Between us will be observed fidelity and modesty. . . ."

Then Piotr affirmed, "I will not have any other wife except the one to whom I now swear." It was his own voice and the warm chambers of his own body that breathed out the word *wife*—and the speaking made it so. He looked at Fenya. She knew it in every fiber of her being.

Their voices joined again: "In conclusion of our promise we swear fidelity and truth forever." *Forever*, the blue depths of her eyes affirmed. The congregation pressed around them. Hands reached out and took their two hands and joined them. Singing broke from the people and washed over them.

"And their seed shall be known among the Gentiles, and their offspring among the people: all that see them shall acknowledge them...." The words were a promise, and Piotr bowed under the giving. The song surged: "I will greatly rejoice in the Lord; my soul shall be joyful in my God; for He hath clothed me with the garments of salvation; He hath covered me with the robe of righteousness...."

And under that covering, they went out to the feasting and the celebration. Makar, as *druzhko*, presided over the bridal pair and their guests in a special tent set up for the wedding. They shared tea and cabbage soup, *lapsha*, *kasha*, and glasses of strained *kvas* flavored with apricots. Hanya gathered the young girls and women, and they pulled Fenya aside and unwove her single braid, brushed loose the flowing flax of her hair, and rebraided it into two plaits—signifying that she was no longer single. Piotr knew that the ritual required that the groom's mother take the young man to the barn and explain what he was to do. Then the young couple would be locked in for the night. He couldn't imagine how this custom would work in their new setting. After all, his mother was lost in Russia, and there was no barn for miles. Besides, he knew well enough what to do. The idea preyed on him every time he saw his beautiful red bed.

But the Molokans had determined that this wedding would be done right. As the last guests began drifting away, Ivan and Aksinia Bogdanoff pulled up with their team and produce cart. Gerassim, Makar and his Hanya, Ilya and Elena Valoff, and a crowd of young people piled in with the bride and groom. They drove out to the shack by the railroad tracks, singing and shouting and joking.

Ilya's face was wreathed in smiles. "You'll not escape, Piotr Gavrilovich," he chided the groom. "We haven't held to our ways for generations to let you slip through the first crack in the fence!"

Meanwhile, just out of earshot, Elena was making demure comments that sent the flock of girls around her into gales of laughter.

Piotr raised his eyebrows. "What am I in for? We don't need any more traditions."

"Oh, yes, you do. We'll do our duty and lock you in tonight in the time-honored way!"

They rolled up to the porch stoop, and the cart emptied into the house. Aksinia put a tray of wedding delicacies on the table. The young people plumped up the pillows and gave joking advice. Then they collected outside, singing and cracking sunflower seeds.

Elena Valoff took Piotr by the sleeve and tugged him aside. "You have no mother here, so I'm your mother tonight. You take heed! Listen, God has given you a girl more precious than rubies. You be kind to her on this night of nights, and the kindness will come back to you. She has a bruised spot on her memory because of her sister, so don't you go touching where it hurts. Blessings on your head."

"Blessings!" shouted the young folk in a shower of sunflower husks. Elena closed the door, leaving the bridal pair alone. Someone threw a handful of grain, and it rattled off the door like rain. Then they sang, "Their seed shall be sown among the Gentiles, and their offspring among the people. . . ." The song poured through the window—Ilya's tenor and Makar's rich baritone and Hanya's beautiful soaring lark-notes.

Then it was quiet. The river sludge was jelled in its bed; the trains were stopped up in their tunnels and yards; the city's life wheezed and sighed and turned over to pull up the sheet. The balmy September night breathed through the embroidered linen curtains, and the girl beside him with her two braids breathed through a lace *kasinka*.

She went to the table and set a round loaf of bread on a napkin and balanced her wooden bowl of salt on top. She came to him then and presented it. He took it from her and set it aside. Constraint dropped with the lace veil, and with joy-strained fingers he undid the work of the bridesmaids who had plaited her hair. When she stood arrayed in knee-length silver-gold more beautiful than any silken thing made by man, he gathered her up, and she came to him.

Piotr buried his hands and face in the shining mass, his fingers scattered the strands and threaded into them. He felt that his touch was inspired—the strength of the bowman's hand, the delicacy of the harper's fingers. Songs came to him—of a sower's seed falling like silver rain, of grain heaped in golden plenty, of water sprung from water—and tumbled with them into the pieced quilt and the strutting red embroidery. Song broke from him in whispers and came back to him in Fenya's echoed murmurs. "Dushok, you are my beloved. You are my heart's home in the strangers' land. You are my soul's darling forever, forever, forever." And there was no shadow of calamity to mar their joy.

"BUT YOU AREN'T MARRIED." Cory was appalled. "Not without a license!"

"Cory!" Phoebe exclaimed.

"I'm married," Fenya assured them. "None of the Molokans need a—a receipt for marriage. It's God who binds us." She flicked her two braids away from the steaming mangle before clamping the top down. Cory's eyes followed her hands.

"Well, there's such a thing as the sanction of the law. Your hair looks pretty that way—over your shoulders. I never noticed it before." She reached out and examined one of Fenya's plaits as though it were merchandise on a sale table.

Fenya opened the mangle and pulled out a pressed tablecloth. "Here—all ready for your luncheon guests."

"Give it to Evangeline."

Evangeline heard her name and poked her black head into the laundry. "I can't take it! Who you think is goin' to make your fancy croquettes and finger sandwiches? You two girls look plenty healthy. You just get in there and set things up yourself."

"Can't Fenya do it?"

"Fenya! You blind? She ironing! You girls get on out there before your company gets here."

Fenya chuckled. Officially, Evangeline was the family's cook, but, in fact, she ran the house and everyone in it. A good thing, too, otherwise Fenya had no idea how the work of managing the home would get done.

Bernice Wentworth was hard-working in her way, but Fenya had a difficult time seeing what she accomplished. From looking at her, Fenya judged that she was given to extremes. Sometimes she'd cover herself with a plain outfit of fine, stiff white linen from head to foot;

next Fenya would see her float by in tiers of floral frills. On Wednesday mornings she went out to a meeting attired with nunnish modesty in a drab walking skirt and austere shirtwaist garnished with a man's tie. On Saturday evenings she appeared in shamelessly low-cut satin. As far as Fenya could see, Mrs. Wentworth had no idea who she was. Everything she wore looked like a disguise.

Evangeline, on the other hand, was a miracle of consistency. When Fenya first met her, she was fascinated. It was the first time she had seen a black woman close up, and Evangeline was very, very dark. Every indentation on her face—beneath her eyes, at the sides of her nose, beneath her lips—was rich with plum-colored shadow. Her chiseled bones contrasted strikingly with her large, soft eyes and lips. When she turned her finely made hands over, the palms were a surprising pink. She was neat in all her ways. Her kerchief was tied over her forehead and lapped over her ears at exactly the same place. Her apron straps—always white and always crisp—were crossed in a perfect "X" behind her back. Her lean figure was always erect, and her pronouncements were always forthright.

When Fenya got over her initial surprise, she began to realize that this woman was more like Semyon Efimovich, the powerful patriarch of the Voloshins, than anyone she had ever met. Evangeline had the same prophetic sureness, the same fire, and the same hidden gentleness.

Evangeline was interested in everyone. She grilled Fenya with questions that even Phoebe had never thought to ask. She was reserved in her expressions, but Fenya noticed that when she was feeling either strong approval or disapproval, more of the pink palms flashed into view, and the shape of her upper lip changed in some subtle way.

"How come your people move all this way from Russia?" she demanded.

"*Pohod*," Fenya said simply. "The pilgrimage. Many years ago God gave a message to my people, the Molokans. The one we call 'the boy prophet' had a vision that came to him as a writing, and even though this young peasant could neither read nor write, he carefully copied it. Terrible troubles. Turmoil in our homeland. That's what it was all about. We were told that when the time came, believers were to flee to a place of refuge. Fifty years passed before the

43

prophet spread the word that the time of *Pohod* had come. And we learned that the place of refuge was a coastland on the other side of the world—California!"

"Here!" Evangeline exclaimed. "Why here? There's believers and sinners here like anywhere."

"I don't know. I only know that many of those who stayed were killed in last year's uprisings. And there will be worse to come, I think. Those of us who came to America escaped those troubles, though some we loved are gone."

"Well, we got troubles here, too. American-style troubles. But we got refuge, too—in the everlasting arms of Jesus."

"That's so. I left my family and set out on pilgrimage, but the refuge I found was not a place, but a Person. Maybe that's where the Holy Spirit was leading me all along."

Evangeline's black doe eyes spurted with fierce understanding. "Huh!" she stated. "You a Pentecostal. Like me."

"But Russian," Fenya offered.

"The Holy Spirit, He don't pay attention to that. He recognize His children by their hearts."

In the coming weeks Fenya would accept the idea that she was probably Pentecostal, like Evangeline. Surely, it became apparent that the two of them shared a point of view different from that of the rest of the household.

But now as Cory and Phoebe took their pressed linen into the dining room, Evangeline muttered, "How I'm goin' to raise those girls, I don't know. That Cory—she don't know what marriage is! To her marriage is clothes and a paper from the county court. Jesus said the body is more important than clothes. And Phoebe—that girl is just as bad. She's all trussed up with works. Marriage is grace! And grace is like—like the stars of the firmament!"

Her eyes ignited with sparkling bursts from beneath her purple lids. Light always spurted from her when she said *grace* or *love* or *redeem*. It gave her words uncanny meaning. Something of her mind and something of her soul and something outside of her leapt out with them. Like Semyon Efimovich, she had Scripture stored up like winter grain. In any need she could rummage around in her mind and fling out comfort or inspiration. Fenya basked in her intense good will as she went about cleaning and ironing the astounding number of frills and camisoles and table linens and shirtwaists required by the family.

Fenya's workday ended at three o'clock. Then she would walk through the wide, shaded avenues of Hollywood to the streetcar stop. Sometimes she would get off near Vignes and visit with Aksinia and the twins, but usually she went home and started a one-dish supper on the new cooktop. Often she had fresh bread from Evangeline's bounty or Aksinia's pastries to add to their simple fare. With the table set and stew or soup simmering, she waited for Piotr's step on the porch.

Then they would share the evening meal on enameled plates and carved wooden bowls on the small poker table. They talked about the men at the lumberyard, about the Wentworths, about everything except the loved ones back in Russia. Cranky freights or the rambunctious fast express would drown them out from time to time.

The days crisped and shortened, but the twisted eucalyptus trees and jewel-like orange groves and fern-fountained pepper trees gave no sign of bowing to winter. The autumn wind grew chill and carried scents from faraway open places to them, filling them with a longing agitation. The pepper tree next to the shack formed hard little pods and tossed them about so that they rattled on the metal roof like rain. Everything that spilled over them drew them closer together, and they wrapped themselves up in each other and awoke breathing in unison.

Shining threads appeared in the river with the first winter rains. At midwinter Alameda Street glittered with fiesta lights, and the Americans began singing as the Molokans had never heard them sing before. The Wentworth home filled up with the scent of a forest and uncanny lights. Fenya loved the stately Douglas fir that towered in feathered layers to the living room ceiling.

The Molokans did not hold with Christmas celebrations, shunning the pagan customs that tainted such feasts in Russia—and here. But Fenya noticed that the Americans, although they became more jittery than ever, seemed more full of heart than at other times. Even the music changed. Songs that were real, true songs poured from churches and homes and even street corners.

Young people gathered around Charlie Wentworth's piano and

sang of a deep blue silent night. Phoebe sang in a sincere off-key voice with her soul in her eyes. The depth and the silence of it filled Fenya's soul. She nurtured it like a candle in the wind and carried it home to Piotr.

Mick Mulvaney was always dropping by to tease Cory and joke with Charlie and watch Phoebe from under his long lashes. Cory twirled through a succession of parties, and Phoebe raided Evangeline's domain for her "care baskets," and Mrs. Wentworth tried to do both. Fenya lurched and swayed on the streetcar full of impressions, wondering how she could explain it all to Piotr.

In January and February real rains battered the city; the river filled, and the downtown streets turned to mud. Wagons and buggies sank to their axles. One corner was so notorious for its swamplike ability to swallow rigs that Mick and Charlie jokingly stuck a wagon tongue and buckboard seat on top of the muck so that it looked as though some poor soul's cart was just about to disappear. Piotr and Fenya happened by, and Piotr put his workman's cap just behind the seat so that it looked as if a passenger had gone down with the wagon.

"Ah," he said nostalgically, "it's just like a Russian spring!"

"It's winter here," Fenya reminded him. "And I'll have to wash your cap."

Sometimes on a clear winter night, they would go out on the doorstep and look at the stars clustered in their swarming congregations. The chiming light spattered across the dark arc of sky, and they listened with their eyes while lyrical light dripped on them. Then a slight trembling, a dark blot beyond the edge of vision would intrude and gather strength and fury, and the hulk of a night express would leap out on its shining path and hurl itself at the eastern ranges. Wheel and rod, wheel and rod, and the rods striking downward, striking power from the rails with harsh chinking blows. And the train would moan its hollow, lonely moan and with smoke draw their eyes along the bend of rails and onto corrugated freight cars or empty flashing windows. They waited until the fierce, moving blot was swallowed by other night blots of trees or warehouses and its shadow sounds swallowed by the still, star-chastened air of winter. Then they drank in a last draught of night sky and went to bed, bound with double bonds of shared beauty and menace.

Winds from the east brought hot, dry air from the Mohave

Desert. The shack banged and rattled, and the wind raked up unquiet, dry things that rustled on the edges of their minds and filled them with a vast, unnameable unease and a deep need of each other. But late in spring, Fenya noticed that seeds fallen from careless celebrating hands at their wedding had sprouted beside the porch and along the south side of the shanty. *Sunflowers!* Fenya thought. *By the time they bloom, I'll know for sure. Then I can tell Piotr.* And she hugged a secret joy to herself.

AGAFYA ANDREIVNA BOGDANOFF WAS DEAD.

"The earth is calling out for her," Fenya told Piotr as soon as she heard the news from Aksinia. "She is kaput."

"Succumbed," he corrected her absently.

"Succumbed or kaput," Fenya said sadly, "Bunya has given up her spirit to God."

And together they went to the Bogdanoffs' to stand with them in their sorrow. Agafya was dressed in the white, lace-trimmed burial garments she had brought from Russia, and her body was laid out on one of the benches in the Bogdanoffs' front room. Her face, loosely framed by a lace-trimmed *kasinka*, seemed younger, less lined than in life. Piotr supposed that the wrinkles she always crunched into place with her tightly tied kerchief had been allowed to relax at last and were lapping around the edges of her face. Her small, waxen nose was yellow and impudent, and her hand with its mushroom-like skin curled around an embroidered handkerchief. There was no doubt that Agafya was ready for her journey. There was something beautiful and touching about her. *I never understood her—or what she was here for,* Piotr thought. But Fenya did. She and Aksinia were weeping in the corner, occasionally touching each other for comfort.

Ivan, as the old woman's son, came in to announce the start of the burial. Two elders appeared behind him. One was an old man with a silky beard, rain-gray eyes, and a bumpy forehead. The stocky one wore an American coat over his *kosovorotka* and looked gloomily about under shaggy brows. His stiff whiskers spumed out as though he had gray-black smoke billowing from his nose and mouth.

Agafya's body was placed in a redwood casket and carried out to the middle of the street where a rug was spread out next to a cloth-covered table. Piotr helped Ivan and the other men position the casket on benches near the table. Then the silky-bearded old man began praying in a strong, practical tone. Piotr's mind drifted, and he forgot to listen to the words. The man's tone and gestures made it seem as though he were sternly instructing the old woman on where to go and how to get there.

Scores of Molokans—men, women, and children—thronged the street and followed slowly, singing and weeping as Piotr, Ivan, and the other men shouldered the casket and carried it to the street-car stop.

The funeral car with its panel of stained glass at the back was already in place, so they positioned the casket at the back, and the mourners crowded into the small compartment. The men wore the customary white *kosovorotka* under a dark jacket. The women, in keeping with Molokan tradition, wore white peasant dresses—not the white of mourning as worn in the East, but the white of rejoicing for a sister whose soul has flown to God. The darks and whites of faces and caps and kerchiefs and hands fell under the spell of the colored patches of light from the stained-glass window as the car rolled sedately toward the Los Angeles County Cemetery for the Indigent.

"She's to be buried with vagrants, our dear one," moaned Aksinia. "It's not fitting . . ."

"Hush, hush." Fenya's voice was tender. "It's all right. We're all vagrants."

But Aksinia sobbed all the more loudly, and others joined in as though it were catching. The women's voices rose in a gale, their laments filling the small space. But Piotr knew that they were weeping not for Agafya Bogdanoff, but for everything, everything—the lost homeland, the missing loved ones, the uncertain future. Unashamed, he began crying with them. The pain in his heart seemed to grow and grow. His cousins—why were there gaping wounds where there should be eyes? Why was there ruin and blood where there should be strong, young men and a girl like a lily? And his own family—where were they? These things were a wound on his mind. And the wound cried out with its open mouth. Had anyone with the name of Voloshin survived?

When they reached the end of the streetcar line, Piotr again shouldered the coffin. They carried it in relays—man replacing man—all the way to the cemetery. But Piotr kept his place. He wanted to feel the old woman's slight weight on him and share his portion of tears with the brethren.

A dozen male voices took up a song, all of them blending in a powerful stream. The women joined in, forgetting their sobs. They were one when they sang like that, Piotr marveled. They took the incomprehensible, captured it in word and note, then absorbed it so that they could continue their journey. The song gathered force. Makar Kashergan stepped beside him, slipping his own damaged shoulder under Piotr's load. Piotr let his pace slow; men and women flowed into the street surrounding the coffin, bearing it up. The wooden casket bobbed and heaved with the pulse and heaving of song. To Piotr it seemed that it was being carried away by a great river, away to a far-off sea.

He turned to glimpse the faces behind him, but other faces intruded. His parents—Gavril, Galina; his sisters—Nadya, Dausha. He remembered the last time he had seen his father's house. His father and mother and the two girls crowded the doorway, their eyes clinging to him as he walked away. Their faces were vague even then. *Where are you, my dear ones? I seek you out during the night, sharpen my memory on faces grown dim and porous. In the day I shoulder my work and my burden with longing. Why have you gone from me? Even when I hold my beloved, my heart is torn between fleet, swift joy and crushing loneliness.*

The mourners were at the county cemetery now. The casket was positioned on benches at the grave site. The singing began again as Piotr and Makar drifted to the back of the crowd.

Makar put a sympathetic hand on his shoulder. "It's not Agafya Andreivna, is it?" He looked quietly into Piotr's eyes.

"No." Piotr wiped his sleeve across his face.

"You're like me. If anything unusually sad—or happy—comes along, my mind flies off to Russia like a bird."

"Russia! Yes. It's as if we're tossed between the two worlds. But it's not just that. It's the cost, the terrible cost."

Makar began humming along with the funeral song, but his brows raised questioningly. Piotr responded to the understanding in his eyes. "My journey has been a strange one," he said. "It wasn't a simple boat ride from Batumi to San Francisco. My whole—my whole way of looking at things changed. My parents took a terrible risk, and to this day I don't know what it cost them. I was in the tsar's army, and they were determined to keep me from going to war. They defied the government to smuggle me out of the country, but I refused to be smuggled. I found refuge with some mountaineers. A Khevsur in the valley of the Aragvi befriended me—Grigol . . ." A tumult of memories broke free. How long had it been since he had spoken that name? Makar stepped back a little from the crowd, his face open and receptive.

"I keep seeing it in my mind," Piotr mused. "The whitewashed block and rubble of the Khevsur village on its mountain perch. We stumbled into it. There were four of us, and everyone of us was changed."

"Who? This Grigol?"

"Yes, Grigol. Grigol most of all." Piotr looked around searchingly. How could he explain it? "The Khevsurs are full of contradictions," he said earnestly. "They're so full of noble ideas and yet steeped in pagan ways and superstition. But flashing from all this confusion would be these Christian images—a cross on a shield, a sacrifice of a lamb—but they had no idea what these things meant. With Grigol it was as though every one of these images was a blazing question in his soul. Well, he was a seeker. And he was one who found."

"Ah, it's Christ's Gospel that sets men's souls on fire," Makar interjected. "But you were the one who carried the spark."

"I wasn't aware of carrying anything."

"Who were the others with you?"

"Nina Abajarian, a girl from my village. She escaped the sham marriage her relatives had planned for her and instead married someone she loved—Grigol. But her half brother, Noe Tcheidze—he was with us along with his . . . his lover, a girl called Irina. They had only loss. She betrayed him to the Cossacks. The last time I saw Noe, he was reeling with the beating they'd given him."

Makar shifted uneasily. "They're praying now. We'd better move up."

When they had shouldered to the front, Piotr saw the oblong pit that sank deeply into the clay, ready for Agafya Andreivna. Makar touched his arm. "We need to help lower her."

They eased the casket into the ground. Runnels of loose sand slithered down here and there and then darted beneath the casket. Piotr started as the first shovelfuls of mustard-colored adobe hit the wood. He noticed that Makar was sticking close to him with a helpful, companionable silence. "We're putting the first of our loved ones into American soil, and my thoughts keep drifting back to that other place, that terrible spring," Piotr apologized as he took up the shovel. He joined several young men who filled the grave until a swelling mound rose below the redwood marker. Then they began tamping it down, hitting the dirt with the backs of their shovels as though to keep the earth itself from rising up against them.

III

Silver Dagger

Transcaucasia–1905

Noe's eyes were steady and agate-hard, but Irina saw that he was shuddering horribly from the beating that had reduced his body to chattel for the Cossacks. *The fiends*, she thought. But his man's soul looked out at her from his uncannily fixed eyes. They were filled with things she had never seen there, and his bitterness was gall in her mouth. The nervous gelding jittered beneath her. She felt her own features tremble, and she stretched out her hand. But even in the best of times tender little gestures were not their way.

Noe wrenched his head back. He lifted a hand to hold the flap of skin ripped down from the corner of his mouth. He held it gingerly while his fingers reddened, and his eyes bore down on her.

"Something for you, my love. A gift," he gasped. *What did it cost him to speak?* "In my saddlebags. A reward for your treachery. You'll know what to do with it!"

Then they dragged him away, their horses' hooves battering the delicate spring grass. The pounding hammered inside her own chest, and she let the high-strung gelding leap into a gallop. Her shaking hands forced him away from the Cossack troop and flung all his wild energy to the east—away from Mtskheta, away from the man with the mutilated face.

But how that face haunted her along the road! Not tattered and bruised, but whole and beautiful as she had known it. The Noe living in her mind was intact even as her own core disintegrated in dust and flying pebbles. "What is, is all that is." He had said that to her often as he traced her features with his sure fingers and summoned all that she knew of delight from her.

"It's enough, it's enough," she had always murmured. And it was. At the time.

The horse flew away to the north and east under the prick of her heels. The day was cool and light, but a darkness began welling up from behind the mountains. The light from the west fought it. The flash of a stream, the sudden glint of porphyry in a rock face, the runic shapes of splayed snowfields—they caught at her eyes, tugged at her in some vague way she could not describe. Something was unfolding before her—a sign, an omen. Instinctively, she reached a hand to her throat, but the charms and amulets of her childhood were no longer there. She had given all that up when she met Noe. "There is no meaning to it; it's all chance; and we, too—we're a cosmic accident," he had said. But chance was there, and Noe knew how to grasp at the main chance!

She had no idea how long she rode. She was weary beyond being able to tell whether her limbs were worn out, and the emotions rising within her crowded out any desire for food. But the horse was thirsty, and she stopped at one of the sparkling Caucasian springs. Irina dipped her hem in the cold rush of water and wiped her face with it. Then she bent to drink from her hands. They were numb when she stopped and began to fumble with the saddlebags.

So, my love, she thought grimly, *we'll see what kind of message you have for me*. She found it at the bottom beneath bundles of clothing and gear. Slim and dangerous and artfully concealed, its oiled leather was cleverly tooled, its point hidden. She paused for a moment before she unsheathed it. Not even the skillful carving of the smith who had wrought it could conceal its deadly intent. The fifteen-inch *kinjal* of the mountain tribes was made for killing. Irina held the dagger up to the light. The reddening sun licked fire along its glittering blade. The mountains to the north repeated its shape in their cold, impersonal thrust while the sloping green lands to the south brooded in the evening.

So that was it! Noe would sever their love in the most final way possible. Irina thought of the story her Kurdish grandmother had told her of the four Ossetian brothers who went out hunting. At evening as they cooked their prey, a poisonous snake fell unseen into the pot, and the four hunters died in agony. Later the worried parents sent out a sister to look for them. The young girl found the campsite and quickly took in what had happened. She wailed for her brothers and then drew the deadly *kinjal* that, like all good mountain lasses, she carried in her belt. Quickly she thrust it into her own heart. The five gravestones, four ranked together and one apart as befitted a mere woman, still weathered in some lost little glen in these mountains. Irina narrowed her eyes and stared at the iced-flanked peaks as if she could find the spot. *You and I will have our reckoning one day*, she told the mountain.

She weighed the dagger in her hand. There was no doubt that it was costly—and old, perhaps ancient. She touched a finger to the tip—and ready for business. Yes, a snake had fallen into the pot. All that she and Noe had had was poisoned. Why not act on his intent and make an end?

If that was his intent. The thought crystalized like the porphyry glints and flashing snow runes. Again she examined the intricate, magnificent workmanship. Could it have been meant as another kind of a gift? She knew that Grigol had given the dagger to Noe as bride price for Nina, along with the gelding that now stamped and snorted beside her. Grigol had given this valuable gift to seal a love, ensure a bond. Could it really be that Noe would want it used to cut off her life? But, after all, what was her life worth now? Her thoughts broke into two warring factions. *Your life is worth much if this is a token of forgiveness—a rich gift to aid your life in days to come . . .*

Impossible. Everything in her culture, in her own nature, and in Noe's last bitter glance told her that this could not be the case. And yet Grigol had meant the *kinjal* as a love-gift. For his lovely Nina.

Irina shivered and turned toward the southern meadows. The overshadowed mountains were now charcoal and purple, but the afternoon sun, licking out from beneath a cloud-ledge, tarried vividly on the lowlands. *Noe is not the only giver.* Then she remembered the hatred in her lover's eyes. Noe's cool gaiety and hot love were gone. "You'll know what to do with it," he had said. Yes, she knew.

IRINA FOLLOWED THE STREAM toward the east until she came to a stone shepherd's hut. She looked around quickly. Pale snowfields and glaciers jutted from the dark mountainsides in fantastic shapes as insistent as proclamations. She turned from them impatiently. Clay, sheep dung, and moldy straw—these were the familiar scents of her childhood. The hut with its rounded walls, its oneness with the river's pebbles, nestled snugly in its triangle between the rush of the stream and the peace of the meadow. It was like a womb—a place to think.

What did life hold for her? Impossible to go back to her family. They would cast her out with a slice of her nose missing! The code of the Kurds did not forgive. A job in the city? She knew where that would end. With another man. The next in a meaningless string of relationships—"protectors"—until she was too old to be attractive. *No, I'm too proud for that.*

Irina built a pyramid of *kizyak* bricks to fuel a small fire. She bent over it, brooding. Her dark cloak fell around her like a web of shadow. Its coarse fabric brushed her cheek. She had worn a *nabadi* like this as young girl in her father's house before the days of her shame. She remembered his hawk's face—gaunt and narrow with cheekbones that sprang from beneath his large, predatory eyes. Below his black mustache his mouth pronounced the Prophet's words. "Men have authority over women because Allah has made the one superior to the other," he chanted with an Imam's voice. "And because they spend their wealth to maintain them. Good women are obedient. They guard their unseen parts because God has guarded them. As for those from whom you fear disobedience, admonish them and beat them." And from the young girl—Amina they had called her then—he feared disobedience and guaranteed it with a rod.

Yet because he had no son, he taught her to read and set her to memorizing *suras* from the Koran while her silent mother looked on.

"Ah, my little Amina—see how quickly she learns," he told her mother. "Her mind is like a man's." But Amina's mother looked away with tightened lips. She was a woman so watchful that the merest glance away made Amina feel lost—annihilated. Her silent attentiveness seldom faltered. As a little girl, Amina imagined that the scissors she always wore at her sash were a second pair of eyes, watching.

Then the days of rebellion swept over the highlands, and strangers came into the high-perched villages. By this time Amina was a young woman with her father's expressive mouth and the same prominent bone ledge that housed her hot, fixed eyes and gave her face its striking beauty. Noe did not fail to notice it when he came into the village. His quick sureness, the graceful verve to all his actions captivated her. His smile and gestures were free, generous, and kind, and she could see the truth in his eyes. "I cannot offer you marriage. You know the price for what you do."

"What is, is all that is!" Her fierce sureness startled even herself. But she knew what was in her own heart even then. "The adulteress may marry only the adulterer or an idolater," said the Prophet. In spite of the hundred lashes prescribed by Muhammad, she had chosen her idolater, and he had cost her everything.

Amina was sure that neither of her parents suspected anything the night before she left with Noe. Her blood boiled with expectation all the night, until at last a dark tide of sleep welled up within her, blotting out her thoughts of Noe. A skittle of stones awoke her, and she sprang up from her cot with a feeling of marvelous lightness and freedom. A moment later she saw why. Her long, heavy hair lay scattered about the pallet, neatly severed. Glossy black ribbons of hair that had once reached to her knees rippled among the bedclothes. Her mother's work. She reached up to feel the cut ends. *I am marked—there's no going back.* Quickly she drew out her bundle of clothing. Then pausing, she wrapped one of the tresses around her hand like a bandage. Grabbing her cloak, she lightly stepped out of the stone hut forever.

It would have been better if Noe had shared the laughter in her heart when she met him in the ravine. "Your hand! What?"

She pressed the severed hair to his cheek, and he reached up for it. She threw back her cloak to show him her shorn head. "I've been punished in advance for my wickedness," she said airily.

But Noe was disturbed. "It's a sad loss," he said. "It was a great beauty."

Cold iron pressed on her heart. Was it her hair he had loved? Too late now. Honor demanded that he protect her. The first awareness of what she had done crept into her mind, and she lurched for the pride that would uphold her. "Do you feel cheated?" she challenged him.

"No. Never that," he said. He took the shining black strand in his two hands and looped it around her neck and pulled her to him. The morning was remade as he kissed her. But as they made their way down the ravine, she looked back. There on the crag near the village was a form back-lit by the flare of dawn. It looked almost like a great bird—black-winged and with a raptor's stoop. But Amina knew it was the cloaked figure of her mother.

"A new life—you'll need a new name," Noe told her as they drew closer to the Christian towns of Georgia. "A name like Amina will set people wondering what pure Muslim maiden I've enticed from her home."

"You choose it," she said.

Noe scrutinized her, narrowing his sparkling hazel eyes. "Irina. That suits you, I think. And, besides, it has a similar sound—so you won't be forgetting who you are."

"Irina," she repeated. "And what does it mean?"

"Peace," Noe said surprised. "It means peace."

She accepted the name, but she knew there would be no peace for her. The love she had given everything for was already tainted by doubt. And only Allah knew what maledictions flew from that black figure on the crag. *I have no past and no future. I can only live for the day.* And she tightened her grip on the handsome, unpredictable man beside her.

"No past and no future," she mused in the dim hut. Even in his bitterness, Noe was right. His choice was the only one for her. And yet, she flared inwardly, how dare he cast aside her life in a flash of rage? No, if any choices were to made, she would do the choosing. *I won't be the meek sacrifice to his outraged love! I'll end it in my own way—so that he'll know it was my own choosing.*

Suddenly, the blue splash of moonlight on the floor darkened. She realized that stream sound was no longer the only noise surrounding the hut. Behind her the movement of flocks, the hoarse coughing and choking of sheep sent a thrill of fear through her. A wailing Caucasian pipe drew out plaintive notes in a repeated pattern. Played once, then cut off, then played again softly but somehow more insistently. Then a third time—sounding farther away this time. But she knew the player was near, near.

She reached for her weapon with a quick, instinctive grasp. But the shadowed shape was too quick for her. A powerful grip shot pain through her wrist; she crouched and writhed but held onto her dagger. Her face was shoved into an armpit smelling of leather and wool and wood smoke—and a strong man's sweat. The *kinjal* snapped out of her fist, but she pounded at the man who held her, and he backed away holding her treasure.

He was a brown, sinewy man, tall and rangy in build. Even in the dim hut she could see the gleam of his gray eyes as he examined the dagger. A small, appreciative grunt escaped from his throat. Then the gray eyes lifted to take her in.

"Where did you get this?"

She maintained a sullen silence. She owed this intruder no answers!

"An heirloom? It's old. You must know that." The oddly clear eyes studied her. The voice coming from that dark, craggy face was curiously mild. He shrugged at her silence. "The maker wanted to show beauty in utility—not carve fury into murder."

"It was designed for killing."

"Killing comes from what's in the heart, not from a tool. But you're right—its task is to cut flesh." He balanced the dagger in his hand. She flinched as he approached her and then brushed her aside and called out to someone. "Jano!"

A young man, probably still in his teens, stooped into the opening.

"Ah, a fire!" He sprang down on his knees like a Cossack dancer. His offerings of twigs and dried grasses stoked the fire's zeal.

The older shepherd disappeared while the younger one began pulling a battered pan from his sack. "I'll make you a *pilaw* such as you've never tasted," he promised her.

"I'm not hungry."

But Jano smiled at her gaily. The old shepherd came in with hunks of mutton; he threw these into the pot and then tossed the blood-stained dagger back to Irina. Grimacing, she dipped it in the boiling pot and wiped it on her skirt. The movement brought her closer to the two faces bent above the fire. The boy was dark-haired with a fine, high coloring and merry eyes. He eagerly prodded the simmering gruel, sprinkling in spices from a packet he drew from beneath his shirt.

"We come with our flocks from the Shirakli steppe," Jano told her. "At winter's end we travel back to our summer pastures in Tusheti. The steppe—you've been there? No? It's a long way from here—many *versts*. The journey takes us twenty days. The steppe—it's as flat and bare as a piece of *lavash!* After four months of it, a man longs for the high places." He glanced eagerly at his companion, but the older man kept his eyes on the bricks of *kizyak* falling to red ruin.

Irina drew her knees up and watched them. She was beginning to feel safe—safe enough to acknowledge the gnaw of hunger in her belly.

"It's good," commented the young shepherd. The remark was addressed to the pot, but so diffuse and hearty was his manner that it took in everything—the warm fire, the snuffling sheep, the silky murmuring of the stream.

The two men ate from the one pot in the manner of nomads, scooping out boluses of the grease-laden, starchy mess and swallowing with the hungry man's attentive silence. They nudged the pan over to her when they had finished—or, as she suspected, before they had finished. Hospitality, even to a lone woman, was the rule of the mountains, whether cot or castle. She unwrapped some rounds of *lavash* that Noe must have picked up in Ananuri and passed them around. She dipped hers into the *pilaw* and bit into it, letting the strong spices burst in her mouth. Jano eyed her with kindly interest.

Later she pulled her cloak around her and slumped into a straw-packed corner. The young man was already stretched out beside the fire. The old shepherd watched by the door, playing his flute. His rootlike fingers searched along the wooden pipe, drawing out his few notes again and again. Irina listened, puzzled. Was there a point to it? Why the same notes? And why did his light eyes gleam so—shining oddly in that dark place?

Over and over she heard Noe's challenge. The pipe echoed itself. *No respite.* And over and over the tough, tenacious root of her early training leached its sap into her blood. Her father's Koran-fed words came to her. "Unbelievers think that their days are prolonged for their own good. They're wrong. We give them respite only that they might commit more grievous sins. A shameful punishment awaits them."

The glowing embers began to wheeze and redden strangely; Irina saw that storm clouds overshadowed the moon. Pellets of rain rattled against the stone walls and hustled the stream into a splashing rush. Cold gusts came in to rifle the ashes and spray sparks into the corners. The herdsman drew in a great gulp of air and began to play again. He had found all the lost notes. His fingers groped along the stops while his clear, grave eyes gleamed in the dark. It was as though the air were full of secret sound, and he was sifting through it to find those exquisite chains and garlands of melody. The pipe exhaled its music, wavering in subtle variations until it touched the wellspring of longing where beauty becomes pain and pain is bliss. The abstract and the commonplace rose up and declared that nothing is accident; note and wind and wood repeated it. The design is perfect and breathes its rich intent into all things.

Irina staggered at the thought. *Intent!* She was pinned between two only—her own and Noe's. She again unsheathed the silver dagger. Its etchings were incised perfection; its shape expressed its purpose. She looked again at the two men. The piper's last note ascended and drifted away. The old shepherd subsided into his corner. She watched him briefly. Then she pulled her cloak around her and turned her face to the wall. She placed the *kinjal* between the wall and her hand. *An odd precaution—the only hand I need fear is my own.*

IN THE MORNING Irina ducked from the dim enclosure and shaded her eyes against the brilliant glare. The crisp air sparkled, and the meadow heaved with the moving fleeces of many thousands of sheep. Jano approached her excitedly.

"You see, even the sheep are eager!"

Irina shrugged. The beasts dourly pulled up the juicy grass.

"We go to the green alpine meadows—north and north! Travel with us if your road lies that way."

"My road lies to the south," Irina said, surprised at her own sureness. "I have business in the city." The thoughts fermenting within her in the long, wakeful night bore their fruit. She would go to Tiflis, to the Metekhi prison. She would confront Noe and uncover what was in his mind. Then she would use his gift as she saw fit. She would lay all the maddening, frustrating enigmas to rest!

A full day's ride took her to the outskirts of Tiflis. She scanned the brown, boiling flood of the Kura as she crossed one of the ancient bridges. Her eyes took in the brick houses, wooden balconies, and cobbled streets, searching. Rank on rank, the old houses teetered on the cliff edge above the river. Mount David swelled in the westering rays; and in the old town, across from Sioni Cathedral and the tall Russian bell tower, the conical tower of the Metekhi fortress sent its pointed shadow arrowing across the earth. Her sureness that she would find Noe there sent a wave of excitement over her.

She came to the old apartment where their work together had begun and where that fierce love had grown between them. The crowded shadows of the Nadzaladevi quarter hid her as she tethered the horse and slipped up the narrow stairs. She opened the door, and the smells of ink and cigarette smoke and the stale waft of her own rose water perfume met her and pounded her with memories. They had been happy, hadn't they? How were they to know that there was something stunted about their love that wouldn't hold for the fate dealt them? Irina sat on the bed stroking the green coverlet like a beloved face.

All her life she had been struck before she knew her crime. This time she had been the one to strike. Was it the old patterns of haphazard punishment that made her betray the only one she loved? Or was it her hidden rage? Her gorge rose, choking her as she thought of Noe's anger at his sister's marriage to Grigol. Nina had married according to tribal customs—but, no, it must be according to all the Orthodox traditions that the anarchist Noe had said meant nothing! What meant nothing was Irina's love—her giving of her whole being, the years of danger and sacrifice. And so she had struck out. The authorities in Ananuri were pleased to learn that the noted revolutionary Noe Tcheidze was easy prey for those who knew where to find him. Nothing in her imagination had prepared her for what it would do to her to see him when they had finished with him.

Irina glanced about absently. The room was much as they had left it—disheveled after a hurried departure. She noticed a rucksack stuffed with provisions. It must have been left by one of the many friends—comrades in the struggle—who came and went.

Pen and paper were positioned on the rough table as though asking a question. She went over and picked up the pen wearily and began writing because her mind seethed with taunting mysteries, because her heart sickness cried for expression, because there was no one she could talk to.

She noticed a volume of poetry on the table, its cover ajar. She turned it over—Shota Rustaveli's *The Knight in the Tiger Skin*. Where did it come from? Irina was familiar with the twelfth-century poem about the Christian knight Tariel and his quest for his lost bride. The great epic was so beautiful that every Georgian bride quoted it at her wedding. It certainly couldn't be Noe's. Even Noe wasn't crude enough to taunt her with that. The book opened to whatever was crammed inside—something blue-black scattering in satin ribbons across the page. Irina stared. It was human hair—her own. *Another enigma.* She carefully replaced the hair and the book. She began weeping, and when she finished weeping, she began writing.

> *Where were you, my knight in a tiger skin, hiding darkly in*
> *your sleek fur?*
> *You held out your hand, and I counted my life into your*
> *palm, careless of its value.*
> *Then your strong fingers flexed and crushed and wrung*
> *from me blood and balm.*
> *Turning my shoulder, I fled the rage of my father's house,*
> *·driven to a deeper, stronger fury.*
> *Your eyes and hands held me and hold me still.*
> *What you desired from me was given;*
> *What you desire for me—will that be given, too?*
>
> *The mountains clash with symbols,*
> *The airs of heaven breathe out through the shepherd's*
> *cracked lips,*
> *But I am deaf, attuned only to you.*
> *Where are you, hiding darkly, while your secret intent*
> *whips my thoughts in the night?*

Can Allah give peace where dark things lie forested, sprung
for a pounce?
Now my offerings are ash and yet to be set before a greater
Prince.
And I look for you, my dark one, still—my fate strung to
the pull of your will.

I must know! She cloaked herself in her *nabadi* and went out on the streets. At Metekhi fortress, the watchman was courteously vague. "Tcheidze? I'm not sure. There have been so many new ones. . . ."

He led her to a desk where a uniformed officer probed her with tired, bored eyes. "Tcheidze? Ah! That one. The Cossacks lost that one." The room spun around Irina, then stopped dead. "The slippery eel—he threw himself over an escarpment, handcuffed as he was. They didn't bother to search for the body."

So, my dark one, you've slipped away—and all my heart's questions unanswered.

Her face was hot and the night air cool as she made her way back to Nadzaladevi. She sat on the green coverlet for a long time. All the bright beauty that was Noe was gone. Her hands were clenched in the rough stuff of black purdah. She loosed them and watched as her slim right hand, pale against the robe, slid down to the pack on the floor to the tooled scabbard where Noe's gift to her waited. She unsheathed it and, drawing aside her garment, thrust the point into her side beneath her ribs. She distinctly felt the point deflect off of something hard, then bite with a pithy scrunch into her flesh. Gasping, she fell back on the bed. *Have I failed? The pain, the pain—it must be mortal.*

But even if it wasn't, she comforted herself. She was so utterly alone that she had plenty of time to bleed to death. She closed her eyes and waited for darkness.

IV

Purchase of Pain

Sirakan Abajarian wedged his cart beneath a rickety overhanging balcony. Shouldering his day's purchases, he climbed the narrow stairway into Noe's old quarters. Someone had left a valuable bay gelding tethered to the railing. *The fool! That'll be gone by morning.* Repulsive odors wafted up from the alleyway, fetid even in the cool of the rain-swept night. *Oh well, it's a place to stay.* Sirakan's welcome in some of his old friends' homes had cooled since his half sister Nina had jilted the wealthy industrialist that Aram Abajarian had picked out for her.

Nina—where is she now? And Piotr—did he make it safely out of the country? How Sirakan's tough common sense had skirmished with his heart when Nina had pleaded so piteously for her freedom! Sirakan knew he'd face all kinds of reprisals, both subtle and not so subtle, if he helped her escape, but what could he do? By forcing the marriage, he'd be sentencing a young woman to a lifetime of unhappiness. Poor Nina! Her choice was certain unhappiness with Mourad Mushegan or the uncertainties of an escape with Noe, her half brother.

Sirakan ground his teeth with the frustration that Noe always brought up in him. The weasel! It was hard enough to turn Nina over to him, but Noe had to bring his mistress—that Kurdish harlot with her proud eyes and sensuous mouth. Certainly not a fit companion for Nina who had been brought up as a sequestered Armenian maiden—even if she was half-Georgian. Maybe it was just as well

64

that she left. Relations in the village were growing more and more tense. Even Noe's hare-brained schemes might be safer than the bitter animosity boiling beneath the surface there. Ah yes, these were days when everyone lived close to the edge!

He set his packages at the top of the stairs and fumbled for the latch. The room was completely dark. A cloying unrest that quickened to fear pressed on him. He felt his way to the table and the paraffin lamp—where was it? Glass shattered as his elbow knocked it over, but only the chimney was broken. The wick flared under his trembling hand. From the shadows on the bed sprang a statue face, gray-hued with perfectly chiseled features and damp hair falling back from a severe forehead. Sirakan gave a violent start that sent the shadows lurching. He set the lamp on the table. A pumping tide of blood soaked the girl's cloak and bodice. Sirakan moved quickly as an immense calm steadied him. He pulled back her garment and pressed the coverlet to the wound. It looked as though the knife had deflected downward from her breastbone and cut deeply toward her diaphragm, narrowly missing the heart and lungs.

Sirakan took a deep breath and began muttering. "For bleeding, apply pressure; make sure the wound is higher than the heart." He followed his own instructions automatically. Still pressing hard to staunch the wound, he raised the dying girl with his left arm. Only then did he recognize her.

Sirakan sank heavily onto the bed. He saw that he could not take his hand off the wound for even a second. He pulled Irina up against his chest so that he could press the wound with his elbow while tearing strips of sheeting with his hands and teeth. When he had enough bandages, he paused and stole a look at the frozen profile. He removed the blood-soaked wad of coverlet and pressed a folded square of sheeting to the wound. Next he would have to bandage it. Somehow he doubted that anything less sure than the weight of his own hand, his own flesh, could keep that terrible flow from starting again. The girl's head lolled against his shoulder; he steadied her with his free hand and shifted his back against the iron headboard.

He pressed hard on the square of cotton that separated him from Irina's wound and held onto the limp young body. *In all my days I've never held a woman like this*. He reached for her hand and felt for the feeble pulse. He knew it was there. Hadn't he seen her heart's work as it pumped out that red tide? The iron pipes behind him bore into his back, and a feeling of awkward tenderness and wrenching fear filled him. *Will she live? And what will become of her if she does?*

God help her, he prayed. *She's so cold!* He held her tightly against his burly chest, letting his own body's heat flow into her. He did not move when the lamp went out, but he continued to hold her through the hours of darkness. The faint rise and fall of her breathing stirred up all the yearnings that he had so carefully kept submerged. Sirakan's deepest instincts told him that the times were apocalyptic. His practical sense insisted that it was a time to prepare for the worst, a time to preserve what could be preserved, a time to protect those who relied on him—not a time to siphon off needed strength and resources in new involvements.

But as he cradled the unconscious girl, he found himself wishing that this were any woman other than Noe's Irina, that he could put aside his fears and reach for the human bonds denied him. The stretch of early manhood behind him that had seemed so productive, now seemed empty because he had not held a woman so, had not given all he knew he had to give.

By dawn Sirakan was cold and stiff, but it seemed that the inert girl was warmer, more supple. A curious peace suffused him as he laid her down on the bed and rebandaged her wound. Strangely, she had a long lock of blue-black hair wound around her left hand. Whose was it? Warily he looked around the rumpled bed and untidy room. *Be on the alert,* he reminded himself. *Whoever did this may return.*

He pulled the blood-stained coverlet off the bed and started as something heavy clattered to the floor. Gray-white light sifted in like ash and silvered the carved handle of a magnificent Georgian dagger. Sirakan held it gingerly, avoiding the touch of the blood-crusted blade. In his market-stall ramblings, Sirakan had seen plenty of deadly weapons—Russian swords, Turkish scimitars, the wicked curved *tulwars* of India, and these mountain *kinjals*. But he had never seen one like this. *A work of art—and ancient. Where did it come from? From some ancient warrior's tomb in the Caucasus? Or the secret cache of a rebel tribesman? Or did it lie hidden in the ruin of a forgotten battle-field to be found—by whom? This girl?*

A mixture of awe and horror crept over him as he gazed at the sleeping Irina. For the first time he realized that her wound was self-inflicted. He stared at the beautiful, remote face. No answers there. What had prompted her to do such a desperate thing? Of course, her situation with Noe was irregular, to say the least, and yet they had seemed happy enough in their intense way. But he had always felt that the vehement love Irina visited upon Noe was somehow dangerous. He looked around the room thoughtfully, wondering how the flare and flow of pride and passion had kept those two together in such dreary circumstances. *Not much of a life for a woman.*

The room, one of many similar rooms that had housed this baffling love, was dingy and comfortless. The sagging bed filled one corner, its metal head and foot leaning toward each other like wiry schemers. Next to it was a small washstand with its flowered china bowl and pitcher. The window was glazed like a pastry so that even the spring morning was colored like winter. The bookshelves were stacked with pamphlets, tins of food, and cooking things among the dusty volumes. A door opened onto a ramshackle balcony screened with an ancient wooden lattice. A spirit stove perched on one end of the long table cluttered with tin utensils, folded clothing, a few scattered books. One of them was lying open.

Sirakan glanced at the title—*The Knight in the Tiger Skin*. He read through some of the beautiful, ancient verses before he noticed the note tucked inside. But it was not a note. Sirakan could see that it was a cry into a void . . . and yet, and yet somewhere in Irina's bruised heart and confused mind she had a glimmer of something beyond despair. ". . . my offerings are ash and yet to be set before a greater Prince. . . ." If only she knew how princely that Prince was. The thought of mercy incarnate brought the sting of tears.

A burlesque review of his own petty thoughts paraded in front of him: "Harlot, Noe's draggle-tailed wench, that Gypsy slut, wanton . . ." Sirakan shook his head to throw off the badgering words. He was bitterly ashamed. Before whom? The answer came striding with its brilliant shaft of light. *The Prince.* Love pushed aside the sour censuring posturings. Suddenly, surely, Sirakan knew that just as Irina had absorbed his own body's warmth in the long night, he had absorbed her, too, as one for whom he would always care.

The morning drew on; the sun stabbed through the cloud cover here and there, potent enough to penetrate the grease-filmed win-

dow and reveal the shambles around him. *What a mess!* Sirakan
absently began dusting and tidying the room. The simple, habitual
movements reminded him of all that awaited him back at the
Abajarian shop. *It'll have to wait.* He hoped that his father's shys-
ter ways wouldn't stir up the wrath of the villagers in these sensi-
tive times.

Sirakan studied the girl on the bed; her face was chalky, and she
looked as though she were receding into the rumpled, gray-white
sheets. Sirakan shrugged uneasily. *My work is cut out for me.
Impossible to abandon her.* Well, his father would have to attend to the
shop. Pray God he won't set the whole village at odds!

Order restored, Sirakan picked up the water pitcher and some
rags. *I'll have to arrange to stable my horses, send word back to the village,* he reminded himself on his way down the stairs. At the bottom,
gazing at him with liquid pleading in its eyes, was the beautiful bay
he had seen earlier.

"Still here?" The gelding blew on him gently as he searched
through the saddlebag. It was Noe's. "Where are you?" he muttered
and twisted his head around as though he expected his elusive stepbrother to waft up from the cobblestones.

"Here's a riddle," Sirakan confided to the horse. "His lady love
is at death's door upstairs; he's suddenly the owner of a matchless
beast like you, and he's nowhere to be found. But what else would I
expect?" The gelding nuzzled him affectionately and began nosing
into the saddlebag.

"Sorry, no breakfast here. Come on, we'll go where there are better accommodations."

At midmorning he returned bringing bread, fruit, and cheese.
He stopped at the tap in the courtyard to fill his pitcher. The slice of
sky that appeared above the buildings showed a day at odds with
itself. Moody clouds hastening from the north would suddenly block
the cheery snatches of sun. The fickle light and sharp shifting shadows of Nadzaladevi made everything seem distorted, deceptive.

Sirakan balanced his pitcher carefully as he mounted the
steps—were they always this warped? He stopped on the landing
briefly. A dark shadow clicked into place. The lattice on the balcony was riddled with damage like moth-eaten lace, the once-pre-
cise pattern all askew. The sun flashed briefly; a pointed angle

licked at his feet, and apprehension prickled the back of his neck. Then he saw that the door was ajar.

He stashed his provisions carefully and stole a quick look inside. A man was standing beside the window staring at the bed. His face was twisted with such loathing that Sirakan made a quick, clumsy gesture as though he could block the hatred in that riveted look.

"What are you doing?" he blustered.

The man turned and studied him with protuberant, unsurprised eyes. Then his skin seemed to bulge as malice distorted his lumpish features. *Like rodents ferreting under a tablecloth,* Sirakan thought.

"The murderess!" He fixed Sirakan with an implacable look. "You've been warming a viper at your breast."

"What do you mean?"

"This woman killed your brother."

"Noe?"

"Exactly."

"Noe is dead?" Cold sweat broke out on his forehead. Noe dead? Sirakan had never considered whether he even liked his stepbrother. Now all the gaiety and charm that the effervescent Noe had brought to the lonely son of a grasping Armenian shopkeeper darted from his mind to his heart. A sense of great loss crushed him, and he sank unsteadily onto one of the wooden chairs.

"Tell me . . . ," he pleaded. Then more sternly he demanded, "Who are you? How do you know me?"

"I know everything about you," the man said. "You are Sirakan Abajarian—son of Aram Abajarian by his first wife. You became Noe Tcheidze's stepbrother when your father married Maria, widow of Davit Tcheidze. I know how much money you squeeze from the peasants each year. I know—" He broke off suddenly, and his face twitched with crafty thought.

Ah, Sirakan realized, *the two-tailed devil is one to use information to whip me with! He's a fox, but the fool has nosed into the bear's den!*

Sirakan let a sigh gust from beneath his full, glossy mustache. He slapped his two hands down hard on his muscular thighs and drew himself up to his full, brawny-chested wrestler's stance. The intruder started; the big Armenian quietly put a heavy hand on his guest's shoulder and guided him to a chair. His hand tightened, and the man squirmed.

"You sit here," Sirakan said firmly. "You can tell me your name, your business, and what brought you here. Then you can tell me what you know—or claim to know about my brother's death."

The man chewed his lip as though its taste repulsed him. Then he shrugged. "Who I am is no secret. My name is Zviad Kostava. If you troubled to look around you, you'd see my name on some of these pamphlets."

"Tell me something new. All of Noe's friends are social-democrats, followers of Zoe Zordania—"

"No!" Sirakan saw that he'd struck a nerve. "Not Zordania. His petty little vision of a free Georgia is vapid, feeble. I follow a man who sees the world as his field. A new world order where workers are supreme! I follow Koba—the son of a shoemaker from Gori—but someday he'll be great."

"So . . . you're one of these Bolsheviks."

"And Noe was, too. Or was turning that way—before this whore destroyed him. She killed him as surely as if she'd taken a knife to him."

"This woman loved him. I don't know much about women, but that much I could see."

"You don't know much about women if you don't know that love can turn to hate with the flick of an eyelash. She turned on him as soon as she felt he'd bruised her pride. He was captured by Cossacks. Did you know that? They beat him brutally. Then they dragged him Georgian-style toward a Cossack outpost—tied to the tail of one of their horses. But he cheated them in the end. He threw himself off the edge of an escarpment. His hands were chained, but he died free! And this snake here—she's the one who betrayed him. All because of a woman's pride."

"Why?" Sirakan was genuinely puzzled.

Cunning stirred across Zviad's face; he pursed his mouth, and an odious glee oiled his eyes. The Armenian was suddenly afraid of what he might hear.

"It was because of Nina, your sister."

"What!" *Nina was dear to him, dear.*

Zviad warmed to his story. "Your sister, it seems, gave herself to one of these mountain tribesmen. Noe demanded that the man marry her in a traditional wedding—priest and all—the whole bourgeois charade. When this one here heard of it, the sparks flew! The idea that the free love that Noe talked her into wasn't good enough for his sister gnawed at her like rust on iron. The next day she disappeared. When Noe, his Khevsur friend, and that reactionary Russian peasant left their mountain hideaway, the Cossacks were waiting."

"My sister?"

"My sources tell me that Noe was captured and died trying to escape; the Khevsur and Russian were taken for questioning and released. I've heard nothing of any woman."

"Prod your memory," Sirakan growled, "or I'll wring it out of you. I can see that you know something. You were there!"

Zviad's face jumped in alarm. "I left. I could see what was coming, and I took off before any of them. When I left, Nina was there, safe with Noe and her new husband."

"Who is he?" Sirakan demanded.

Zviad shrugged. "A Khevsur smith from one of the villages above Passanauri. His name is Grigol. Noe seemed to use him as a contact for fleeing refugees—and he was great friends with the Russian, Piotr. That's all I can tell you."

"If she has come to harm—" Sirakan's voice shook with the force of his warning.

The Georgian threw up two hands, palms outward. "Don't blame me. I had nothing to do with it. If you want to blame someone, look behind you. That wanton is responsible for your brother's death and for your sister's disappearance."

"Get out!"

Zviad thoughtfully rubbed his hands together and then made for the door with infuriating slowness. He shot a last look of rancor at the bed. "I'll be back," he said softly.

Sirakan bolted the door. His head was throbbing. Little steel hammers tabored at him and set up a ringing in his ears. *Where is she? Could Nina really have done that?* His only chance of finding her was to locate some mountain savage—*Grigol. Was that it?*—out of all the tribesmen of the Khevsur valley. Sick at heart, he turned his eyes back to the girl on the bed.

She was watching him. Her eyes glittered with fever. *I never saw that her eyes are like gray-flecked granite, not brown.* Flying fragments of thought and feeling blended into coherence in those eyes. Sirakan felt suddenly alienated from her.

"You heard?" he asked. She nodded.

"Is it true?" She nodded again.

"Nina?"

"It's true. The Cossacks were badgering Nina and the boy. But when they came to arrest Noe, they said she'd been taken—by some Georgians."

"Where?"

Irina closed her eyes; her voice was weakening. "No one knows. Grigol . . . he'll find out. He'll find her . . ."

"This Grigol—is he a good man?"

She nodded, then pressed her cheek into the pillow.

Sirakan eyed her, thoughtfully stroking his mustache. What to do? Every sinew in his body wanted to rush out and search for his lost sister. But a pinprick of thought insisted: *If I leave her, she'll either do away with herself, or someone like Zviad will come and finish her.* The clear need would have to take precedence over the remote possibility that he could be of help to Nina. He'd have to leave that to God—and to this Grigol. The decision filled him with peace and purpose. He felt that something new, something beautiful had taken place in his soul, but he shied away from the thought and turned quickly to practical matters.

It was a comfort to him that Nina's new husband was, at least, friends with Piotr Gavrilovich. Piotr, he knew, was a good man. He'd protect Nina from harm if he could—plus Sirakan had always suspected that the young Russian had a soft spot for his pretty sister.

He took up his pitcher and some clean rags and with his sure, practical hands began cleaning and dressing the wound on the pale girl who had brought so much woe on his family.

THE HAZE THAT PUSHED around Irina was thick, viscous. Too heavy to permit movement. But she could hear the accuser's voice: "Murderess! Wanton!" Then another voice, rich and heavy as gold. The deep voice cleared the room, and a big man-shape guarded her bed. She closed her eyes. *Safety.* She opened them and recognized Noe's stepbrother, Sirakan.

The big Armenian was slumped in a chair, chin on chest, sleeping heavily. She had never paid much attention to him. She moved in circles where shopkeepers were not admired. But now she studied him carefully. He was so different from the wiry, slender, swift-moving Noe. Sirakan's bones were massive and thickly muscled. His whole trunk planted on the flimsy chair was just that—a trunk in might, girth, and steadfastness. Yet his hands, feet, and ears were neatly made and set. The lavish mustache did not quite conceal his red, generous lower lip.

And for a big man, he was strangely graceful in his movements. For nearly a week he seemed to hover on the perimeter of her dim world, preoccupied and quiet; yet those things that needed doing seemed somehow to be done. She weakly let go—let herself flow under the current of his unobtrusive care. From somewhere outside came a spatter of gunfire. Stuttering bursts rang out between irregular pauses; then came a final single shot like a period ending a mad dialogue. She recognized the sound, but a soft-cushioned inertia left her meek and compliant. *Let them shoot*, she thought indifferently.

She sank into slumber. When she awoke again, the room was bright with a new day, and everything in it seemed sharp-edged, clear. Sirakan was standing over the spirit stove, stirring something with precise movements of his large hand. But when she cautiously eased her body into a sitting position, he turned with quick alertness and a warm smile.

"So you're ready for gymnastics. Don't do too much," he commented. "Your wound is doing nicely." She flushed uneasily. She was wearing a clean shirt, and the bandages around her midriff had obviously received conscientious attention.

"Perhaps," Sirakan added, "you're watertight enough to hold some of this."

She took the bowl and began to eat hungrily, astonished at how good the simplest gruel could taste. But the effort soon exhausted her, and she set it aside. Then, looking at Sirakan, she knit her brows. "I'm better," she said. "Much better. You can go."

"Go where?"

"Home. Back to your business."

"I think for now you're my business."

"Why? Why do you stay?"

Wry amusement bristled the dark mustache. "I'm not sure myself."

To escape his clear, attentive gaze, Irina let her eyes drift about the room. The window sparkled, and the scattered contents of the room had been neatly stacked on the bookshelf. The table had been cleared except for a few bowls, the stove, and a vague glint that she recognized as her *kinjal*. She looked away quickly, her fingers cold on the counterpane. It was as if all its glittering menace had sheared into her diaphragm again. Sirakan reached for her discarded supper.

"Why did you do it?" he asked brusquely.

All her defenses sputtered to life. "Why should—," she flared, then stopped. Somehow she felt she owed this man an explanation. She raised her eyes and looked deeply into his. "Noe is gone. Do you know what that means to me?" His face moved, and he looked away. His compassion cut and cut.

Her voice was swollen with all the pain of the past weeks. "And it's what he wanted, what he wanted for me."

"What! That's—but wait. You turned him in. Still Noe wouldn't want that. He's too confident in himself, in his ability to weasel out of any situation. He wouldn't hold you to that."

"He would. I saw his face. He hated me."

"The rage of the moment. An hour later he'd have forgiven you."

"Was that," she nodded toward the dagger, "the gift of forgiveness? He gave that to me—just as they dragged him away. You know he had one purpose, one only."

Sirakan walked over to the window, stroking his mustache with a smooth, deliberate gesture—as though calming a wild beast. Then he picked up the dagger, and, holding it across his palm, he let the light play on the carved pommel. Irina stared, fascinated. *What mind had imagined those whorls unwinding with all the grace and power of nature and that strange geometric device—stark as an omen.* It was a thing of rare beauty. Entranced, she reached for it. But Sirakan held it away.

"I'm no expert on antiquities," he said, "but this is ancient. It probably belongs in a museum. And it's valuable. Noe must have realized that when he gave it to you. Where did he get it?"

"From Grigol. It was part of the bride price for Nina. That and the horse and some other things."

"Not bad. This Grigol—is he a rich man?"

"No. But he is a skilled craftsman. You know how important a good smith is in the mountains. Maybe this was a family treasure."

"Maybe. He must have loved her," he added, almost to himself. "A man needn't have paid so well for a girl in such a precarious position."

"Not so precarious as mine," Irina said hotly.

"And yet you are the one with the gift. I wonder, what will you do with it?"

"Give it to me."

Watching her intently, he handed it to her. It was warm from his hand. "What will you do?"

"You ask? Noe had only one thought in mind—to punish."

"Maybe there's another plan. You could sell this—I could get you a lot for it—and start a new life."

"Doing what?"

"Living. Just that is gift enough. I think that in the times ahead, many will have that gift wrenched from them unwillingly. How do you know that you weren't chosen for this just so you can have a chance at a new life—a new start?"

She snorted derisively. "That wasn't what Noe had in mind."

"Forget Noe. There's a purpose higher than his. Do you think he's the one who should shape your fate?"

"Who then?"

"The One who ordains all things."

Irina shrugged impatiently. Allah. The omnipotent. The capricious. The punisher. Allah or Noe—what did it matter? They had the same style. But out of long habit, she muttered, "Allah the compassionate . . ." She stared blankly at the exquisitely carved pommel.

"Not Allah. Christ. A God of forgiveness. Noe intended evil; God intended it for good."

Irina listened attentively, but dry little thoughts warred in her mind. *Good, indeed. What good is left for me?*

"He has a plan—a design," Sirakan began, searching for words with his well-shaped, hairy hands. "Listen. Just as the mountains and forests express a form, a harmony—so your life does if you put it in the hands of that same Designer."

The dagger's carved device winked as she turned the handle.

There was something about what he said, something familiar that she had known or wanted to know long ago. It came to her in images, not words. The might and beauty of her native mountains; a mother's face—was it hers?—turned lovingly toward a child; skies strewn with stars, each seeming to spin a silver thread that attached to her heart. She had for so long felt herself to be on the outside that she had forgotten that there was an inside—her soul's homeland—where she longed to be. The idea that this world really existed and that she had carelessly forfeited it filled her with an aching loneliness.

Sirakan was still waving his hands about in a frustrated attempt to explain the unexplainable, but she felt that she was deadened to all the worn phrases. *Hope—what is that to me now? Don't despair—why not?*

Then he said something that cut right through her. "He will give you beauty for ashes." Something in her awakened. Her own words haunted her. ". . . my offerings are ash and yet to be set before a greater Prince. . . ." Why had she written that? What did it mean? Part of a design. The answer blew softly on the ashes.

Agitated, she thrust it aside. "Stop tormenting me," she demanded. Then, contrite, she added, "I'm tired. I can't think."

"I'm sorry. I didn't mean to offend you. But someday you'll have to think."

"Not now." She closed her eyes wearily. But the thoughts still came. *No magician or alchemist on earth could conjure the black soot of my life into loveliness. I've cast my lot with my lover.* And the more she turned from Sirakan's clumsy phrases, the more it seemed to her that Noe was beckoning to her, drawing her to be where he was.

This attraction began to exert a powerful pull on her. She urged Sirakan to go back to his village. She needed to be alone to keep this appointment! Sirakan refused to leave, as though thinking, *I'll see this thing through.*

Meanwhile, the days settled into an oddly comfortable pattern while the fighting in the streets intensified. Cossack bands patrolled the working districts and factories. The strike of steel on stone echoing in the cobbled alleyways stopped their conversation for a moment. They exchanged glances, then continued talking quietly. As soon as night fell, random shots pattered nonsensically in the darkness.

Sirakan chose a quiet morning to go out for food. Irina pushed herself from the edge of the bed and dressed quietly. The effort left her exhausted, but she forced herself to search the room for Noe's dagger. However, the dagger, which had been glowing in her mind like fox fire, was nowhere to be found. *He's taken it—the interfering boor!* Chagrined, she started at his step on the stair.

"You see," she told him, "I'm well. You can go."

"I'm afraid not," he answered with heavy finality. "No one will be going anywhere for a long time. The city is under martial law."

But the next time the Armenian went out, she found herself with an unexpected ally. Zviad Kostava turned up again, accompanied by a short Georgian with a pockmarked face and an iron manner. She recognized him immediately. Koba—the Bolshevik who had so captured Noe's interest. Although he wasn't much older than she—twenty-five perhaps—he reminded her of her father. He used his Marx much as her father had used his Koran: to control, to bludgeon, to divide all people into two camps—friend or enemy. Yet she felt a sympathy for him. She knew that he had lost his young wife— and with her had seemed to bury all human emotion. She used to be afraid of him, but not now. She envied him—the man who could no longer be hurt.

Noe had told her that Koba had been sent to Siberia last year but had managed to escape and, after trekking through the vast, gaunt taiga and frozen wastelands, had returned to Georgia more adamant than ever. The stern inner core of him seemed to have hardened to steel. In fact, some were beginning to call him that— Stalin, man of steel.

Zviad's malice had curdled to contempt. He ignored her. He and Koba began rifling though the paperwork—pamphlets, news articles, posters.

"I'll keep these for the meeting at the Town Hall," Zviad offered.

Koba glanced dismissively at one of the pamphlets. "Pablum." He shrugged. "Insipid pap for these juveniles playing at revolution."

"You're right. Why take this liberal line and give the government a chance to right itself? Better to force the issue—make compromise impossible."

"There's only one way to do that. Violence. Those who have seen the blood flow won't be so quick to accept halfway measures."

"But that's what this meeting is all about. The liberals and 'legal' socialists will bandy about some kind of fake reform, and the tsar will mete out just enough concessions to blunt the rage of the people. And that rage is what we need!"

"I think the Cossacks will help us with that," Koba said quietly.

"Ah! An incident. Will you tip them off?"

But Koba retreated into stolid reticence. "Someone will," was all he said. He eyed Zviad distastefully as he gloated, "So an incident. We'll whip the people to fury and then invite the Cossacks in for a show that will burn in the mind of Georgians for years! Now you said you had guns."

"Yes. Here, here."

Surprised, Irina watched as Zviad pried up two floorboards near the balcony to reveal a cache of rifles and revolvers. It occurred to her that they were being very careless in her presence. Then she saw the gun in Zviad's hand, and she realized why. *So be it. As long as Sirakan doesn't return.* It was bad enough that he'd come back to find her body, but that couldn't be helped.

Koba wrapped their treasures in the green coverlet and stashed the printed material in a flour sack. Zviad glanced at her briefly, then began scanning the ceiling. She thought she had nothing to fear, but something in that look and his strange smile sent a shudder through her. Involuntarily, she, too, looked up. A trap door to the crawl space above. She'd been staring at it for days but not seeing it. Her eyes met Zviad's, and a rising horror engulfed her. Then she heard Sirakan's heavy tread just outside the door.

"Not a word," warned Zviad with a jerk of his revolver.

But she shouted anyway, screaming for the Armenian to go away. Maddeningly, his footsteps only quickened on the steps. "Go away," she sobbed. But Sirakan was already in the room, and Zviad, with a snakelike movement, twisted behind him, covering him with his gun. Koba slipped quietly out.

"Put it down," Zviad demanded. Sirakan cautiously set his bundles on the table. A packet of cheese and Irina's silver *kinjal* slid onto the table. Both Sirakan and Irina looked at it longingly. Their eyes met.

"None of that," Zviad chided Sirakan. "There's work for you—wrapping up the merchandise. Something you're used to. Tear up the sheet. That's right. Gag her. Now! No slackness, or I shoot. Tie her hands. No. Tie them properly. Don't worry—I'm not going to hurt her."

He kicked a chair so that it stood under the trap door. "Now take this floorboard. Get on the chair. That's right. Reach up and open the trap door."

Fascinated, Irina watched as the baffled Sirakan pushed the cover away from the dark opening. Plaster sifted onto his dark hair. What was up there? She saw nothing but a black square. Following Zviad's instructions, Sirakan positioned the floorboard across the opening.

"Fine. Turn now. If you're quiet and don't move, your traitress lover will survive. I'm telling you the truth." He gagged Sirakan and securely bound him to one of the two chairs. Zviad set the second chair behind Sirakan, precariously positioned on stacks of books. The Armenian's brow puckered with dark confusion while Zviad forced Irina to stand on the second chair. "Close your eyes," the Bolshevik instructed above the cold gleam of the gun. "Both of you."

She obeyed, trying to guess what he was doing—throwing something, something not hard, up at the ceiling. Fear wrapped its cold coils around her heart. She felt a powdering of plaster falling softly on her shoulders, then a harsh twisted rasp of something against her cheek, on her neck. He intended to hang her! *Not that way!* she pleaded inwardly. She glanced down at Sirakan. His prominent eyes were bulging in horror. She knew that the worst of it was that he would be her killer. He'd been forced to set up the makeshift gibbet, and the slightest movement of his burly form on the fragile chair would send hers toppling and her body swinging from the ceiling. Irina set her jaw. She determined that she would not poison this gruff, kind man's future by making him her executioner.

"Now," their tormenter said softly, "you see I keep my word. I haven't touched a hair on your head. You'll have plenty of time to be together. No one will be calling. Word is out that the 'safe house' is no longer safe. You see your position. Of course, your greatest enemy is your need for sleep. Whoever slumps first will be responsible for hanging this Jezebel."

As they left, Zviad turned to Sirakan. "The news," he said. "Your brother is not dead. He has been found by Svanetian tribesmen."

Instinctively, both Zviad and Sirakan looked at Irina. *Noe. Alive. But it's too late for that.* All she could do was stare at Sirakan with her whole soul in her eyes. *Forgive me, forgive me.*

THE SLOW DANCE OF HOURS sent their misshapen shadows groping along the walls. Sirakan strained to see Irina. She was standing stock-still, white, and drained. But her face was filled with intense resolution, and her dark eyes flamed with all the life that was missing from her face and limbs. *She looks like Joan of Arc—with her short hair and that soulful air about her. Was it because of Noe?* He twisted his neck; their eyes met; and he dropped his before the beseeching pain in hers. What was happening to her? She had wanted to die. Now it looked like she'd get her wish. But some sort of fervent, brilliant life had awakened in her, and it sparkled from her eyes as the red twilight spurted from the riddled gaps in the latticed balcony.

Sirakan groaned through the painfully dry wadding that packed his mouth and throat. But although the stiffness in his back and joints was turning to throbbing pain, he did not doubt his endurance. The girl, on the other hand, was still trembling with weakness. He wanted to look at her, communicate somehow that she must hold on. But how? Moving his upper body required such contortions that he was sure that his eyes communicated nothing but agony. But he tried it. Her eyes were pleading—for what? Mercy? Forgiveness? He felt his own expression shift. A light of assurance sprang from him. He saw that she understood, and a few tears sparkled on her face.

Sirakan turned back to the work of holding his body upright. He was exhausted, as though a great wrestling had wrung the pulp from him. But something he could not name had been won.

Darkness seeped up around them; then random shots punctured the quiet. Sirakan's body jerked to alertness, and Irina's chair slipped and teetered. One leg slipped from the book it was perched on; the chair rocked like a cradle and was still. Sweat broke out on his whole upper body. *I almost killed her.* He forced himself not to try to look at her. He forced himself not to think of the brutal tug and choke of the rope on that slender throat. Or of what it would be like to wait for help while her decomposing corpse dangled behind his shoulders.

By morning he spent all his strength trying to control the violent trembling of his tortured limbs. Bathed in his own sweat, he was bitterly cold. He was astounded that Irina held out. What secret source of strength had buttressed her during the long night? One thing he was sure of. They could never survive another such night.

The morning wore on; he revived when the sun slanting through the window doused him with warmth and light. But it slipped away again, hiding behind the old brick houses of Tiflis. His gag tormented him; every cell of his body cried out, except for his hands. His hands had no feeling at all. He prayed for deliverance.

The evening shadows leapt about them. Street sounds flattened out so that he clearly heard the precise snick of the catch on the door. The door opened, but he saw nothing. *Am I hallucinating?* Then he realized he had been looking too high. A child, a young boy, materialized.

Completely unafraid, the boy quickly took in the scene. He grabbed the Georgian dagger and cut Sirakan's bonds. Irina's chair tottered madly. Sirakan steadied it and cut first the rope, then the bonds. Irina collapsed, and he carried her to the bed, rubbing her hands and calling to her. He waited until he was sure he saw life flickering beneath her eyelids before he turned to study their rescuer.

The boy couldn't have been more than eight. He was tanned to a healthy brown, and his rough tufts of hair were sun-bleached at the tips. His deep blue eyes devoured every detail of the room. Then he picked up the mountain *kinjal* and held it up with a touch of ceremony in his manner.

"This," he said, "was my grandfather's."

V

The Pierced Screen

Sirakan gaped at the ragamuffin apparition in front of him. "Who are you? Where did you come from?"

"I'm Loma! We come from the mountains." The boy's comically raised eyebrows slipped back toward his ears.

"We? Where are your parents?"

"They're coming. They went to find a place for our horse. And mule." A quizzical look never left the lad's face. Sirakan gathered that it was his normal expression. "Wait! I hear them!" He spun toward the door as Sirakan tensed.

A well-built man wearing the mountaineer's *tcherkeska* with its grouped cartridge holders and belted waist blocked the doorway. His drooping mustache with its scorched-looking ends did not conceal the fact that he was a larger version of the boy. They had the same squarish features, the same swift, swooping attentiveness. But the man's eyes were golden, not blue. They quickly sized up Sirakan, the room, the girl on the bed. Then he bared two rows of healthy teeth in a grin with no stinting in it. He was pushed aside by a Georgian woman in a rich blue dress that sculpted the slender grace of her figure. Her sober, wondering eyes beneath the velvet headdress flashed their dark splendor at the Armenian.

"Nina!"

She reached up a hand to touch his face. "What happened to you?" she asked in dismay. "What happened to you?"

Then a cry broke from her as she took in the dangling noose, the prone girl on the bed. Her startled eyes searched his face. Then she sprang toward Irina, her trembling fingers searching the throat—for a pulse or rope burn?

"Did she try . . ."

"Yes—no." The strain and exhaustion slammed into Sirakan with tidal force.

"Never mind. Rest. You can tell us later. But wait. I have to tell you. I'm married." She did not move, but Sirakan had an impression of her whole body lunging toward the man in the *tcherkeska*. Her beautiful, slightly tilted eyes grew tender.

"This is Grigol, my husband. A man of Khevsuretia. And this is my son, Loma." The boy nudged up to her with the butting movements of a young goat seeking its dam's attention. Grigol put up a hand and pulled down the hangman's rope as though putting an end to the sinister episode. Then he came and bowed to his new brother-in-law. Sirakan studied the three of them. A family. The whole atmosphere of the room changed.

"I'll sleep now," Sirakan said roughly. He staggered to the mattress that had been his bed for the past weeks. His consciousness slipped into that most wonderful of resting places—a body that feels no pain.

NINA STARED AT THE ROPE in Grigol's hands. She sighed and met her husband's eyes. "What happened?" she murmured.

Grigol glanced around the room. Sirakan's bearlike form lay prone in the corner while Irina was flung across the bed like a sacrifice.

"It's like walking into a sorcerer's cave and finding his victims cast into an enchanted sleep," she told Grigol, "but something's wrong. No one sleeps like that!" She touched Irina's forehead. "She's burning!" Then she gasped as she noticed the bright red splotch on Irina's shirt. Quickly, Nina bared the girl's midriff and found the wound bleeding in a trickle across a sweat-stained bandage.

What had happened? A terrible foreboding filled her. What had this rash, headlong girl done? *Something's happened to Noe—something horrible.* She rebandaged the wound; it was small but obviously very deep. A *dagger wound.*

"Don't block the light," she said as Loma drifted near. He edged away. Silver flashed in his hand.

"This was my grandfather's," he remarked displaying the *kinjal*. "I remember it. It has stories on it."

Grigol captured his restless son in his arms and pried the dagger from his fingers. "It does have stories on it," he said. "More than we know! This is the gift we gave to your Uncle Noe—as bride price for Nina."

"So it's not ours?"

"Not anymore. We traded it for your stepmother. I think we have the best of it, don't you?"

"Well, yes. But where is Uncle Noe?"

"We're not sure. As soon as it's light, I'll go see if I can find out."

NINA WATCHED FROM THE BALCONY as a red-gold sunset punctured the riddled lattice. Splotches of light played across her face, her hands, as she peered through the gaps in the wooden railing. At one time, Nina remembered, in the early days of Russian rule, the governor had declared that all the wooden balconies in the city were to be torn down. He had no grasp of the Eastern custom of shielding its women. The private, shaded courtyards and balconies where a secluded Muslim lady or Georgian maiden might secretly view the life of the city were alien to him.

But the people of Tiflis were not about to give up so easily. Too much imagination, too much of the city's grace and charm, too many intimate family scenes were carved into their beloved balconies. After vehement local protests, the governor backed down. The balconies stayed. Tiflis remained Tiflis.

The glossy leaves of the mulberry tree in the courtyard shimmered like foil. Then the buildings and balconies and stiff-branched plane trees chopped the last of the twilight into rosy fragments. Nina turned and looked back into the room. Grigol had already lit the lamp—his blunt, rugged features softened by the light and by his look as he glanced up toward her.

Loma was sleeping with his head down on the table. Grigol wrapped him in a blanket and put him on the floor near Sirakan. She couldn't hear what was said—a soft, sleepy murmuring from the child and the man's muted voice. The lamp-lit scene filled her with long-ing and loneliness—but a different longing than she had experienced before. Now she knew that the ache would plunge into sweet, pierc-ing joy as soon as Grigol left his son and came to her.

A thousand threads of fine-spun thought and feeling stretched between them. In these first days of their marriage, every hour was suffused with acute awareness of each other. His breath stirred her hair, and the beating of her heart was the beating of wings—soaring. She touched his arm, and gladness leaped to gold in his tawny eyes. She loved to sit beside him and press her smooth cheek against his rough face while her whole soul contracted with the wonder and joy of it.

The street lamps woke and breathed out a hazy glow, and the air turned damp. Grigol was beside her, his hands on her face, her hair. The diffuse light and her husband's quiet breathing, his scent, the quiet words between them, and the deep core of peace that filled them bound them into a sort of pod—safe, but permeable. She could still hear the shooting in the street, was still aware of her own fear for her brother and her anxiety about their own future. But all these things were changed as they transversed the membrane that secured her to this unexpected, unimaginable love.

This is the happiest time of my life—and the saddest. She could not shake the feeling that the news—burnings of manors, shootings in the streets, uprisings in villages—that had hounded them along their way would strike them in some specific way. *And what of Noe?* They had come expecting to find him in prison—and perhaps he was—but Irina's condition and Sirakan's strange silence boded no good. Perhaps Sirakan was peeved at her. After all, she had married with-out permission, and she was sure he had taken some unpleasantness for that. Maybe he didn't accept her marriage. But, no, it had to be something worse than that.

"What do you think?" she asked Grigol. "I feel that something terrible has happened, but I don't know what."

"I'm sure of it. Your brother was like a man who has come to the end of himself. But we'll have to wait until morning before we learn anything." A few shots scattered in the darkness. The spatter of sound seemed to match the holes in the balcony screen.

"This is it," she said quietly. "This is the revolution that Noe has waited for, worked for all his life. Now it's here. But where will it take us?"

"I don't know. I don't know." Grigol smoothed back her hair. "I only know that we have to stay together somehow. I'd always hoped that when these days came, something good would spring up from the ferment. A free Georgia, a better life for common folk. But now I wonder. Something dark and powerful has been unleashed. Who knows what will come of it? In the old days the tsars and eristavs and mighty men meted out justice or injustice. But they chose their victims. This revolution is as diffuse as a bomb's debris—anyone in the way gets hurt. It doesn't matter who they are or what they believe."

"Are you afraid?"

"I ask myself that. Yes. I am afraid. Afraid as I've never been!"

She felt an odd thrill of joy. Not because this man whom she knew to be brave and good had admitted something, but because he had learned to open his heart to her. The swagger, the bravado—and the man's true courage sometimes broke through to a moment of openness when his need of her was a deep, rough cry. These beautiful, trusting moments were her reward in the anxious, turbulent days, and she drank them in greedily.

"What kind of life will we have? How will we make a place for our children?" Grigol asked while his eyes narrowed, searching the pierced screen. More and more noises came up from the street: voices arguing, a woman's wail, the percussion of hooves. Nina twisted around and glimpsed a Cossack band cantering across the alleyway. Grigol put a shielding arm on her head and arm and pulled her inside. He held her with convulsive tightness.

"You're my fear. What if I lose you? What if you are wrenched away from me . . . after all we've been through? We know what that's like, don't we?"

She nodded mutely. She knew what he was saying. They were like two children who had found a priceless treasure but could not protect it from the crafty eye, the violent grasp. *But we have another protection*, she reminded herself.

Grigol again took in the ransacked room. "Some outsider has been here," he asserted. "Someone who may return. I'll sleep by the door, and we'll learn more tomorrow." He stretched out in front of the door, and Nina nestled beside him.

Nina awoke to the sound of moaning. Irina was still in a deep sleep, but a repeated groaning escaped from her white lips. *She must be unconscious*, Nina thought, *or she'd never let herself show weakness like that*. Irina's face did not move, but a trembling gray shadow fluttered over her throat as an insistent childlike complaining rose from her. Nina began to sponge her face with water from the basin, and the girl began sucking on the wet cloth. Then suddenly she was fully awake, looking at Nina with lucid eyes surrounded by dark, bruised shadows. "Water!"

Nina pressed a cup to her lips, and she drank thirstily, never taking her eyes from Nina's face. Finally, she drew back. "Nina! You . . . here? How . . ."

"We came to see about Noe," Nina explained. "And I had hoped to go home to see my mother if that's possible."

"They told me Noe was dead. But then I heard, I think I heard that he was alive. Maybe a dream . . . Sirakan would know. Where's Sirakan?" Irina lurched forward.

"Don't! Sirakan's here. Lie down. He's sleeping. He'll tell us all about it."

"I'll tell you." Comprehension and suffering rose up in her and stiffened her face. Nina remembered her as she had last seen her; her face, her whole being had seemed to fly to pieces as they saw the Cossacks come in and knew that the stroke that would change everything for them had fallen.

Irina told her story. Nina stilled her inward flinching. "I understand, I understand," she kept saying. But she didn't understand. She only knew that where there is pain, there must be soothing. The shock she felt when Irina told her about her suicide attempt was on the surface. On a deeper level, Nina knew that the first jab at the inner harmony that was Irina came much earlier. When she had betrayed her lover? No, earlier, much earlier.

In a flat voice, with pauses as she garnered her strength, Irina described the long hours of agony when she and Sirakan had been suspended between life and death. Her dry tones bled the story of its gruesome power, but Nina could see that something momentous had happened, something that Irina could not or would not explain. The only thing was to wait until Sirakan could fill in the gaps.

Dawn stole into the alleys, glazed the windows, and slipped

beneath balconies and stairways. Gradually, the streets filled with people: hawkers, *kintos*—the petty tradesmen of Tiflis, and workmen. But few were buying, and the workmen did not go off to their jobs. Most were on strike. They clotted on the corners in dark, tense groups.

Nina spied a woman carrying birch-bark panniers filled with bread rolls and went down to buy some for their breakfast. The woman shouted to a gang of railway workers in a hoarse, gibing voice. They waved her away with jokes, but she kept craning her neck back toward them so that she almost bumped into Nina.

"Now, dearie, what are they up to?" she asked with a conspirator's wink. "Always talking, never working." Her thick fingers gripped the heavy baskets. The shanks of her heavy forearms hung loosely from the bone. Her face slid back and forth in the dark cowl of her shawl; when she turned her head, Nina thought of the moon at three-quarters. Her tone had softened to an insidious rasp.

"You're new here," she said, turning her head sideways. *Danger!* Nina thought with a pang. The days when a young wife could run out into the street to buy bread were over. Why had she been so stupid as to forget?

"Not new," Nina stated. "My brother lives here. I've just returned from my—my wedding journey."

"Ah! A bride—and such a pretty one. So you've just returned?" she mimicked.

"Only last night," Nina said levelly. "What news in the city?"

"You see for yourself. The Russians are swarming like ants on carrion. But they haven't stopped the strikes or the rioting. Oh no! The day of retribution is come, dearie." She lowered her voice, and the cowl swallowed the left side of her face. "Those who have stepped on the necks of their neighbors are choking on their riches now. Landlords are driven out, factory owners killed. And the Tartars have risen. They're killing the Armenians."

"Here?" Nina whispered.

"Haven't you heard the shooting? Some they catch and douse with kerosene and set on fire." The hawker seemed almost approving, but Nina's skin beneath her Georgian dress turned cold and clammy. Would this odious old woman see that the dark, rich tones beneath her pale skin, the slight tilt to her eyes, and the shape of her nose came from a man named Aram Abajarian? And who would she tell?

Nina paid for her rolls and slipped quietly up the stairs. No one must know that the unquestionably Armenian Sirakan was peacefully sleeping in the flat of a known Georgian revolutionary! Looking up, she caught a glimpse of Grigol's face behind the balcony lattice, watching her. She joined him and told him what she had heard, then flushed under his intense scrutiny.

"You're looking for my Armenian blood, aren't you?" she challenged.

"No one could see it. You're dressed like a Georgian. Just keep it that way." His voice was matter-of-fact, but she didn't like something in his tone. She felt as though something were being taken away from her.

"Maybe you'd rather I were a full-blooded Georgian rather than a half-breed!" she flared.

"It would be safer," he said practically.

"Oh! I'm sorry I've brought down danger on your head!"

"What are you saying?" He was genuinely surprised.

"You seem to feel that my Armenian side is a problem."

"Of course, it's a problem! They're shooting Armenians in the street. Do you think I want you killed?"

"No." *Why am I feeling like this?* she asked herself. It had been easy to set aside her Armenian heritage when she married Grigol, but now when her people were in trouble, she was ashamed to detach herself from them. *Will I always be divided like this?*

Sirakan began stirring in his corner and stared about with hollow eyes. Loma leapt up like a young deer. They breakfasted on rolls and tea.

Sirakan shot a brooding glance from under his brows. "It's not safe here," he said morosely. "I have no idea whether Zviad and his comrade will return. It's better if they think Irina is dead, but it's not going to be easy to find a place for her. I think that she'll balk at doing anything until she finds out about Noe."

"And Noe?" Nina asked.

Sirakan sighed. "Impossible to know. Irina had gone to Metekhi fortress to find him and was told that he was dead. Later . . ." He paused and looked up at the black hole in the ceiling. "Later we were told that he was rescued in the mountains by some Svanetian tribesmen. I suppose the only way of finding out would be to go into Svanetia and look for him."

"No! You can't. You'll have to stay in hiding. There have been uprisings—atrocities against Armenians."

Sirakan surveyed her with unsurprised eyes.

Yes, she thought, *he's changed.*

He began speaking in a deliberate but strained way—as though he were cutting out chunks of himself and setting them out on the table. "That night—she told you about it?—I kept seeing over and over again in my mind a young man and woman holding tightly to each other and burning like a torch. No. I mean literally a torch. They were on fire. *Am I delirious?* I wondered.

"I wanted to think that. Once while we were still living in Turkey, we were visiting my mother's sister. She lived in a mountain village. I was quite small at the time, but I remember them out in the yard taking down laundry from a line. One minute there was this secure little yard. Then my aunt pulled down a clean sheet, and I saw that the clothesline was right on the edge of a cliff! I wanted her to put the sheet back up so that I could pretend that that chasm wasn't there!

"Sitting on that chair all night was like that. When your body screams for release and your nightmares come alive in the night, you haven't the strength to keep up the barriers. I knew that the young couple was real. I had seen them as surely as I'm seeing you now. It was during the massacres of 1896. The Turks had poured kerosene over them. They never stopped clinging to one another. My mother knew them; she was distantly related to them. In all the years of my boyhood—up until her death—I never saw her smile. My uncle was killed during those uprisings. Someone put an axe through his chest, and he struggled to breathe for three days. But we escaped."

Nina put a trembling hand under Grigol's arm. Her fingers touched a cold cartridge case, and she felt his muscles swell and tense with anger.

"We each of us have an enemy," he said. "But for each it's a different enemy. The Tartars are massacring the Armenians; the Cossacks hunt down revolutionaries and uncooperative tribesmen like me; and the revolutionaries punish the masters and supposed traitors—like Irina. We must be careful, or we'll be scattered to the winds."

"And who is my enemy?" piped a firm childish voice.

"Loma!" Grigol rubbed the side of his nose, obviously chagrined that the boy had heard their talk. "Your enemy," he muttered, "is the future."

Loma widened his eyes, and his brows slipped back toward his ears.

"But you have a Friend, too. One who controls the future," Grigol hastened to add.

"How can that be if the future is my enemy?"

"There's a greater future that will swallow up the smaller one."

"Like a fish?"

"Just like that."

Nina was relieved that this seemed to satisfy Loma, and he wandered out to the balcony.

Sirakan smiled pitifully. "So you see why I never married. There's a charred memory within me that tells me that this will happen again. And yet as we were strung that night between life and death, beneath the pain and terror I felt like a conqueror. I felt that I had a glimpse of something that I'd never understood before."

Irina began to stir, and they quickly fell silent. She propped herself up on spindle-thin arms and drew their attention with her black-shadowed eyes. Sirakan quickly got up and sat on the edge of the bed. Something soft and living was cradled in the look suspended between them. *Things ceded and things forbidden meshed in that quick glance*, Nina thought. But Irina pulled her gaze away and thoughtfully considered the blanket.

"Was it true?" she asked. "About Noe. Was I dreaming?"

"I heard it, too," Sirakan said. "According to Zviad, Noe was rescued by Svans. But how we'll find him, I don't know. We'll have to wait until he contacts us."

"He won't. To come back here is sure arrest for him. I'll have to find him."

"You can't search every crag and valley in the Caucasus."

"No. But if he's at all able, he'll come to that meeting—the one Zviad and Koba were talking about."

"What is it?" Grigol stopped his pacing and stood over them.

"A meeting to protest the harsh treatment of the Christian

priests. The authorities have been hammering away at them, and the people have risen against it. They plan to meet at the Tiflis Town Hall at the end of the month to protest."

"I'll find him," Grigol declared. "If he's not there, we'll go into the mountains and search for him. I know the Svans."

"This meeting—it will be dangerous. When Koba and Zviad were talking about it, they seemed to expect trouble. In fact, it looked like they were arranging to have trouble."

Sirakan shrugged. "It takes no special arrangement to have trouble these days. We'll just have to chance it."

"No," Grigol insisted, "I'll go alone. You shouldn't be seen right now."

"So I'm to crawl in a hole and pull it in after me? No thanks."

"Grigol's right," Nina pleaded. "Maybe none of us should go. Let's stay here until all this is over."

"We came here to find Noe—and to try to see your mother." Grigol frowned. "Let's at least try to learn what became of your brother. A public meeting in the city's Town Hall shouldn't be dangerous for a Georgian."

"That's right," Sirakan put in. "Meanwhile, I'll go back to the village. Who knows what's happening at home? What if I'm needed? Then I can talk to your mother, Nina, and try to arrange a meeting. I'll have to do it behind Father's back. He was furious enough when you escaped his marriage plans for you. This other matter will throw him into a red-hot rage!" He glanced at Grigol from beneath lowering brows, but Nina could see that he liked her husband.

"But I know your mother will want to see you," Sirakan added kindly.

The next day he left taking the bay gelding and leaving them with enough money for their needs.

But as the midsummer days stretched out toward autumn, Sirakan did not return. The rest of them kept to the room as much as possible. Grigol and Loma made excursions into the city for food and news while Nina nursed Irina and tried to make a comfortable life in their cramped quarters. Beyond the tattered balcony, the city continued to heave with distress. Cossacks roamed the streets— sometimes preventing violence, sometimes inflicting it. Black Hundred bands, members of the ultra-patriotic monarchist society, held counterrevolutionary demonstrations in the streets and assaulted Georgian workers and their families. Strikes paralyzed the city—sometimes leaving the residents without lighting, running water, regular food supplies, and public transport. And the killings of Armenians continued.

Grigol stopped taking Loma with him on his forays, and the boy's pent-up active nature found outlet in rigging chairs and stray boards into elaborate structures. If Nina wasn't tripping over someone's body, she was tripping over one of Loma's edifices. But their captivity had some pleasant moments, too. In the evenings Nina would spin out stories—as fanciful as she could make them—and watch Loma's whole face reshaped by the intensity of listening. Before sleeping, they huddled near the lamp and prayed for those they loved and for their own safety in the dark, uncertain days.

In August the streets were buzzing with the news that Tsar Nicholas had issued a manifesto establishing a state council or Duma.

"But it's a sham," Grigol reported. "It's not going to satisfy the democratic yen of the people. Instead it's pricked them to even greater fury. This Duma is the idea of the tsar's chamberlain, Bulygin. They'll set up a fraud assembly of the middle and upper classes with a few monarchist peasants thrown in. Everybody—from the moderates to the Bolsheviks—see it for the lie it is."

Nina groaned. "Now things can only get worse! What can we do? Should we try to leave? Maybe things are safer in the countryside."

"I don't think so. The villages near here are going the way of Kakhetia. The peasants are attacking the landowners and gendarmes— sometimes even the priests. And they're paying for it. Just outside of town forty-eight peasants were killed in a fight with army units."

"Those who live by the sword will die by the sword," Nina murmured.

Grigol's eyes locked with hers for a long moment. "It's not those who live by the sword that I'm worried about," he said grimly. "I expect that we face dangerous days ahead. You two," he included Irina with a nod, "and Loma will have to stay here as quietly as you can. I'll lie low also; we'll just have to survive on what we have for a while. But at the end of the month, the Social Democrats are having a meeting to discuss Bulygin's project and other things. I'll be going. As Georgians we need to take up the tsar's challenge and show him that we, too, have some ideas about shaping our country! Besides, the meeting will draw many out of hiding. Maybe I'll find Noe or someone who has heard about him."

Irina's voice was eager. "I know he'll be there. Unless he's dead or crippled, he'll be there. But it will be dangerous. When Zviad Kostava and Koba were here, I somehow gathered that the police will be alerted to this meeting. Koba seemed to foresee all this. It wouldn't surprise me if they tipped off the gendarmes just to stoke the violence."

"Don't go," Nina cut in. "It's not worth it! We can find out about Noe some other way."

But Grigol was adamant. "It's not just Noe. It's the future of a nation. Look at how our life is now! We aren't even safe on our own streets just because of who we are! Through all of history, we've been battered by Byzantines, Persians, Turks, Arabs—and now by Russia. And our way has always been to flee to the mountains. Find a snow-barricaded, rock-strewn ledge where we can eke out a bare existence. Some place where no one can find us—for evil or for good. I've had enough of it! This is a new century—and the opportunities lie in the city. What will Loma learn in an eagle-haunted medieval village? I want more for him and for our children. If we are weak and passive now, it will be wrenched away from them."

Nina shrugged. *No point in arguing.* That telltale scar on Grigol's cheek was as white and obdurate as a barricade at the end of a street. But in her own heart she wanted nothing more than to fly to the strong, sheltering ranges of Caucasia.

"He's right, Nina," Irina put in. "It takes courage to fight injustice—but we must fight it." Nina looked at her thoughtfully. For the first time, Nina glimpsed the idealistic underpinning of her apparently heedless choices. *But they think they'll find solutions this way, and I just don't believe it.* She held her tongue but stiffened inwardly. *I don't care what they say. I still don't want him to go.*

GRIGOL HELD HIS WIFE in the wash of clear dawnlight that surged over the balcony. He pulled her to himself with everything in his being. His hands, his arms and shoulders reached out for her—not only bone and sinew, but even the grasping life of blood and cell. Nina melted into him with the nudging tuck of her head into the hollow between his jaw and neck. Her breathing against his collarbone distilled joy and blessing from the gray morning air. He gave himself up with gladness to the God-breathed unity that was his greatest comfort.

But later the sweet lethargy of mind and limb began to seep away as the sounds of the city coming to life prodded him. Grigol's thoughts broke from the wordless fusion with the woman beside him to the specific problems of the day. He must have moved slightly as his thoughts drifted away. Nina was instantly alert, her beautiful eyes—brimming with love like a dark liquid—flashed at him, and a brittleness of knee and elbow edged her soft body.

"It's too early. You can't go yet," she insisted.

"I have to. I'll need to find out what's happening in the city. Then this meeting . . ."

"No. No." She put her hands on his temples and kissed him insistently. Voices came to them from the street with hoarse shouts and whistles: "Bread, bread—milk, milk." The sharp cries of the *kintos* and hawkers in the square jabbed at the mulberry boughs and latticework screen.

"You—you are my life, my heart's sustinance," Grigol whispered. "And for you I must go. A man doesn't shape his life by clinging to his woman."

"Bread, milk," sang the hawkers.

Bread, milk, Grigol thought as his fingers slid across Nina's cheek.

"Oh, my love, don't leave me," Nina begged.

"If I don't leave you, I'll be a hollow man. You can't live with a man who has let the core be scooped out of him by fear."

Nina moved her hand from his temple to his lips to silence him. "I know, I know. Go, husband of my heart. And God go with you."

GRIGOL FOLLOWED the narrow street uphill. Climbing to a spur of the Solalaki Ridge, he paused by the crumbling stone wall of Narikala Fortress to get his bearings. It was one of those late August mornings that hint at the crisp autumn days to come. The crystalline air allowed the sun's rays to exaggerate the color and sparkle of this extraordinary city. At the crossroads of Europe and Asia, Tiflis was a magical habitation where history assumed the power of myth—and legend was absorbed as fact by the Georgians, Tartars, Armenians, Russians, Gypsies, and Jews who lived there.

Grigol narrowed his eyes and looked north where the river Kura cut deeply between ancient streets and houses. He remembered the story of the city's founding. The Georgian king, Vaktang Gorgasali, came down from Mtskheta in the fifth century hunting a wounded stag that staggered into one of the hot springs in the area and bounded out healed of its wounds. The king decided to move his capital to this place of the life-giving water, and Tiflis was born. Across the river the Metekhi fortress called down light on its pure, conical cupola. King Vaktang had built a church on the site as a memorial to one of Georgia's most beloved saints, St. Shuchanik, who was tortured by her husband when she refused to convert to Zoroastrianism.

Drawn by his musings, Grigol strolled down to Vorontsov Street along the river. Here near the stone-domed Goglio Baths, Georgians paid homage to the three hundred heroic knights of the Aragvi. These men of Grigol's own mountain homeland had rescued King Herekle II in 1795 when the murderous Agha Mohammed Khan tried to capture him. Herekle's grandson, Ioane, learned of his grandfather's imminent capture and mustered the warriors. They saved the king, but not one survived. *But their honor—that survived*. Grigol stared across the torpid, brown swash of the Kura where the old houses clung to the steep cliff so precariously. *A dear price for such fragile, fleeting gains*.

Grigol's gaze caught the radiant gleam of Mount Kazbek jutting from the Greater Caucasus in the far north. Struck to unbelievable brilliance in the morning sun, Kazbek thrust forth its majesty and beauty and power. Grigol breathed out, feeling that the muscle-sheathed strength of rib and chest were not enough to keep his heart from flying straight to that loveliest of mountains—the Mountain of Christ. Kazbek had loomed on all the horizons of his world as he grew to manhood in the fastness of Khevsuretia. And it loomed still, an everlasting image in his soul's memory. And honor—what was honor? Hadn't he learned in the mountains that the supposed honor of country and custom shriveled next to the great honor and sacrifice of God Himself?

As he circled back to the bazaars of the Old Town, Grigol noticed that many of the stalls of Armenian rug dealers, merchants of eastern silks and satins, and restaurateurs were boarded up. The gray stones of the Armenian quarter in Avlabari seemed to lock the streets up in a funereal somberness. Had the Armenians been ferreted out by the gendarmerie or fled in fear?

But lower in the Old Town, the narrow, crooked streets and open shops buzzed with activity. He found a stall selling thick, sweet Turkish coffee and sipped it as his ears pricked at the vehement debates on every side. Grigol studied the crowd at the street corner, the mob under the coppersmith's awning. Bodies tensed with anger, an arm flung out in menace, swift gestures of fury, flaring nostrils, and spark-struck eyes. There was no doubt that the Georgians were stoked to protest Bulygin's flabby reforms! Grigol grimaced at the gritty sediment in the bottom of his cup. This meeting would be interesting.

Grigol made his way past Sioni Cathedral, its yellow tuff facade mellowing to gold in the sun. A cluster of black-habited nuns disappeared behind one of the polygonal apses. Men strode along beside the *caravanserai* toward the town square. The walkers congealed into larger and larger groups as they neared the Town Hall. Grigol guessed that there were many hundreds of men and women. The mob surged, then seemed to break on the stones of the Moorish-style building. Threading his way through straining knots of people, Grigol saw that armed police barred the doors. The crowd milled in aimless eddies around the facade, then caught by a sudden undertow surged forward, and forced their way past the gendarmes. Grigol recognized Zviad Kostava and another short, dark Georgian urging the town folk into the building with word and gesture.

Once inside the people were eager but peaceful. The numbers had swelled to about two thousand—liberals in city suits, Bolsheviks in workers' caps and jackets, Georgians in flaring *tcherkeskas* and soft boots like his own. Most of the women wore town dresses with hats or shawls covering their heads. Grigol noted that although the organizers were "legal" Social Democrats, many people seemed to be ordinary citizens who had come from sheer curiosity. There was some confusion at the podium. Then Grigol heard the noise of a scuffle

97

coming from behind him. He turned and caught a glimpse of a police officer at the entrance.

"You are ordered to disperse. I demand that—," he shouted, but his words were drowned in a roar of derision. Pandemonium broke loose, and Grigol edged toward a doorway. *No point in staying if it turns into a free-for-all.* But the speaker at the podium managed to calm the crowd and began outlining the "burning issues" people had gathered to discuss.

Still, Grigol sensed danger. He scrutinized the hall carefully. Was that a movement outside the window? Yes, every window— Cossacks. Shouts and hoots greeted a renewed order to disperse. Then a shot rang out, and the orator slumped at his tribune. Glass shattered, and the Cossacks stationed outside opened fire on the assembly through the windows. Others invaded the hall and shot into the audience from the platform.

The mob turned frantic. Grigol wrenched out his dagger, but it was useless. It was impossible to see where the shots were coming from. He saw a slender teenaged boy bend groaning to the floor. A screaming woman in fashionable boots stepped on him. A refined-looking man in a Western-style suit clawed at his belly, convulsing as a blood-drenched pocket watch swung from his waist. Furniture splintered under misplaced sword strokes, and bullets riddled the walls. A hellish chaos of noise never ceased.

Grigol pushed through the frenzy looking for an exit. He looked up as one of the chandeliers exploded, sending a rain of crystal on the terrified citizens.

Now he could see his enemy. Cossacks were pouring into the auditorium; one sprang at him with a flashing saber. Grigol dodged and twisted and suddenly found himself before a dark corridor. At the end of it he could see two Cossacks, their muscular backs straining beneath their gray uniforms as they hacked at a huge bearded man. He was holding a shapeless woolen cap—such as the Svans wear—in front of him in an almost religious pose. A woman slightly behind him shrieked again and again in horror.

Grigol raced down the hall and launched himself at the larger of the two Cossacks. His fingers dug into the hard ridges of the man's trachea. The other Cossack turned from his victim, but Grigol used the larger man as a shield. Beneath the sheepskin cap of the small man were the blue, alarmed eyes of a teenager. This Cossack with his healthy Russian face and the shimmer of a blond mustache on his upper lip merely looked confused. His saber dripped with blood, and his lips moved soundlessly. It seemed to Grigol that the keening cry of the woman behind him was coming from this young man.

Suddenly, a squatting, brownish shape lunged out of the darkness, and the young Cossack's confused look turned to one of disbelief. The groan that broke from him now was his own. He collapsed with a steel dagger buried deeply in his back. The woman shuddered, still gasping with cries of horror. The brown-clad warrior emerged from the shadows. With a springy movement he retrieved his dagger and plunged it into the wildly struggling Cossack in Grigol's hold. Grigol dropped his arms.

His ally was a slender, wiry man with a handsome beard strangely divided on one side by a scar that meandered like a path through a forest. He, too, was wearing the Svanetian's felt cap. The hatred flaming in his hazel eyes was snuffed for a brief moment as he grasped Grigol's arm.

"Jibiani—do you hear? The village of Jibiani. Upper Svanetia. Bring her. Better for you, too." The woman behind them was still screaming. Grigol's rescuer shook him gently. "Do you hear? Bring her. Jibiani. If she's alive."

Grigol stared into the gleaming hazel eyes. "Noe," he choked. "Noe Tcheidze!"

Noe sprang away as panicking people began spilling into the hallway. Grigol shoved his way back into the main auditorium. It was quieter now. Most of the Cossacks were outside, hunting down the fleeing crowds in the streets. The dead and wounded littered the floor. A middle-aged woman was bent over a wounded worker, tearing off strips of her clothing to bind his wound. Her movements were awkward, and Grigol saw she was nursing an injured arm.

"Let me help you," he said gently.

"No. No. I'm a doctor. Too many casualties. Go help that one—yes, the old man. Tear up whatever you can find for bandages. Go. Go."

The old man was sitting up, holding tightly to the gash in his thigh. When he looked up at Grigol, his eyes were still bright and alert. But Grigol knew that without help he would bleed to death in moments. He found a woman's scarf and began binding the bleeding leg.

"Hold still, grandfather."

All at once the old man began hissing maledictions: "You Satans. You filthy offspring of the devil. Killing a woman! May you burn in Gehenna. May the pit swallow up your souls . . ."

Turning, Grigol saw the woman doctor slumped over her patient. The Cossack behind her wiped the blood off the rifle butt he had brained her with and then took careful aim at Grigol. Grigol stared back at him, gathering his soul into his eyes. His heart thudded, and the old man hissed and flung out his arms.

Jesus, I am in Your keeping, Grigol prayed. A powerful surge of strength and acceptance leapt through him like an electric current. The menace of the lean-faced Cossack, the curses of the flailing old man, the puddles of blood in the desecrated auditorium became vague, unreal. Bouncing back from the stare he fixed on his enemy were his own images—the love-filled blue eyes of his son, the soaring beauty of the mountains, his wife. *Nina, you are my unforgettable love. We'll always be together. My wife.*

The shot cracked. The old man fell over backward with a hole in his temple. Grigol sucked in cold air and faced his executioner.

"Get up," the Cossack snarled. "We have work for you."

The streets were dark—the lamps dead on their iron poles. Grigol could see little, but there were cries and moans and shouts everywhere. A constant wailing seemed to rise from the stones. A caravan of carts pulled into the square. Blanched faces of men, women, and even children floated around these carts and their drivers. They were begging for the bodies of loved ones. Grigol shuddered as the tide of anguish reached out to him. What about his own loved ones? Would Nina and Loma be pleading with outstretched hands for his fallen carcass? And where would his body be at this night's end?

But the soldiers kept to their duty. Infantrymen and several strong young Georgians, like Grigol, were forced to bundle the corpses into the waiting carts. Grigol was paired with one of the foot soldiers who had been posted outside the hall. The young man stared at the tangle of mutilated bodies with a dazed look. A nudge from the older Cossack's rifle prodded him to action.

These victims would be buried ignominiously. Their families would not even have the comfort of mourning them. As they worked, Grigol let the younger man take the victim's feet while he himself hoisted the upper body. He made a point of studying each face as they passed by the light at the doorway. *You were precious to someone. God rest your soul. You are my countryman.* With holy respect, he tempered the might of his shoulders and gentled his hands as he touched and grasped and lifted. He had never had such a strong sense of belonging. Before that night, when he thought of Georgia, he thought mainly of the land—the green tillage and gracious orchards and glorious mountains. But now his heart was full of these faces.

Grigol fully expected to end his life in a ditch after burying these unfortunates. But he was not thinking of that. He was experiencing a peculiar strength and freedom of thought completely untethered from the horror around him. The young soldier working with him must have noticed, for he kept looking at him oddly.

Loaded, the carts lurched forward with their gruesome cargo and rolled toward the outskirts of the city. A full harvest moon climbed up over the buildings, shook itself free of the reaching plane trees, and floated serenely above them. Its brilliance brushed feather-shaped shadows at the base of the poplar trees that lined an empty field. Here they stopped. And here their night's work began. Under the blue slant of pointed rifles, Grigol and the young men with him broke into the peaceful earth with pick and shovel. Others began piling the corpses alongside the widening ditch.

When Grigol reached a depth of three feet, the ground turned damp, and a scent arose, a scent of earth only—no dry grass or rank leaves or animal droppings—just earth. A fierce, clawing anguish took hold of him and shook him. Every scrape and chink of the shovel and every thud as the clods rained on the ground above tore from him the inner cry, *My God, my God.* And all of his man's strength of pleading and of worship were in the cry.

NINA WATCHED through the lattice. The moon was so bright that spangled dots of light burst through the screen and splashed across the balcony. The stones of the angled alleyway shimmered and sluiced a spreading pond of light into the square. But beneath her the top of the mulberry tree was dark and secretive. She could see nothing beneath its glossy, oval leaves. The night was as lucidly alive and ominously silent as a watchful beast. Nina's heart contracted in fear. Where was he? No meeting could have taken so long.

Inside, Irina was deep in the stupor of a sleep she had fallen into. Loma curled in a peaceful little coil. Nothing broke the glass-bright night. Nina spread out the bedding she shared with Grigol, but she could not bring herself to lie down. Instead she settled on a shabby cushion and waited, peering constantly at the fractured moonlight infiltrating her third-story perch. *I've waited like this before—not knowing, but full of hope and expectation. This time . . .*

Her heart recoiled before the abyss that opened before her. This time, she acknowledged, she was filled with dread. The air chilled, and she began trembling. She wrapped herself up in the blankets. The night stretched out—unbearably shiny and frail. Then it burst in a din of shouts and wailing. Nina flew to the balcony's edge. The darkness filled up with noise—the rattle of loud, agitated talk, the drone of hopeless weeping. *Something horrible has happened!* But she could see nothing. The street beneath the mulberry boughs was unperturbed.

Nina rushed into the room, flung off the blankets, and grabbed her shawl. Irina sprang up.

"What? What?" she asked.

"Grigol—he's not back."

"Wait. You don't even know where you're going. Wait 'til first light. We'll get news and decide what to do. And maybe he'll be back by then."

"I can't. I need to find him."

"Yes. Just wait," Irina soothed. She got up from the bed quickly. She had filled out during the past two weeks, and she was much stronger.

"Sit down," she whispered with a cautioning glance at the sleeping Loma.

Nina sat, pulling her blankets around her. Irina pulled up a chair and waited with her until daybreak. Suddenly all the church bells of Tiflis began tolling, and people appeared in the street. Nina threw off her blankets and clattered down the stairway. She spotted the old bread woman with her huge basket and ran to her.

"Well, pretty lady, how about some fresh *penovani* with good strong cheese?"

Absently, Nina doled out a few kopeks. Maybe Irina was right. Maybe Grigol would return, and they'd sit together and have rolls and tea. She didn't want to tell the old hawker that her husband was missing, but she had to get some news.

"Why do the church bells ring so early? Mass is not for an hour or more," she asked.

"Why, bells always sing out for death, pretty lady. And there's been death in the city!"

"What? Who?" Nina's lips turned stiff. All at once several shouting youths dressed all in black appeared, moving together in a swooping group like crows.

"Massacre! Massacre!" they yelled. "The innocent killed! Massacre!"

Nina rushed at the nearest young man and grabbed his sleeve.

"Tell me," she cried running alongside of him. "My husband is missing."

The youth drew up. "There was a massacre. At the Town Hall. They were meeting. Innocent citizens—talking, just talking. And the Cossacks came in and murdered them." He panted and stretched out his mouth as though the words burned like acid. "We're heralding to all the city."

Nina's knees buckled, and she sank onto the stones. Irina was beside her questioning the young man.

"How many killed?" she asked coldly.

He paused and shuddered. "All," he said. "I think all. It was a massacre, I tell you!" His glance strayed to Nina, and he lowered his voice. "Cossacks surround the hall still. They won't even let relatives in to bury their dead. I've heard they've buried them already. In an unmarked ditch."

The old bread woman sidled up to them, holding out a packet. "Pretty lady, you forgot your *penovani*." Irina reached out a hand. But the old woman eyed Nina. "You take your tears to Avlabari. You don't fool me. I know where you belong." Nina raised her eyes uncomprehendingly.

"I belong nowhere," she said in a dead voice. Then she sprang up wildly and started running.

Irina stopped her. "Wait! I've learned something. Come." She led the way back to the room and closed the door.

"What?" Nina asked. Loma nudged against her sleepily, and she held her hand to his eyes with a cupping motion as if protecting a candle flame.

"Two things. First, if your Grigol is dead, you won't find him. They've already taken them away. Second, the old woman is an enemy. Didn't you hear what she said about Avlabari? We both know that's the Armenian quarter. She knows your blood. It's too dangerous for you on the streets. We'll have to wait here for word."

"What are you talking about? Avlabari! I don't care about Avlabari!"

"Be sensible, Nina. We'll have to wait here for word."

"Word? From whom?"

"Sirakan. Or Grigol himself. You don't know for sure that he's dead."

"That's why I have to find him! What if he needs me?" Nina flung herself at the door, but the other girl barred her way. And Loma clung to her.

"No. I won't let you," she said. "The city will be full of fury. You will thank me later. And Grigol, if he returns. And Sirakan. Sirakan will thank me for keeping his sister from throwing her life away!"

"Let me out!"

But Irina only shook her head and turned an impassive profile toward the window.

Stunned, Nina sank onto the bed. Her stepson sank beside her with exactly the same motion. His deep blue eyes were troubled, but his voice was clear. "He'll come back. Just as he did before. I know him; he'll come back."

Numbly, she went out to the balcony. The tree jittered with sparrows and finches. Their purposeful frolics and cheerful squabbles were like a flimsy barrier between Nina and the troubled discord on the streets. Then the deep-throated Russian bells from Sioni Cathedral tolled a summons, ringing for the morning mass.

"Don't try it," Irina's voice wafted out to her. "It's three stories down."

"I'll try it," Loma whispered beside her. "I'll go find him." His strong, agile fingers hooked into the screen, and he had found his first foothold before Nina grabbed him. She tugged him back into a long hug. "No, little warrior. If we go, we go together. You and me."

"We'll always stay together. Right?"

"Right. No matter what."

They held onto each other for a long moment. When they went in, Irina scrutinized her carefully. What she saw must have unsettled her. The smooth, resolute calm on Irina's face cracked into bewilderment.

"Why? Why?" she asked. "My love was full of passion and pain and riddled with confusion, and its end was catastrophe! Your love was set on a rock—sure and serene. But look what's happened! What's the use of it? It's all futile—all of it!"

"No. No, it's not futile." Nina thought of what Grigol's death would mean to her now and for all the long years to come. And yet she knew that she had something to say. She looked steadily into Irina's eyes. "God gave Grigol to me. I know it. Even if it's over, our love lived for a time to mirror a greater love."

"Why did He smash the mirror then?" Irina asked acidly.

Nina paused, thinking. In spite of her terrible fear, she was overshadowed by a sense of beauty and harmony. *No, I won't let this troubled girl and her bitter warrings with God rob me of what I know!*

"It's not smashed," she replied. "It lives in my memory. I am changed forever because I know that this kind of love exists. And the greater love that it reflects is as powerful and true as ever. My heart is bereft, but my spirit knows that I'll see him again.

"Besides . . ." Nina reached for the book on the table, *The Knight in the Tiger's Skin*. "Answer me this. When we hear a story of love beyond hope won after much strife and suffering, we call it beautiful. Yet a story where all comes easily is no story at all. Why? You know there's some great truth in it though we don't fully understand."

Irina shrugged, but her attitude softened a little. "For you, I hope he comes back," she said, but she held her position by the door.

At midafternoon they heard steps coming up the third flight. Nina was sitting on the bed trying to coax Loma into a nap. Her heart labored heavily as the footsteps paused at their door. Hope and fear clashed in the glance she and Irina flung at each other. Then with a graceful movement Irina moved aside, and a man stood in the hazy lozenge of daylight. He was filthy, stained with black blood in ugly, crusting splotches and begrimed with earth as if he had, indeed, crawled out of a grave. His oblong jaw was blue with stubble, but his eyes flared golden. Nina stretched out her arms.

Grigol stumbled toward her and, falling at her feet, buried his head in her lap. The great shoulders heaved, and his arms, as they clasped her, shook violently. A harsh, strangled sound came from him while Loma's adept hands pattered on his back. "Father! I knew it."

Nina looked at Irina, who hugged the little boy. "Come," she said. "Let's go out and share our gladness with the sparrows. We'll take them a special treat."

Irina took the boy out to the courtyard while Nina held her weeping husband. She stripped away his fetid clothes and cleansed his body, relieved to find that the blood was not his own. She kissed his skin in thankfulness where she found it whole. Then she held him until he could relax and look deeply at her and seek from her his joy and comfort.

"My wife," he said, "my true wife . . ."

THEY STAYED IN TIFLIS until September was past. Then just after the wheat harvest, Sirakan appeared. Nina was overjoyed to see him, but his news was grim.

"The shop has been burned to the ground. We can never return," he told her. "Our parents moved away in fear to an Armenian village to the east—a mistake, I'm afraid, but who knows? Perhaps there's safety in numbers. But all kinds of horrors broke out in our village. The landlord and his bailiff have been killed. The Voloshins—not Piotr's family, but his uncle's—have been crushed. They took those two young men, gouged out their eyes, and left them in the forest for the wolves and bears. Natasha, the daughter-in-law, the beauty with the blonde hair, was raped and killed. I heard that Mikhail and his old wife fled to Persia; I also heard that about Piotr's parents."

"What about the girls, Piotr's sisters?"

"They were alive and with their parents last I heard—God protect them. The sixteen-year-old was a pretty girl, and such girls are prey in times like this. Some said they followed Mikhail into Persia. Others said they'd been seen on the road going north from Akhalkalaki. But all the roads are crammed with refugees, and cholera is rampant in the countryside."

Grigol told him about the havoc in the city and about his meeting with Noe. That seemed to decide something for the big Armenian.

"We'll go to the mountains; I'll be safe as long as I'm with you. We'll find Noe—and perhaps hear news of Piotr's family as we travel."

Nina noticed that Irina looked at him with thankfulness and something more than thankfulness in her eyes.

They remained long enough to collect supplies, knowing that they would journey into autumn and meet winter along the way. On the fortieth day after the tragedy at the Town Hall, the bells of Tiflis rang out as Georgians flocked to the churches for *Panikhida* or requiem for the victims. That same morning nine bombs exploded near the Cossack barracks. The Cossacks went berserk and began shooting down people in the streets, including a German Lutheran pastor. Chaos reigned as criminals used the revolution as a cover for their murderous activities.

The next day Grigol, Nina, and Loma along with Sirakan and Irina turned their back on beautiful, tragic Tiflis and set their faces toward the mountains of the north.

VI

The Caves of Uplis-Tsikhe

The road from Akhalkalaki was clogged with travelers—in carts, on foot—moving sluggishly or stopped along the dusty roadside as though tethered to the bundles and cases piled around them. Vaktang guessed that many of them were refugees uprooted in the convulsions that shook all Georgia. But Vaktang Rukhadze and his brother Nodar were no refugees! Both young men were *tergdaleulni*—those who had drunk from the river Terek—that is, studied in Russia. Both were fluent in Russian, and both were eager to throw off Russian domination and shape a Georgian homeland. Because of this, Nodar had been fired from his post as a government clerk and was returning to their village in Svanetia. Vaktang, who worked as a surveyor's assistant, always had his winters free.

So the two of them scraped up the wages that would help their family survive the long winter and set off for the town of Gori. From there they'd take a challenging trek across the Bakh-fandak Pass and connect with the Mamison Road into Svanetia.

The thought of his native mountains always filled Vaktang with unquenchable happiness. Even the morose plodding of the fleeing Russians and Armenians couldn't cloud his joy as they drew closer and closer to the Caucasus.

Vaktang shot a quick look at Nodar, who was stepping along as jauntily as he himself. A cart load of Russian peasants lumbered by, and a pretty blonde girl with a snub nose gave the young men a thorough inspection. As well she might! Vaktang did not doubt that he and Nodar were fine young men and well worth a second glance. He honored her with a beautiful smile and swaggered a little—not too much. Nodar attacked him with a broadside shove, and his pack dislodged and swung awkwardly, catching on his damascened gun.

"You dog, you jackal! She's not looking at you! She's looking at me!" Nodar argued laughingly.

Vaktang tilted his curly wool *papachka* across his eyes and threw a playful punch at the younger man. "What do you know about women? They all love me!" He threw out his arms in a mock embrace. "I'm irresistible!"

The girl in the cart was much smaller now, but it was clear that he had made an impression. She was flushed like a rose, and her impertinent face was bunched up in giggles. Vaktang flung out an expansive arm.

"See. Look how I spread happiness. God made me like a bird. To be happy myself and to make others happy!"

"Stop cackling, bird," said Nodar, "and pay attention to the road. Here's the fork. Do we go up toward Gori?"

Vaktang narrowed his eyes at the off-turning. The autumn day was brisk with a hard brilliance to it. The mountains were green with forests, then blue with distance, then white with springing glory. A day for wonders! A day for miracles! Not a day to be shut up in a small town.

"That's it," he told Nodar. "That's Gori. But I'll tell you what! Let's turn aside and see the caves. Who knows if we'll ever come this way again? We have to spend the night in Gori anyway. We'll tramp around the old cave sites and then get into town in time for a nice dinner."

Vaktang noticed that many of the travelers—he assumed they were fleeing from troubled villages in Kartli—turned off toward the town. Others kept on. Where were they going? He supposed that refugees could sell their belongings and take the train from Gori across the Surami Pass to the ports of the Black Sea. If the trains were running. Or maybe they'd try driving their carts north across the Georgian Military Highway to Vladikavkaz. Perhaps, being Russian, they'd feel safer in a Russian city. He shrugged. *Well, let them go. We've had enough of the Russians!*

But when they had crossed the bridge over the Kura and mounted the steps into the fabled cave city, he was almost sorry they'd come. The city carved into the soft stone of the mountainside swept from east to west. Man's delvings had punctured hill and escarpment, honeycombing them with palaces, cathedrals, and the dwellings of ordinary folk—long dead. *A bleak, eerie place*, Vaktang thought.

The city, he knew, had grown over a period of hundreds of years in the first millennium before Christ. In antiquity it was an important center of Kartli, and in the Middle Ages it straddled one of the prime trade routes that linked Byzantium with India and China. A flourishing community of merchants and artisans, its beauty was trampled by the warriors of Tammerlane, damaged by earthquakes, then leached away with the passing of Byzantium and all its rich trade. For hundreds of years the noble stone chambers and ruined palaces were a haunt for the shepherds of the hills.

From where Vaktang stood, both the scraped, eroded hills of nature and the crumbling work of man looked as though they had been gnawed by the same despoiler. The brown land buckled in warped dips and folds rakishly turfed with rusty scrub. Gaping, inhospitable caverns tunneled into the low cliffs and escarpments. The arched hollows of doorways reminded him of the eye sockets of skulls.

Nodar's spirits, too, seemed a little dampened, but he cheered up when he saw the Three-Church Basilica at the summit.

"Let's go up," he suggested. The climb was exhilarating, and their youthful spirits returned. They turned aside to see the Hall of Queen Tamara—a luxurious cave dwelling where ancient kings wielded power beneath the weight of living stone. Vaktang studied the curious ceiling that was carved to simulate wood beams.

"How did they do it?" Nodar asked, but his voice echoed in a dreary, lonely way, and they soon went out again into the sunlight.

Like everything else, the steps going up to the church were carved right into the hillside, but a thousand years of use had rounded their edges, and the hills had adjusted to them so that they looked like the work of wind and water—which in part they were. The church, though, was clearly the work of skilled hands. Its walls were crafted by ninth-century masons, and its tile roof had resisted nature's assaults for a thousand years. But in Uplis-Tsikhe even a thousand years is young.

They circled back to the southeast part of the town where the ground was riddled with small pits that had been used for pagan ceremonies. Later, after Christianity came to Georgia in the fifth century, they were used for food storage. And, Vaktang noted with a start, they were being used for something now. He shaded his eyes, trying to decipher signs of habitation in the striated patterns of glare and shadow. He caught a blur of movement in one of the smaller artisans' caves and nudged Nodar silently.

They crept up to the cavern and saw what was obviously a family living there. Peasants on the run most likely, and apparently they had been there for some time. The stench was hideous. He thought he saw a woman rocking in pain, huddled in a far corner. He recoiled and put out a hand to keep Nodar back.

"What?"

"Sickness. Stay away. There've been rumors of cholera," Vaktang advised.

Nodar backed away, and they sprinted past the crumbling defensive walls.

"More refugees," Vaktang noted as they passed a ragged group. Judging by their appearance, he guessed these people had been here for weeks. How had they survived? And how would they survive when the winter snows came? That would be soon. Already the nights were brittle with frost.

"Let's go down to the river. I know a secret way," he said. He wanted to restore the day's cheer and forget about these forlorn vagabonds. What could he do? Thousands—Georgians, Armenians, and Russians—had been swept away in the tumult. It was like an avalanche. Impossible to put out a hand and stop it.

"Secret way?" Nodar gibed. "If you know it, it can't be a secret."

"I'm a surveyor," Vaktang bragged. "It's my job to know the lay of the land and the mind of the builders. Here, look." He paused before a gaping tunnel. It was too dark to see anything, but a freshening breeze and a scent of water came up to them. Vaktang dived into the dim, clay-scented space; his gun caught on a rough jut at the opening, but he twisted free and strode easily down toward the light.

"How far?" Nodar asked carelessly.

"Only about 150 feet—then we'll be at the river." He drew up suddenly, and Nodar slammed into him from behind.

"What! Don't stop now!"

Vaktang did not answer. A bent, gray shape fell across the haze-fogged oval of light at the tunnel's end. Instinctively, he reached back for his gun, squinting into the murk. The shadow-figure wavered in the thin, milky light. Drawing nearer, Vaktang made out a face sunk in a cowled shawl. A woman. Her long, ash-dirty hair mingled with the shawl's tattered fringe. A bleating cry rose from her. It seemed to come not from her lips, but from the misshapen center of her being. The cry echoed and stopped and was swallowed in Nodar's harsh exclamation. But it was too late. It had already reached out to Vaktang and wrapped around him with clinging fingers.

The young woman backed away, and he followed. In the sunlight he saw that she was covered with a weird assortment of garments. At least three skirts—red, green, and a rose-colored print—layered her rather tall body. These were covered by a huge man's greatcoat, topped by the shawl stiff with grime. She was walking in front of him with an ambling, lopsided gait like a wounded bear. But she seemed strong and agile enough as she climbed over the rocks at the river's edge. She stopped several hundred feet down from the tunnel's mouth and stooped with a heaving motion—as though she were sick. Vaktang came up behind her, and he too heaved inwardly.

At her feet lay a beautiful little girl dressed in peasant fashion. She, too, was covered with dust, but her embroidered coat was finely made, and her small feet were carefully booted. Her hands like pale petals were neatly overlapped on a lace-trimmed linen handkerchief. She was dead. And because the day had been hot, the black ants had come out. They scurried across her cheek and poured into her eyes in black, glittering pools.

The older girl peered at him. Her eyes had an odd, blind look. They asked nothing of him. But the beauty of the flashing river, the kindness of the beaming sun—these cramped his heart and demanded—something.

"Vaktang, where are you going?" Nodar, halted near the tunnel, was still in another world.

But Vaktang clenched his fists. Because he had stumbled on this kind of death mirrored in the eyes of this girl—this kind of girl—everything was changed for him.

"Wait!" he yelled. "Don't come too close!"

Characteristically, Nodar drew near and stood on the embankment above them. When he looked down toward the river, his gray-green eyes filled with horror.

"Who is she?" he asked.

The hollow-eyed girl tried to open her mouth, but her lips were stuck together in places. "Dausha!" she managed.

Vaktang was instantly alert and coaxing. "Dausha—was that her name? What is yours?"

"Dausha!" cried the girl as if trying to summon someone from a long way off. And again a bleating whimper rose from her. But this time she opened her coat and drew out an emaciated infant. The baby squeezed its eyes to shut out the sun and, in spite of its thinness, thrashed about as though happy to be set free. Vaktang and Nodar exchanged a shocked look. The baby boy opened his eyes and fixed Vaktang with a wide, knowing stare. Then flexing all his fingers and toes, he stretched out toward the sparkling river.

"A lively little one," Vaktang commented. "But how on earth are we going to feed him?" Only when Nodar seared him with a half-grinning, half-disgusted glare did he realize how fully he had committed himself.

NODAR WENT INTO THE VILLAGE across the bridge to buy food and a milk goat while Vaktang buried the little girl on a sandy shelf a little way from the Kura's bank. The older girl followed him apathetically, seeming to look right through him as he vigorously attacked the layer of crumbling sand and moist firm soil beneath. He worked with only his dagger and a flat rock, so progress was slow.

The Russian girl swayed slightly and moved her hands as though scooping something. Her expression did not change until a sudden gust blew the pretty little handkerchief into a tangle of bushes. It clung there like a fallen bird, and her wide-set, fawn-colored eyes flew to it with an expression that made him jump up clumsily and fetch it back. He replaced it in the dead girl's fingers with a delicate, gentle tuck and looked up at her sister hopefully. But the girl was impervious. She bundled the boy baby in her shawl and set him beside a tangle of bushes.

What has happened to her? Vaktang asked himself as he worked. He had heard reports of all kinds of horrors and inhuman acts in the villages. He pulled the tiny girl's kerchief over her face and brushed away the last few ants. Then he gently lifted the dead child and laid her in the crude grave as though it were a cradle. Vaktang waited for a few moments. Again he glanced at the young woman, but she did not respond. The light was failing, so he shoved a mound of earth into the grave with his booted foot. Then, from reverence, he scraped up a handful of dirt with his bleeding hand and held it over the small form. Suddenly there was a movement from behind him, and two young hands were cupped beneath his. Vaktang let the earth slide from his fingers into hers and then sift into the child's grave.

Turning, he saw a flicker of understanding in those wide, staring eyes. That brief connection, fleeting through a chink in the dead crust of whatever had been done to her, was the most potent thing he had ever encountered. But it was gone in a second. He turned back to the grave. All the diffuse, formless agony of revolution had hardened and condensed and lodged heavily on his heart. It was no longer the faceless suffering of the masses, but the very specific pain of this one girl.

When Nodar came with his newspaper-wrapped bundles and bleating goat, Vaktang was glad to see him. But at the same time, he felt that he was years older than this brother who was born only a year later.

"How is it in the village?" he asked.

"Peaceful now," Nodar replied. "But folk are careful, and the gendarmes are prowling about. It may be better to stay here for the night." He indicated the girl with a lift of his heavy, slanted brows. Then he lowered his voice. "No need to raise suspicions. Do you know who she is?"

"No. I've tried, but I can't get anything out of her. I think she's in shock."

"Well, let's get comfortable for the night. Then we'll see if we can get her to talk. With a child that young, she must have a husband—or family of some sort."

They shouldered their gear and supplies and motioned for the

Russian woman to follow them. The sun was gone by now, and the mouths of the caves looked blacker than ever. Smoke from hidden fires curled along the ground and lost itself in the indistinct scrub and vague outcroppings of Uplis-Tsikhe.

Vaktang avoided the southeast area—too many refugees—and led them up the central street to an arched doorway flanked by carved pillars. Inside was a sizable chamber. Its coffered ceiling swirled with ancient botanical designs that sent back the men's voices changed and chastened. A second cavern yawned on one side. Nodar ducked in quickly, then sprang out again.

"That will be a good place to sleep. But not until we have a fire going. It's too dark." His bright eyes gleamed as he scanned the fanciful ceiling and relief work on the lintel. "This place is strangely beautiful, but it makes my skin crawl. It's like stumbling across a lovely woman—only to discover that she's a corpse." His voice died in the stone foliage overhead. The girl flinched.

Vaktang turned away to hide the trouble in his face and studied some niches cut deeply into the rock. He began to stow their belongings while Nodar set out the provisions he had purchased in the village. Every movement, every word stirred up things best left undisturbed. Nodar's knapsack scraped stone, and a scent of clay and dust arose. The girl stood rocking her baby, not even watching them.

"I'll go out and see if I can find something to burn," he told Nodar. He knew that the area around the cave city would be denuded of wood and brush, so slinging his rifle on his back, he went back down to the river. A strong night wind funneled through the river bed. The low-lying elders fidgeted while the treetops thrashed in agitation. The cliff face towered darkly at his left hand, but the Kura snatched light from the sky and carried it back toward Gori.

Vaktang hiked up toward the higher hills where he found some dried sticks and wind-fallen branches. The slim moon with its two piercing cusps nipped at the fleeing stars. Vaktang felt as if something sharp and bright had entered into him—something he could not escape—and which, in fact, he would miss if it were gone.

He bound the wood to his back and retraced his steps. Nodar and the girl sat near the cave's entry, crouching in the arched pool of light. The girl was as still and stolid as ever, but Nodar was cheerfully bouncing smiles and gurgles from the skinny baby.

"Watch this," he said as soon as he caught sight of Vaktang. He dipped his finger into a bowl of country yogurt and offered it to the infant. The baby clamped down his quirky little brows, and his soft mouth sucked with fierce concentration. "Whoa! Leave some skin on!" Nodar protested laughingly. He scooped up another dollop and eased it into the pursed little mouth. "He's a strong one! Not too many babies are this strong. Look how he holds his head up!"

"Is that right? That shows he's strong?" Vaktang peered down with interest as the tiny boy scowled and craned his wrinkled neck. His spirits lightened, and he felt a surge of pride for the little fellow. "Well, he's no ordinary baby," he commented offhandedly.

"He's a lion of a baby! Sister Katai's baby lolls its head like a drunkard."

"Well, let's set up camp," Vaktang suggested. He built a small fire close enough to the doorway that the smoke could escape and set on a pot of beans to cook. He unwrapped Nodar's bundles and laid out bread, cheese, grapes, and yogurt. His clever little brother had even thought to buy some *basturma*—dried beef strips—and some *churchkhela*—the delicious sweet made from grape skins and walnuts. He had found a bottle of cow's milk for the baby, but after tonight they'd have to rely on the goat.

Vaktang bit off a piece of bread and chewed it hungrily. As he glanced up, he found that the girl was looking at him—with no expression, but the bread turned to ashes in his mouth. He tore off a fresh piece, dipped it in yogurt, and offered it to her with a courtly dip of his head.

"Refresh yourself." He bowed.

She took the bread and, for some reason, moved her hand up and down as though weighing it. Then her small even teeth sank greedily into the thick crust. In a moment it was gone, and she was looking at him again. With a gesture, he told her to take whatever she wanted. "Honor us," he said, and she squatted near the fire and supped on bread and beans and beef. They shared out the grapes. Then Vaktang made tea, and they sipped it gratefully as the night turned cold.

Finally, Vaktang turned to the girl. "Tell me, you must tell me who you are and how you came to be here. Do you understand? Who are you?"

"Nadya," she whispered, and the name was a groaning negation.

"Nadya who?"

"Only Nadya."

"Where is your village, your people?"

"Gone."

"Where? Can't you tell me?" In the red firelight he saw her eyes—which had been so expressionless—widen and fill up with such horror that he dropped his gaze.

Carefully, he positioned a few sticks on the blaze. When he looked up, Nodar was wriggling his eyebrows trying to get his attention. They exchanged a long look.

"Well," Vaktang offered, "you can come with us. We're going to our village in the mountains. It's not an easy journey, but you can come if you will."

But the girl had retreated; her eyes were as empty and staring as before.

Nodar knelt beside him. "What does she want?" he muttered.

Vaktang shrugged. "She's beyond wanting anything. We'll have to take her. If we leave her, she'll die and the babe with her. If we turn her over to the police, who knows what will happen? These are violent times."

"Will she be strong enough for the climb?"

"We can get a troika in Gori and drive as far as the pass. After that she may be stronger with some food and the air. But we'll all need our strength, so let's try to sleep."

He and Nodar stretched out on one side of the fire while Nadya, the goat, and the baby huddled on the other. Nodar dozed fitfully while Vaktang stared at the stone forms that sprouted overhead and seemed to wave like seaweed as the fire flared and guttered. Just past midnight he heard a snarling in the distance. He took up his gun and stole through the pillared entry and up the street. Low growls and a single howling yelp rose up from the river. *Jackals*, he thought with a pang. *Maybe I didn't bury the little girl deep enough.* He thought of the lace handkerchief he had placed so carefully in her tiny fingers and of the small boots. *What of all that now?* He decided that they would have to leave the cave city by crossing the bridge and skirting the village. It wouldn't do to have Nadya see what was left of her little sister.

A dark, webbed sadness settled on him. Too many had been hurt—too many children given back to the land—too many young girls marred. He scrutinized the moon-blanched shapes of ancient dwellings—some comely, others grotesque—left behind by a lost civilization. *When all is said and done, all monuments are only tombs.*

He turned to go back to the cavern, and his eyes were caught by a blaze of whiteness. Rising from the somber forests, the mountains of the north lifted up their highest peaks to display the first of the autumn snows. Glimmering light leapt back and forth as moon, snow, and stars exchanged their night-subtled brightness over the peaks of Sarkineh and Zedazeni.

Steel-bright resolve hardened in Vaktang, and he lifted his head as though he too had light to barter. He made up his mind that he would pour out all his brawn and cunning to get that stone-faced girl, her fractious baby, and the troublesome goat over the mountains and into Svanetia. At least there they would be safe for the winter. After that, they'd see.

Vaktang was happily weary when he returned to the cavern. Plans bulged in his head, and his fingers were jittery for action, but he was bone-tired. He remade the fire and lay beside it, drifting pleasantly.

An outraged squall jerked him into wakefulness. Nodar groaned, and the goat pleaded with an offended quaver, but the babe clenched his fists and screamed lustily. Nadya rose up in the firelight, dazed and confused. Vaktang groped for the bottle and began milking the protesting goat.

"Nodar, hold her . . ."

His brother straddled the goat and grabbed her horns. "She misses her kid," he explained.

Vaktang said nothing while the baby's yells echoed through the cavern and Nadya watched them through her raised fingers, her loosed hair falling around her like moulting feathers. For the first time it occurred to him: *This baby can't be hers. If it were, she'd be nursing it.* He cast a sideways glance at her. She had been using the clumsy greatcoat as a blanket instead of wearing it, but she still had plenty on. An open blouse peeled back over a rose-printed dress that showed through a dirty cream-colored smock. But in spite of the concealing layers, it was evident that Nadya was amply supplied to keep even this voracious baby happy—if she was a mother. Evidently she was not.

But where had this fierce, noisy baby come from? "Hold him, Nodar," he yelled. He capped the bottle and offered it to Nodar who was patting the thrashing red-faced baby. "Come on, little friend, take it," Nodar begged. But the little boy wrenched away from the nipple, still screaming angrily.

So much for secrecy, Vaktang thought as the shrill cries rang out. Aloud he said, "A lion of a baby, Nodar! A lion of a baby."

THEY RENTED A TROIKA IN GORI, agreeing to leave it in Tskhinvali, twenty-nine *versts* away. "It will save us two days of walking," Vaktang explained as he counted out the precious rubles. He scanned the clear autumn sky and the towering snow peaks. Winter in the high passes could kill even vigorous young men. What about Nadya and the babe? An unknown. He felt that the tall, inert girl and the vital, life-grasping baby were pulling him in two, and he had to push forward powerfully to tow both of them. Nodar hobbled the shaggy goat and tossed her into the carriage.

Vaktang took up the reins, and they followed the road along the churning Liakhva's stream. The road dipped and swelled between harvest-shorn fields and sparkling groves of apples. Occasionally, the stream rose up to cover part of the road, but these places were easily fordable, and the three horses scarcely slowed their pace.

The land began to change, and the hills bristled with pine and fir as they came into the Ossetian town of Tskhinvali. They spent the night at the post station. The babe fought his bottle, then guzzled greedily. The girl fell into a restless sleep. Vaktang could see her limbs twitching as he and Nodar talked quietly with the postmaster. An Ossetian with a deeply scored, angular face, he told them that the sudden thaw had sent avalanches hurtling down on the ancient villages of Jibiani and Ushguli in Upper Svanetia. *My native village!* But Vaktang's pang of fear was unnecessary. The frozen flood had flung its fringe over some of the watchtowers, but no villagers were caught, and spring would release the stone towers soon enough. As for Ushguli, it was the highest continuously inhabited village in Europe and had survived many such catastrophes.

"But there's a scent of snow in the air," the postmaster cautioned. "Make no delay in getting over the Bakh-fandak."

Before dawn they hired a pack horse and found the track that follows the Patsadon stream up to Jomay. Now the snows were more than a far-off glimmer. Gleaming white fingers reached down to meddle in the valleys. Smoke from the Ossete settlements smudged the mountain face with puffs of defiance. But the snow masses gathered their strength into knotted fists and waited.

Vaktang was familiar with the area. A few years before he had helped survey the nearby Roki Pass for a railway. At noon they stopped at Jomay, but their rest was short. The taciturn mountain folk cast suspicious glances at the disheveled girl in her man's greatcoat. *What is it to them?* Vaktang chaffed, but he choked down his temper with his hot tea. These were not times for lashing out heedlessly at offense.

He looked thoughtfully at Nadya. She was bent over her glass of tea, cradling its warmth while an ashen wilderness of lank hair tented her features. Her delicate nose was pink with cold and wet with steam. *She does look . . . odd. People are bound to think something evil of her—or of me.*

Shrugging, Vaktang strode out of the dark hole of a *chaikana* and squinted uneasily. The drab village was transformed. Every branch, every roof, every ledge was frosted with a translucent sheen and glistened like ground glass. The snow sifted down in leisurely drifts and swirled aimlessly at his feet. *God help us, we're trapped*, Vaktang thought and stamped as though putting out a fire. Nodar came up behind him, peering up at the laden clouds.

"Dancing on it won't help. Save your strength for the high passes," he said. "Let's chance it. I don't want to stay here."

The girl came out, her face blanched and drained in the soft light. She held the baby with her right arm and shielded its eyes with her other hand. But the boy kept squirming so that his bright eyes pierced through her spread fingers and the snow flurries. The sight of her stabbed him with an acute pity. Vaktang turned away. Why was it, he wondered, that this pity—that for him was usually mixed with disdain—had now become the most powerful force in his life, influencing his every decision? Vaktang flung a flamboyant gesture of frustration at the untimely snow and the needy girl and the fussy baby.

If it were only he and Nodar, of course they'd chance it. But to hike over a pass almost ten thousand feet high with a dazed girl and a helpless infant in falling snow was pure folly.

"The pass is only a few *versts* away," Nodar urged. "In a light snow like this, we should be able to get across it quickly and be on our way."

Vaktang peered up at the sky. A mist of snow touched his face with hesitant delicacy. The sky still had a tarnished, heavy look to it, but it seemed to Vaktang that the cloud cover was growing lighter, more translucent. "We'll go," he agreed.

But as they climbed, the snow gave up its airy spiraling and settled into a steady, slashing blizzard. The girl was perched on the pack horse, but they took her down so that the three of them could walk alongside the horse, letting the sturdy animal take the brunt of the storm. They slogged on that way for an hour or so and then stood in a weary, shivering clump while Vaktang took his bearings. But the storm had swallowed any signs of the trail, and the familiar mountains hid behind a veil of snow.

Then the veil drew aside, and the snow settled. Vaktang saw the Bakh-fandak Pass before them. A steep ramp led them between the snow-flecked flanks of soaring mountains. Rising on either side, but especially high on their right hand, the ice-barbed tines of the main Caucasus range sheared at the low-ranging clouds and tore great rents in them. Blue rifts opened in bright sky chasms, and they kept craning their necks to take in the glory of the sun-ignited snow-peaks and the opening sky.

Heartened, Vaktang hastened up the incline until he stood at the top of the pass. He gulped in the cold, rarefied air while a shuddering joy lurched through his body from knee to chest. These were the mountains of his boyhood! The white crest of Shikara held back the sky to the north. The new snow clotted densely on her ridged spine and clung in fanciful patterns to her granite sides. And behind Shikara was Ushba—the storm-thrower. Its majestic twin horns crowned with crenelated diadems, Ushba reared its seventeen-thousand-foot bulk to catch the moisture from the distant Black Sea and hurl it into the valleys with swift fury. But now all its looming might was silent and serene.

With all my learning in the Russian lands, I've never been able to tell anyone what these mountains mean to me. Science told him that they were crushed into their massive forms by great pressures within the earth. Theology told him that God existed everywhere. But the massed splendor of these sky-cleaving peaks caught at his heart and reminded him that God revealed Himself in the high places—on Sinai and Carmel and the Mount of Transfiguration. Law and prophecy and redemption. The glittering spires were full of expression, and he felt himself pierced and receptive.

He turned suddenly to see Nadya by his side. Her face was tilted toward Shikara. Its light fell full on her face, which looked as scrubbed and clean as a newborn babe's. Her lips were parted, her mouth soft and tender with the wonder of it. Her wide-set, light brown eyes had lost their dead look and were deep, clear pools filling with the light around her and with an inner light that she had kept hidden. She did not look at him, but he felt that her secret inner light called out to the light of the mountains and to him. The wrenching pity he always felt for her drained away, and its place was taken by something else. Vaktang stared at her in awe. *You are beautiful, beautiful.* He longed to reach out and touch her face, but she had retreated again into some deep refuge where he could not follow.

She turned from him without a glance and began toiling down the incline with her peculiar halting gait. By the time Nodar came up leading the horse, Vaktang wondered whether the moment had ever happened. And by the time they descended into the Nardon Valley on the north side of Bakh-fandak, the light had failed, and the land stretched out in dark, velvety folds.

The outlying fields were silent, but odd echoes arose as they approached the cultivated lands surrounding the villages. The noise became deafening as they drew near. The horses began to shirk, and Nadya shrank back. The night seemed to leap with scattered blazes of wild fire and gamboling, impish shadows. Then Vaktang saw that the menacing shadows were men and boys stationed around each newly harvested grain field. They were beating on kettles and drums or waving torches in wild, flaming arcs. The baby set up a sympathetic squall, but the girl was breathing heavily; a spasm of terror and a sort of heavy disgust distorted her features.

"It's only for the bears," Vaktang explained, briefly touching her arm. But she jumped back with a frantic look.

"Look," he continued, "the bears come down from the hills at night and forage among the ricks. The village folk are trying to frighten them away. They do it every year this way."

But he could see that he was not reaching her. A reflection of torch flame jetted across her eyes like a red comet. Her whole body shook as she stood holding the baby. She continued to shake as they set her up on the horse and led her into the village. And it was as though they were leading her to her death.

VII

The Storyteller of Gebi

Tossing torches and hammering clamor and the shouts of men—for Nadya the descent from the serene mountains into the valley's red and black tumult was a return to nightmare. A nightmare that continually moved before her eyes since that night when she had watched in terrible fear the destruction of a family. A screaming girl—they were tearing her like beasts. *No! Shut her away!* Agony on a young husband's face—then the agony swelled and bloated because his face was no longer recognizable. They had stabbed his eyes out with sharpened stakes. *Shut it out!* Her heart pounded so hard it was like the trampling of a herd of horses! *Stop it!*

She clung to the horse's mane; the baby screamed and screamed. *Put him away!* She let him slip, then started as arms reached up to take him. The racket subsided, muffled by the clutter of dark stone walls. They went down a village lane shaled with moon-struck stone, led by the young man who had taken her up as a river takes up a fallen leaf. *Be still*, she told herself, and her thoughts were swallowed up in the trembling of her body.

The young Georgian—she could not remember his strange name—was consulting with some village folk dressed in ragged sheepskins with shapeless felt caps pulled down over unkempt locks. Their eye whites flashed as they stared at her. The young man was further away now. Women in sacklike dresses under sleeveless coats sidled up to her and began fingering the packs, her shawl, her coat, jabbering all the while in a tongue unknown to her. The other young man was waving his free hand while he held the baby with the other—trying to protect the supplies on the pack horse. "Vaktang!" he yelled.

More men, women, and children funneled down the dark chute of a street and mobbed Nadya. Grasping hands pulled her down and began snatching at her and stripping away her coat. *My father's coat.* She shuddered as Gavril Voloshin's last protection for his daughter was wrenched away. Drowning in terror and a clamoring confusion, she couldn't remember the word for help, and she too cried, "Vaktang!"

A shot rang out, and the young man appeared, laying about with the butt of his flintlock gun. He pulled her into a dark, enclosed space—a barn by the smell of it. The brother followed leading the horse and goat. Vaktang shoved both nervous animals into the stone barn. Then he turned to face the mob from the doorway. The other man joined him. Both assumed hardened, vicious expressions as they confronted the villagers. She caught only a glimpse of their faces, but teeth and daggers and guns all flashed with befitting menace. Then Vaktang aimed his gun at the slender curve of the moon and fired. The villagers scattered, and a wave of his hand sent Nadya stumbling deep into the black interior.

The two brothers stood in the block of blue light from the barn door. The younger shrugged and wriggled his heavy eyebrows. Vaktang punched him lightly on the arm, and the two laughed lightheartedly.

"Not bad," Vaktang pronounced as though nothing were out of the ordinary. "We haven't lost anything."

"The girl's coat—a couple of old witches grabbed it right off her shoulders," said the brother.

"She's shivering. We'd better give her something, Nodar. I have a sheepskin in my pack."

"I'll wear it. She can wear my *tcherkeska*." Nodar paused judiciously. "That way she won't look so . . . Russian." He pulled off his red Circassian coat with its dark brown trim and flaring skirts. Nadya shrugged into it gratefully. The stone barn was ice cold. The coat fit perfectly. Nodar was just about Nadya's size, Vaktang only a little bigger.

"It looks good on you," Vaktang commented. But something in

his black-fringed, gray-green eyes frightened her. She turned to find the baby snugly stowed beside a heap of dung bricks.

"The baby . . ." Vaktang hesitated. "He's not your son?"

"My brother," Nadya said. Her voice sounded strange even in her own ears. She had talked so little in the past weeks.

"And his name?"

"Semyon. Semyon Gavrilovich."

"So your father's name is Gavril. Is he . . ."

"Dead. My mother also. Cholera." Nadya tried to push away the thought of those two days when first Gavril, then his wife had burned with fever and died within hours. Semyon gurgled happily on her lap. Only he had survived. Only this meager bundle of flesh whom she did not, could not know.

Vaktang was silent. Then he returned to his prodding questions. "So little Dausha was your sister, and this is your brother. Were there any others?"

"A brother Piotr. Twenty years old."

"Ah! And this Piotr, where is he?"

Nadya gave him the most direct look she had allowed herself so far. "Los Angeles."

Vaktang exchanged a glance with his brother, and they both raised their heavy brows over almost identical eyes. "Lazengales! Where is that?"

"America." The word was final—a cutting off—and they knew it. The brothers lapsed into silence, and Nadya began feeding yogurt to the survivor—Semyon Gavrilovich. She did not want to talk. In fact, it was hard for her to find words even for her own inner thoughts. Words were crowded out by two images—black shadows lurching among jostling torches and the blindingly white mountain that stabbed her with its beauty and purity so that a flood of longing poured from her.

She felt that these things had risen before her out of nowhere, that they had complete power over her, and that she had been given over to them by those whose love she had trusted—her parents. *I'm too tired. I can't think about this.* But the ugly insistent thought goaded her. Just as Gavril and Galina Voloshin had chosen America for Piotr, so they had chosen this for her. The precious son was redeemed—the daughter surrendered. *No! It wasn't their fault. How could they know?* But this idea tormented her and made her feel that she had lost her loved ones in way more profound than death.

She imagined herself talking to Piotr, explaining, justifying: *I couldn't help it, I couldn't stop it. I couldn't even bury them.* A dark blot appeared in her mind. It was the mouth of the cave on the outskirts of Uplis-Tsikhe where they had watched Gavril die and where Galina had pushed them away, swaying and sweating in her fever. But Dausha had clung to her in a wailing frenzy, and Nadya had pleaded, and the baby had screamed. But Galina was adamant. "Go! Do this one thing for me, Nadya. From heaven I'll thank you. Go!"

But Nadya could not. She stayed and hoped against hope that she could nurse her mother to health. But there was no water and no heat. In the freezing morning, Galina sank into her death sleep. When her last breath vanished like a ghost fleeing the murky cavern, Nadya took Dausha and the boy and left. As she looked back, the distinctive shape of the cave's mouth sprang out and branded her mind, a constant black reminder of everything that had gone before.

She found the tunnel that went down to the river. By that time Dausha was flushed with fever. *I've killed her. We should have left.* Desperately, Nadya mopped the small face and tried to squeeze water from a rag past Dausha's swollen tongue. The little girl moaned weakly while baby Semyon's fierce bawling bounced off the cliff wall. And again she had failed. Dausha slipped away. Nadya was exhausted—torn between blood-sapping inertia and a wild, clawing panic. *Let me die,* she prayed. A dark, blotting hex of a shape rose up to numb her mind. *Let me die.*

But Semyon screamed in resolute, lusty gusts. She picked him up and rocked him to silence and cradled him close to her heart in the big coat she had taken from Gavril. Then she had staggered toward the black mouth of the tunnel, and there Vaktang's gray-green eyes had gleamed so strongly, sucking all the will out of her and leaving her pliable and doomed.

And even now as the two brothers made a fire of *kizyak* bricks and set out food, the brooding shape of a cave's mouth came and sopped up her living thought so that she spoke no word to the eager young men.

BEFORE DAWN Vaktang hustled them awake. Nadya saw that he had everything packed and ready to go. They slipped out and stole up the stone street, finding their way to the Mamison Road. Fairly new, it cut a rain-washed swath through forests and rugged hills. The sun played yellow and gold across the towering ranges to the east. Occasionally the black silhouette of a ruined monastery would lift its cross against the dawn-glow.

The road followed the white, churning Rioni River up to Sori, but Vaktang pressed on to the village of Oni. As they traveled, Nadya kept her eyes on the river. The sun spread molten gold from across the mountains and overlaid the water with a rich gilding. Gray rocks along the bank were filigreed with ice, which gradually shrank into lacy, dreamlike patterns as the day warmed. Then the road climbed into a forest, and green-brown shadows changed shape on the moving water. They passed a village. Nadya was relieved when they did not stop, and she turned her eyes back to the river.

All day Nadya watched the river, turning from it only to swallow a roadside meal or feed her baby brother. From time to time she glanced briefly at Vaktang. His ice-green eyes were colored like the river and the mountains.

They toiled up a steep hill where the stream broke free with a white churning down a rocky incline, then flashed with fire as the sun went down. The scents of night crept out from the rocks, and the river settled into a broad, silken stream brocaded with silver wavelets.

That night they spent in the starosta's way stop in a village called Glola. The next morning they left the main road to follow the track to Gebi. Nadya found that she had trouble remembering where they had been. Was it three days they had traveled—or four? But this lapse was as welcome as cotton wool to a wound. Let the ranges and rivers and long hours of travel make a barrier! The more that lay between her and what had gone before, the better. Nadya found that the inner haze had thickened so that she could focus her outer attention on the stupendous, the bizarre, the curious—anything that she could pile onto her wall of defense. Silently she took it all in—and found that the medieval villages and hawk-haunted cliffs and mysterious forests were generous in the stupendous, the bizarre, and the curious. She began to wake up and look around her.

As they walked, Nadya noticed scythed clearings around wooden homesteads patched into the woods. They were coming to an inhabited place. A brawling stream on one side havocked down a rock-chasmed canyon. But on the other side, the smooth velvet of a shorn field was arrayed with precisely placed ricks trussed into elongated shapes. *Like golden straw warriors enforcing a strange peace,* Nadya thought.

At midmorning they came into the village of Gebi. Then Nadya saw the reason for the odd silence of the fields. All the folk of the district thronged the town for the harvest festival. A band of Mountain Turks in black sheepskin bonnets and flying cloaks prodded along herds of horses from the green downs under Mount Elbruz. A knot of women in colorfully patterned, flamboyantly flounced skirts gossiped at the corner of the church. They were surrounded by an assortment of market baskets spilling sheaves of corn, apples of many kinds, and vegetables. "From Latal," Nodar explained. "Only the women of Latal dress in this way."

A tall, tawny-bearded noble mounted on a black horse sliced between them, his long *bashlik* hanging loose over his shoulders and his sword, dagger, and pistols clattering on his belt. "A Mingrelian," Nodar muttered when he caught up to Nadya again. Just ahead of them, Vaktang was shouldering through the mob. A pack of large, wolflike dogs and small children gamboled by. The children were beautiful, their shapely limbs flashing through the rags that scarcely covered them.

Vaktang led them to the *chaikana,* but it was empty. They pressed on to the village green where an old man was sitting amidst the big, grasping roots of a mountain ash. Flocks of birds skittered through the branches pecking at the clusters of bright red berries. But the tree had given up most of its leaves, and they made a rustling carpet for the assortment of village folk surrounding the man.

The crowd shifted and murmured with anticipation. What a strange group they were! The men looked as rugged and sinewy as weathered wood. Their tattered clothes contrasted with their extravagantly decorated weapons—flintlock guns and ancient swords and engraved daggers. Their ragged skirted coats glittered with silver clasps, metal studs, and crisscrossed belts of cartridge cases. Each wore a rude felt cap that almost covered the forehead but allowed a fringe of wild locks to escape.

"The caps go under helmets," Nodar told her with a tweak of his own. "The old-timers never take them off. That way they're always ready to clap a helmet onto their head in case of sudden warfare." Sudden warfare—he spoke of it as though it were like a storm or avalanche. No warning. No escape. Just the armor to face it.

The women of Gebi wore vivid red robes adorned with necklaces of seashells, pieces of amber, and many-patterned beads. Their proud heads were crowned with colored turbans worn over white cotton veils that draped stiffly down their backs.

The storyteller himself looked comical. His red, puffy face was furrowed with wry wrinkles and tweaked with sly little corners at the eyes and jaw and beside each nostril. He lacked the beautiful aquiline nose so common to Georgians; his snout had no bridge at all, but bulged out with snub impertinence as though it had remembered just in time that this creature would need air. His eyes were as blue and cloudless and innocent as a child's. His hat looked like an old eroded mountain—and was about that color. It perched far back on his head, exposing the deep creases in his forehead and the shiny skin between.

He held up a hand, and the villagers tensed in silence. His flat tongue moved in and out over the gaps in his teeth like a shovel ladling out the words. But in a moment Nadya forgot the old seer's ugliness. His voice was beautiful.

As soon as he held out his hand, the crowd gave themselves up to him and bent or swayed or sighed like a field of sunflowers. His stubby brown hand conducted them, and the muted, modulated voice warmed them with gladness or stung them with grief. Nadya found that she, too, would bend or sway or sigh as the story unfolded, though she could not understand the words. Vaktang came and sat cross-legged behind her, quietly translating snatches of the story into Russian. He murmured a few words, and she leaned into his murmurs. The listeners sighed. Their sighs upheld the storyteller's art, which roots up deep images and compels teller and listener to conspire together so that the tales could do their work of shaping a people's mind and heart. The clownish old man exhaled his story, and they swayed in the wind of it.

It was a story of love lost beyond hope—a story so ancient and so powerful that for the first time Nadya felt that she was not Russian but part of a people much older, a people who had no name. Vaktang's whisper took up the music of the other voice and breathed a current of meaning into it. A feudal world of hunters and forests, queens, and lost towers opened up before her. And always moving through the hunts and battles and heroic journeys was a single dark figure—the melancholy knight Tariel riding on a horse "black as Merani" and clad in a tiger's skin. "And beauty such as his has ne'er been seen by man . . ."

Nadya glanced back at Vaktang. His gray eyes gleamed with the beauty of the legend. She looked away and let her body relax and float as the story took her up. The villagers groaned, and Vaktang described three brothers—one wounded, "his spirit almost fled." Nadya stiffened at his next words: "If you cannot help us, add grief to our grief and make it complete . . . weep with us who need pity—weep . . ." Nadya turned with a sharp, stealthy twist and saw that the gray eyes were glistening with tears. But she did not cry. *Only the tears of my own people—the Molokans—can add grief to my grief.* The time of completion was not yet.

NADYA COULD TELL that the temperature was changing rapidly. The glade around them and the encircling highlands wheezed and cracked in the frost's grip. The sky darkened, and the mountains sent down threats of winter. As they climbed, beautiful Shikara rose up again, the brightest thing in the landscape. Nadya's eyes trailed the curving sweep of a glacier the color of thin milk, its mosaic-like segments outlined in blue. Then a sea of gold opened before them. She caught her breath as they looked down onto a vast golden forest of birches transformed by autumn. These were not the slender Russian species, but the great Caucasian birch. Each leaf glimmered at the sun, and clusters of gold would part here and there as some large, glossy bird broke free in dark escape. The wind lapped gently and billowed the gold in a lift and fall, lift and fall, like a mother settling a blanket on a much-loved cradle. Wild crab apples fringed the wood, and they gathered as much of the dappled fruit as they could carry. The forest floor, too, was gold as they plunged in; they were all drenched with it as they followed a woodland path, eating tartly delicious fruit. Then the trees darkened to russet and stopped.

Again they were climbing—this time along a crumbling ridge of slate. Somber and hostile, it threw dark shards down at them. One of them grazed Nodar's cheek, and he brushed at it as though it were a gnat. A river flashed in the gorge below them. Nadya caught a glimpse of a dark tower with fanged horns rising on its battlements. They went down into a glen that opened into a larger valley. The grass in the valley was the whitish straw color of a meadow just at the tip of winter when the light licks at it from under a ledge of cloud. It crackled like glass as they walked across it.

Nadya halted, astonished. A stalking company of watchtowers—dozens of them—clustered in three separate knots. Each square tower was spackled with crude white plaster and crowned with a slate roof and battlements pierced for musketry. Low barnlike dwellings of slate lapped around their bases. The farthest clump of towers was partially buried in snow—as though the mountain had swooped down to swallow up these insolent intrusions.

The whole valley had a brutal strength to it. *I'll never get out*, she thought, but each of her footsteps mimicked the steps of the two brothers. She followed them across the harsh, slicing slate down to the ancient village of Ushguli.

The brothers were arguing quietly. Nadya gathered that they would have some difficulty explaining her and the baby and the goat. But she did not trouble to wonder where she was being taken or for what purpose.

Again the villagers mobbed them, but this time there were friendly greetings for the brothers and curious stares for her and the baby. The group thinned out as they turned off a slate-strewn lane. A branch of the river forked into two streams and in the "Y" between them was a slanted tumble of buildings—mostly low farmhouses but guarded by a tower at the front and a cluster of three towers on the hillside behind. A squat tower perched right in the center—shorter and broader than the others, huddled next to a stone barn and a two-story house. Tilted fields hemstitched by short-slated fences flanked this collection of buildings.

Vaktang approached with his swaggering step. They all stopped when a black-clad woman slid out of the house and moved down toward them. Vaktang squared his shoulders. The little woman—she was much shorter than Nadya—came right up to them and flicked a glance of her gray eyes at Nadya. *Their mother!* Her fine-featured face and those flashing gray eyes left no doubt. A string of tense questions flew from her. Was she angry about her unbidden guest? Vaktang began waving his arms around, and Nadya saw that most of his gestures were aimed at the goat. After a while she gathered that the woman was berating her son for buying a goat when the barn was full of them. Nodar grabbed Semyon from her and shoved him into the fray. Here, he seemed to say, this is the reason for the goat!

Vaktang was still explaining with his hands, and Semyon, too, flailed about with his fists as though to enter the debate. Nadya tried to dissolve into the pack horse. But Semyon made a quick grab for the woman's hair. She tilted her face up toward him, flashing her eyes. Then she grinned and snatched him up from her son.

She was a wisp of a woman and, in her coloring and movements, reminded Nadya of smoke. Her dark garb looked as though it had been smudged with charcoal. Her curling gray hair wafted from the confines of her headdress, and the uneven tint of her eyes wavered in shades of gray. Her arms and head flowed with graceful curves, but she kept her feet firmly planted so that only the top part of her body moved. But for all that, she was a handsome woman with smooth, young skin and a supple body. She flung a few more spirited phrases at the two young men; then they all trooped up the hill to the medieval tower and the stony farmhouse.

The trio of buildings—tower, barn, and house—stood cheek by jowl so that it was easy to move from one to the other. They entered through the barn—an ancient building with no windows, but slivers of light came in through the unmortised stones. Dozens of sheep milled about in the semidarkness. They ducked through a low doorway into the adjacent building and found a byre with four cows, several goats, and, disgustingly, a grunting collection of tiny, greasy-looking swine.

A wooden passage led them into the main homestead. The hearth dominated the long main room; a table with several stools and a shelf for kitchen utensils were grouped nearby. On the other end of the room a loom set up on blocks stood next to a great pile of rusty white fleece. The oily scent of lanolin filled the room. A tiny window set high on the wall near the stove and two others on the opposite wall offered a frail light. Through a narrow doorway, she caught a glimpse of two iron beds and a curtained alcove that screened a third bed. Another doorway led outside to a south-facing balcony that ran the length of the house.

A *cave*, Nadya thought. There were only a few touches of wood—the table, the stools, a few shelves, the loom, and the plank floor. For a Russian, wood was considered the most healthy material for a home. Windows were prescribed—always three, representing Father, Son, and Holy Ghost. They were set right at the front of the house facing the street so that people could see their neighbors and the comings and goings of village life. Bowls, utensils, and the beloved carved sills and lintels—all were wood. But here the hard deflection of stone and metal were more common. The kitchen things were brass or tin. On an occasional shelf or niche were brass and glass railway lanterns—there must have been at least half a dozen of them. But the warming, familiar sight of a piping samovar graced the crude table. *Still*, Nadya thought, *these Svans are a proud and lonely people who revel in their isolation and use dark stone and shining metal to ward off human invaders and the ever-present threat of the mountains.*

The Svan woman set the baby near the fleeces and went out. In moments she came in again, bringing a basket filled with smoked meats and cheese and pears. Again Nadya thought of smoke—her presence permeated every corner of a room as soon as she came into it. She laid out the food with swift, pirouetting movements, and they ate hungrily while she filled glasses with hot tea from the samovar.

Later she handed Nadya a sheepskin and a blanket and nodded toward the loom. Nadya settled her makeshift bed next to the loom, but then she rolled over so that she lay partially beneath the woof and warp of woven wool. She nestled into her fleece-cushioned haven and studied the webbed design above her. The brunt of the day's exertion caught her up, and she floated in the ebb and flow of strength and exhaustion. A soothing rocking sensation came over her, as though she were being carried away by a boat. She fell into a stupefied sleep.

By THE END of the week, the days of false starts and passing frosts were gone; true winter was upon them. The two streams turned black, and snow packed every nook and cranny of the rocky village. Then even the river froze, spun into fanged ice shapes as its tumble over rock ledges was arrested in midcourse. Crystal beaded the willow scrub beside the stream. Snow sifted over all the towers, houses, and fields, joining them to the patient, waiting mountains. Overnight the rugged valley was transformed into a tranquil white sea that lapped dreamily at the harsh, stubborn stone. And the dreams prevailed while the stone receded.

This soft, muted, white world filled Nadya with peace and spoke her inner language—hush, be silent, cover it. During the day she combed wool and spun it while Vaktang's mother—her name was Esma, but Nadya called her auntie—clacked away at the big loom. Nadya learned that she wove for much of this village and nearby Jibiani as well as for her own family. Her attitude toward her guest was hard to read; she seemed to take her for granted in some ways. Nadya began to suspect that she expected payment from the Voloshins when they returned her to her own folk. *But I have no folk.* Return to her own village was unthinkable, and she was careful not to mention its name.

Occasionally, Esma would nod in a proud and friendly way and make some comment. "What did she say?" Nadya asked Vaktang.

"Oh, she thinks you're a fine worker." Then he'd smile enigmatically.

The days spun out like the coarse thread between her fingers. Days of snow like fleece and fleece like snow. On sunny afternoons she would put on the red *tcherkeska* Nodar had given her and sit out on the balcony, spinning. The sun flattered the snow into sparkling iridescence and conjured mysterious blue shadows from every hollow and crevasse. Sometimes Vaktang or Nodar would come out and talk to her. They were the only ones in the village who spoke Russian, yet Nadya accepted them passively. She had no need for talk.

But Vaktang apparently did. "Your village . . . your home . . . your family?" His questions pricked and tried to pin her down, and sometimes she fluttered wildly beneath them. But many times she let a deep, sifting whiteness within her stifle them.

"Your brother—this Piotr—you say he lives in Lazengeles,"

Vaktang said. "When first you told me, I thought you meant a place of the Laz. They are an ancient people who once lived near the Black Sea many hundreds of years ago. But their kingdom was shattered by the Mohammedans when they raided the seacoasts and drove many to the mountains."

"No. Not that Laz," Nadya said patiently.

"I know. America, you say. What can you tell me about it?"

"Little. Those who go travel to France or Germany and take a big boat across the ocean. Then there are more travels. And then they are in Los Angeles."

"How do the people there live?"

Nadya struggled to remember. "It's a city," she hesitated, "with many, many people. We have not heard from my brother, but others say that men labor on railways or in lumberyards. There are few farms, I think."

"And why did your brother go to this place?"

Nadya studied her opponent. His ice-gray eyes were full of a kind of tender curiosity. His dark head was bare, and his fair face was as chiseled and black and white as the snow-flecked granite around her. He was, indeed, a beautiful young man.

"Our people are Molokans, and we are pacifists. We believe that a prophet told us to flee this land and go to this other on the far side of the ocean. Because Piotr was in the army, my parents were eager to send him away—so that he would be saved from killing or being killed. And they sent him, and he is there—in a place of refuge."

"And why not you? Didn't God want you to flee?"

Nadya's hand shook on the distaff. *How can I answer you? Why was there no refuge for me?* She drew herself up and flung a hostile look at him. Maddeningly, he only smiled.

"Why do you smile?"

"Because you're angry. It's good to see you show feeling. Usually it's as though you feel nothing at all. Perhaps I'll try to make you angry more often."

Nadya ignored him and went back to twisting the wool in her lap into a strand. But the thread was uneven and crude. *I'll have to start all over*, she thought.

But his question troubled her and rose to the surface in a dream that left her wakeful and staring in the middle of the night. In the dream she was walking through a landscape of unbelievable beauty—green hills looped with flashing streams like necklaces and garlanded with lush flowers in every color. And thrusting out above the hills, the mountains caught all the light of heaven in crystal, silver, white and lavished it on the meadows and fields. Then the sun changed, and the mountains reared and threw down shadow. A black chasm opened at her feet, a chasm with a unique, familiar shape to it, an evil shape that had branded her mind in Uplis-Tsikhe. Voices called to her as the dark blot swelled and grew. "Nadya! Nadya! Do this one thing for me. From heaven I'll thank you!"

But the darkness was swallowing her, and she could not fight it. She surfaced, gasping, and opened her eyes wide, seeking light. But the night was moonless, and the room was unbearably dark. She longed for light, hungered for it—so that she felt that her bones would extrude right though the pores of her skin. She turned over and clawed at the loom, raising herself and lurching toward the door. A feeble red glow came from the hearth, not enough to light the room. A milk can clattered, and she jumped with fright.

Vaktang appeared. "What?" he whispered.

"It's dark," she moaned. He looked at her for a minute. He understood. He quietly lined up all of the railway lanterns and filled each with kerosene and lit them all. One by one, the lanterns contributed a dose of warm, healing color. Vaktang placed them around the room with a serious, businesslike air—but clumsily. After all, he was still half-asleep. Nadya began to relax. She let the amber glow wash over her as she watched Vaktang's earnest, awkward movements. And something welled up within her, something that made her want to laugh and cry at the same time. *He's so clumsy! So eager to please and so obstinate; so precise and so extravagant!*

He glanced at her with a bleary question in his eyes, and she couldn't bear it. She started laughing. He recoiled, ran his hand through his hair, and stared at her in bafflement. Then he swaggered a little, placed the last two lanterns on a shelf just so, and laughed with her. That made her laugh harder. There he was—the clown, the hero, the mighty one of Georgia, his whole soul sparkling with mirth because he loved to see her laugh!

A grumbling complaint came from the other room, and Nadya swallowed her giggles. Esma wafted into the room, her gray hair coiling over her billowing shift. She stared aghast at the flamboyantly lighted room. *Just like a big city on a feast day*, Nadya thought guiltily. But Esma only smiled and shook her head and drifted back into her alcove. Vaktang began putting coals from the fire into the top of the samovar, and soon it was piping merrily. The baby awoke. His mouth opened in astonishment as his bright eyes traveled from light to light. He was too amazed to work up to his usual scream.

"He's so stung with surprise, it's made him shy!" Nadya giggled. Then they both shook with stifled mirth, for Semyon was certainly not shy and would never be shy.

They drank glasses of tea and joked in whispers about the perplexed baby and Esma's confusion and the whole house lit up like a train station.

Then Vaktang leaned forward. "Tell me your dream," he said. And she told him. It was the first time she had opened her secret life to another, and there was a tearing to it, but a mending also. She described the beauty and dread of her dream and the deaths that shaped it.

"I see it always, that black blot. The cave mouth of Uplis-Tsikhe. I feel that it's gobbled up my whole life."

Vaktang was silent. She could see her sadness settling on him. *So it will sop you up, too.* But then a new thought came to her. The black shape had lost some of its power. Instead it seemed that Vaktang had siphoned off a little of her pain and taken it into himself. She remembered the storyteller's words: ". . . add grief to our grief . . ." that the full tale of sorrow might be complete.

She stumbled off to bed, and he moved around the room snuffing the wicks. But he took one light and set it on a shelf near her loom-canopied bed. He had been thinking about what to say, she could tell, and he said it as he positioned the lamp. "A peaceful sleep to you. May your dream flowers bloom without shadows."

LATER SHE LEARNED where all the railway lamps came from. "Come," Vaktang said beckoning, "we'll see a friend who speaks a little Russian." Along with Nodar, they set off to the edge of the village where Shavleg lived with his wife and children. Shavleg was as big, pale, and shaggy as Vaktang was dark, slender, and acute. He wore his sheepskin coat fleece-side-out and pulled a whitish, pointed cap low over his forehead.

His two-storied house was tucked into a copse of firs and had no windows. What little natural light there was came through the cracks between the stones. The lower floor where the animals were kept was as dark as the tomb, but Nadya could barely make out an odd, fuzzy-looking blur along one wall. When her eyes adjusted, she saw that it was a huge pile of the bone-white horns of the Caucasian ibex. The milling sheep had left snagged bits of fleece hanging from the prongs like moss on branches, and the whole edifice seemed to wave in the wind from the door. Peeking out at them from here and there were children, rather dark-skinned but with aureoles of wildly tufted blond hair.

But the upper floor was different. Unlike most of the villagers, Shavleg did not rely on sputtering birch torches. Instead, dozens of railway lanterns filled his home. Two of them were lit even in the middle of the day.

"He's always giving me one as a gift." Vaktang shrugged. "Soon we won't have room for them."

In addition to the shiny lanterns, Shavleg's home was crammed with all kinds of metal junk and odd artifacts of unknown purpose.

"He gets it from the Franks," Vaktang explained. "Many a time he's gone on excursions with foreigners—some from Britain and Germany and France, as well as Russia. No one knows the mountains like Shavleg, and he's in demand as a guide. They reward him with money and with these—these gifts." Nadya gathered that "Franks" referred to any European other than a Russian.

Shavleg pulled off his cap, lobbing it onto another bristling tangle of horns near the door. Nadya bowed to his big, diffuse smile. In spite of his size, he seemed to her like someone in the process of fading away. His big teeth were brown near the gum, gradually becoming a yellow that was darker than his hair. And his hair, too, was yellow at the roots, but the sun had bleached it almost white at the tips. The fleece of his coat blurred around him; his grin disappeared into his rimelike mustache. He called out, and a small, dark woman came into the room. She flashed black eyes at them and with a bird-like, brittle grace handed a small object to her husband.

"A Frankish knife," Shavleg told them in his broken Russian.

"A knife?" Nodar studied the rounded oblong in the Svan's big hand.

"A knife!" exclaimed Shavleg with a child's delight. He began prying at it with thick fingers and painstakingly extracted a short blade. He shot a gleeful glance at his audience and then began solemnly sawing off tufts of his beard.

"What?" Nodar's and Vaktang's astonishment brought two tousled blond heads up the stairs as the children crowded in to see.

"Give it to me," Nodar said. "What kind of a knife is that?"

"A Frankish knife. I got it from an English explorer. He wanted to climb Shikara, Ushba—all the big ones. And this knife—well, he left it behind somehow."

"It's an English knife then," said Vaktang. "Look, there are more tools in here." He pried out a can opener.

Nodar grabbed it and, holding it up, began laughing. "What a knife! Hardly longer than a finger!" He pulled out his long, wicked *kinjal*, comparing the two. "What warriors these Franks must be!"

Vaktang, too, started chuckling. He snatched the knife and with a quick, fierce movement pirouetted into the Georgian dagger dance. The others burst into laughter, and Shavleg rumbled into a dance song. Vaktang twirled and crouched, flourishing the stunted Frankish knife with practiced menace while the others laughed and sang in accompaniment. Shavleg's swift, wiry wife came in and began moving with graceful, complicated steps. Her skirts flared, and the veil beneath her headdress billowed out. The wild, tousled children joined in, spinning like flossy tufts of thistledown. Nadya clapped her hands and laughed. *Strange, strange*, she thought. And she loved the strangeness. Only the familiar was dangerous to her.

NADYA LET THE STRANGERS' WAYS catch her up in a soothing, turbulent wash. She made no attempt to understand. She sat on the balcony and stared at a cloud-streaked sky collecting sunset over the western peaks. The valley was locked in blue and gray and black, but the sky flamed until the ball of the sun doused itself in the austere ranges. The towered hamlets and stony farmsteads and shrouded fields held no reminders for her.

Then Vaktang came out and began telling her in his easy way of the villagers—smiths and herdsmen and hunters. Then with one of his gleaming looks, he asked, "And your father—how did he live?"

"Farming."

"Ah. What crops?"

Nadya shrugged uneasily. She did not want to talk about her father. "Wheat, grapes, zhito . . ."

"Your growing season is longer then. Where is it—your native village?"

She froze. She would never tell him! And she would never go back.

He put a hand beneath her chin and forced her to look at him. "You will never go back?" he echoed as if she'd said it aloud. His voice was deeply serious, but there was a smile at the back of it. He dropped his hand and took up her wrist with its big bones and milk-white skin. He shook it a little. "You are strong, Nadya. Strong and beautiful." Then he kissed her, and she closed her eyes and thought of the river sliding along through field and forest, winking and wincing in the sun.

VIII

Ice Haven

On a day when new snow offered a sure footing, Vaktang decided to hike out onto the Benzingi Glacier along with Nodar and Shavleg. They blackened their faces with soot to protect themselves from snow blindness and set out. Nodar was slim in his dark, fitted coat while Shavleg loomed shaggy and diffuse in sheepskin. His blond beard and blue eyes contrasted curiously with his blackened face. They set out carrying food and, of course, weapons.

Nadya came up the path with them as far as the white-shrouded barley field. Vaktang looked back at her. She was wearing a pale smock and Esma's soft, gray shawl. In the bright slant of morning light, she looked faded against the ponded snow behind her, but her shadow sprang to the west crisp and dark—the most distinct thing about her. Her slow wave made him think of a wing dipping into the colorless wash. *Swan-girl, swan-maiden*, he thought.

They had walked as far as the turnoff to the village of Jibiani when they caught sight of a man in a brown *tcherkeska* toiling across fresh snow, churning a blue wake behind him. He hailed them in Georgian. His breath's moisture settled in icy needles on his mustache, but his tawny eyes were warm and curious as he approached them.

"I'm going to Jibiani," he announced in a strong voice. His accent was different, Vaktang noted, the accent of a Pshav or a Khevsur, he thought.

"I am looking for a man called Noe Tcheidze," the stranger continued. "I hope to find him in Jibiani, but others say he may be in Ushguli."

"We come from Ushguli," Vaktang said, "and there are no travelers in our village." Fear roughened his voice so that the stranger's face stiffened, and the scar on his cheek whitened. *Someday someone will come looking for her like this.* Vaktang pushed the thought away. Eager to amend for his rudeness, he offered, "You may find him at Jibiani. These villages are in a cluster of three, and sometimes people say one and mean another. We can take you there."

"I see you have other business." The stranger hesitated. "Tell me the way, and I'll find it."

"We—we're going that way. We'll escort you. Besides, I know the elders and can help you find out whom to ask. Folk are cautious these days and slow to talk to outsiders."

The stranger thanked them courteously, and they made their way to the hamlet of Jibiani. As they tramped through the soft snow, they learned that the stranger was named Grigol, a man from Khevsuretia. He told them that he was staying in Gebi with his wife and son after a summer's sojourn in Tiflis.

"Tiflis!" Nodar exclaimed. "We heard that great things were happening in the city! Even the tsar's concessions of last autumn couldn't douse the flame!"

"Great things?" Grigol's voice was heavy. "Is that what they call them? I myself have stood in pools of Georgian blood. My boots were soaked with it, but that blood is on the head of the tsar and the Bolsheviks. Both alike are stained with it."

"But the Bolsheviks are for the common folk!" Nodar argued. "It's the Cossacks who murder the people."

"Once I thought like that, too. But not now. I've seen too much. Ah—we'd like to grasp the guilt with tongs and hold it to the anvil, but it's too slippery for that."

"But there is right, and there is wrong, and there are workers of each," Nodar challenged.

The newcomer kept his silence, and Vaktang was glad for it. But at the same time, he saw that this man knew things that his boyish brother had no concept of. The ardent, young-man's phrases that could have come from Vaktang's own lips a few months ago now rang hollow.

Vaktang turned the conversation to the mountains and found an eager listener. Grigol wanted to know all about the three villages and the surrounding areas. But the impression of Grigol's knowledge stayed in the back of Vaktang's mind, and he held it in reserve. *Someday I'll talk to this man,* he told himself. *Long and deeply.*

As they talked, it came out that Grigol was especially interested in a pass over the northern ranges into the steppe near Vladikavkaz.

"There is a pass," Vaktang assured him. "Beyond the valley of the Sadon. But it is not an easy way in winter. Not many know of it, but Shavleg has gone that way." The blond giant assented with a show of his brownish-yellow teeth.

"My hope is to find work in Vladikavkaz for the winter," Grigol explained.

"Why do that?" Vaktang exclaimed. "Between Gebi and the three villages there's more than enough work for an extra smith. Stay on and travel from village to village. You'll find enough and more to keep you."

When they came to Jibiani, there was a flurry of movement and then an unnatural hush. A foam of snow spumed on all the black rocks, but the stolid stone towers presented an impervious front. A village elder came out and questioned them warily. His beard above the heavy chain that bore his medal of office was as stiff and regal as an Assyrian king's. He scrutinized them carefully before assuring them that there was no Noe Tcheidze in the village. A sharp-visaged woman peeked down at them from a high window; a rag-padded child sidled behind a balcony post.

Then a dark man with a slim elegance to his movements emerged from a shadowed doorway. He was dressed like a Svan except that instead of the usual leather sandals stuffed with dried grass, he wore fine leather boots. His handsome aquiline features were fringed with a short, dark beard furrowed by a pale scar. There was no shrinking in his step as he approached them. Ignoring the three Svans, he turned a direct look on Grigol.

"So," he said in an emotionless voice, "is she dead?"

"No," Grigol replied. "Are you sorry?"

The man shrugged and smiled grimly while his scar-strung beard pulled strangely—as though it had a life of its own.

"Let it go," Grigol said softly.

Vaktang could see that there was both compassion and a yellow glint of vigilance in his eye.

"She's here. In Gebi. Come and talk it over, Noe. We've all been crushed in something too big for us. It's time to heal."

Noe smiled again, cynically, and his beard slid oddly. "Healing? Ah. The poorly set bone will always be crooked."

HE IS TOO COMPOSED, Grigol thought as they trudged back toward Gebi. By the time they reached the village, Shikara was gathering rose light from the sun's setting while Ushba moodily drew in storm clouds. Amber rectangles of lighted windows floated in the evening wood smoke, and the aroma of roasting meat met them as they strode down to the homestead. Grigol stole a look at his companion. Light in sheets of blue and flicks of yellow played across his handsome features. Yearning and bitterness—which would win?

Then his own yearning won out, and his thoughts turned to his wife. What bliss to come in out of a cold night to her warm arms—not to mention the fine meal she'd probably have ready. Grigol opened the door so that Noe could pass into the room. Nina was at the far end by the stove, Sirakan and Loma perched on the wooden sleeping platform, and Irina was setting out bread and cheese on the table. They all turned at the rush of cold air, and Irina drew her breath in on a sharp hiss. Noe only looked at her, then smiled, his beard shifting askew.

Irina supported herself with two hands grasping the table. Then she unsheathed the dagger at her belt and, holding it across her two palms, held it out to her lover, never taking her eyes from his as she slowly drew near. Noe watched her, his lips twitching. That stare strung out between them until both their eyes were drawn down to the shining *kinjal*.

"Your gift," Irina said in a hoarse whisper. "You see, I give it back to you."

Noe drew his head back as though the silver blade were a snake. But Irina continued insistently. "Tell me, would you rather have had it buried in my flesh? Is that what you wanted?" The two wells of dark torment that were her eyes traveled upward again. "The truth, Noe. Is that what you wanted?"

"Yes. That's what I wanted."

An oppressive silence filled the room, and Grigol sought his wife's eyes, but she was staring at her half brother in horror. A brass ladle clattered from her fingers, and she started forward, but Noe spoke again.

"So. It seems we've all had a surprise. You weren't expecting to see me alive, and I didn't expect to see you." He put out a hand and touched Irina's face caressingly. But his eyes were hard. "We have so much in common."

Irina flushed, then blanched, the bridge of her nose a livid band. Grigol expected her to lash out—he'd seen her that way before—but she merely looked away toward the blue-lit window. She seemed to draw in a white stillness like the stillness of the snow.

"We'd heard you were alive, and I was glad for it. Because I wronged you, and I carry a soul's weight of guilt from that wrong." Still holding her dagger like an offering and with her eyes steadfastly on his face, Irina sank to her knees. "I beg your forgiveness. From my heart, I beg it."

Noe smiled. Grigol felt himself recoiling from the bitter irony of that smile, but Irina did not recoil.

"Well, my love, it's convenient for you that I'm around to see this performance." He flung out a hand. "And these others!" He flashed a brittle smile at Nina and Sirakan, dismissing the girl at his feet.

Sirakan shouldered past them with a gruff, "I can't stand this!" But Nina extended her hands and welcomed Noe. It was fitting that a man returned from grave danger be succored by his family.

"Welcome, brother. Thank God you are with us! Come, and we'll eat and forget past trouble."

Nina had prepared a lamb stew flavored with scallions and tarragon. Noe, Grigol, and Loma ate hungrily, but Sirakan did not return. Irina waited on them with a pale, averted face. As soon as the meal was over, she wrapped herself up in a heavy shawl and slipped outside.

IRINA SCANNED the snow-enameled street as it spread into luminous blue fields. The night was dark, cloud-smothered. But occasionally a break would open and send down a spear of light toward the silvered massifs of Svanetia. It looked as though the mountain had shot forth light to pierce the cloud rather than the other way around. Then crusted snow scrunched behind her, and she spun to face him.

He was smiling still. How she dreaded and mistrusted that smile! *Don't smile, Noe. Don't you know what we will create or destroy in the next few minutes?* But she held her ground. A cool inner calm steadied her. Both the coolness and the calm were so foreign to her that she experienced it as a sort of deadness.

"Well, Irina. I had forgotten how beautiful you are." He was as cold as she was. His smile held—the smile that moved his lush black beard but did not touch his eyes. Then he lifted a hand to his chin. His touch on the horrible scar sent a jolt of anguish across his features.

"Wake up, Irina! I don't need your ice-maiden pleas for forgiveness. Do you know what I've been through?"

"What else can I ask? Your hatred for me was clear enough. You yourself have said you wanted me dead. And dead by my own hand."

"That's it! That is what I wanted. And like you, I would have taken it back. But it was too late." His hand whipped out and grabbed her arm. "Do you know what it was like? They had me tied to the tail of a horse, blood spurting from my face so that the horse's rump was red with it. I'd loosed my hands enough to pull away, but I waited until we came to a ledge where I knew the fall wouldn't kill me. I threw myself into the darkness—then lay there with crushed ribs and a broken arm until morning.

"And during that night, I followed you in my thoughts. *Now. Now*, I thought, *she'll be stopping; she'll pull out that kinjal. Will she use it now or later?* I saw the stars spin back into a tunnel of cloud, and I wondered. The jackals began baying in the ravine, and I knew in the morning I'd face the vultures. *Is she dead*, I wondered, *and where does her body lie?*

"The jackals edged in. I saw a humped shadow, and I wondered if we two would make a feast for the same scavengers. Then a pelting rain came and washed away my thought."

"I remember the rain," Irina said. The old herdsman with his pipe came fluting into her mind.

"I didn't want to die with that wish for you. Yet, as it was, I couldn't help hating you."

"And God didn't let you die." She thought of the shepherd's groping fingers coaxing the wood of the forest to fashion an ascent of music. *A rich intent infuses all things.*

Noe stared at her. "Not in that way," he said. "But enough of it. All that is past. All we can do now is salvage what's left of our love. We're scavengers, too, on the earth! Something, after all, is left." A fierce glitter passed over his eyes, but it touched the surface only. Irina could not fathom what waited behind. His hand moved up to her shoulder, her neck. "We'll stay here for a week or two. Then at midwinter I'll go to Mestia, and you'll come with me."

Irina's cool poise disintegrated. "Go with you? What do you mean? Too much lies between us!"

Noe shrugged. "We've seared each other with the same iron. We are quits. Much is lost." His voice slid into soft insinuation. "But much remains. What is, is all that is."

Irina stared at him aghast. Truly, something in him was dead that he would so glibly accept this blemished compromise.

"It's not enough!" she cried. Her hand flew in front of her face to block out the snowfield and the mountains, but other mountains rose before her. She could see them so clearly! Silver shining from tier after tier springing straight from the ashen moraine and blue-tinged glaciers. The face of the mountain spilled forth its radiance in jeweled rays. In her spirit there was a leaping ascent and a falling away. Great heights invited her cool soul's footprints. An abyss fed on old tottering images—the god of revenge and the black box, the demanding idol of false love, the petty despots of revolt.

"It's not enough!" she exclaimed, and her fingers furled as though to catch a fleeting impression.

"And where will you get more?"

"Somewhere, somewhere!" She wrenched herself away and strode back toward the village, her skirts dragging on the ice-needled path. Chimneys trailed ribbons of smoke, threading the cinder-gray clouds. Here and there narrow windows shone like topaz against the grimed stone walls. The doorway spilled honeyed light over the snow, and a man's barrel-chested form appeared. He began calling her by name. She stopped, recognizing Sirakan. She stood fused to the track like iron on ice. Her eyes widened until she felt that they would glaze over with the cold. Her ears strained in an exquisite attentiveness. *Where are your accusers? Gone, Lord.*

A swirl of images caught her up—the face of the mountain, beauty from the far north, the city of refuge. The oblique clicked to clarity on a precise corner in her mind. *He has a face! And a voice. He is not the featureless avenger or the inscrutable despot of history—but a God with a face. A God who can feel pain.* Stung by such an astonishing idea, she cast about for everything she could remember about the Christian deity: the God-man who subtled His power to come among men in blood and a woman's anguish; the Crucified whose racked arms flung open the floodgates of joy; the flesh-sheathed Word whose speaking was heard on the ramparts of nature. *And in me.*

"Irina!" The voice had a heavy, golden quality to it.

He will give you beauty for ashes.

"Irina!"

I don't know anything. But I have hope! She held onto it with both hands.

NOE SPOKE OF MESTIA, and Grigol speculated about work in Ushguli, but no one went anywhere for many days. A blizzard hurtled down through the passes, lashing the stone houses, howling through the towers' ramparts, and shaking the windows like a thwarted demon. Their life contracted into a ring around the hearth. But while Nina, Loma, and Grigol nudged each other in a comfortable little circle, Noe paced nervously, and Sirakan was morose and withdrawn. Irina herself felt like a chick in an egg, and she attacked her white capsule with beak and claw. She felt that she was alive in ways she had never been before, and their imprisonment galled her.

But when she stood on the balcony to look out, her restlessness fled. Beyond the stone towers of Gebi, the great snow peaks were encased in an icy sheath full of subtle lines and delicate flutings. Enormous firths of ice spread from their flanks, and snowfield upon snowfield opened in their secret hollows. Corniced crests threw blue bands of shadow on the pure snow. An exquisite, living silence lulled and comforted her.

"What are you thinking about?" she asked Sirakan one day.

"My future," he replied. "Our shop is charred rubble, our home gone. What now? I'm not even sure whether my parents live."

"Can you go back and rebuild?"

"It wouldn't be easy, but it's not impossible. Somehow my heart's not in it. I'm weary to death of the old hatreds. I want something new." He looked at her as he said this.

"Go to America," she said.

His lips twisted in an ironic smile. "Yes. And exchange the old hatreds for new ones." He was silent for a moment. "But at least they do not kill Armenians. Yes," he sighed. "That would be something new. How about you?"

"I also want something new." She lowered her voice. "Maybe I'm new already."

Sirakan searched her face with his deep, probing eyes. She did not turn away.

"I have thought little about God—about things of the spirit," she continued. "My flesh was trouble enough, wasn't it? I was raised to honor the words of the Prophet, and his words were vinegar in my mouth and violence in my breast. The friends that Noe and I knew were idealistic young rebels and bitter revolutionaries. Most of them had been raised as Christians, but they pushed away the old ways as though they were sweeping aside heavy drapes to let in the light. They let in only darkness."

"That's true," Sirakan agreed. "I've seen many make that trade and be left empty."

"Worse than empty—filled up with anger and sour futility! But still they railed against anything religious or made coarse jokes. Narrow bigotry, they called it. A drug for trance-trussed fools. And this was all I had ever heard about Christianity—this and my father's horror at their blasphemous woman-born god. Then that night with you I stood on a threshold . . ."

"And recognized that the narrow way frames a universe of stars," Sirakan finished for her.

"Yes! And the other way begins as a wide, flowing stream—easy to dip into but hard to pull away from—and it sucks you into a funnel that ends in darkness where every color is black."

Sirakan's face was eager, fascinated. "And so do you know this way?"

Irina shook her head. "I don't. I only know that it's there—and that it has to do with the God-man, Jesus." Her manner grew shy. It was hard for her to even say the word. *Jesus! An abomination to the Muslims and a joke to the revolutionaries. Jesus—the One who stood in the path and turned away my accusers.* She wanted to talk about Him. She felt that any question would be an intrusion, yet she longed for just this intrusion.

"I find that, in spite of myself, I want it. I want beauty for ashes . . ." Her voice sounded stripped and chastened in her own ears, like the voice of a little girl.

When she looked up at Sirakan, his face was beautiful—like a father or a lover or a teacher. "I can show you how to make that trade," he said. "The ashes—that's your will and all that it has brought to you. The beauty is what His will can create in you. And faith—well, that's the coinage!"

They talked long into the night while the storm thrashed outside the window slits. Irina opened her fingers and let the ashes sift away. As the Muslims of the mountains vow allegiance of war to an Imam, so she vowed her allegiance of peace to Christ. She affirmed what a thousand voices told her—that He had the power to change her and the love to want to. The storm flung itself around the house, but deep within her a soft nurturing well opened up, and from it sprang the first shoots of something new and tender. That anything so lovely should grow within her astonished her, and her mind closed around it in cherishing wonder. Irina felt that she was utterly changed and yet more intensely herself than she ever had been.

Peace, she marveled, *my name is peace.*

AT LAST THE WIND exhausted itself in the rough ridges, and quiet came to the sky. Grigol set off for Ushguli. He passed through wintry, branch-etched orchards and crossed over the rugged slate hills, their churlishness restrained by a delicate netting of white. In the village the homesteads and towers were sinking in a slanted sea of drifts. The air was so still that the smoke sprang straight up from the chimneys. A gap-toothed farmer in a stiff sheepskin led him to Vaktang's house.

The young Svan welcomed him with a stiff reserve that quickly melted to his usual friendliness. *What is he afraid of?* Grigol wondered. Inside Esma was feeding gruel to a rosy-cheeked baby. The child couldn't have been more than a year old although the woman was past the time for children. Perhaps the boy was Vaktang's? But the baby's wide-set, dark eyes were nothing like Vaktang's. They reminded him of something.

Family by family, Vaktang described what work might be needed, Nodar chiming in with suggestions here and there. Esma put the baby on the floor and began setting out tea and bread. The boy started crawling with fierce resolve over the hard floor, slapping his plump hands down adamantly. Occasionally, he sat up and scrutinized them all with a stern look: *Who are you and why are you here?* Grigol gave him a disarming smile, and Vaktang laughed, but the little one only scowled in perplexity. He scooted over to a pile of shorn fleece near a loom, occasionally turning to give them a look over his rag-girded backside to see if they were still watching. Then he began grabbing at tufts of wool and picking them apart with a fierce, worried expression as though he were looking for something.

"A serious boy," Grigol joked. "He's chary with his smiles."

"Not always," Vaktang said.

"He reminds me of someone—the way his brows peak up over his eyes," Grigol commented. Then he noticed that his companion grew slightly aloof. *Women's talk, I suppose.* But Grigol couldn't shake the impression that this baby looked like someone he knew and that Vaktang did not want to talk about it.

In spite of his discomfort, Vaktang did not forget the code of the mountain tribes. Grigol was welcome, he said, to lodge with them as long as he was working in the village. Esma and another obscure relative would go and stay with Vaktang's sister so that there would be plenty of room.

Just then a young woman came quietly into the room, and the baby's whole face lit up with a gaping, gummy but beatific smile. Grigol felt his mouth pull in a sympathetic grin. *The mother, no doubt.* Then he turned to the newcomer. What he saw surprised him. This woman was no Georgian. Russian blood had shaped every feature from the broad ledge of the high cheekbones to the magnificent shoulders and sloping line from chest to hip. Her hair was fair—a color neither brown nor blonde—and her soft, wide-set eyes had the sheen of a fawn's coat. She was wearing a pink smock over a cream-colored peasant blouse, and her milky, very white skin took on an apricot flush. Her face was wide, with a rather heavy jaw, but her nose was delicate, and her lips parted in childlike tenderness. Where had she come from—and who did she remind him of? As soon as she caught sight of him, her eyes went blank, and she retreated with a limping gait.

While Grigol stayed in Ushguli, meals were prepared either by Esma or by her daughter Katai. Sometimes Katai brought her little daughter, but Grigol saw no more of the strange Russian girl or the determined baby boy.

One day about a week after he had started up the cold forge near Shavleg's house, Grigol asked about her. Again he sensed Vaktang's inward recoiling. But this made him more persistent. Her odd resemblance to someone he had seen somewhere niggled him as he sweated over bent plows and sprung harrows.

But Vaktang was as elusive as ever. "A girl from another village," he answered vaguely. Then he added in a rush, "She's to be my wife." And the hot, red blood surged behind his fair skin.

Winter began to sigh and weaken. The snow shrank up over the stones, revealing signs and portents in the rock shapes. Slush dripped from pine boughs, and the boughs sighed as they released their burden. Every day brought new changes, and Vaktang was filled with pulsing, crushing, restless gladness long before the first green blade stabbed defiance at the hanging glaciers and snowfields. The snow took on a look of illusion. After cold nights a translucent silver meshing like spider web appeared.

And Nadya was changing, too. She began humming tunes in dreary, repetitive snatches. At first this heartened Vaktang. *She's cheering up, coming out of herself.* But then the songs became longer, and words drifted up from the slow-pulsed melody. Russian words. Vaktang began to fear these words because they seemed to take her away from him where he could not follow. He thought of Grigol and his curious sidelong glances at Nadya and baby Semyon. *Impossible that a Khevsur brave would know them!* But it worried him all the same.

Vaktang also noted that her attitude toward him had subtly shifted. Since the time of her dark dream and the lighting of the lanterns, she seemed to accept him in a new way. Of course, she had accepted him before—just as she'd accept a crow flying by or a sheep tearing the grass. In fact, she accepted everything with a porous absorption that maddened him. But now her acceptance contained a glint of the notion that he was a human being—that he could feel. He would hear her sing. *Sing, Nadya, wake up and sing!* Then jealousy seized him, for these were songs of the Russian lands, Molokan songs. And they transported her far from him.

Esma sensed it, too. Daily Vaktang saw that his mother grew more and more attached to the baby boy. Although less than a year old, he was a bold, adventurous baby. He'd pull himself up holding onto table or loom, then lunge across the room in a careening walk. Esma was enthralled. He was also beginning to say his first few words, and they were all Georgian. Vaktang knew that his mother smiled on the idea of Nadya staying, not only because she liked the tall Russian girl, but also because she could not bear giving up Semyon Gavrilovich. And so they eyed each other warily and exchanged worried glances when Nadya began singing with that faraway look.

Vaktang would walk out on paths of tarnished ice and stand on the spur of the mountain. Warm, scented air rose up from lands where spring was already in full sway. Then even in Ushguli winter collapsed in a black-rimmed shambles, and rain came up from the Black Sea. The tilted barley fields turned to vivid green. Vaktang was filled with longing. And the fragrant west wind told him that the time for decision was near.

One evening they were sitting side by side in the hearth glow. Nodar was polishing his gun by the door while Esma stitched at the table. The firelight sprang back from the metal barrel in Nodar's hand, and Esma's needle dipped with the flash of a dragonfly. Nadya got up to check on Semyon sleeping in his wicker basket. When she came back, she sat a little closer to Vaktang. He was absurdly pleased—like a man who has coaxed a shy bird into his hand.

"He's wheezing a little," she remarked, "but he sleeps as fiercely as he does everything else."

"A lion of a baby," Nodar joked from the door. Esma chuckled.

But Nadya was thoughtful. "His eyes are the eyes of my mother—and of my brother Piotr. When I look into them, I feel that there is something I need to do for him, that he belongs with them somehow."

"He has a good home," Vaktang said. He shifted uneasily.

Esma threw them a look as sharp as her needle. Then her stern face softened, and she came and stood before them. She smiled. Then with a lithe dip of her body, her hand darted out, and the shining needle quickly basted a crude seam joining Nadya's skirt with Vaktang's long tunic—just at the thigh. Nodar laughed, and the girl scanned Vaktang's features with a bemused smile. Esma broke the thread with a sharp tug.

"She doesn't understand," she told Vaktang in Svanetian.

"She will," he answered in the same tongue.

Nodar straightened and wiped his greasy hands on his trousers. "If that's to be it, we must celebrate!" He grabbed his brother, and Vaktang stood, pulling the confused but attached Nadya with him. Vaktang strode around the room laughing, and Nadya followed him perforce. She began to giggle. Her eyes were gentle in the firelight.

He answered the question in them. "Don't you know? It's a marriage custom! My mother's saying she wants us betrothed."

Nadya seemed to understand, he thought, and to accept. Occasionally she idly picked at the binding threads, but they held, and he took it for a sign. At the end of the evening, Esma cut them apart with her scissors. Nadya yawned and curled up in her sheepskin as though nothing had happened.

"COME," VAKTANG TOLD NADYA early one morning shortly after this. "I'll show you where spring is."

He packed *basturma* and bread and cheese, and they set out for the south and west. "A valley so beautiful you'll—you'll . . ." What would she do? Share his joy? Open up to him in some new way? Stay forever? All of them! "You'll see," he finished lamely.

They crossed a forested ridge, the dark, silent pine trees still wad-ing in snow. But lower down, the spring melt snaked between stones, slid beneath leaves, sought out its kind until every gully and ravine sparkled with it. The air around them whispered with the barely perceptible stirring of these hungry, seeking tendrils of water.

The higher ridges gave way to slate hills covered with broadleafed glades. Beeches and maples were already in full leaf. Then the trees declined, and a gentle promontory invited them to look out over a sunny, open meadow lavished with an extravagant growth of giant flowers. Vaktang knew what he'd find, and he did not look at the rare scene spreading before them, but at Nadya. Her face told him that all his pains were worth it. She was stunned, radiant! He drank in her expression, then turned his eyes to the radiance that created it.

"The garden," she murmured, awed.

Vaktang laughed eagerly. "Some say that! Eden in full bloom. Shavleg brought some Frankish botanists here once. How they scurried for words, trying to figure it out. *Macroflora*, they called it. As if a word could take away the wonder!"

Following a moss-cradled brook, they plunged into a forest of white-umbreled flowers higher than a man's head. Golden lilies nodded shoulder-high as they passed, and blue campanula tossed in a silent ringing of their bell-shaped blossoms. Azure columbine trembled at their passing. The hollowed stems of pink and red ranunculus broke at their feet. Mounds of a lilac gentian stippled with black bowed with stiff, pointed leaves. Every blossom, every petal splashed pristine white or zealous color in massed profusion. Drawn up by the brilliant upland sun and warmed in a mold formed by the decay of immemorial woods never touched by the woodman's axe, the giant flower meadows of the Caucasus opened to the spring. Their heady, complex perfume grew stronger as the day warmed. Larks launched themselves at the sun, dripping gold song with the gold warmth. Sated bees droned at easy tasks.

Vaktang and Nadya found a knoll of rock, an atoll in the high seas of bloom, and shared their meal. A drowse of sleepy sounds rose up. From across the western ranges, curling fronds of cloud unfurled—white, translucent, carrying no threat. Vaktang stretched out, his weapons clanking against the rock. Nadya sat facing him, her broad brow peaceful and smooth. He was utterly content. She began humming. Russian words drifted up:

> "'Whither do you fly, little cloud, on the wings of the wind
> Over the earth—or do you carry a sign of love
> To water the land of Paradise?
> Oh, speak the real truth.
> Whither do you go so fast—or do you strive
> To water the cool valleys?
> To speak truth, I water the narcissus
> And the lily and to give them drink for life.
> I have the dew of nature.
> You have the dew from heaven. . . . '"

Vaktang sprang to wakefulness. She was singing about love! Fascinated, he watched her delicately cut mouth round out the Russian word, *liubvi*. But her eyes were fastened on the curling spume of cloud, and she did not look at him. Still his limbs surged with exuberance. He sprang down from his rock, unsheathed his sword, and with a swooping dance began scything at the tall flowers. Now she was looking at him! With knees bent in the Georgian dagger dance, he laid about with his sword, and the toppled blooms fell in a circle around him.

"What are you doing?" Her face flushed with emotion.

His feeling poured out of him in laughter. "It's for you! A bridal bouquet!"

"What! Why are you doing this?"

He looked at her nonplussed. He stretched out his hand toward her. "Love!" he said, as though the word glittered between his fingers.

He began gathering his extravagant harvest in huge, ruffled arm loads and dumped it onto her spread-out skirt. There! She was beauty surrounded by beauty. No one in the universe had ever seen what he was seeing now. And there was more in store for him. Someday.

Nadya sat as still as a statue. He leaned over and kissed her forehead, scattered her fair hair over her shoulders, then kissed her more fervently, crushing her and her flowers to himself. The lilies held their waxy shapes, but the ranunculus shed rosy petals all over the rock.

He looked into her eyes—like a tawny river calmed so that the glinting bottom and all the gliding life within were visible. Something deep within her had changed shape. She edged away. When she stood, her pink smock was stained with wet red splotches where the stalks had bled their rich sap into the fabric.

Vaktang took her hand, and they went back through the forest and the highlands into the valley of Ushguli. As they came down-hill, he saw Nodar hastening toward them.

"Wait!" Nodar pulled his brother aside with an urgent hand. His heavy band of a brow pressed concern into all his features. "We have visitors. Grigol has come back with his wife. She thinks she may know the girl. I told them that she is no longer in the house. That was true, right? But they are asking questions."

Vaktang's stomach dropped sickeningly. He froze to the track. So. He knew it would come! He looked at Nadya, who was staring down at the black and white towers as though she'd never seen them before. The divided river flashed its "Y" at the hard, bright sky. They could skirt the village, go on to Jibiani. No need to torture her with questions from strangers. What if they weren't strangers? Vaktang groaned, and the girl gazed at him curiously. He had seen something new in her eyes today—a genesis amid the flowers of rev-elation. All he wanted was to see that new, tender thing grow until it was a mate for what was in his own heart. *But she has never chosen you! Chance threw her at you. Give her a choice.* A desolate fear seized him. If he let her decide, what then? A great love if she chose him. A great void if she did not. His fear grew until he felt crushed and cornered. He lashed out with a quick jab of what was most typical of his character—largess.

"Nadya!" he called loudly though she was only a few feet away.

For her the agonizing choice evaporated. "A man of the Khevsurs?" she asked flatly. "I've never heard of him. No. I did not rec-ognize him that time he came for work. How could I know his wife?"

"She lived in a village with some Russians who were driven out," Vaktang offered.

Nadya shrugged. "A rare chance. Many Russians have been dri-ven out. But if they really are from our village, I can go with them."

"No!" He did not touch her, but the air around them filled with touchings. She lifted her head as though they brushed her face.

"Nadya! You must understand! I don't want you to leave. I want you to be my wife!"

She smiled in a motherly sort of way. Then she edged past him and trudged down the path.

Grigol was on the balcony. His hands spanned a hearty welcome. He didn't know that his hand's span measured Vaktang's grief!

But she may stay.

Inside, a comely woman with dark, curly hair sat near the stove. As they came in, she turned, and her shawl parted to reveal her face, icon-oval and icon-pure. Her black-rimmed, tilted eyes widened as Nadya came into the room. "Nadya Gavrilovna!" she whispered. Nadya glided toward her. The meeting was dreamlike; the women were so slow and awed in their movements, the room throbbed with significance and danger. Vaktang felt he must move, throw himself between them, stop it, but just as in a dream, his limbs were paralyzed.

Then Nadya did something he had never seen her do before. Her shoulders convulsed, and she began sobbing. Nina reached for her, drew her into a comforting embrace. Then she, too, began weeping, and the stone walls did not hold their laments but gave them back in echoed wailings. Vaktang's mouth clamped down on bitterness. Her tears had never wetted his shoulder though his arms cried out to share her burden. He couldn't bear watching them. Nodar was ducking around the doorpost, and Vaktang lurched past him. Grigol stood on the balcony near the door. Vaktang paced to the other end, looking south and west where the glade of giant flowers lay sheltered unseen behind its ridges. Grigol came and stood beside him.

"There had been news from the villages in the south," the Khevsur offered. "Order has been restored, and some of the refugees have returned. It seems that this girl's uncle is one. So she has family and a home. They will be glad to have her alive and well."

Vaktang did not respond.

"You cannot take what hasn't been given. . . ."

Vaktang turned away.

"If she wants to be your wife, she will stay and send word back to her family," Grigol suggested.

Vaktang groaned from the depths of his being. "You don't understand! She cannot want anything! She was just beginning to get to the point where she could, a little. She's like a leaf on a current. Now yours is the stronger pull. Yours and her mother's."

"Her mother is dead."

"Yes, but Nadya's had it in her mind that her mother wants her to take the babe back to her own people. As for herself, I don't think she cares one way or the other."

"And yet you have done a noble thing—to succor her and restore her to her own folk."

"Yes. And she'll smash my soul on her way out and not even notice what she's stepping on!" He shouldered past the other man with abrupt vehemence and spent the night tramping on the mountains.

In the early morning he saw them—a cluster of two women and a man and a bundled babe on the trail toward Gebi. A scream pierced the dawn-peace. He saw his mother behind them on the path and Nodar struggling with her. Her cries broke on the rocks and shattered into the undulating death cry of the Svan women. Baby Semyon echoed her wailing, and the glen filled with keening, like needles in Vaktang's temples.

Nina turned and called out something, raising her hand to her face, but he could not hear what. Nadya kept on, her head down and her shawl pulled over her face as though to shield her from rain. Neither of them saw him on his slate perch above the trail. But Grigol scanned the mountainside intently. Vaktang knew that he was looking for him, but he did not call out. Then the Khevsur spotted him and lifted his arm in an odd wave that tilted his hand toward the sky. But Vaktang's limbs were too heavy to return the comradely gesture. He kept his eyes trained on the tall girl with her gray shawl and dour gait. Long after the group had merged into a single lump, he could pick her out.

They disappeared around a bend, and he lunged toward an eastern outcropping. He clawed at the screening branches and was rewarded by a last glimpse of the three walkers. He stared hard at the girl, willing her to turn around and look at him. But she did not turn, and she did not see.

IX

Wrestlers with the Earth

A s 1907 drew on, the Americans began talking of reces-
sion. What was receding, Piotr learned, was the dream of
quick prosperity. Even Los Angeles, which had grown
steadily since the boom-town days of the 1880s, was beginning to
feel the pinch of shrinking opportunities. *And we're at the bottom
of the heap*, Piotr worried as the word *layoffs* began to be whispered
around the San Pedro yards.

"Walkouts, layoffs," Ilya Valoff joked, "we don't know if we're sitting or standing."

"Lying or standing," Piotr corrected him with the grin that Ilya
always managed to pull out of him.

"Don't worry. These Americans are a clever lot. They'll dream
up some new scheme that'll give us our fair share of blisters and
paychecks."

"They already have. The aqueduct."

Ilya grabbed a fluffy handful of beard and squeezed it thoughtfully. "Yes. That's an amazing thing."

William Mulholland's plan to bring water hundreds of miles
across deserts and mountains to the parched city both appalled
and thrilled them. That these cocky engineers and developers
would set their shoulders against all the inert, unhewn might of
rock and hill and carve out their own will in the wilderness
smacked of presumptuous sin. But it wrung from them a half-
mocking, half-awed admiration. And the fact that this arrogant

manipulation of nature would open new lands to the plow stung them with their old longing for land. Piotr's mind worked as his fingers absently searched with a gleaner's intentness among the silky new growth of his beard.

Later that week this conversation came back to him as he stood with the silent, shuffling crowd of men who picked up their last paychecks and "notice." Their rough hands strayed to pockets and cap peaks with curbed quietude—strong, powerful things being settled to a futile rest. Makar stood beside him, his blue eyes screwed up against the glare as they searched the quays and docks. Their glances crossed, and they shrugged. *He's wondering how to tell Hanya.*

The ginger-haired clerk handed them each an envelope. "You're good workers," he said apologetically. "If things pick up, I'm sure they'll want you back."

Makar smiled awkwardly. They went and waited for the streetcar, fingering the change in their pockets. Past the alleyway, the scalloped water of the harbor jittered with white flashes.

"What now?" Makar breathed. "No work. And nothing in sight."

Piotr studied the sliver of winking water between the warehouses. "I'm thinking something I don't want to think."

"What?"

"Mulholland's aqueduct."

"No. We can't leave our wives. You know that."

"That's why I don't want to think it. But—"

"No, Piotr! We'll find another way."

"I hope so. But I'm thinking of all these men thronging the desert while we sit idle."

"Well, we haven't been idle for long. Let's look around."

"Right. We'll look."

Fenya received his news quietly. "I'll see if I can get more hours at the Wentworths'," she offered. But something within her seemed quashed, oddly reticent. More than ever, he hoped that he could find work in the city. After dinner he found her outside letting the evening breeze cool her face.

"Well," he joked, "at least we'll have sunflower seeds to eat. Look, they're sprouting up everywhere!"

She smiled—a quashed, reticent smile. Something about the sunflowers hurt her.

"Makar and I will go out tomorrow and see what we can find. Don't worry, little bird. Something will turn up."

"I don't want to be uprooted. We've been happy here."

His heart full, he set his arms around her. "Dushok, my berry, we have been happy. But I have in mind for you a deeper rooting. We'll find a place for it. And it won't be beside a railway track."

"I like the trains," she insisted stubbornly. "I've gotten used to them."

He laughed delightedly. "So. That's how it is. Will you be able to love your husband with a plowed field outside the window? Or a stream flowing beyond the door?"

"Well," she said reluctantly, a quirk of unwilling humor nudging the corner of her mouth, "I suppose I could manage it." Then her small, rough hand shot out and grabbed his arm—hard. "If you're there."

"MORE WORK? Of course there's more work!" Evangeline brushed aside Fenya's question. "I'll tell Miz Wentworth. She can make enough work to keep everybody busy. I'm countin' on her. Your man lost his job?"

"Yes. Layoffs in San Pedro."

Evangeline cocked her head. She had a way of turning her face so that the starry depths of her eyes, rimmed by two white quarter moons, drew in more of Fenya than she was willing to give. It was an odd night-sky sort of look—both velvety and piercing. Fenya tried to deflect her bright, sharp intuition with a noncommittal glance. The woman's inspired "huh!" told her that she was unsuccessful. Evangeline's "huh!" always expressed some deep sword stroke of inner knowledge, and Fenya squirmed under her knowing gaze.

"So-o-o-o," she said calmly, "when you expek this chile?"

Fenya flushed. "I'm not sure."

"Well, when did you start missing your monthly time?"

"A couple months."

"And you haven't tole your husband?"

"No . . . I meant to. Then this layoff. I didn't want to trouble him."

"Trouble! That's *good* trouble, girl! Don't you stint on glad news. That kinda trouble put heart in a man. The good Lord not goin' to let you slip outa His hand. You go home and tell your Piter this very night. And you be glad-hearted when you tell him. It's an insult to the Almighty to mope and groan about His good gifts."

"I'm not moping," Fenya defended herself. "I'm worried on the surface, but inside I'm—I'm happy." Happy with the first frail touch—something fleeting and delicate that she felt not in her womb but in her heart. Something wondrous was floating in hidden unguents, and she wanted to cherish it in secret.

"How did you know?" Fenya asked suddenly. "I haven't been sick."

Evangeline hooted in wise glee. "Not hard! Sometimes I catch you with that look, like you listenin' to somethin' faraway. I know what you listen for. That voice of God shaping His chile in your womb. All things come into being through His Word." This seemed plausible to Fenya. The mesh of blood and vow, sinew and sworn promise, flesh and word were one to her and did not cry to be dissected. Already her babe in its dark puddled cove was attentive to the mystical shaping word, the sculpting hand.

"'My frame was not hidden from You when I was made in secret and skillfully wrought in the depths of the earth,'" Evangeline added in the precise English she always used when quoting Scripture.

"What will Piotr say?" Fenya wondered.

PIOTR LURCHED, AND his thighs under the flimsy poker table sent the soup bowls wobbling. His hand reached out to her, then retreated into the now-lush growth of brown beard. "A child?" His face stiffened under the brunt of some emotion that Fenya had not yet learned to read.

His thoughts were strewn and throbbing with the rending rush of great winds, the peaceful, engulfing hush after love, the prowl of huge dark machines across the land. These were the things of his life—and somehow from this a new being had been flung from its place as a thought-nub in eternity to a refuge in his wife's belly. He looked at his young wife with respectful awe. The job of life-giving would be hers. But the job of place-making was his. This urgency drummed on him: a home—land, security—land, sustenance—land. But there was no land! His frustration overtook his joy before he expressed it.

"How . . . ," he murmured.

Fenya's eyes darkened with retreat. "I know. I know it's a hard time," she apologized and began biting her lip.

He came over to her and picked her up easily and began rocking her on the bed. "No. No, that's not it—I'm happy! It's just that . . . I want to make a good life for us."

He was sorry to have tarnished the shining joy in her for even a moment. "But we'll think of that later." He held her tightly, laughing. "For now I'll rock my wife and babe at the same time!"

Fenya's muted voice relayed to him her body's silent stirrings, her mind's poignant vision of the mysterious little stranger while his own mind tramped over barren fields, shut-up warehouses, and closed doors on city streets. "We'll find a way," he assured her as he wondered where in Los Angeles he could find a job.

Early the next morning he and Makar flung themselves against these same fields and warehouses and sharp-edged businesses, but they found no work. Day after day he threw himself into the brawling clamor of the city, looking, listening, searching for clues as to how he could uphold his role as husband and father.

Voices at busy corners and streetcar stops and in front of coffee bars jarred with disgruntled prophecies. It was easy to overhear the brayings of derbied businessmen as they fumbled in striped vests for watches, cigars, business cards. Stagnation. Ruination. The Democrats were destroying the country. The Republicans were ruining the country. The unions were leaching away profits. A monocled cowboy was running roughshod across the hearts of America. The Broadway was having a sale. "Did you hear about that new hotel going up in Pasadena? Deluxe." "Have a cigar."

But the workmen with big, lank hands were silent. The hot August days drew on, and still they found nothing. The idea of William Mulholland's aqueduct began sparkling in Piotr's mind like distant water. "Let's talk to Mick Mulvaney about it," he suggested to Makar. "He knows about everything." He decided also to ask him about the monocled cowboy and the dismal prophecies.

"Ruination, stagnation?" Mick listened with the serious attentiveness that Piotr liked in him. Then a grin quirked around his features. "Ha! That's funny. But you're right. That's how we talk. The greedy cads. By stagnation they mean they aren't getting everything they want just when they want it—which is right now. Don't worry, the country's not going to rack and ruin—at least not before lunch!" Then Mick showed him a cartoon with President Teddy Roosevelt mounted on a knock-kneed old nag and the word *Economy* patched on her rump. "There's your cowboy," Mick said. Piotr explained it to Makar, who laughed uproariously.

"You won't see that in the *Times*." Mick grinned. "It's an American custom to whine about hard times. Usually it's the ones with the big bank rolls who whine the loudest. These cycles come and go. You just have to ride them out. But there are some people who are hurting. . . . Layoffs? Yeah, I'd heard. Wondered whether you'd get hit by it. Tough luck," Mick sympathized. "Your best bet is the aqueduct. Now that's a project! They'll scrape and rasp and blast their way 250 miles across the roughest terrain in the country to bring water to Los Angeles. Nothing like it has ever been tried! When they've finished, there'll be enough water for millions. Millions!"

Mick stared off into a swarming vastness of people. "Quite a job! They're using a lot of miners—fellows left out of work from the mines of Colorado and Nevada, but they'll need some plain ole pick-and-shovel men, too."

"We can do that!" Piotr offered eagerly, but Makar blinked dejectedly.

"I guess you could!" Mick grinned. "But, hey, what about your wife? I thought you wanted to stick to L. A. because of her."

"Well, it looks like I may have to leave because of her. I can't find work in the city."

"Hmm. Let me do some asking around. I've heard that they're hiring only Americans, but then Mulholland himself is an Irish immigrant! Besides, I'll remind them of how you boys shut down the union. That'll stir up some warm feelings for you."

"Warm feelings!" Makar echoed. "It'll be more than warm when I tell Hanya. But what else can we do?"

Piotr had a hard time imagining the meek, doe-eyed Hanya as a spitfire, but he had similar qualms when he thought about Fenya. "Well, we aren't hired yet. Let's see if it's even possible."

"I'll go with you," Mick offered.

At the Department of Water and Power, they found that it was possible. The crews who scoured out the rough, rocky troughs for

Mulholland's vision of water in the wilderness were an unpredictable lot.

"They're an ornery bunch," complained the nervous clerk. "We get a lot of blue-jawed drifters who slouch onto a job site long enough to scrounge cash for a grand spree. Then they disappear."

"We won't disappear," Piotr assured him.

"No." He surveyed the two big-boned Russians thoughtfully. "You two don't look likely to slither into a crack in the rock. That's what we need. Plain ole brawn. But Russians? I don't know. Let me talk to a supervisor."

The supervisor eyed them, asked a few questions in a loud voice, and grunted his assent. "No skills, but they'd make great muckers. Send them up to Mohave."

Makar groaned and lapsed into Russian. "Not so fast! We have wives."

Piotr frowned. "Yes. And someday a child as well. But how will they eat? Maybe we can work just until the economy picks up."

Makar shrugged unhappily. "Hanya can stay with the Samarins, but how about Fenya? You can't leave her pitched at the side of the tracks like forgotten baggage."

A hard lump swelled in Piotr's throat. How studiously he had steeled himself to make this break "for the good of all," but how it stuck in his throat when it actually came down to it!

"If you're interested," the water and power man intruded, "you can report here next Wednesday. We have some wagons going up with supplies. You can ride along. If not . . ." He scrutinized the young men, then burst out, "Listen, boys, this is a chance to work on one of the great engineering feats of all time! This aqueduct is right up there with the Erie Canal and the Panama Canal. Some day you'll tell your children you worked on Mulholland's 'Big Ditch'!"

Makar swept a hand over his damp curls. "We'll take it!" he said loudly. Piotr stared at him. Then with lead in his wrist, he turned his hand to receive the application forms.

"I'm jealous," Mick complained.

"You won't be," muttered the clerk, "when you see the kind of work these men will be doing."

Later Piotr explained it to Fenya. "To the far north is a lake filled with snow melt from the great mountains that go up California like a spine—the Sierra Nevada. Except for a few cultivated valleys, all that land is desert, wilderness, and the water is wasted. So this engineer, William Mulholland, has thought up a way to bring the water all the way down here—250 miles, I'm told. That way the people of Los Angeles will have enough water and to spare so that more people can come here from the East."

"But if they're coming from the East, why don't they just go and live by the lake and get their water there?"

"There's no city there, no railways, no reason for being there."

"In Russia bringing the railway out to virgin lands is easier than moving a big lake hundreds of miles."

"It's not that simple, Fenya."

"No! It's very hard, very complicated." She was beginning to get suspicious. "How will they do it—with ditches?"

"Yes, ditches. And open channels and siphons and tunnels." He took a deep breath. "And that's where I come in. They've started work on the biggest tunnel, the one that goes under the Sierra Madre. The Elizabeth Tunnel, they call it. And they need workers. Muckers to go in after the dynamite crews and clear away the rubble. Makar and I will be going."

"Not me?" she ventured.

"No. The workers live in barracks like the army. My old training will be of some use now, except that we're battling a heap of rock instead of a flesh-and-blood enemy." She did not smile. Her lower lip began trembling, and she started biting it. She was flushed with the August heat and with cooking and with the soft padding of her pregnancy.

"Find another way! You can't leave!"

"I've tried, little bird. You know how I've tried. We can't live on the little you earn. I don't want to. And how can we make a life for our child unless we can save money? This tunnel—it's only sixty-eight miles away. I can come home for visits. You can stay with Aksinia. Now that Bunya's gone, she has plenty of room, and you can pay her something. She'll welcome you. And you and Hanya can put your heads together and gossip about your truant husbands."

"I want to stay here. At least I'll be in my own home waiting for you."

"No. It's not safe."

"And mucking after dynamite crews is?"

"It's something I have to do!" he snapped. "Why are you making this so hard? Don't you see that we'll lose our lease anyway? We have no money. We can't live on our own without work!"

"I'm sorry, I'm sorry!" Her voice was agitated. They both became afraid when anger flared between them. "You know what it is. You know . . ."

"I know. I know." He tugged at her two fair braids, pulling her to him. "It's hard. I don't want to leave. Especially now."

Piotr watched his wife carefully during the rest of the week. Fenya seemed to accept his decision. But she won the tussle about their rented shack. She would stay in their own home to wait for him and nowhere else. And she always referred to the "big ditch" with a touch of asperity, regarding it as an arrogant and futile attempt to wrest control of nature away from God-appointed powers.

"They won't be able to do it, Piotr," she predicted. "No one could."

"I think they'll do it," he replied. "But then they won't fully realize what they've done."

Her antagonism to the American aqueduct remained. But they drew close together in the shadow of his coming departure. The trains swept down on them, mincing the balmy twilight with wheel and rod. His mind rumbled uneasily. *In Russia I left them, and look what happened.* He went out at night to bare the fear in his soul to the cleansing music of the stars. *Lord, bring Your water, Your heavenly dew, to water my loved ones. Keep them safe for me. Give me strength.*

"I'll be back before the baby comes—or if you need me."

"I know."

How could he leave her? Her lovely, quirky features expressed all he needed of human love. The strands of her hair were threaded into the weft of all his thought. Her body, ripened with the luxuriant womanliness of pregnancy, filled him with joy and longing— and carried their future in secret cherished cache. How could he not be here beside her?

"It's only for a time."

"I know."

Fenya was dressed for work in the early morning, her braids shining beneath her crisp kerchief. Makar appeared looming in the doorway, smoothing back his curly mop of hair. Piotr looked at Fenya. Their glances meshed and pulled them together, and Makar's call from the porch pulled them apart.

At the Department of Water and Power, Piotr and Makar met with a surprise. Two disreputable-looking men perched on an old buckboard wagon began waving wide-brimmed slouch hats and shouting, "This way!" "Inyo or bust!"

Piotr turned away and scanned the piled-up wagons for a sign of aqueduct workers. The renegade buckboard driver wheeled and pulled up. "Are you blind?" yelled a familiar voice. Mick Mulvaney's blue eyes were laughing at him. "Hey, we've got an express—exclusively for Russians—all the way to Mohave. A deal you can't refuse!"

Makar's face creased in his slow smile, and Piotr found himself chuckling. "You look like muckers, but don't try and tell me you'll be sweating with a shovel instead of a pen."

"Not me. Actually Alan Kelly is the reporter for this project, though I'll try to squeeze a feature or two out of it if I can. If not, it's a lark—and a chance to see the beginning of the project of the century. Now Charlie," he jabbed an elbow into his friend's ribs, "Charlie has nobler things in mind. He wants to camp out in the desert and then take a look at the big trees in Sequoia. But Mohave is right on our way. You're welcome to drive with us. We checked with the works department teamsters, and they're only too happy to be free of the responsibility of dragging you two hulking fellas across the desert."

Piotr and Makar exchanged a glance. "Okay. Why not?" Piotr assented, and they clambered on board with the two Americans and a wagonload of camping gear.

Mick's exuberance grew as they left the city and suburbs behind them. They crossed the Hollywood hills and glimpsed the wide dryland farms of the San Fernando Valley. The land broke into canyons, and tawny hills rose through a green-gray tussle of chaparral. Charlie eased the buckboard over the dry wash of the Big Tujunga River and then, for good measure, the Little Tujunga River.

"We're going just the way Bill Mulholland and Fred Eaton came a few years ago—when they first saw the Owens River and all its potential for Los Angeles," Mick commented. "Old Bill Mulholland took one look and figured there'd be enough water there—not for

two hundred thousand people—but for two million! Staggering."
But the cold immensity of that number and the thought of that far-off water glittering like steel sent a chill dart into Piotr. The young American, with his quick eye for moods and nuances, quickly added, "But tomorrow, Piotr, I'll show you something that'll be a real treat to you."

At Newhall the unpaved road bent to a strenuous grade, and they all piled out and walked, encouraging the straining team as they climbed the hill. They camped that night in the Santa Clara Valley, listening to the tumble of a small autumn-swollen creek and the remote howl of coyotes.

"A lonely sound," Mick remarked. Charlie's glasses flashed as he looked up.

"Maybe. But it's a comforting kind of loneliness. In the city—or in the 'bosom of one's family'—you're still lonely, but it's an unhealthy, bitter loneliness. I suppose because you feel that you *shouldn't* be lonely. But there it is. For me, I'll take the dark side of a hill and the howl of a coyote over a posh party and all the social yelpings."

"Ah, you're a cold man, Mr. Wentworth," Mick said. "Sadly lacking, I'm afraid, in the love of one's fellow man. After all, isn't that what socialism is all about? Share and share alike? Where's your communal spirit? Here, have some beans—and coffee. Come on, Piotr, Makar—the chow wagon's dishin' it up."

Piotr grinned, gathering that Mick meant to share his supper with them. "We brought our own," he explained. "But we have plenty of good Russian bread. Hanya sent it fresh from the oven this morning. You must try some."

"See! He's got the hang of it. These Russians know all about how to live the communal life," Mick joked, thumping Piotr heartily on the back.

"Communal life—that's right! The Russians know something about that," Charlie said. "Here not even the families live a communal life. At least, *we* don't. We each follow our own purpose but under the same roof."

"The Russian city folk and gentry are like that, too," Piotr explained. "It's only the peasants who are different. I suppose we are what you call communal because we have to be. If we don't all pull together, we won't survive. It's the land that compels us."

"Land—yes. But here the coinage of life is work—production. Not land. But your revolution sent out a cry for justice heard all over the world—even though it failed. Someday it will succeed. Somewhere. If not in Russia, then in Germany or England or here in America!"

Piotr's throat tightened around the harsh rebuke of an answer that pushed up from his chest. He turned away, studying the fire. Terrible images leaped in the flames. Around them swarmed the night with its stealthy sounds: the rustle of a scaled creature, the slither of a rock-clogged creek, the piping of a fickle wind down the dry throat of the arroyo, and—to remind them that they were alien here—the occasional howl of the coyote.

You, You are my rock. My shelter in a dry and thirsty land, he told his Comforter. *Though I dwell in the remotest part of the earth, there Your hand will lead me. For darkness is not dark to Thee.* His thought carried far into the secret places of the valley, hills, and canyons and into habitations where humans stirred behind windows, suspended in amber light. Beyond the scalloped hills, past fields ribboned with silver tracks, in a clapboard box, a girl, his wife, waited for him. *How beautiful you are, my wife. You have dove's eyes.* And within her were other membraned eyes, tiny and perfect as glass beads. And beyond them, the eyes that gleam with all knowledge and all beauty. The night was dark, and it was mysterious, but it was not blind.

Piotr turned his attention to his companions. Makar was staring at the fire with a bleak, puzzled expression. Mick, his head jerking with the quick snatch of his perception, glanced from Charlie to Piotr. And Charlie waited with his detached curiosity, his long, pale face floating in the darkness above his drab jacket.

The strangeness of all that surrounded them was stronger than the strangenesses that lay between them. They were no longer two Russian peasants and a streetwise son of Irish immigrants and an educated American—but four human creatures drawn to a focal point of light and warmth and comradeship.

"Look at me," Piotr said laughing. "I've had to—what do you say?—bite my tongue. I was all ready to be hot and quick with my words. But it's all because of things that you couldn't possibly know. For us, Mr. Wentworth, the socialist revolution did not bring justice. Nor did it bring this ideal community to us. It brought only horror—

horror . . ." He shook his head, wondering how he could describe the time-rooted pride of the rich, the ancient rancor of the poor to someone who lived in a land so new. But these things were in America, too, and hatred needs be only one generation thick to be vicious enough to kill.

"My own family is lost, probably dead. My uncle—a wealthy man by peasant standards—wrote to me two years ago. These seekers of justice dragged his two sons, my cousins, and his daughter-in-law into the glare of his burning barn. They raped and killed the girl in front of her husband. Then they took up wooden stakes and stabbed out the eyes of my cousins. They died in the forest, probably mauled by bears. My mother and father and two sisters fled." His story—he had not told it for a long time—became so heavy that he began gasping with it as though he too were fleeing.

"Who knows what became of them? Did they meet some terrible end at the hands of rebels—or of gendarmes? Or did disease strike them down? Or are they lost and distressed in some remote place where they cannot send word? But that's a foolish hope," he added in a rush. "I know they're dead."

Makar, who knew the story, stared morosely at his hands. Mick's face was set with all the morbid, absorbed compassion of his Irish soul.

Charlie shifted uneasily. "That's an outrage," he began, then caught himself. "Whoa! I'm sounding like some foiled society matron. 'There should be a law!'" he mimicked. "Fact is, there are laws. But what good are they in the face of something that's like a force of nature? Laws won't do it. But don't you—how is it that you—doesn't this sort of thing challenge your beliefs? After all, would a good God allow such horror?"

Piotr grimaced inwardly. He had encountered this amazing trait before—as though a human soul could grab God by the scruff of His neck and call Him to account!

"I never have felt God's presence so powerfully or been so moved by His love as on the night that tragedy was hammered into my soul. But I can't explain it."

Charlie's straight mouth twitched with impatience, but Mick's eyes smoked with a deeply emotional look of understanding—and of pride. "Good for you!" his expression cried although he spoke no word.

Charlie's face floated remote and alienated in the firelight. Piotr was filled with an oppressive sense that things weren't as they should be—that he needed to say something to make this central fact of his life clear. He ransacked his mind for the English expressions that would move this sophisticated young American.

"We Molokans are taught all about God, and so we know about Him, but that's not the same as knowing Him. When men were lost in darkness, He sent His Son, Jesus, to give a face and strength of action in history to His character. And when we see Him as He is, we know that He can do no evil. But it's our connection to God through Christ that brings something to life in us so that we can know this. Without this connection, we're still numb in our souls. If the cord is broken, the stirrings of God within your soul cannot be felt."

"Well," Charlie said with a wry flicker about his mouth, "I must be living with a severed cord because I can't feel a thing."

"You're a hard case, Charlie, m'boy," Mick said, only half-joking. "Bloated with pride and cocksure you're going to save the world by replacing the greedy, pompous capitalists with greedy, envious socialists." He punched his friend playfully. "But you're still connected to us! That'll have to serve until you're sick of being numb inside."

The next day they traveled across rugged canyon country with the San Gabriel Mountains, shagged with chaparral, looming on their right. An unnatural heat swept toward them from the unseen valley ahead. Then the road bent, and a desert opened before them. *No wonder this land is crying for water!* Piotr thought.

"This is the rim of the Mohave Desert—the biggest desert in America and the lowest spot in America," Mick told them.

"Rather formidable," Charlie commented. "Isn't it?"

"Let's get over it as fast as we can," Mick advised. "I want to be in Mohave early. Charlie and I'll be going on across the Tehachapis and up toward Sequoia. The sequoias," he bragged, "are the biggest trees in the world. Their trunks are so huge they've made a tunnel in one big enough to drive a cart through. And a little further north is Mount Whitney—the highest mountain in America!" The

Russians smiled indulgently. They'd heard all about the Western tall tale!

They stopped briefly at the weather-beaten town of Palmdale. Then Charlie spurred his team across the summit of the Tehachapi Mountains. Desert terrain opened in the distance—a desolate vista of mountain peaks and dry lakes. "We'll take a detour here," Mick said. "I'll show you something, Piotr, that you'll like."

They urged the horses over stony washes, occasionally getting out to push the buckboard up steep-walled, rocky creek beds. The Tehachapis were a slumbrous, camel-skinned hump of mountains with mange-gold hides hot and plush in the afternoon sun. Then the hills folded away, and a wide flat land opened out until it met a misted line of sky. The land was as bleak and featureless as the desert, but there was something different about it, a secretive fecundity of rounded curves. Here and there in green squares precise as emeralds glistened new crops. Piotr, with Mick at his shoulder, stumbled out of the cart and climbed a rough outcropping. The soil scrunched under his boot soles; his hands and legs pulsed with a heavy surge. Possibilities, wondrous and elusive but subject to the straining of shoulder and sinew, waited in the mist. And these possibilities swelled and raced in all the conduits of his body. He felt as though his life's veins and cords had grown out through his feet and into the land beneath him.

Mick said nothing for a few moments. His silence had a respectful attentiveness to it that Piotr liked. And when he spoke, his words flashed quick and sparkling. "I knew you'd like it. Farms—hundreds of them—all along the valley. Farms like jewels strung along the rivers that come down from the Sierras from the Sacramento in the north down to the Kern here near Bakersfield. And all the rivers in between—jeweled with little farms! The Stanislaus and the Merced and the San Joaquin, the Kings and the Tule, the Kaweah, the Tuolumie. A whole litany of rivers! Really, it could be the biggest agricultural valley in the world."

Piotr did not smile. The soft mists and the flick of sudden water and the vast unawakened land was ripe to any possibility. Far away from them, a tiny man with a team of ant-sized horses ranged slowly over a cross-hatched field. And the land scrolled out between the Tehachapis and the coast ranges, ciphered with plow and harrow.

Mick began a second litany. "Grapes in Delano; cotton nearer here where it's hot; peach and orange orchards up toward the foothills; alfalfa, lettuce, tomatoes, almonds—you should see the almonds and walnuts in the orchards near the Kings River! Anything can grow. Anything."

But Piotr looked down with a great bursting longing. "My son," he told himself, "must grow up on land like this—and not in the streets of the city." Makar's compact bulk stirred behind him, and Piotr saw his own longing in the eyes of his friend. In mute understanding, they made camp in a grove of scrub oak. Faraway a train crossing the Tehachapis plunged into the receptive hills, and the wail of the train hung on the air and was drawn off into the hills. Above them a scythe-shaped moon poised with gentle and patient attentiveness.

The next day they rode into a vast, dead land bordered by desiccated ridges. The fearful power of the brilliantly blue sky had sucked the color from everything else. Gray-green juiceless scrub and blanched burdocks huddled abjectly. A lone saguaro cactus lunged toward them with outstretched branches that seemed to cry, "Get back! Get back!"

It was still early when they came into the town of Mohave. The dusty main street swarmed with men and animals. Knots of thin, hard-faced men watched them with indifference, their eyes gleaming from under the shadow of slouch hats. Mule skinners, deft and cunning men who could hold teams of forty or fifty beasts under an iron-fisted sway, sang out sharp commands. Mick and Charlie directed the Russians to the camp doctor and then made their way to the Mohave Hotel.

The next day Piotr and Makar found themselves facing down a defiant, rocky outcropping of the Sierra Madre. They joined an army of eager young engineers from the mining colleges of the West, seasoned miners from recession-hit stakes in Nevada and Colorado and Arizona, and muckers—a scruffy collection of vagrants willing to wield a shovel until it suited them to drop it and head off to Los Angeles for a week-long spree. The stone-browed indentation that would become the north portal of the Elizabeth Tunnel eyed them warily. But all the men stared back confidently—from the fresh-faced college boys to the jaded transients. Hands bent for a grapple, they were going to punch in the face of this mountain and push a five-mile tunnel into her granite innards. Piotr and Makar exchanged a grim, admiring glance.

"They'll do it," Makar murmured.

Suddenly a deafening blast tore at the vitals of the Sierra Madre and spewed out dust and debris. "There's your job, boys!" yelled John Gray, the overseer. He grabbed a shovel, dove into the tunnel, and attacked a hill of broken rock. A seasoned miner with years of wet-tunneling experience in the mines of Colorado, Wyoming, and New Mexico, the energetic Gray didn't balk at getting his hands dirty. The team of muckers followed, Makar and Piotr among them.

It was blessedly cool inside the tunnel. Outside, temperatures ranged from 10 degrees at midnight up to 120 degrees during the hottest part of the day. The tunnel crews preferred inside work despite the constant danger of falling rocks and dynamite blasts. Their goal was to bite eight feet per day out of solid bedrock. A second crew was excavating the south portal, and a fierce rivalry arose as to which team would reach the center mark first.

The dogged, relentless Gray worked out a fast-paced relay system. Sometimes his men ate their meals standing waist-deep in mud, snatched a few hours of sleep, and returned to battle the mountain. They grumbled, but they did it knowing that Gray didn't ask anything of them he wasn't willing to do himself.

The days unraveled to the percussion of dynamite and the scrape of shovels. Piotr began to develop a sense of the dangers they faced day to day.

"Listen, boyo, if you hear the blast fizzle, and the smoke of it billows out red instead of black, run for it," advised one of the muckers, an Irishman who, though begrimed with sticky clay, sported a dapper derby hat. "So's me brain won't crack when the rocks fall," he explained.

"Name's Dan Calloway, but they call me Derby Dan," he offered. A humorous and imaginative man, he referred to the solid granite core of the Elizabeth as "the beast" and attacked it with jaunty waves of his shovel and a rolling cascade of Irish maledictions.

By late November they had bored deep into the mountain's flank, but now they were hitting more and more pockets of water. Once the crisp pops of the charges were followed by an ominous swoosh, and the tunnel filled with tons of saturated sand and gravel and fleeing men. Derby Dan, still gulping air, shook his fist at "the beast." Makar heaved his relief and shook his head. "She's fighting back," he noted with a nervous smile. Later they mucked out the sodden gravel while standing thigh-high in icy water.

At night as they wolfed down a hot meal in the mess hall, doubts would pour out of Makar, but Piotr's mind was full of the land calling to him on the other side of the hills—and of the girl waiting for him back in Los Angeles. While the boisterous "blanket stiffs" sought out whiskey and women in Mohave, the Russians walked in the foothills. A crystal night expunged the rubble of granite and basalt debris and the clutter of machinery. In the morning they were back on the job.

Sometimes Piotr would catch sight of some tanned, keen-eyed young engineer staring out at the unfolding mountains that flanked the Antelope Valley. Other crews, Piotr knew, were out there digging ditches, excavating tunnels, laying the huge siphons that would carry water across the most desolate desert in North America. And the young American's eyes would narrow piercingly—like a strict housewife surveying a cluttered room. "These things are in my way," the keen eyes said, "and I'll sweep them away!" The granite-rooted monsters of the Sierra Nevada were no more to him than the flimsy scrub of sage and greasewood or the fleeting verbena and lupines of spring.

"It's an unnatural way to live," Makar complained. "Our wives are miles away. There are no children, no families—only these grasping men and the slinking creatures of the desert. I'm going home."

"One more week," Piotr wheedled.

"There's something amiss in the whole idea—something flawed. No good will come of it. In Russia they build the big towns near the rivers—not the other way around! Moscow, Petersburg, Kiev, Novgorod, even Tiflis—they're all set on a river. That's how it should be. These folk are too apt to stick their spoon in the pot and stir things up."

"But that's why they can make a new and different kind of life for themselves," Piotr argued.

"You've gotten greedy for what God hasn't given you, Piotr

Gavrilovich. If He wanted us to possess the land, He'd have given it to us."

"No! You're wrong. I just want to provide for my wife and child."

"Yes, but this is an unnatural way of doing it," Makar insisted.

"Every way seems unnatural to us—unless we could somehow work the land. And you want that, too, just as much as I do," Piotr challenged.

"I admit it. But this isn't the way. Even Ilya thinks we don't belong out here!"

"Maybe not. But it's the only way I see right now." But Makar's words clung to him like burrs. Piotr was seized with times of agitation and something like remorse. *Perhaps he's right. Should we give it up?* The idea of seeing Fenya again shook him to the core.

"Don't light out yet, boyo," Derby Dan advised. "They'll pay extra during Christmas."

But by midwinter Makar was even more insistent. "Let's go back to our wives. Your child is due soon."

"You go. I'll stay another month and go back with plenty of time before the birth—and some extra money in my pocket."

Makar shook his head, then was quiet. Deeper in the tunnel the miners were setting the charges, and the two friends instinctively fell silent, waiting for the loud "pop, pop, pop" of the explosion. Instead, a reptilian hiss flicked through the tunnel's mouth. Then the space filled with noxious gases, and the fumes clawed at the throats of men. Piotr threw himself toward the light, shoving the confused Makar in front of him. Makar gasped headlong into daylight and fell on the ground. Piotr skidded on his knees beside him. He shielded his streaming eyes with his hands and bent double in a wracking cough. Makar was gulping air with a hoarse desperation, his eyes a terrified blue in a face the color of beet root. A little way from them, Derby Dan was sprawled out on a heap of rubble with the camp medic leaning over him.

"Let me be . . ." He struggled. "Let me be. I'm better . . ." Then his body arced with explosive coughs that spewed blood across the ground and spattered the medic's coat.

"Bring up the wagon," yelled a foreman. The team was already galloping up from the tent camp.

"Too late," said the medic. Derby Dan's face changed, and he lay still.

"Red fumes," muttered a miner. "One minute you're gasping for air; then you feel better; then you start coughing your lungs out."

Makar and Piotr exchanged a glance. Piotr cautiously drew the air into his lungs. How long before they knew whether they had survived or whether the horrible cough would tear the tissue from their lungs? Makar was looking off into the distance where the Sierra Madre reared between the Antelope Valley and the city. His eyes took on a peaceful, dreamy expression.

"No more of this for me," he whispered. "Tomorrow I go home to my Hanya."

Piotr began to speak but could not. The next day he saw his friend off.

"My heart goes with you. I'll be coming soon," Piotr said. "I don't know . . . there's something here for me to do. But I'll be coming soon."

The miners buried Dan Calloway near the camp site. Like many of the muckers, he was a drifter with no family and no past. In the greasewood-lined hollow, he had found roots at last. Flanked by miners and a ragtag assortment of muckers, William Mulholland read the service. The men's dark clothing fluttered like wings in the wind. "'I am the resurrection and the life . . .'" The words sprang into the wind from beneath Mulholland's field-marshal mustache. The Sierra Madre brightened in the morning. A blue shadow tinted a root of the mountain that reached into the dry little hollow where the lean redwood marker already tilted to the wind. A weathered miner came up and placed the jaunty derby on top. His face was hard, but his hands were gentle. The derby rollicked on its post but did not blow away. And as he watched, a crushing loneliness rose up in Piotr.

The miners returned to drill and charge, and the engineers strategized against the mountain, and the solitary tumbleweed muckers chewed on their tossing thoughts, and across the Tehachapis farmers scratched their mark upon the land.

I am like the pelican of the wilderness, like an owl of the desert. I lie awake and am like a sparrow alone on the housetop.

His heart swelled and burst with his cry, and his cry was heard in the wilderness.

X

The Vineyard

In the quiet after upheaval, the Russian lands continued to disgorge Molokans—and the streets of the eighth ward swelled with new arrivals through the months of summer and autumn. Winters were quieter; the big boats coming into San Pedro were fewer. The Molokans in the house churches of Russian town had time to take stock and prepare for the next influx. *As I am preparing*, Fenya thought, *for a new arrival!*

But she was not prepared for what the last ship from Odessa brought her. Unmarked except for her name and city, a large wooden crate was brought to Aksinia's by a family from Kars. "It was given us by a man in Delizan," a middle-aged Molokan explained. "He gave us money to ship it with our things. His name? Kobzeff—he was one of the Kobzeffs, but it wasn't his. It was put in his care by a man from a village near Tiflis. His name should be there. Look at the writing."

But not even Ivan, who could read, was able to find a clue as to who had sent the box.

"Open it!" Aksinia prodded her husband excitedly.

He tapped the boards with a hammer. The crate split, and boards parted to reveal something wrenchingly familiar. They looked at each other through the web of silence that had fallen on them, their eyes shining with recognition and pain. Fenya's hand flew protectively to her mounded belly and up the slope to her heart.

Before them stood a carved chest. The marbled graining of birch had been coaxed with knife and chisel into the curving branches of a fruit-laden vine, each grape juicy with the shine of lovingly burnished wood. *My father's work*, Fenya thought. She could see that Aksinia and Ivan recognized it immediately. This was the dower chest for Natasha's *pridanoe* that had been given at her betrothal.

"Open it," Ivan said tensely.

Fenya pried her fingers under the lid, then let them fall. *What will this open for me? Irrational fears buzzed around her. Something painful? Something that will hurt my baby?*

"Don't—," she began, but Ivan had already lifted the hinged lid. The chest exhaled the scent of pent-up cedar. *I'll line it with cedar and have it ready by August*, her father had said. There was nothing inside.

But the long-locked wood scent engulfed her with her father's words. *A vine, you see. I can't read the Scriptures, much less carve them in wood, but the idea I wanted to send off with my daughter is that of Christ as the true vine. "I am the vine, you are the branches . . ." Abide in Him, in His love, and you will bear much fruit, and your joy will be full as He promises.* Vassily's voice with its diffident pauses shaped something inside her—working with the grain. *The chest—it's to be a reminder of that. . . .*

And yet these words were spoken to her sister—the sister whose August wedding was followed by that autumn of terror. *How can it be? Why was the bride who smiled in the hope of joy and fruitful years cut down so brutally?*

A heat of emotion scalded her so that her face and feet felt hot and swollen with it. The life within her stirred with delicate, bone-sharp proddings. She raised her face to Aksinia's, and their eyes locked and held.

"I don't know," Aksinia said, her usually light voice dragging. "I don't know why . . ."

Nails groaned and screeched as Ivan pried away the loose boards with a claw hammer. Aksinia rubbed her hands down her apron and turned on him with quick wrath. "Stop that noise! And close the lid!"

But for Fenya, a door had opened in her mind, and vague forebodings pursued her as she went about her daily tasks. Her own marriage and the months of happiness with Piotr had crowded out the thought of her sister's death, but it was still there—a dark spot in the far corner of her mind. And now it was growing, and her mind kept returning to it. She longed for the bulwark's bend of Piotr's shoulders.

Phoebe noticed her sadness and responded with her absorbent, spongelike sympathy. "You need to focus on something else," she offered.

But Evangeline's crystalline spirit deflected any darkness into a splash of light. "The Lord have His hand on you," she insisted. "You seein' darkly now, but someday you see face to face." Her eyes swept around the small laundry room, gathering in her vision.

Fenya knit her brows over the steaming mangle. "I don't even know who sent it. My father? Or Mikhail Voloshin? Who? And why?"

"*God* brought this carving to you from Russia to show you His hand! Jus' don't you forget what your father says. Those are wise words. You know what we call a chest like that? A *hope* chest. You store up hope in that chest, and God will show you everything you need to know."

But I don't know, Fenya thought. "You know so much," she said aloud. "You seem so sure . . ."

"The Word is my sureness," Evangeline insisted. "Thy statutes are my songs in the house of my pilgrimage! I got no sureness about anything else, but I *know* what God says to me."

"You can read?"

"'Course I can!" the black woman replied surprised. "Can't you?"

"No. My younger brothers were learning—back in Russia—and we were so proud of them! But none of the girls had time to learn, and my parents don't read."

For once Evangeline was silenced, but Phoebe spoke up. "I can't take away your questions, Fenya, but I can teach you to read. We'll concentrate on it, and you'll be able to read stories to your little one by the time he's ready to listen. Your day here is over just about the time school lets out, so the time will work out perfectly."

"Can we work here?" Fenya asked.

"No. It's actually closer for me to come to you. My apartment is in the city, remember? We'll start tomorrow."

"An American? Coming to your house?" Aksinia raised her eyebrows in surprise. "Our way is to keep to ourselves—even here. But it's a wonderful thing to learn to read! Just think, soon my little Nikolinka and Valentina will be off at school reading away like deacons! The girl as well as the boy. But," she added, lowering her voice, "don't tell Ivan. He'll think it's foolishness. So will you offer her tea?"

Fenya was taken aback. "Tea?" She had been so enthralled by the idea of reading that she had forgotten she would be hostess to this educated woman. "What shall I do?"

"Well, surely you should have some tea for her—and look! We'll make Russian tea cakes. We'll have to be quick about it. Then you'll have a nice little repast for her."

"Yes! And in my own home!" She was glad now that she had convinced Piotr to hold onto their tiny home. It seemed a grand thing to be able to regale Miss Phoebe Wentworth with tea and pastries in a house of her own.

She and Aksinia set to work and soon had a plate of the ball-shaped, sugar-coated cookies arranged like a mound of snowballs. "Here, take some lemon leaves to garnish it with. Be sure and put them in water for tomorrow! And here—some raspberry jam. And take this—just a little apricot *kvas*. That will be a real treat."

Fenya happily packed her provisions in a basket and hurried home to clean the shack. She had grown a little careless with Piotr away, but this gave her a reason to give everything a good scrubbing. It was late when she finished, and she surveyed her work with happy exhaustion. The quilted bed covers glowed richly against the red frame; the curtains tidily framed the two small windows, and the carved birch chest showed its warm artistry beside the bed. On the card table covered with its lace-trimmed cloth, she had set out glasses for tea and the plate of pastries. The jug of *kvas* was cooling in the tub of water by the door. Fortunately, Phoebe would be visiting in the afternoon, so the lack of heat wouldn't be too uncomfortable.

"It's a good thing," she told the little stranger within, "to prepare for the coming of a friend!" Her own words surprised her. She had thought of Phoebe as a helpful outsider, a good and kind woman, and, since she so seldom saw Mrs. Wentworth, her employer. *Is she a friend?*

She asked herself the same question as Phoebe walked up the path littered with broken glass and odd bits of paper to her home. Phoebe looked about with narrowed eyes and a serious expression. She jumped guiltily at Fenya's greeting.

"I'm early, I know," she apologized. "I've been near here before—

visiting the peon colony. See, it's behind those bushes. You can smell it." Her lip curled with disgust. Fenya knew that many Mexicans lived across the river in shacks not too different from the one she and Piotr shared. Except that there were many of them—men, women, and lots of children along with dogs and chickens—crowded along crooked little alleys that stank with sewage.

"It's a shame," Phoebe murmured, "that they have to live that way." Then she turned toward the Voloshins' shanty. Fenya could see that she was trying very hard to appear open and comfortable.

"We have an outhouse," Fenya found herself saying.

"Oh, I'm fine—I don't need to . . ."

"No, I mean . . . in case you did . . . or anyone. We have one."

"Well, Fenya, thank you."

Fenya studied her fresh, scrubbed face. Her glasses flashed as they went up the steps, hiding her eyes, but not before Fenya caught a glimpse of their sadness. *She feels sorry for me!*

Fenya opened the door, letting the older girl step in front of her. *I'd forgotten how dark it is in here.* Phoebe stopped in confusion, almost bumping into the bed. Fenya went to the smaller of the two windows and pulled aside the curtains.

"It's not enough, I know—the light," she apologized. "I thought we could work here at the table." And she flushed as Phoebe looked down at the cheap glasses and wobbly little table. A torpid fly had settled on the tea cakes, refusing to move even when she tried to shoo it away. Embarrassment and a vague loneliness swept over her, and she longed for Aksinia's effusive naturalness. That made her remember the tea and the lemon leaves. She backed into the alcove with the sink and stove.

"I'll make some tea," she offered.

"That would be lovely," Phoebe said a little too heartily.

Fenya set the water to boiling. She noticed the lemon leaves in a glass beside the sink. *Aksinia said to put those on the cookie plate. Too late now!* But she retrieved the *kvas* from its tub and set it before her guest. Phoebe had already set out two books and some alphabet cards. Fenya went back to the kitchen to pour the tea.

"It must be lonely for you without Piotr," Phoebe called out.

"A little. He sends letters, and Ivan reads them to me. But it would be nice to read on my own."

"It will be. I think you'll make a quick student."

"I hope so," Fenya said, bumping into the sink. After months of barely showing, her pregnancy had gotten proudly out of hand, and her belly was always in the way.

She threw some tea leaves into the enamel-ware kettle, brought it to the table, and poured tea into the glasses through a cloth. Phoebe watched her curiously.

"Take some of this jam—it's very good," Fenya insisted, offering the jam pot.

Phoebe took the jam with a confused expression. She reached for a tea cake and used her spoon to apply jam to the cookie instead of stirring it into her tea. The rounded contours of the tea cake didn't take well to jam, and a red sticky blob dripped onto the tablecloth.

Trying not to notice, Fenya stirred a spoonful of jam into her own tea.

"Oh! You use it in your tea. I've never seen that!"

"I have sugar. I can get you some!" Fenya jumped up, but her bulging belly played another trick on her and sent the table lurching and the tea glasses flying.

"Sorry! Are you wet? I'll make some more."

Phoebe scraped her chair back. "No, never mind. I had a sip. It was just enough. We need to get to work. Maybe we can have some of this—what is it? Juice?"

Fenya knitted her brows. "It's apricot . . . apricot *kvas*."

"Oh, apricot juice. That's just the thing. I'm thirsty for something cool. That'll be lovely."

Fenya poured, and Phoebe drank. "This is delicious—just what I needed!"

She drank some more, becoming more relaxed. Fenya moved the jug to the other side of the table, but as Phoebe was setting out her tea-stained alphabet cards, she absently reached for it and poured herself another glass.

Fenya struggled for words as Phoebe became flushed and effusive. "Kvas is . . . it's a little more than juice," she explained. Phoebe focused on her with a dim effort. "It's, well, it's a little like beer—"

"Beer?" A temperance advocate, Phoebe had never tasted beer. A shocked expression crossed her face. "You've given me beer?"

Fenya tugged at her kerchief with a horrified expression. "Not as strong as beer but . . . what have I done?" she pleaded.

Phoebe tilted the golden, milky liquid in her glass thoughtfully, then burst into laughter. "Well," she said giggling, "I have a lot to learn—more than you, I think!"

Fenya, too, began giggling.

"So," Phoebe teased, "are you giggling in English or Russian? We can't have any Russian giggles in this class."

"These are American giggles," Fenya insisted.

"Well, we'd better settle down. You'll have to be a diligent student to learn anything from a half-tipsy teacher!"

"You're not tipsy! Just a little—unbent."

"So—I was bent before?"

"No," Fenya laughed. "A little stiff maybe."

"Well, I'm not stiff now!"

In spite of their rough start, they made great progress in the two hours before Phoebe went back to her downtown apartment.

She left two books on the little table. One was the first *McGuffey's Eclectic Reader*. The other was a small, blue-bound *New Testament and Psalms*. "You'll soon be reading *McGuffey's*, and the other I've left as a sign of hope. I know it's your goal to read that one."

Filled with excitement, Fenya drew her over to the carved chest. "Look! This is the chest that came from Russia." With a muted sound, Phoebe knelt and caressed the exquisite curving lines of branch and leaf and fruit.

"What a beautiful, beautiful thing, Fenya! I've never seen anything like it!" She looked into Fenya's eyes as the cool November twilight dimmed the room. "I hope that someday you'll be able to look at it and feel the joy your father wanted this piece to bring—instead of pain."

Fenya glanced away, hiding the stab of feeling that thoughts of Natasha's death brought. Then she knelt beside her friend. "See, there's the Bible reference written on it—the one about the vine and branches."

"From John's gospel," Phoebe said. "Shall I read it?" She opened the testament and read, "'I am the vine, you are the branches. He who abides in Me, and I in him, bears much fruit; for without Me you can do nothing. If anyone does not abide in Me, he is cast out as a branch and is withered; and they gather them and throw them into the fire, and they are burned. If you abide in Me, and My words abide in you, you will ask what you desire, and it shall be done for you. . . . These things I have spoken to you, that My joy may remain in you, and that your joy may be full.'"

As Phoebe's soft voice rose and fell in the crude shack, Fenya was carried far away to another wooden shack where her parents and brothers and sisters had clustered around the lamp, and a small boy's voice had read these same words. Natasha was there, and plump, pretty Tanya, and tow-headed Misha and Vanya. The words lost none of their power in the foreign tongue. And all the heaving peaks of oceans and fortress walls of mountains and cold thrust of the cities could not break the light-spun strand between her and that time and those people.

The shanty seemed quiet and lonely after Phoebe left. Fenya longed for Piotr. She turned up the lamp and leafed through the McGuffey reader, studying each of the engraved illustrations. Then she opened the testament, but the tiny English markings were a parading riddle. In the distance she could hear the fast express gathering itself up, and the little stranger began stirring in her womb. She went to the window, watching as the train came up beside the river. Rod and wheel, rod and wheel, wands of power striking a churn of motion from the earth. The little one lurched within her, and she clasped her belly protectively with her two hands.

THE DARK, POWERFUL NIGHT TRAINS prowled her dreams, but a festive spirit sparkled over Fenya's days at the Wentworth home. With Christmas drawing near, Evangeline threw herself into a baking frenzy, and the kitchen was aromatic with cinnamon and orange peel and chocolate. The stately fir tree, resplendent with remarkable baubles, breathed its forest scent through the house.

But in spite of the rich beauty of their surroundings, the family seemed to Fenya broken and divided. Each went about his or her business separately, then came home, each to a separate room. Fenya supposed that the bonds of love and work that made a family were there, but they were hard for her to see.

Our life was so simple though we felt so often the nip of want. The

Kostrikin family went into the fields together, spent evenings around the table with its single lamp or candle, and slept together. *We had a shared life.* But the Wentworths were divided by their many walls. *They are crushed by a weight of bounty,* she mused, *and yet we were crushed, too. I am here across the sea, and Natasha is dead.* But in spite of that, Fenya felt that those early bonds had given her something, an unquenchable sap in her that could flow out in this new land to send down roots and begin something new. A family.

But for now she felt cut off—not only from the Kostrikins in Russia, but from her own husband and even to some extent from the Molokans. Her lessons with Phoebe opened wide fields of new thought to her, and her working association with the Wentworth family made her life different from that of Aksinia or Hanya or Elena Valoff. While some of the brethren looked at their new home with wide-awake eyes, quick to recognize their kinship with Angelinos of like spirit, others shuttered their vision and complained of American godlessness and sinful practices—including the celebration of Christmas. Leaders like Philip Shubin gathered together the best singers into visiting choirs and filled the churches of Los Angeles with Russian song. Others held themselves morosely apart from the "pork-eating *nynash.*"

Before Christmas Makar returned. "It won't be long now," he told Fenya. "Piotr wants to get his extra wages for Christmas. Then he'll be coming back, too."

Hanya glanced at the bulge under Fenya's apron and whispered, "It won't be long for you either!" They laughed merrily. Hanya, too, was expecting, her pregnancy dating from September when they had said goodbye to their husbands.

But Makar's description of camp life and the dangers of excavating the Elizabeth Tunnel were disquieting. "I've seen men cough out their lungs, blacken, and die—and I watched helplessly." He told them that in addition to the menace of rock and water and dynamite, there was the menace of angry men. Threats came from unionists and the defrauded homesteaders of the Owens Valley. "But don't worry. There've been no problems at the tunnel, and, God willing, Piotr will be home soon."

On Christmas Eve Fenya was asked to help serve the formal dinner at the Wentworth home. She eagerly accepted. The more money she earned, the sooner Piotr could come home. Plus, she was curious. She wanted to see this American family together.

"This is much harder than washing and ironing," she told Evangeline as the older woman showed her how to set the table. The astonishing array of different forks, spoons, knives, plates, and glasses for each person fascinated her. She was eager to see what they would do with it all. But, she acknowledged, it did look pretty when the lighted candles sent prismed flares and silvered flashes off of the crystal and silver.

"That look festive indeed," Evangeline approved. She had a sumptuous feast of turkey, dressing, sweet potatoes, vegetables, and all kinds of condiments ready to set out as the family gathered. In addition to the five Wentworths, the guests included Mr. Wentworth's elderly mother, Bernice Wentworth's sister and her husband from Pasadena along with their twelve-year-old son, and Charlie's friend Mick. In their Christmas finery they all made a handsome picture, Fenya noted as she poured out the water. Evangeline filled the wine goblets. Due to her Molokan beliefs, Fenya declined to serve the alcohol, which caused Phoebe to swallow a paroxysm of laughter.

"I know you're too much of a prude to drink wine, Phoebe," Charlie gibed, "but you're acting like you've had a few glasses already."

Phoebe laughed harder while Mick's vivid blue eyes sparkled at her. She did look unusually lovely in her green velvet jumper over a creamy lace blouse. Fenya often intersected Mick's bemused stare.

"Your girls look beautiful tonight, Bernice," noted the aunt. "They're quite the young ladies."

"A toast to the ladies—and especially our hostess," proposed her husband.

Bernice Wentworth inclined her pompadoured head graciously, but her husband interrupted. He held up a glass of water. "This is what we should be toasting with, Silas. We made more money from water this year than the richest vintner in the country has made from grapes."

"That's so." The brother-in-law set aside his wine goblet with a grin. "That tip about the San Fernando Valley was pure gold. Here's to ya!"

Fenya watched as they gulped at the water or jokingly held it to the light like finicky connoisseurs. "Good stuff, brother. No finer anywhere." Fenya knew that while miners and muckers and ditch diggers grappled with the desert and the mountains, these men were raking in dollars as the land prices in the once-thirsty San Fernando Valley skyrocketed. Evangeline glared, and Charlie shot a disgusted look at his father.

"The old paterfamilias is never happier than when he's squeezing a profit from someone else's sweat," he muttered to Mick. "He's exuding Christmas spirit. You see why I'm a so-called socialist."

But the older man wasn't fooled. "You have something to say, son? Go ahead and say it."

Charlie shrugged. "'Tis not the season," he quipped. Evangeline noisily plopped a drumstick on his plate with a flashing stay-in-line-boy look.

Charlie subsided.

On a cue from her mother, Cory began brightly describing the Christmas cotillion. Her aunt listened with lively interest.

"I'll bet you girls are surrounded with beaux," she declared. "Such a fun time of life! And how about you, Phoebe? Did you have a good time?"

"I didn't go."

"Not go! Why, that's the event of the season for a young woman."

"I'm not so young anymore, Aunt Eunice. I've been out of college and on my own for a few years now."

"Well, that's no reason to shun a party and a chance to have a little fun! You're not a nun."

"Almost." Cory giggled. "She's been spending her time down at the peon colony across the river—when she's not teaching our maid how to read."

"Your maid is illiterate? Is she Irish?"

Mick's blue eyes darkened, and Fenya flushed. Phoebe's lips tightened as she caught their chagrin.

"No, Russian." Cory threw an embarrassed glance at Fenya. "That's her—serving."

"Well, Phoebe, that's a fine thing to do," Eunice said sanctimoniously. "But the peon colony—I'm not sure that's the place for a young lady."

"Fenya has ears—and feelings, Aunt. As for the colony, it needs attention, and that's why I think it's exactly the place for a young lady. This young lady anyway. The children are half-naked and undernourished. The shacks have no heat in the winter, and the streets are flowing with untreated sewage."

"Perhaps," Bernice Wentworth cut in stiffly, "we could speak of something more savory."

"Righto. Have some dressing, Mother," Charlie offered. "Phoebe just has one of these psychological complexes. She's trying to pay for her father's sins."

Harold Wentworth turned his heavy, pouched eyes on his son. "She wouldn't be able to try and pay for my sins or anybody else's if I weren't footing the bill," he growled. "I'm the one who gave her an education—and you, too, if you'd care to remember. But what are you doing with it?" They all blinked at the hot, angry silence for a minute.

Then Mick poured some Irish charm on the smolder. "That's it, sir," he soothed. "What are we doing with the opportunities we've been given? Something to think about. Especially at this time of year."

But Fenya could see that Phoebe was too hurt to let it go. "I don't know about Charlie, but I'm just trying to help people. I'm not trying to insult anybody or pay for anybody's sin. You all think I'm eccentric because I'm too busy to be out there looking for a husband." She flushed painfully. "And you, Charlie—you think that what I try to do is worthless because it's not part of some big political picture. You think you've got a corner on what social justice is—you want change from the top down. But you can't have it. There's no justice without love, and you can't love 'The People' with a capital P. You can only love persons, real men and women—and some of them are Mexicans and live in conditions you wouldn't tolerate for a minute! So if you love justice so much, be fair!"

Fenya and Evangeline exchanged a look of pride. Usually Phoebe kept her intense, ardent nature hidden behind her good manners. Mick applauded solemnly, never taking his eyes from her face.

"Absolutely, absolutely," intoned Harold Wentworth. "A man

likes to see a woman showing some Christian virtue in the community."

Phoebe rolled her eyes helplessly. And Fenya bending over with the dessert plates heard Mick mutter, "Couldn't be more true, Phoebe. You can only love a person—and, believe me, you've found a husband."

Phoebe vanquished him with an exasperated glance.

IN THE NEXT SEVERAL WEEKS, Phoebe showed Fenya some freelance articles that had suddenly appeared in the local newspapers. The features described conditions in the peon colony and called for city action.

"At least it's getting some attention now," she remarked. "I suppose you can guess who wrote them."

"It's not hard. Your future husband, right?"

"Not in any future I can see," remonstrated her friend.

"Why? You'd make a good team."

"I'm not ready to be a team."

"But at least you're a team with me. And maybe someday I'll be reading Mick's articles and writing to Piotr about the latest news, but hopefully he'll be home long before then."

"I think he'll have to be," Phoebe joked with an exaggerated sideways glance at Fenya's stomach. And, indeed, the time was close. Fenya had locked up the shanty and was staying with Aksinia "just in case." While she was there, a letter addressed to Piotr came from Russia. Aksinia excitedly gave it to her as soon as she came in from work.

"Ivan says it's from Piotr's Uncle Mikhail—from your native village!"

Fenya looked at it doubtfully. Her heart tripped and took up a new rhythm. How the last letter from this uncle had shattered them!

"Shall I open it or send it on to Piotr?"

"Better to open it. What if there's something Piotr needs to know right away? You may have to send a messenger. See if you can make anything out of it."

Fenya tore open the envelope and smoothed out the rough paper. But, though she was beginning to read English, she could not read her own mother tongue. Ivan Bogdanoff came in and offered to read it to her.

Mikhail Voloshin's letter was almost incoherent with rambling phrases—some about his poverty now that he and Marfa had returned from Persia. He included news of the farm and countryside, but the words *harvest of fire* kept cropping up. He also repeatedly referred to his son Andre who, Fenya knew, had been killed just after her sister's murder. Finally he came to the point. "I'm writing to let you know, Nephew, that your sister Nadya survived the bloodshed of 1905. She was lost to us for a while, but she has turned up and has been staying with us along with Semyon. Though she is a good worker and we have needed her help, we have decided to send her to you in the spring."

Mikhail mentioned Semyon again, saying that he would accompany his niece. Fenya, stunned that after two years of silence, this one member of Piotr's family was restored to them, could think of nothing but of what Piotr would say when he heard the news. And with Nadya, doubtless, would come the answers to the gnawing questions about the rest of his family. But Aksinia snatched the letter from her husband and stared at it with puckered brows as though she could draw further meaning from it.

"A miracle! His sister—after all this time! God be praised! But who is this Semyon? Mikhail sounds half-crazy, as though he can't tell the difference between those who are here and those who have given their souls to God. Do you think he means the old man?"

"Semyon Efimovich?" Fenya shook her head. "Maybe. He keeps talking about Andre, and, as we all know, Andre is dead."

"Or maybe it's some other Semyon. Maybe your sister-in-law has found a husband, and he's coming with her. Could that be?"

"Who knows. It's enough for us that she's alive! We'll have good news for Piotr. This will bring him home!"

But it wasn't the news from Russia that brought Piotr back to Los Angeles. Fenya was pressing sheets at the mangle—ignoring Evangeline's protests that she was doing too much—when the horrible gripping pains began. *It's too early, much too early!*

Evangeline half carried her to the downstairs bedroom with muttered prayers and scoldings. A call for help brought Charlie. "Ring up the doctor," Evangeline cried and held Fenya like a mother.

But Fenya hardly felt the strong, tender grip of her black hands. Something struck the lower part of her body with such violence that she bit the pillow. The pain shook her and then let go. She breathed in the lull, noticing her own breathing and the wild beating of her heart. *Something's wrong, something's wrong.* An iron-clawed dread worse than the pain dug into her. Then the pain came back, more acute and prolonged this time. When it stopped, her heart's cry came out of her mouth. She looked at Evangeline with agonized eyes. "Something's wrong!"

"Hold on, baby. Hold on to me and hold on to the Lord. That's right, baby." Evangeline's rich, soothing voice reached out to her in her tossing sea of pain. *Is she talking to me or the baby?* And Fenya, too, began talking to her cherished one, *Hold on, little one, hold on.* But her encouragement gave way to a high, piercing scream.

The doctor came in, but Fenya clung to Evangeline. "No, no . . . I need a midwife, a *babka!* We don't use doctors." Evangeline's voice was comforting, but her hands helped the strange man lift up her skirt and examine her. Fenya sweltered in an agony of embarrassment. Then suddenly it didn't matter as she writhed and kicked out her feet in pain.

The doctor in his brusque voice was saying something that she didn't want to hear. She didn't hear it, but retreated far away. The distance she flew into was filled with tiny pricks of light that flittered in airy chaos. Then they assembled into a whirling pattern, heart-catchingly beautiful. *He is coming.* . . . A gasp fled from her raw throat. She was filled with an excruciatingly joyful expectancy. *He is coming. He is coming.* . . . The babe? *No, you'll know Him. You know Him.*

She felt a call upon her—a fleeting, winged touch upon her face. She was being called by name. Not Fenya or Vassileyevna but another name—a name like music that summoned all the meaning from her history, all the beauty from her nature, and extruded a life's blood of significance from the dry stuff of her circumstances.

When Fenya awoke, all was still. The absence of pain and the absence of movement lodged on her like a cold stone in her hollowed middle. The lamp had been lit, and in its glow Phoebe's face looked down at her. The expression on that face told her everything she would not hear from the doctor.

"My baby is dead."

Phoebe bent her tear-marred, swollen face over the bed and began smoothing Fenya's hair with a gentle, motherly hand. Fenya closed her eyes trying to remember the only thing that could help her bear it. *He is gone from me, my precious one, my little berry. Gone.* Barely, barely, she could remember the clear-voiced Glory that had called him up—and had called Natasha and Andre and all those who had gone before. *I understand.* And barely, barely, she remembered that there was a name for her that would dispel all darkness and leave her seeing clearly. But she could not remember what it was, only that it existed and that she would know it when she heard it again. *But for now, my arms are empty.* And she wept for the emptiness.

Finally she slept. When she woke, Piotr was there holding her hand, a cipher of pain carved into his forehead. The loss of their son rose in front of them and lived between their two glances. Stupefied by her ordeal, Fenya felt like some cold, limp thing that had been washed up in the tide. At the same time, as she held tightly to her husband's hand, there grew in her a warm awareness of a teeming sap moving secretly through all the hidden conduits of her being. This sap branched from other richer sap, and it was meant for life—to seek rooting and to bear fruit. But for what purpose was a mystery to her.

XI

The Steppe

In the second year since Nadya's departure, Vaktang watched spring scale the mountains as he and Nodar led their herds to lower pastures. It had been a winter of change, and he was glad to see it over. They shared a meal on a rock ledge where the warmer air of the low meadows lapped at them in scented eddies. Vaktang knew what he would find in those fertile, Edenic glades. The thought of it struck at him like thrown stones. *Nadya!* Her name breathed up to him with warm fragrance. But it was a wafting memory only. Nadya was off in some nameless village somewhere in the Kura valley. *She probably barely remembers me. But here I am like a mountain goat on the spine-ridge of a great peak, and I must go down one way or the other.*

Nodar glanced at him curiously, reluctant to break into his thoughts, a quickly suppressed glint of exasperation in his gray eyes. This combination of awkward deference and secret impatience was typical of his relations with his brother in recent months. *And why not? Wouldn't I feel the same?* Vaktang was being offered everything that Nodar wanted—and yet Vaktang couldn't quite bring himself to reach out his hand and take it!

Esma had grieved for the lost Nadya and baby Semyon, her pain grinding and whirling within her until it spun out the idea that one of her sons must marry, take up management of the household, farms, and flocks, and provide her with many grandchildren. Who else but the eldest? Already she had entered into negotiations with a family in Mestia who had a beautiful, lively daughter. But it was Nodar, not Vaktang, who was netted in the sparkle of her black eyes.

Nodar began gathering up their gear. "One moment," Vaktang said, still absorbed in his thoughts.

"Take your time." Was there something coolly bitter in the way he said it? Maybe not, but Vaktang missed the old comradely joking ways.

"I will," he shot back. "My time is my own—and my thoughts!"

"Your own . . . yes! But they affect others—many others! Why do you wait? Is this beauty not good enough for you? You know *she* will never return. Why cage me in this misery? Have done with it! Marry, and God be with you. And when you're settled and Mother is secure in her life, I'll go. Far away. It will be easier that way."

"Maybe I'm the one who should go."

Nodar spat. "That's impossible, and you know it! You would be foolish to give up your place in the family—and a girl any man would want to marry."

Vaktang shrugged. He understood the hot hurt in his brother's eyes.

"Maybe we should both go, eh? Like the old days when we'd tramp off to the cities of Russia and Georgia. Remember?"

"So long ago . . ."

"Only two years," Vaktang reminded him—and yet Nodar was right. A tedious wasteland of time stretched between that time and this.

Their white, wolfish dogs began barking. A dim figure appeared on the rock-rubbled bank of slush that rimmed the dell—a moving blur of dirty white against the jetsam of the recent thaw. It was Shavleg. The dogs quieted immediately and went back to their business among the sheep and horses. The blond giant's dark yellow teeth showed briefly in his pink face as he squatted beside them.

"Well, brothers, the Franks are up to their old tricks. A group of them has arrived in Nalchik, and they're eager to set their footprints on the snows of Elburz! I traveled with them four years ago, and they politely request my services. Last time they left me this souvenir." He pulled out a big, outlandishly carved pipe with a silver mouthpiece, filled it with home-grown tobacco, and began puffing.

"Where are these Franks from?"

"Germany. Usually the holiday climbers come up through Tiflis. But these Franks think that since they've crossed half of Russia to come here, I can cross the ranges to meet them in Nalchik." Shavleg pulled thoughtfully on his pipe, becoming even less distinct as he breathed out. "And this I will do. For money. And souvenirs."

"And I will go with you," Vaktang found himself saying, "as far as Nalchik. We need to buy a stallion for the herd, and a Kabarda stud would be best. That way you'll have company through the passes and across the steppe."

"Good." Shavleg passed the pipe, and Vaktang took a puff, narrowing his eyes to look at the mountains hazed with the smoke of his breathing. *They are fading away from me*.

"It will be good," he explained to Nodar. "I need to think."

"Take your time."

"I will."

And he did. Through the passes of Svanetia, along the spring-swollen surge of the Sadon River, and across the worn shambles of the Bezingi glacier's moraine, he took his time, letting his brother's sudden rancor and his mother's grasping dominion seep away from him. The blond giant trudging beside him was mostly silent.

The first night they shared tea and *basturma* beside a small fire of rhododendron stalks. All at once the starry stillness was broken by the crash of a tumbling ice cliff, its fall lit up by a sudden sparkle of innumerable lights. Vaktang had seen such luminous avalanches before. Tonight its strange beauty ached within him. Shavleg grunted with interest, and his light eyes gleamed.

"The Franks claim to know all about this miracle," he said. "They call it a phenomenon brought about by friction, but only when the air is just so." He laughed hugely, shook his head, and then hunched forward with a conspirator's wink. "The Abkazians tell a story of a lost valley where men look down into an abyss of darkness; yet they can hear the voices of men and the neighing of horses and crowing of cocks. They say that the darkness befell by a miracle of God when a cursed emperor of Persia came upon Christian men to destroy them and force them to bow down to idols. But when this haughty and evil man rode forth with his host, a great cloud came out of heaven and covered them. And since then the heathen host has wandered in darkness."

"I've heard the story," Vaktang said.

"Well, I told this tale to the Franks, and, behold, an Englishman claimed to know all about it. He said that the Arabs tell a like story about a lost valley swathed in cloud where folk look down to see tiny men and houses, but none can go down; nor can the people of the valley come up. And he determined that his lost valley of legend is Svanetia—our home country!" He slapped his knee, and his eyes prodded Vaktang for a reaction. "Are we heathen living in darkness? Or idolaters of Persia?" Vaktang let his face register rueful disdain, but his eyes drifted to the fire at Shavleg's next question: "Is our Svanetia a lost valley?"

When they came into Balkar, Shavleg surveyed the hill dwellings of the Mountain Turks with his wide, childish eyes. "Look," he said, sweeping his thick arm toward the outlying stone huts, "the dead abide in houses while the living delve the earth." He laughed, showing his dark yellow teeth in the vague outline of his mouth.

Vaktang shrugged. It was true that the village houses were built deep into the rocky hillside while the town was surrounded by ancient tombs built in clusters like beehives. Shavleg laughed his empty laugh. "It's a sad business when a man's customs give the bones of his fathers better fare than the children of his body."

But Shavleg was silent when they crossed the downs toward Nalchik. He turned aside to the forest of Urvan and there shot some pheasants, which they feasted on that day and the next.

"Don't the Franks expect you?" Vaktang asked.

"They will see me soon enough." His teeth tore into white flesh, and golden juice threaded the blond beard.

Nalchik was bright with green roofs and whitewashed walls as its picturesque cottages shone in their garden plots. Shavleg strode off toward the government building. There he met a nervous Mountain Jew—one of the *Tati* of Nalchik who had lived in the mountains since the time of the Babylonians. Vaktang watched as, with much expression and flailing of arms, they reached some kind of agreement. Then with a gesture, the big Svanetian lumbered off to where a mounted party had gathered. He swung himself onto a horse and, with a last wave at Vaktang, cantered toward the town's stockaded wall. The small square filled with a confusion of dust and horses.

Shading his eyes, Vaktang could make out Shavleg's dark mount, but the outline of the man himself was obscured by pale road dust and the glare of whitewashed walls. It looked as though he had faded into time like one of his strange legends. *I'll never see him again*, Vaktang thought with conviction. Then he went off and haggled with a Kabarda horse dealer for a strong, dark bay stallion.

Later Vaktang strolled the marketplace where he bought an embroidered scarf from an old woman. It was a deep azure patterned with the fine-spun gold and silver embroidery for which the Kabarda women are famous. He held it to the sun, stretching it between his hands and watching the sparkling play of color. *But whom is it for?* Twitching with chagrin, he shoved it impatiently into his pocket. *You're a fool*, he chided himself. Mounting his stallion, he set off across the steppe.

Along the edge of the town, the dogwood was in bloom. Fits and spurts of Russian-style settlements clustered here and there, then stopped. He left behind the green grain fields of Kabardino, galloping into the lands to the east and north. The mountains had fallen away into low, blue dreams behind him, and the vast steppe stretched out—empty and without memory. The steppe called him with its flatness and its openness. Speed and mindless flight and a mad flinging of self against the nothingness! All of these things rang out across the stretched distance, and man and horse heard them together and together flew with swift forgetfulness and flung with madness and fury. The stallion stretched out his neck, and Vaktang bent to his speed. When the horse was lathered and heaving with exhaustion, Vaktang twisted his hands in the reins and pulled him roughly back. They halted on the brink of a steep-sided ravine.

Now! he thought. A metallic wink caught his eye. Looking down, he saw that the embroidered scarf had worked its way out of his pocket and was flaunting beneath his cartridge holder in a sly feminine way. He snatched it up and flung it from him. It caught on a tuft of feather grass and twinkled coyly at him. Goading the confused stallion, Vaktang rode headlong at it again and again until it slipped to the ground and was pounded under hooves. *You're a fool*, he told himself. He stopped and looked about.

To the east, to the north, and to the west the great Russian steppe spread its silver mantle of feather grass across the earth. Flung into the rich Ukraine, fringing the Black Sea and the Caucasus, and sweeping across the Urals into Mongolia, the steppe imposed its broad rule of hawk-haunted loneliness. *And I am on the edge of emptiness.* Panting from his hard ride, Vaktang listened to the hollow wind in the ravine echo in his own breast. Something in the beckoning expanse whispered that there would be peace and forgetfulness. *It's a lie. Peace and annihilation are not the same.*

The dour, expressionless land wrinkled with ravines had nothing to say to him. But he himself, Vaktang Rukhadze, had something to say! His heart filled with a blind outrage. *I gave, I gave—everything I knew of love, and I was given nothing in return!* The steppe answered him back, *I gave, I gave—everything I knew of love, and I was given nothing in return!* The diffuse, chaotic echoes assembled into a hierarchy of cogent thought. *I gave, I gave—everything I knew of love! And I was given nothing in return. Return, return to Me, O man.*

Vaktang squinted across the empty lands; he fell silent—even in the word-forming nub of his brain. But his soul cried out across the steppe, *Where are You?* There was no answer, but a fleeting impression of smiling came to him with warmth and with summons. Could he trust his own impression? It was such a small thing, and the vast, tugging emptiness was so huge. A soft wind changed the face of the steppe as the feather grass bowed to reveal its silver-lilac underside. *I will not plunge my soul's distress into nothingness, but I will seek.* Vaktang swept the land with keen, expert eyes. *After all, I am a surveyor.*

He retrieved the battered scarf and slapped it a few times across his thigh to remove the dust. Then he mounted the Kabarda stallion and returned to the track to Balkar. As he rode, his confusion began to assemble itself around a burning ember of intent. *But whose intent?* It seemed impossible to him to go back to Ushguli, to take up a farmer's life, to marry a beauty who had no hold on his heart. The ember within him burned and ripened to a flame of desire. *But what for? What am I to do?* Follow. *Follow?* And Vaktang thought of how the men of Svanetia will carry an ember for starting fires in a hollow fennel stalk—sometimes for great distances. *This I will do.*

Coming to Balkar, he turned his horse toward Gebi rather than toward the passes into Svanetia. He allowed himself a leisurely ride through the pine and birch forests and flower fields of the northern

Caucasus and then spent the night at a crude way stop in Oni. At dawn he rode straight to the new church in Gebi. A trio of stacked arches housed the church bell, and behind this tiered edifice was the church itself with the familiar conical tower. But Gebi's new church was a poor version of the old Georgian style. In his own country of Svanetia, the churches had little of the medieval Georgian but hearkened back to older times—the days of Byzantium.

Vaktang, bludgeoned by something huge and nameless and drawn on by a minute spark of an impression, shouldered through the doors and into the sanctuary. The skirts of his *tcherkeska* flared about him as he threw himself, splay-kneed, onto the cold floor. A great inarticulate cry rose from him. His bent-fingered hands grasped at the elusive. *Hear me, hear me.*

The familiar silver icons studded with crude turquoises and other precious stones gleamed mutely. The stone curve of the apse held his inner cry. Then he had a sense of walls falling, of piercing newness. Every fiber in him was stretched to breaking, and he felt himself exquisitely attuned. *I am the One whose hand spans the heavens, and My hand's span will measure your life and fill it to its utmost filling. Give it to Me.*

"I give it, I give it," Vaktang murmured. Then dragging thoughts of all he would not give took hold of him and shook him. "I lie, I lie," he groaned. His mind filled with the flocks and ploughland and the castellated farm—all of the precious things held out to him. And his heart filled with the memory of the dour-gaited girl walking away from him though he had never let her go. "I give it, I give it," he repeated. *God help me, I'm purged.* His sense of inner cleanness was so acute that he jerkily looked about the church to see if some change in the atmosphere had caused it. There was nothing—only the strong figure of a rough-haired man striding toward the iconostasis. The man turned, and Vaktang recognized Grigol of Khevsuretia.

The Khevsur knew him immediately and smiled with such warmth that Vaktang wondered, *Can he know?* He scrambled to his feet, weapons clanking. With a friendly gesture, Grigol beckoned to him.

"Let me return your hospitality," he urged. "Come and stay with us."

Vaktang followed to a balconied stone house on the fringe of the town. It was set in a dell with the towers of Gebi looming on its knoll, green cornfields sweeping up to the mountains, and the icy torrents raging below. A young boy played under a walnut tree, and inside were two beautiful woman. One was Grigol's icon-faced wife; the other was a woman with lean, chiseled features and black hair—a Tartar perhaps or a Kurd.

Nina set out the samovar, and the two men drank tea together. Hesitantly, Grigol touched on their last meeting. Vaktang turned away in sudden distress; the memory of Nadya stolidly walking down the slate path away from him hazed his mind. But he let it go and looked back clearly at the Khevsur.

"What became of her?"

"We took her back to her native village—near Tiflis. She went to live with her uncle, a rich man who lives in a big brick house with a mill. But his sons were killed in the uprisings. My wife was loathe to leave her. The outbuildings were still blackened by fire, and the whole place seemed desolate. The two old people were half-crazed with grief. But my wife's kinsman does business in the place, and he has promised to look out for her. And, too, there was talk of sending the girl to her brother in America, but that is unlikely. The uncle and his wife need her labor."

"Was she glad to see her people?"

Grigol studied his hands and then flicked one of his direct looks at Vaktang. "No. She did not have any kind of feeling at all. It's as though she were heavily moving in all the black smother of what had happened. Perhaps if she could rejoin her brother, it would be different. But as it was, we never saw her smile."

Vaktang was filled with an odd excitement. *But I did. I saw her smile.*

The Khevsur shot a keen glance at him. Then he said something strange. "You are a faithful man. Your faith will set you free."

I was right! He knows! Vaktang exulted. "That's true! Today I feel that I've squirmed out from under some weighty oppression . . . and that I'm free as I've never been." He explained all that he had experienced on the steppe and in the church at Gebi.

The Khevsur's blunt-featured face ignited with understanding.

"So," Vaktang concluded, "I'm free—but empty as the steppe."

"It's the steppe that bears the richest soil," Grigol answered.

"Good, black soil for fruitfulness and abundance. But what has happened within you is more important than houses or farms. And that is what you must act upon. It's as though you carry within you a map, and you'll have to tread its ways to find the intent of the Mapmaker."

This thought reverberated in Vaktang. What had seemed to him an impossible tangle of cross-purposes and warring desires now became as simple as taking a walk. He was filled with excitement. "Now! Tell me about this kinsman of your wife, and tell me about this village of Russians!"

"My wife is half-Armenian. Her half brother Sirakan ran a store in a village partially settled by Molokans. But rioters destroyed the shop. Somehow he continues to trade in the area, but he prefers to use a covered wagon—like a Gypsy. If you want to see the girl, he would be the one to contact. The Molokans would bar you from her."

"I know. But should I?"

Grigol shrugged. "I don't know. But this odd meeting between you and me, brother, is not for nothing. . . . Besides, can you prevent yourself?"

Vaktang laughed. "Probably not—not since I heard that she may not be happy. . . . Yet it's different now somehow." The grasping bitterness in him had loosened, and now he only wanted to assure himself that all was well with this girl who was so precious to him.

"It won't be easy," Grigol warned. "But Sirakan may think of a way."

Vaktang noticed that the black-haired woman pricked up her ears every time they mentioned the Armenian shopkeeper. Later she approached him as he was bidding his host farewell.

"If you go to the village," she asked, "will you take this to Sirakan Abajarian?" She slipped a folded bit of paper into his hand.

As he left Gebi, Vaktang noticed the storyteller holding court on the village green. He remembered the afternoon when he had echoed the story to Nadya. And he remembered how she leaned back to him, listening to the tale of the lamenting Tariel going forth throughout the earth seeking his lost bride. *Only now do I understand it!* And this was because he was not thinking of Nadya as the lost one but of himself—cast forth into the empty steppe but sought out and found.

Later he stood on a high ledge overlooking the valley of the three villages where the barley fields of Ushguli were greening under the sun. He knew he was leaving it. He would go down and kiss his mother and take a second son's portion, leaving his inheritance to Nodar. He looked hard at the little homesteads and fields spangled with miniature sheep and tiny horses. *So far away.* And he remembered Shavleg's story of the lost valley. *Svanetia,* he thought. Where year after year the snows of winter are replaced by the snows of mountain rhododendron, where rivers spring full-grown from the ice ledges of glaciers, where the avalanches of the great ranges fall on beds of yellow lilies. *You are my lost valley.* . . . He thought of the Mingrelian storyteller's formula: "There was and there never was . . ."

It looked to him as though the whole collection of hamlets and fields were something that he could hold in his palm and give away. To mark the significance of the moment, he took out the azure scarf and, holding it over the cliff, let it drift into the chasm. It flared and floated in the warm upward currents. A *flag of surrender—or a pennant of triumph.*

Then he set off on the stony switchbacks, letting the broadleaf glades and pine forests mete out occasional glimpses of his home village. But even as he drew closer, the proud towers and winter-etched stones and miraculous flower meadows of Ushguli seemed distant, remote—something from another time.

"Sirakan Abajarian? He is not here. I think you will find him on the Post Road to Delizan." The young sower cradled his sack of seed and swept his hand toward the south. Vaktang leaned over the sprightly head of his dun-colored gelding. His heart was pounding as he got out, "And Mikhail Voloshin—where is his house?"

The peasant's open face darkened as he measured Vaktang with a suspicious look. "You have some business with him?"

"Yes. A family matter." Vaktang held his eyes, trying to break through the young man's hesitation.

"Well, it's no secret," the peasant answered finally. "His house is the big brick one. Follow the lane upward toward the hills, and you'll see it right in front of the grain mill."

Vaktang followed the track, letting the gelding pick his way along a path that was half lane, half muddy river. *What if she's there? What if I see her? Maybe it would have been better to see Sirakan first.*

But the horse kept plodding through the mire until they came to a brick house with blue-painted eaves and shutters. Vaktang could see that it had once been a rich house, but it had fallen into disrepair. The whole yard and homestead had a forlorn, disheveled air. The blue woodwork was weathered, and some of the shutters hung disconsolately awry. What had once been a barn was charred rubble. The threshing floor behind it was awash with ashes and mud and the droppings of the lean and scrappy chickens that pecked about the yard.

Vaktang started as a side door opened, and a woman as lean and slovenly as the hens appeared. Blue-stockinged scrawny legs stuck out from one end of a bundled lump of clothing; a red scrawny neck stuck out from the other. Her faded eyes took him in and spat him out.

"Go away!" she shrieked.

"Wait! I'm looking for someone. Tell me where she is, and I'll go."

"They're dead. All dead. Get away, you devil. And take your gun . . ." Her voice came out in a shrill mewling, but Vaktang could hear the rumbling of a deeper voice from within. "All dead!" she screeched. She was suddenly jerked into the darkness, and the door slammed.

He stared at the desolate house for a moment. "I'll be back," he promised. "If she's here, I'll be back." The barnyard fowl answered him with their mad cacklings.

It was late evening when he found Sirakan, not on the Post Road, but on the side road to Vorontsovka. He was leaning against a canvas-covered, tub-shaped wagon nestled in a birch copse. His brawny arms were folded across his chest, and his eyelids flicked as he took in the abuse being flung at him by two peasant women.

As he drew nearer, Vaktang could see that the upbraiding was half-joking, and the big Armenian twitched his mustache and grimaced like a bull being plagued by flies.

"You've given up!" scolded one of the women. She pushed her tongue into the gap between her teeth. She had a broad, bland face lit up by kindly, merry eyes. "You're letting evil have the upper hand. We Molokans have been burnt out and beaten, yes, and had our kindred—even our children—snatched away from us. But we always come back and rebuild our villages and replant our fields."

"Oh? And how about those who flee to other lands. That happens too," Sirakan countered.

"Of course! Of course! Sometimes God leads us to rebuild somewhere else, but you're rebuilding nowhere. Just lopping around the roads like a homeless Gypsy."

"But truth be known, I am homeless," Sirakan groaned exaggeratedly. "A homeless orphan. So be kind."

"You're too big to be an orphan. I don't feel sorry for you."

"A hard-hearted woman—you just want a place to buy salt and calico. It's your own convenience you're thinking of."

"What's wrong with salt? It's true. I need things like every housewife. A village needs a store, but we have a shopkeeper who thinks he's a holy pilgrim."

"What do you need?" Sirakan began rummaging in the wagon with mock eagerness. "You name it—I've got it. A wagon's as good as a shop if it's well stocked. What do you want? Rugs from Azerbaijan, silks from Persia, tea from Sochi, salt—our specialty—straight from Siberia. You can taste the taiga in it." The women laughed at his clowning, but they fell silent, and their eyes rounded in alarm when they caught sight of Vaktang. The Armenian frowned and planted himself firmly beside his wagon.

"Do you want something?" he challenged. His deep-set eyes with their dark circles took in Vaktang's sturdy gelding and gleaming weapons.

The Russian housewife found her voice and chided, "God be with you, but no man needs such guns and daggers. You've put me all in a fright!"

Sirakan, who apparently had decided that Vaktang meant no harm, shushed her. "Nothing would frighten you enough to freeze your tongue!" But the second woman, a plump peasant with a corn-colored braid, was still speechless.

"You are Sirakan Abajarian?"

The Armenian nodded, his eyes still holding Vaktang's.

"I need to talk to you." Vaktang flushed red and glanced sideways at the women.

"Let me finish our business, and then I'll talk."

When the women had made their purchases, Sirakan turned back to the young Svan. "So. What is it you need?"

"I'm looking for someone. I was told that you would help."

"Told by whom?"

"Your sister and her husband in Gebi." The Armenian's manner warmed, and Vaktang explained his journey.

"You've come for nothing," Sirakan said gruffly. "The Voloshin girl left for America. Let me see—only a few weeks ago. She went with a whole crowd of Molokans who took the train to Bremen. Right now she's somewhere in the middle of the Atlantic Ocean." The deep, pensive eyes registered Vaktang's reaction.

"Lazengales!" Vaktang whispered. "So far!"

The Armenian only sighed. "So-o-o either your journey is over, or it's just beginning." He paused, studying the young man. "But stay. Have some tea and tell me about my sister."

"Your sister—she is well, happy, I think. Things are well in Gebi. The boy, Grigol . . ." Vaktang gasped. He felt as though his body had been plunged into the cold waters of the Atlantic. "But Lazengales! So far!"

Sirakan's mouth hooked down on the pity that darkened his eyes. He pushed a glass of hot tea into the young man's hand. "Sit down," he said.

Vaktang was too exhausted to hide his shame. He sank onto a birch log and sipped his tea while Sirakan made up the evening's fire.

"So. You've come to love a Molokan girl," he said brusquely. "The Molokans don't give their daughters lightly—and never to outsiders. You know that. But this one—Nadya, I mean—she has no father to give her, and her uncle is a broken man. They made a workhorse out of her, and there was little joy in her life even before that. So I talked her people into sending her to America. A holy calling, I argued, and the tight-fisted old man finally gave in. I thought she'd have a better life with Piotr."

"You did well. But I—I would have cared for her."

"You must be the young man who found her after the uprisings. Well, God will reward your faithfulness. But a mountain tribesman and a Molokan?" Sirakan shrugged at the hopelessness of it.

"Your sister is married to a tribesman. And every time she looks at her husband, her eyes shine with joy."

"Well, yes. It's true that Nina has found something." Sirakan became morose. "No, you're right—but there's something in the times. In times of upheaval, it seems that some of the ways of people are challenged. Some respond by seeing things in a new way, and they reach up to something higher, something that transcends the cultural differences. Others become even more entrenched, and they revert back to old tribal warrings that should have ceased centuries ago."

"Exactly. That's exactly what I want—to reach up and transcend the differences!"

Sirakan looked at him curiously. "So. You would marry a Russian—a woman from the people who have tried to take over your country and have oppressed Georgia for the past hundred years?"

Vaktang shrugged. "What does that have to do with her—or me?"

"And I," Sirakan marveled softly, "I can love a woman whose people have tortured and killed mine."

Vaktang jumped up as if he'd been stung. "I forgot! A note—from the woman Irina . . ." He patted his pockets, then remembered he had the note rolled up and stuck into one of his cartridge holders. "For you. She was eager that you get it soon."

Sirakan glanced at it briefly and then silently tucked it into his vest.

"So," Vaktang asked raising his brows, "has the Kurdish woman transcended cultural differences?"

Sirakan's voice swelled and broke. "She's obliterated them."

THEY PARTED in the morning. "Where will you go?" Sirakan asked.

"Today? I'm not sure. But someday I'll set my foot in Lazengales. I knew when I left the mountains that I'd started on a long journey. Little did I know how long! But I'll have to take it bit by bit and find work along the way."

Sirakan grimaced beneath his mustache. "That could take years. And I think that the open door to America will be shut soon. Better keep your way stops short. What work do you do?"

The young Svan narrowed his gray eyes. Above him leaf and twig of the overhanging birches snipped the blue-pink dawnlight into fluttering flags. Beyond him the road stretched toward Tiflis and the Surami Ranges and the far cities of the coast.

"I'm a surveyor."

Sirakan watched Vaktang's upright figure mount and ride away. At the off-turning the rider spun and waved his cap. "Maybe we will meet again! In Lazengales!" he called.

Sirakan grinned and shook his head as he waved him away. Then he loaded his wagon and urged his team back toward the village. The square was quiet in the morning. Three tall pines spired as serenely as always, and most of the squat buildings had not budged in all the turmoil of the 1905 revolution. But the Armenian shop was still a blackened pit. *Blackened and stocked with memories best left packed in ash.* If there was anything of value left, it had been taken long ago. Charred beams sagged from the upper floor where they had lived. He recognized a distorted twist of iron as part of his parents' bedstead.

But Aram and Maria Abajarian had flown from destruction to destruction. They had gone to Khankend and had been slaughtered there with all of the other Armenians. Sirakan had searched for them in the days following that terrible autumn, but he found nothing. *As I find nothing here.*

But burning in his vest pocket was a challenge. To meet it, he would have to put a tombstone on all of his past life and truly begin to live as another person. "Impossible," he ground out between his teeth. "I am an Armenian! Now more so than ever!" But, eager to be argued with, he pulled out the note from Irina and read it again.

Then he shrugged as he looked at the shambles around him. "There's already a tombstone on my past life." He studied the heap of rubble that had once been the stove with a practical eye. The part adjoining the back wall was still recognizable. Carefully, he pried a loose tile from a concealed alcove and pulled out a metal box. The box had been Aram's. Sirakan knew it contained something he would need to start a new life in a new place. Capital.

Sirakan wrapped the box in a rag and tucked it beneath a bolt of calico in his tinker's wagon. He took up the reins and clucked at the horses. With their usual reluctance, they lumbered toward the Post Road. As the wagon swayed and creaked, he calculated how long it would take him to go from Tiflis to Kutaisi and from there north on the Mamison Road to Gebi. Three days? Four maybe? Four days at most, and he would meet again the woman who had the courage to sever everything and begin anew. He thought of her severe forehead and tender mouth, her outer intensity and inner softness. He wrapped the reins around his left hand and took out her note again. He shook his head as he read it. *Unbelievable! I have been given beauty for ashes.*

XII

A Portion for Jackals

In Galveston, Texas, one of the pilgrim Molokans—a notorious prankster—returned to the ship wearing a Western shirt, a ten-gallon hat, and cowboy boots. His beard had been neatly shaved. His young wife frantically threw herself from one side of the stern railing to another—desperately searching for her delayed husband. She gasped when an oddly attired stranger kissed her heartily. A crowd of waiting Molokans exploded into roars of laughter.

"But, Manya, you were saying I should dress a little more Western for my job search in Los Angeles," the jokester pleaded meekly. His shocked wife was speechless, and the travelers guffawed again. Even Nadya smiled. The woman gulped down her stunned surprise while, beneath his twitching eyebrows, her husband's merry eyes searched the chuckling Russians. When he caught sight of Semyon Gavrilovich, he came over and presented him with a small cowboy hat.

"Perfect size for a three-year-old Russian head—that's what the salesman told me. I had to get it for somebody, and you're my favorite three-year-old." He grinned.

Semyon was fiercely fond of the hat and would not be parted from it even when Nadya struggled to find room for them to sleep in the crowded steerage section. By the time they reached Los Angeles, the combination of salt-spray and bedtime clutchings had reshaped it into something that had little resemblance to a hat. But Semyon still insisted on wearing it. On the train he'd fix fellow passengers with a challenging stare and spout out the expression he'd learned from his joking friend, "Yippee yi ayee." Then he would smile in a way that would pull a grin even from the most cantankerous traveler. Nadya looked at him curiously. With the dented cowboy hat slammed over his brown curls and his best *kosovorotka*, he did look a little strange. *We may be seeing Piotr in an hour or two.* Fighting protests from the owner, she took the hat and tried to brush and shape it. *Not much use.* Semyon grabbed it and pulled it down over his eyes. "Yippee yi ayee!"

"What a little showoff," teased an old bunya. "He's got a mind of his own, that one. Where does he get it? You're not that way at all."

No, I have no mind of my own. It's been blotted up . . . She could bring to mind and dismiss the whole of the past two years in her home village with a single image. A curiously shaped black opening and beyond—a dim, empty flatness. Very little stood out: The day she had gone back to her family's *izba* and left again; the day Sirakan had come to her saying, "This is no life for you. What do you want? Do you want anything?" She shrugged even at the memory. And then there was the day that her uncle told her that she would be going to America.

"My life is over," he said, "but yours is just beginning. You don't believe me, do you?" She didn't.

They stepped out onto the platform in Los Angeles, Semyon forging ahead. It took her a moment in the crowded confusion to spot Piotr and Fenya. By their faces she knew that they had seen her. She grabbed the boy and carried him, watching Fenya's face flush with fascinated awe. Semyon and hat were almost crushed in the long family embrace. Then Nadya set him down and tilted the hat to reveal the unmistakable Voloshin features. The wide-set brown eyes stared up at eyes almost exactly the same, and the high, broad cheekbones—these, too, Galina had given to both her sons. The angled cut from cheek to jaw was almost covered by Piotr's beard, and in Semyon it was still padded with baby fat, but it was there.

"This," Nadya said simply, "is Semyon, your brother."

Piotr was stupefied. "My brother! How . . ." He did not look at Fenya, but he kept touching her, her arm, her kerchief.

"Our mother gave birth to him about five months after you left. She knew—even when she was saying goodbye to you. But she didn't want to give you another reason for staying in Russia. She knew what was coming! Now . . . well, as things turned out, I knew that she would want him to be with you." Nadya watched Fenya flame with excitement, then kneel, and, putting two fingers beneath his chin, stare intently at the little boy. Fenya could not take her eyes off him, as though the looking were a thirsty drinking, slowly filling some hollowed reservoir in her. He stared back with that who-are-you-and-what-are-you-doing-here look characteristic of him. Fenya was enthralled.

"He's . . . he's so strong! And so . . . so plucky. But I can see the sweetness. Why, he's just like old Semyon Efimovich." Fenya smiled all over her face, and Nadya noticed Piotr watching his wife, his mouth quivering within the soft brush of his beard. Fenya drew closer to Semyon, and he rewarded her with one of his quick, fierce hugs. She was more smitten than ever.

"Well, he's always been that way," Nadya said offhandedly. "From the very beginning! A lion of a baby as they used to say." For some reason she felt like weeping.

"Are you a little lion?" Fenya asked him tenderly.

"Yippee yi ayee," he affirmed.

An evening mist began to gather as they walked back to the eighth ward. Piotr pulled Nadya's arm through his and kept squeezing it. As they passed under puddled light from the street lamps, he slowed and looked at her intently. Fenya followed with Semyon, who kept up a good pace on his sturdy little legs. His wondering, combative eyes followed the clanking, swaying bulk of a streetcar with its glowing windows. Light from storefronts and pool halls and street lamps caught the silver in the streetcar tracks and made a dotted line pointed toward the milky river mist. Nadya's feet and eyes became heavier and heavier, and the weight of what she knew she must tell Piotr dragged at her.

"Are you tired, sister? It's a terrible journey, I know!"

"No. Not tired."

They came to a small shack, much smaller than their *izba*. But inside, it was scrupulously clean. A red iron bed piled with Russian quilts and embroidered cloths took up most of the front room. Fenya lifted Semyon onto it, and he sank down comfortably. For good measure she wrapped a bit of quilt around him and hugged him in that. He squirmed, half-smiling, and she went out to the kitchen.

"It's small, I know," Piotr apologized. "And the trains . . . well, you'll hear soon enough."

"But we're comfortable, and we'll all be together," Fenya cut in. "I have some good soup, and Aksinia has sent you some *piroshkiya* and pastries for your first day."

Nadya ate hungrily. But Piotr put down his spoon and began pacing. Semyon climbed down from the bed and, after taking a few spoonfuls of soup from Fenya, stomped around inspecting the hut and looking carefully into all the corners. Nadya watched the two of them through her hair, waiting for them to collide.

"We had no idea!" Piotr was saying. "When Uncle Mikhail kept mentioning a Semyon—well, we wondered! His letters were so odd. Does he mean our *dzedha*, Semyon Efimovich, dead these three winters? It even crossed our minds that you had married and were coming with a husband."

"But this little one," Fenya interjected.

"Yes! That this life, this person exists, and has been living and moving closer to us these few years, and we never knew! It's . . . it's too much." Piotr started as he backed into his young brother and then swooped to pick him up. "And you, yippee-yi-ayee cowboy, what are you looking for?"

Semyon squirmed down to his usual independent stance, and the three adults laughed. Then, suddenly serious, Piotr turned to his sister. "What *is* he looking for?"

Nadya stared at him while the gray of river mist and the gray of memory thickened to a dark blot in her mind. "Uplis-Tsikhe," she whispered. "The caves. That's where I lost them—all of them. All but him."

Piotr came back to the table and sat, his head in his hands, while her words conjured up Gavril and Galina and Dausha.

"Our mother—I knew she wanted me to bring them, somehow bring them to you. Both Dausha and Semyon. *'Do this one thing for me—from heaven I'll thank you!'* But Dausha had the fever and died beside the river." Nadya paused, thinking of her small sister's sweet face. She decided not to tell Piotr about the ants.

"I couldn't bury them. I left mother and father in the cave. And

Dausha . . . A young man came and buried her. . . . And I—we left with him. The young man."

Piotr's head came up. "Did he harm you?"

"No. He was good. Full of honor . . . and, and . . ." All the things that Vaktang was full of swooped down on her with bright flashings. She fought them away.

"But I wasn't able to save them. I couldn't even bury them. At night I heard the jackals . . ." Burial was of utmost importance to the Molokans, and Nadya shuddered, avoiding her brother's eyes. *Shrieking, laughing, whining—the jackals closed in* . . .

"Don't look like that, Nadya. That doesn't matter. They rested in hewn cave tombs like Christ Himself. And, like Him, they will rise on the last day. No scavenger of the earth or of hell itself could change that. You have done well—better than you know! To bring this child through just when our hearts were yearning for a child . . ." He glanced at his wife who was softly crooning to the little boy while her eyes held Piotr's.

"But you, sister, you've walked through a terrible valley—and alone."

"I did little. It seemed almost as though I were being carried along by something."

"Well, you are here, praise be. Maybe it was this little fellow's strong will that pulled you along. He has no doubts about what he wants."

"Maybe so. It's true that I kept hearing Mother's voice—it filled my dreams—telling me to bring him. And now I have." Nadya spread her hands in a flat gesture.

"And you've brought yourself—don't forget! Mother wanted that, too."

Nadya stared at the blue emblem in the bottom of her soup bowl. "I don't know. I'm not sure she thought of that."

"What are you saying? Of course she did! She believed in *Pohod!* She wanted all of us out. It was just a matter of timing."

"No. It wasn't like that. She knew they could send only one. And that one was you."

"You're tired, Nadya." Her brother's tone was soothingly dismissive.

But Fenya came over from the bed. "No. Wait, Piotr. She's saying something important."

Nadya raised her head and let the other girl's deeply azure eyes pull from her what she thought she would never say. "I was not the one chosen for life. I was chosen for death. . . ."

"Chosen!" Fenya breathed out the word. "I know! But it works both ways. When Natasha died, I asked myself, 'Why her? Why not me?' But I was brought here by strange ways. And I know at the time, it seemed to my parents that I was given over to harsh circumstances in a foreign land while my sister married a rich man. They couldn't have known how things would turn out. As Gavril and Galina did not know."

"That's not what I'm saying though. Nothing horrible happened to me. In fact, I'm the only one that nothing horrible happened to. But I kept having to choose, and those choices linger uneasily in my heart," she confessed.

Piotr's mouth twisted in his beard. "And I felt that choice was the very thing I was denied. And when I did choose, I killed a man to save myself. I was crushed by the weight of that choice until I put it in hands strong enough to carry it. We have been born into an unlucky time—troubles and turmoil as the prophet said! We've been buffeted by so many things, in Russia and here. The only way we can survive is to shelter under the rock of Christ's love. He is our cover in the tempest."

Nadya coiled into herself. "I understand the tempest. I don't understand love."

FENYA AND PIOTR HUDDLED on the porch stoop. The two silver strands of track stretched toward the San Gabriel Mountains but were dissolved in mist long before reaching them.

"It's as though she's numb inside and can't take hold of her life," Piotr was saying. "Has she lost her faith?"

"No. I don't think so. It's sleeping inside her, but she's too blunted by everything that's happened to attend to it. But God will send her something. I know He will. When she was saying, 'I was not chosen,' my heart cried out, 'You are! You are!' I can feel the love hovering over her head waiting to crash down on her. No. Something will come to her. As it has to us."

"The boy, you mean? A brother! Who would have thought it?"

"A brother who looks at you with the eyes of your son. I couldn't believe it when I saw his eyes. How many times have I imagined those eyes in a child's face."

"Yes, you're right. God brought him to us. Nadya has been a mother to him all this time, and yet I can see she's not attached to him. Not the way . . ."

"The way I am," Fenya finished. "He fills my heart, that little one."

Piotr gently touched her face. "Dushok, my little berry, are you happy?"

"My arms—they were so empty. Now they're filled."

"And mine," Piotr said, holding her. After a moment, he joked, "And our house is filled. And our bed . . ."

Fenya laughed. "It's not so hard for me. There were eight Kostrikins in our little *izba!* I'm used to stepping over bodies on the floor at night. Besides, it keeps the house warm."

"And who will keep my bed warm with a crowd all around the house?"

Fenya's blonde eyebrows puckered over the problem. "Well, we'll have to figure something out."

Figuring something out proved easier than Fenya had imagined. When she told Phoebe about the new arrivals, her friend was eager to meet Nadya and the little boy. She visited a week later, kneeling to peer under the cowboy hat at Fenya's new brother-in-law. Semyon, always moving, ducked away from her and began his usual circuit about the room. Then he became intensely preoccupied with rearranging the canned goods in the kitchen.

But now his wanderings were punctuated with occasional lapses, and he would gravitate back to Fenya, giving her a brief touch or showing her the label from a tomato can. He sturdily eluded hugs, except at bedtime.

"He needs you," Phoebe observed. Fenya bent over the teapot to hide her flush of pleasure. Then, with Fenya translating, she asked Nadya how she liked her new home.

The girl shrugged and with a preoccupied smile said, "Very well. It's nice."

"It's hard for her," Fenya confided later. "She's home with Semyon all day while Piotr and I are at work. She's a hard worker and always has the house clean and something prepared for dinner, but there's not much joy in it for her."

"Listen, I have an idea. You'll know if it's right for you and for Nadya, but I think it is. Mother has been wanting to have a live-in maid, and I've been fighting her on it. I know that wouldn't work for you, and Evangeline would have a fit if I even asked her to consider it. And she's right—you both have husbands. But Nadya would be perfect. Her days off would be Sunday and Wednesday, so she still would have plenty of time with her own people."

"I don't know. Usually single Molokan girls don't stay away from home."

"From what you've told me, Nadya has already stayed away from home. She'll have a nice room, fairly easy work, and she'll learn English much faster."

"That's true," Fenya replied. "I learned faster because I had you and Evangeline."

"And it will be better for Semyon because you will be with him all day. To mother him."

Mother. In the past weeks since Semyon's arrival, she had held that word at bay. She was afraid to admit that it was exactly what she wanted to hear.

"But Nadya is his sister and has been the one to care for him all this time, all this way. I can't take that away from her."

"Ask her," Phoebe argued. "She doesn't feel about it as you do. And someday she'll marry. A new husband may not want a toddler in the house. She brought him all this way—to you! And to Piotr. He's your little boy, a gift from God like all little boys. He just got here in a roundabout way."

The idea of spending her days with Semyon was so appealing to Fenya that she approached her sister-in-law with guilty hesitation. But Nadya readily agreed. She turned aside to the tasks at the Wentworth house with her usual pliability.

"Maybe it will be good for her," Fenya told Piotr. "There's so much to learn there, so many strange things. Maybe it will awaken her somehow."

LIKE FENYA, Nadya spent most of her time at the Wentworths over a steaming laundry tub or at the ironing mangle. But she had her own room. The upstairs sewing room had been rearranged to accommodate a narrow maple bed and side table with a pretty fringed lamp. A long table along one wall was neatly piled with linens that needed mending, and the Singer sewing machine with its black iron pedal was situated beneath a window with dotted-swiss curtains.

The unsettling weeks of travel and the meeting with her brother had stirred up something within her. She both hungered for distraction in the odd ways of an American household and at the same time wanted to dull it with routine. In the summer evenings she cloistered herself behind the curtains and watched the neighborhood while she sat mending at the sewing machine. She liked sewing, letting her mind go blank. *It's a little like spinning. I can drift and let my thoughts flatten until they're as relentlessly empty as the steppe.*

When the mending was finished, she would take bits of discarded linens and stitch seams just to hear the soothing rhythm of her foot on the pedal and the hypnotic whir of the machine. She soon knew her other tasks well and had time in the evenings for sewing. Also, her knowledge of English increased until she understood much of what was said around her, although she kept this to herself and only spoke the foreign tongue when she absolutely had to.

A few months after she started her job, the gentle Singer purr was drowned out by a panting racket outside. A new automobile pulled right up to the house and gave out a demanding wheezing bleat. Nadya stopped her work and peered out. A shiny green door opened, and Mr. Wentworth appeared and looked hopefully up at the house. Cory and Mrs. Wentworth fluttered out in light summer dresses.

"Ours! Ours!" Cory's shrill excitement shot across the lawn. The women flew back to the house for their shawls. After a few moments of hesitation, Mr. Wentworth stuck his head in the doorway and shouted for Charlie. Nadya listened, but she heard no reply. In a minute Mr. Wentworth was outside again, striding toward the new motor car. Again his hooded eyes flanked by the bushy muttonchop whiskers scanned the house. Then he shrugged. It seemed to her that his manner was a little more sedate when his wife and daughter came out for their first evening drive. The machine was still putt-putting alongside the curb when the first bars of a ragtime tune clambered up the steps.

So he's home. She went to the top of the stairs to listen.

"Can the tune, you chump. At least have the decency to wait till they're gone." The voice was Mick Mulvaney's. Nadya wasn't sure what he was saying, but his disapproval was obvious.

"Why? He knows what I think of automobiles. They're a rich man's toy. And, mark my words, they'll do more to foster the cause of socialism in America than anything else."

"You're nuts."

"I'm right. And I'm not the only one who thinks this way. It's one of those things that panders to greed. It paints—in bold colors—the difference between the haves and have-nots in this country."

"You're not only nuts, you're a prig. What do you think a piano is if it isn't a toy for the privileged classes? How many pianos do you see at the peon colony or on Alavera Street or in the eighth ward? Wanna know what I think? I think your pater bought the automobile mainly for you—to try and reach you. But you're too smug to play his game."

Nadya went back to her Singer. She was afraid of Charlie. His contempt for the elders, his talk of haves and have-nots reminded her of Russia. Could it be that something as comical as this machine that could move without horses would cause revolution in America? The need for land or fair wages or a say in the government—these she could understand, but an automobile? Besides, the Americans already had a say in their government, didn't they?

The madcap, jangling music began again and threw off her rhythm as she worked. Agitated, she stopped and waited until she heard the front door slam. Then deep in her throat she let the rich, paced tones of a Molokan song rise from her. The words rose up from long ago, but it seemed to her that they were shaped by her own journey, and they flew out from her mouth and nestled in her heart. Something long hidden in her had leapt out to the scattered challenge of Charlie's ragged music. She felt it and wondered at it. Throwing her braid over her shoulder, she opened the door to let some of the hall light in and went back to her sewing, singing softly as she worked.

"'Why is my soul troubled. . . .
Do not despair, but live in hope,
and pray with earnestness.
Thus hope and be not troubled,
But trust in the Lord. . . .
You knew many griefs,
and can reason soundly.
Seeing terrible happenings,
You will suffer with others;
You will sympathize with sorrows,
Being pressed by grief for ill-fate. . . .'"

Something sliced across her light, and she looked up to see Charlie. His blue-gray eyes beneath a wayward dollop of blond hair were intense, but his voice was oddly muted. "What does it mean? Your song," he asked.

She drew stolid calm around her like a woolen *nabadi* of the mountains.

"I can't say it in English," she said, turning away from him. "I will ask Phoebe to write it for you."

"I want to hear you say it. Try."

She looked at him blankly. She did not move when he reached out his hand and touched her neck where her side-swung braid left it bare.

"Your skin is so white," he murmured. "And your eyes are like honey." He looked at her for a long moment. "And you are so-o-o . . . inert."

He turned, and she heard his footfall fade away down the hardwood floor of the hall. She let out the caught-breath fear in her, and, trembling, she closed the door and pushed the sewing machine in front of it. She waited until she heard the family return before she removed it. Later when she curled up to sleep, she kept seeing his gray eyes flickering, and they filled her with unease. Other gray eyes gleamed from the dark tunnel of her memory—Vaktang! She remembered how they had come and swept her along. *And these others—will they sweep me along, too?* Part of her wanted to slacken and bend to the flow, but another part of her had somehow gained strength and wanted to contend, to stand firm.

. . . You knew many griefs
and can reason soundly . . .

"Reason soundly," she affirmed to herself as she fell asleep.

WHEN NADYA TOLD FENYA about Charlie's visit, Fenya was not overly concerned, but her forehead worked with interest so that the white kerchief slipped back over her fair hair.

"They're all at odds with each other in that house," she explained. "Sometimes they get stirred up and ruffled like feisty hens—and then break out in some strange way. Like Charlie. But I don't think he means anything by it."

Fenya knit her brows in thought for a moment. "But maybe we'll tell Phoebe. We'll ask her to write down the song he asked about. That way she'll know, just in case."

"In case what?"

Fenya tweaked her kerchief into its customary peak over her forehead. "I'm not sure. We'll ask Phoebe. That family is like chaff—driven this way and that. It's hard to tell what anything means! But at heart they really love each other. They just haven't found out about it yet."

"No," Nadya mused. "Mr. Wentworth seemed so anxious to please his son, yet the son holds himself apart—with such anger!"

Phoebe was intrigued by the Molokan song. She and Fenya spent a long Saturday afternoon translating it, Phoebe writing as Fenya hunted for English words to capture the Russian thoughts.

"It's beautiful, beautiful—so powerful. Sing it again."

"Well," she remarked later, "Charlie can be a real nuisance, but this time I'll have to thank him. Otherwise I'd never have known. And when I give this song to him, I'll be sure and tell him not to frighten you with unexpected visits. What was he thinking?" She seemed as baffled by Charlie's behavior as they were. "Maybe he was feeling agitated and out of sorts. He knew that Father bought that automobile with him in mind. Now it's just sitting in the carriage house, but I've decided that I'm going to learn to drive it. It'll make my work easier; and just think, it'll be so easy to take a spin over

224

here or to Aksinia's for a visit! In fact, maybe you two would enjoy an outing some time."

Fenya bent her head and flicked an earnest look from under her kerchief. "It's not our way," she apologized.

Nadya noticed that Phoebe accepted this readily, although she herself was not sure why it was "not our way." As the American girl threw a light cardigan over her shoulders and started for the door, Nadya suddenly found herself asking, "What does *inert* mean?"

"Inert?" Phoebe removed her glasses and began polishing them on the empty sleeve of her sweater. "It means lacking the power to move or act. Sort of dull or slow. And one way of avoiding inertia is to ride with me in my automobile," she joked. Her hazel eyes sparkled.

Nadya wondered at it. But it was more than a year before she found herself riding with Phoebe—and not in any "pleasure outing."

On October 1, 1910, news spread through the city that the *Los Angeles Times* building had been bombed a little after one o'clock that morning. Mr. Wentworth returned early from his office with the news that a hundred people had been caught in the inferno. "You can still see the smoke downtown."

"Dynamite," Wentworth said. "Planted by some union arsonist. The whole building went up in a few minutes. The blast ruptured gas mains, and the lines fed the flames through the whole top three floors." He paused, squashed his cigar into a brass ashtray, and looked at his son. "People were desperate to get out. The flames kept lashing the fire equipment—ladders and such—away. The people inside were frantic, and they jumped."

One hundred people! Nadya's mind had no place to hold the enormity of it. None of the disturbances in Russia five years earlier had taken such a toll. As the afternoon wore on, they learned that twenty people had been killed and the rest badly injured or burned—some crippled for life. *That this should happen—and here!* Again she felt that something huge and nameless was set in motion and that it would carry her into dark regions. *How can I stand?*

Charlie paced nervously, pausing to push back his rebellious forelock as though he were rubbing out part of his head.

"Stop that!" Evangeline upbraided him. "You wearin' out the carpet! What's gotten into you?"

"It wasn't supposed to be like this," the young man muttered. "People killed! It doesn't make sense. I'm going to find Mick. He'll know about it."

"Well, ring him then," she advised. "You're too dithered to start traipsing all over the city."

Charlie muttered again for a while, but finally he went to the hall telephone and rang up Mick's apartment house. Nadya was dusting busily, but something in his tone stilled her hand.

When he hung up, Evangeline came out from the dining room. "What's wrong?" she demanded.

Charlie looked at her in a dull way. *Inert*, Nadya thought. *As though a frozen dart has traveled through the wire and stung his heart.*

"What's wrong, son?" the black woman repeated.

"It's Mick. Somehow—he was there, at the *Times* in the middle of the night. He was there, and the building exploded around him. He's at the hospital. I don't know what's wrong, but something's terribly, terribly wrong." He clutched at his ear as though the news had burnt it. Then he lunged for the door and was gone. Nadya and Evangeline exchanged a long glance. Then they heard the sound of a horse galloping away.

"Pray," Evangeline said. "We better pray for that boy—and I mean Charlie."

"We'll pray for both," Nadya whispered. Their hands clasped, and Evangeline began addressing her God in the beautiful, powerful way she had.

Her prayers are like singing.

Later Mrs. Wentworth and Phoebe came in. Phoebe's smile died as she took in the two women.

"Tell me . . . Something's happened, hasn't it? Where's Charlie?"

"Calm yourself, child. Charlie went to the hospital to visit Mick Mulvaney. He was at the *Times* office last night. Appears he was hurt—"

"Mick? How badly?" Phoebe's voice shook, and she began biting her lip.

"That's what Charlie went to find out," she soothed. "I expek he be back—"

"I'm not waiting for that. I'm going—"

"Phoebe! What are you saying?" Mrs. Wentworth threw her hands up. "You can't go."

"I will. I'll take the Franklin."

"You can't drive! It's after dark! I won't let you."

"I'll take Nadya. I'm going." Phoebe's face was white with determination, and her eyes flashed as Mr. Wentworth appeared holding an extinguished cigar.

"Let her go, Bernice," he said in a flat tone.

Phoebe flew at him with a hug, then rushed out the door. Nadya followed. When she glanced at Mr. Wentworth, he pointed his cigar at her and said, "Stick close to her, you hear?"

But Evangeline was staring at Phoebe with one of her star-spurting, knowing looks. "Huh!" she said.

The city looked completely different at night—both moving and oddly static like something captured under water. Nadya recognized nothing—buildings in dark chunks and street lamps dripping light and light puddled in odd places on greenish black lawns and curbed sidewalks. Phoebe's hands on the wheel bent their direction this way and that, and the machine carried them right up to the hospital with its blazing windows.

Nadya hurried to stay close to Phoebe. She hung back only when they reached a curtained alcove at the end of the men's ward. Phoebe's headlong rush stopped abruptly. A blank expression crossed her face, and Nadya realized that she had no idea what she was doing or what she would say to the tousled young man looking at her with his long-lashed eyes. Phoebe reached out her hand and took a step backward at the same time. Mick roused himself with an effort. He opened his mouth, and Nadya could see his waggish expression and quick readiness with some whimsical joke. But then he looked hard at the girl in front of him. His expression changed, and he roughly turned away.

"Are you all right?" Phoebe asked.

"No," he said truthfully. "Charlie was just here. He was going to tell you all about it. I'm a little singed here and there—that's not bad." He held out a blistered arm. "But the worst of it is that I've lost a leg."

"I'm so sorry."

"I knew you would be." He kept looking at Phoebe through

drowsy eyes. *Drinking her in*, Nadya thought. But his voice was edged with asperity. "I'm bound to be much more appealing to you now. . . . But you see, my girl, it's no use. I won't marry you." His lips quirked in a droll line, but his mouth kept hooking down in a bend too stern for drollery.

"Too late now. It'll take more than a little accident to let you off the hook," Phoebe parried.

"Nope. I'm out. Tagged at first base. Nowhere near home. I couldn't even walk up the aisle."

"No need. I can drive."

Mick raised one brow in exaggerated surprise. "You were thinking of getting married in the street?"

"If necessary."

"Miss Wentworth! I wouldn't have thought it of you! But listen, seriously, I need to say this quick—before this latest dose of morphia fogs my mind. I'm out. I won't have you marrying a . . . a cripple. You want to know why?" His sleepy eyes questioned her, and she sat down on the edge of the bed.

"I'm listening."

"Because, Phoebe, there's something in you that's made it hard for you to distinguish between being needed and being loved. When you finally marry, and in your case I do mean finally, you have to be completely, extravagantly, ridiculously loved. Not needed. Get it?"

"I've got it," Phoebe said calmly. "I've always known what it is to be needed. Now I know what it is to be loved. Thanks for the lesson."

Mick jerked to wakefulness. "Wait! What are you saying?"

"Just what you told me. No one can love me more ridiculously and extravagantly than you."

"That's not what I meant."

"That's what you've done."

"Get it out of your mind, Phoebe. It won't work. I'm not cooperating."

"We'll see." Phoebe stood gracefully and, ignoring Nadya, stooped to kiss the baffled Mick.

It took him a moment to collect himself, but when he did, Nadya saw that he wasn't at a loss for words. "Too little too late, Phoebe," he joked. "I would have enjoyed that a week ago."

Nadya gave up trying to dissolve into the wall and started laughing, but Phoebe was unperturbed. "You'll enjoy it a week from now, too," she said.

"Can't argue with that," Mick muttered as they walked away.

WHEN THEY GOT BACK to the house, Charlie was pounding a morose dissonance from the piano. Evangeline met them at the door.

"He's going to be all right," Phoebe told her.

Evangeline folded her in a tight embrace. "That's right. He'll be fine. That Mick—he don't stand a chance."

Phoebe pulled back, her mouth twisted with amazement, but Evangeline just laughed and went out to the kitchen. Charlie brushed by them, and a moment later they heard an automobile engine turning over.

Mr. Wentworth blustered in. "You! Phoebe! Who's cranking up the Franklin?"

"Charlie! It must be Charlie."

"The idiot! He can't drive!"

The older man hurried to the porch, Phoebe and Nadya crowding behind him, but the motor car was already out of sight.

Wentworth sighed heavily. "He's despondent about Mick. Blames himself somehow. Stupid thing. He can't control what the unions do. Can't reach a boy when he's keyed up like that."

None of them slept that night. Mr. Wentworth retreated to the parlor and stayed there, smoking and waiting for his son. Mrs. Wentworth, who usually refused to go near him if he had a lit cigar in his hand, came down and sat quietly beside him. Phoebe and Nadya waited in the kitchen drinking tea and assenting to Evangeline's murmured prayers. "He's gone out to wrestle with the Lord—that boy," she assured them.

At two in the morning, Charlie returned on foot. He trudged into the parlor, hollow-eyed and disheveled.

"Your motor car is out in Trabuco Canyon," he said tiredly. "It's crumpled into a ditch."

Bernice Wentworth gasped, but her husband just looked steadfastly at the young man. "It's all right, son. The car doesn't matter. You're here." He slowly approached his son, gripped his shoulder affectionately, and went upstairs with his wife. Charlie caught

Phoebe's eye, shrugged, and went to the piano. Nothing more was said, but to Nadya it seemed that something great and simple that had long been obscured had come to light and was doing its work among these wayward and complicated people.

Later she lay in bed thinking of Phoebe and Mick and how she had watched as the forsaking of love had somehow created love— right there in front of her. *Why, why?* she wondered. A young man rose before her and held out his hand; in it a word glittered like snow and stars. She marveled at it and acknowledged what lay hidden in her heart. *I am not inert.*

The dotted-swiss curtains were beginning to blush with dawn when she heard Charlie's music. The melody took shape, not in the usual skittish, rapscallion bursts, but in a measured, sonorous rank- ing of chords. It called to something deep and familiar within her. Then she heard him singing. The words were in English, but she knew their heart-meaning.

> *"'Seeing terrible happenings,*
> *You will suffer with others,*
> *You will sympathize with sorrows,*
> *Being pressed by grief for ill-fate. . . .'"*

XIII

Valley of the Nine Rivers

The curved grade that went up to Gebi was too steep for Sirakan's heavily laden cart. The back wheels locked into a spring-sodden rut and would not move. Sirakan sighed and looked about for a timber to lever the cart back onto the road. He had just come up from the spreading beech forests of the Racha—the highland along the Rioni River—where the towering boles and webbed branches nourished a thousand thousands of flame-green, heart-shaped leaves. In that forest with its ancient columns supporting newly awakened life, he had felt young and ready. But now this midday crossroads had thwarted him. His old grumblings boiled up in him. *What am I doing?*

He groaned and glanced back at the forest-fringed barley fields. The land swept out beyond the road on one side; on the other stood a ruined tower and what had once been a house. Only one wall remained now, its precisely placed window rimmed with hewn rock and looking out on nothing. But the thicket behind it jittered with flicks of movement and with the calls of many small birds.

Sirakan went up and strained with the troika of three horses, but the cart remained stubbornly mired. The dappled shaft horse snorted and shook his rangy shoulders while the trace horse rolled her eyes dismally. Sirakan glared at the slate-strewn track. Evergreens struggled for a hold on the rock at either side, and somber forests curtained any glimpse of the village. *Should I go up?* The utter impossibility of what he was about to do clouted him with such force that he sat down on a rock and began stroking his mustache.

I'm at a crossroad, Sirakan acknowledged. He was seized with agitation. *If I go to her, I leave everything behind. What everything? My people, my culture, who I am. Yet I have so little to lose. I am a wayfarer, a vagabond.* An overwhelming sense of how he had been punished and defrauded crowded his heart. He rummaged in the wagon and pulled out the packet that was all that was left of his family's personal belongings. There was the abacus that his father and his grandfather had used, an old Armenian Bible, some photographs, and a leather pouch of jewelry. He opened the Bible and leafed through the book of Jeremiah.

A wayfarer's book, he had thought as he studied it by lonely campfires.

"Stand by the ways and see and ask for the ancient paths, where the good way is, and walk in it; and you shall find rest for your souls," he read.

Ancient paths, Sirakan mused. *And where is there any way more ancient than the Armenian?* Below him the open basin of the Rioni stretched for the mountains. The river's banks were clothed in smooth-stemmed beeches mingled with the dark cones of gigantic pines. And at the base of the snow-peaks and tumbling bays of ice were birch groves and flower-meadows. Farther south he could see the waters forcing their way through a labyrinth of green ridges down to the pomegranate gardens of Kutaisi. That was a river of ancient legend, the Rioni. Called in former times the Phasis, it was the river where Jason sought the golden fleece and was ensnared by Medea. Even today the hillsmen would fasten a pelt of sheep's wool in the waters to catch the gold that washed down from the mountains.

But even these legends of the Greeks were not old to the Armenians—a people who trace their ancestry to the book of Genesis. Sirakan's grandmother insisted that the language spoken before the scrambling of tongues at the tower of Babel was Armenian. And growing up as he did in the shadow of the Ark-bearing peak of Ararat, he half believed her. His lineage paralleled every jotting of human history. He had always sensed behind him this vast antiquity—and within him the fine tracery of time. The Urartians who took arms against Assyria nine centuries before Christ and the earliest Christians of Asia Minor shared his blood. The scholars who gave Armenia its Bible four hundred years before the Slavs or Franks and the great medieval kingdom of the Bagration kings—these were his heritage and his blood. And blood cannot be severed like a limb.

"Ask for the ancient paths." Were these paths not rooted in the life-bearing conduits of his own body? How could he turn aside from them to a new way of life, to a woman alien to him and to his people? He broke out in a sweat of agitation. *Not your blood but Mine. There is a more ancient path.*

"I know, but I will tread it as an Armenian," he said. Immediately he was filled with a sense of the sterile impertinence of his words. Into his mind came a sureness that there was a kindred who were born out of blood and anguish into a cherished unity. And that this unity sprang up the instant man's sin called forth the intent of sacrifice in the mind of God. *An ancient, ancient way.* And he knew—surely, he knew it—that both he and Irina were of this kindred.

A mob of ragged Mingrelian peasants came by on their way north. *More wayfarers,* Sirakan thought. He pulled four bolts of colored calico from his wagon and offered it to them. A grizzled man wearing the medal of a village elder stepped up and fingered the cloth suspiciously, as though he were paying a great price for it. Then his leathery lips parted in a smile, and he bowed low, setting off a commotion of whispering and nudging and bowing. The peasants took his wares and scrambled up the trail with backward glances. Sirakan folded his arms and leaned his shoulders against the wall with the empty window, waiting.

Soon a priest dressed in the flowing robes of the Georgian Orthodox came toiling up in the midday heat. Sirakan bowed and offered him a tin of fine tea from Sochi and a jar of honey. The priest blessed him and went up to Gebi. Later an old woman came huffing up, flanked by two little girls. She flashed a spry, roguish look at him from under a veiled headdress that looked like a heap of washing. He gave her two jars of raspberry jam and a bolt of silk in the same fruity red. Laughing with delight, she held the vivid cloth up to the girls' faces.

"For our wedding," explained the eldest in broken Russian.

By the time the ruined wall had thrown its shadow with the window shape to the east, Sirakan's cart was lighter. But although he heaved with all his might, he still couldn't break it free of the mud. He wiped the sweat from his eyes and squinted up to see the huge shape of a blond-bearded man wearing a sheepskin coat, wool-side-out. The giant bared his deep yellow teeth and set his shoulder to the back of the cart. The wheels lurched and loosed, and the horses trotted free so quickly that Sirakan had to rein them in.

His helper ambled up. Sirakan noted that there was something stealthy, hard to interpret, in the man's light blue eyes and in his sly, sure-footed gait. Sirakan ducked beneath the shaft horse's head and gathered tins of caviar, tea, and kerosene, and a box of matches and gave them to his rescuer. The goods were quickly swallowed by the clumsy sheepskin, but the stranger scanned the clutter inside the wagon. His big hand with its rough calluses reached out and fingered the abacus; his brows raised a little, and the abacus disappeared into his sleeve.

"This I will take," he said, "for a souvenir."

Sirakan started to protest, then stopped. "Take it," he enjoined. "Take it and welcome. I'm no longer counting."

He exchanged a nod with the two peasants who had stopped to stare, grabbed his last bolt of cotton, and gave it to them. The older of the two stretched his mouth out in bewilderment, showing black, rotted teeth.

"What are you doing?" gibed a voice from behind him. Sirakan found himself smiling broadly even before he turned. He knew that voice!

"Lightening my load," he said. His eyes swept up and down the woman who had caused all the trouble and travel and load-lightening. Irina had the same abrupt grace and supple strength to her stride. Her hair was bound up in a vivid kerchief, and her russet skirt flared about her heelless blue boots. Her mouth twitched with a touch of humor and a touch of something softer, more yielding. Her flashing, granite-flecked eyes met his so peacefully and candidly that all his petty doubts drained away. He felt his face contort with a chagrined gladness.

"And where do you come from?" he asked.

"Nowhere. I've walked this way every day since the first thaw."

To look for me. He knew it, surely.

"To look for you," she echoed boldly, seeing his thought. "And to get away. Noe is there."

Sirakan glanced away through the stone-rimmed window. A flock of small birds rose from the thicket and swept in swift tumult to a wayside pine.

"Have you talked to him?" he asked, his face still averted.

"I have."

The birds could not settle, but sprang away from the pine tree in rash flight.

"I have," she repeated, and her face darkened with trouble. "What do I owe him? It's as though he seeks some kind of solace in me, and I—I keep denying him. And yet I feel responsible—as though this were a hurt inflicted by my hand." She paused, and Sirakan was silent. How deep were the bonds between Irina and Noe? He could not say. The thrust and parry of rational thought were swallowed up in his own heart's cry.

Irina turned her dark, troubled eyes on him and pulled his gaze away from the wheeling birds. "And yet Nina says that he cannot take solace of me, but only of God. And she says that I am a new creature." A little half-mocking smile hovered about her lips—as though she were waiting for him to deny it. "In spite of all, I am a new being, and all the old things have scattered like ash."

He put his hand to her face just below the lovely cheekbone. "You are. You are new," he said, his voice muffled with emotion. She flung at him the same courageous, challenging look, but it too was bent on something new. Sirakan folded his arms abruptly. They were aching with the strain of the day and with the need to reach out and hold her as he had on that first day when he had found her, white and still. But now she was lithe and strong with a healthy color behind her golden skin. She had no need of him.

"He wants to marry," she was saying, "now that I, that I will not have it another way. Once that would have meant everything to me, but now the thought of it fills me with weariness. Like going back to an old scratched-out sum that's been done over and over, and the page is too marred to hold meaning anymore."

Sirakan bound his arms on his chest more tightly. "What does hold meaning?" he forced out.

"A new life," she answered with a frank look. "And a marriage where the union is of the spirit as well as of the body. But maybe I've forfeited this in my old days of wandering. Why are you holding yourself like that?"

"Because if I let go for an instant . . ." He shrugged, and his arms reached for her. "This." He held her tightly and immediately was suffused in an odd combination of heart-pounding excitement and inexplicable peace. After a while she bent back to look at him. He could see the ridges on the white arc of her throat and then the wide wonder in her eyes.

"If you go with me, it will mean a great severing, a cutting off," he said. "Your people cannot accept me; mine will not accept you."

He felt her shoulders lift and fall in a shrug. "I have little to lose. You, more."

"We will have to go to a new place. A place where few will speak our language. And those who do will shun us."

"I've been shunned before."

"And there will be no security. No way of knowing how or whether we'll survive."

"There is no security anywhere. Except with God. Are you trying to talk me out of it before I've even agreed?" she flared.

"Haven't you? Agreed?"

"Yes."

"Well, then. I love you, Irina. I love you."

"I love you, too." She dipped her head in one of her rare spurts of shyness. Then she buried her face in his shoulder. "I love you, I love you, I love you." Her voice was muted in his flesh and the stuff of his clothing.

"Then come," he said and helped her onto the cart.

The freed wheels rolled merrily, chuckling and creaking with every jolt as they followed the track to Gebi. They came to the rim of a dell and looked down on the house where Nina and Grigol were staying. It was of fitted stone, in the Georgian fashion, with a wooden balcony much newer than the house. In the old days, Sirakan knew, few of the mountain villages had any wood on barns or houses because of the fear of enemy tribesmen and sudden destruction by fire. But here the balcony must have been built about the same time the walnut tree in front of the house was planted. For the balcony was much weathered, and the tree reached to span the house with its arced branches and drooping clusters of greenish flowers. But the southwest side of the house was gay with crocuses and the clumps of thyme, marjoram, and tarragon that Nina used in her cooking.

"He's gone," Irina breathed with relief. "Noe's horse isn't here."

They went in to a warm welcome, and Nina set a meal before them: *chakhokbili*—a tender dish of pheasant stewed in tomato and fragrant with coriander—and browned portions of the goat cheese pie called *khachapuri*. Sirakan saw that his half sister was as radiant as ever and noticed that her figure was rounded with pregnancy.

Both Nina and Grigol were eager to hear of their plans. Sirakan kept chucking and shaking his head when he saw that they had thought of some of his difficulties before he himself had. "What! You know more about my business than I do. I didn't know until last week that I'd marry."

"We knew," Nina said. "I could see it even in Tiflis! But it's good that you are emigrating. This will not be easy news for Noe to hear."

Irina's face clouded, and Sirakan exchanged an uneasy glance with Grigol. "Well," he told them, "we'll set out for Batumi tomorrow. I'd hoped we would travel as man and wife. But who would marry us?"

Grigol smiled at their dilemma. "We were similarly forestalled," he said. "How well I remember the grim impatience I felt! But a way was provided for us. When neither of your traditions can meet the need, you'll have to seek a third way. Why not go to Vorontsovka? I've heard there is a Baptist pastor there. If he knows of your commitment, I'm sure he'll marry you."

Sirakan recoiled inwardly. A Baptist marriage? For an Armenian? But a glance at Irina's happy face scattered his reservations. Why not? In these past few years, Baptist meeting houses had sprung up all over the Caucasus. *What is it they call it? A revival. Well, we have been revived.* And he was pierced by a poignant happiness every time he looked at the beautiful, angular face of his ransomed bride.

In the evening as they packed their few possessions, Irina unsheathed the silver dagger and showed it to him.

"Remember?" she asked, her voice was swollen with memory. She traced the cunning workmanship on the pommel. "So much of shame is written here, yet Loma used this to cut us free that night. Remember it?"

He took it from her and drew her into his arms. "Put it aside. We've come far since then."

Later she gave the *kinjal* to Grigol's son. "For you, Loma. Once you said it had stories on it, and now it has one more!"

The boy took it from her with a glance at Grigol. "It was my grandfather's and his father's before that. But I'll remember the stories."

Sirakan and Irina went out to the garden. It was rimmed with fruit trees foaming with bloom. Moon-blue light splashed through the lace-hung branches and fell precisely on a pale flower or a tangle of herbs as if to say, "This! And this!" Sirakan was drenched in the night-cooled fragrances. They settled into his soul and stirred up deep things lying there, things from his childhood and the earliest days of his young manhood. He took Irina's hand, and they walked in the dark of the trees, speaking quietly of their plans. They would not go to Los Angeles but to a smaller city in a valley north of the city. Many Armenians had settled there. "Though we won't be a part of that community," he warned Irina. "Yet it may be easier to find our way among people who at least speak the same language."

"And what kind of people live there?" she asked.

"Farm folk, I think. They grow grapes and nut trees and cotton."

"Like Armenia." She smiled.

"Well, the land is lower, from what I understand. But as Armenia has its beautiful rivers—the Tigris, the Araxes, the Pison, and the Euphrates—this land is watered by nine smaller rivers fed by the mountains to the east. And where there are good crops, there are farmers with money who need supplies." And he began speaking of practical matters. But the more he spoke, the more it seemed to him that these things were unimportant and that the vagrant spangles of light playing across Irina's face and shoulders were more significant.

A sliver of a smile quirked about her lips as his talk grew more and more distracted. Finally she tugged at his arm and said, "Come, let's forget all that. And go back to the garden."

FOR NADYA, life in Los Angeles had flattened out into a dull routine. She shouldered her tasks, eluding Charlie Wentworth's stealthy glances and the occasional advances of Molokan young men. But these were few. There were rumors in the church that the babe she brought from Russia was her own and that she had been ruined in those terrible days of revolution. She shrugged at these idle tales, yet she was aware that Piotr was greatly disturbed by them. He did not see that a great inner work was going on within her. "You are of sound mind," she reminded herself every day. She allowed memories that had once been unspeakable to rise within her, and she grasped them with firmness and strength and took them to the throne of grace. The secret wrestlings and hidden bitterness were overpowered when she acknowledged the simple things of her faith: that God loved her and intended good for her, that her parents had not forfeited her but had been overtaken by things too great for them.

Meanwhile, their fortunes had improved. Piotr was working steadily for Ivan Bogdanoff. Ivan's attempt to sell fruit and vegetables from his wagon had failed. He could not compete with the quick, enterprising Chinese vendors. But he had stumbled on a business hauling rubbish—first for the railway, then for private citizens and businesses. Now he had more work than he could handle, and he and Piotr took turns as trash carters, making the run from the town to the dump. As a result, the Voloshins were able to save enough that Piotr began talking of getting a bigger place for them. "Then you'll be able to stay with us always, Nadya. It will be a happier life for you maybe."

But in the early autumn, news that came from Russia changed their plans. Mikhail Voloshin's wife, Marfa, had died. Crushed by her losses during the 1905 uprising, she had never regained health.

"My needs are simple, my life almost over," Mikhail wrote. "Therefore, I am sending to you the inheritance I had saved for my sons. Use it well, Piotr, for you know what it cost me, and you are the last Voloshin son to survive. Set your roots deeply in this place of refuge that God has brought you to. Care for your sister, for she, too, is broken and feebleminded."

Piotr stumbled over the words, and Fenya cast a quick glance at her sister-in-law. Nadya averted her eyes, but Fenya knew! Then she stole a look at her brother. He was stunned, still staring at Mikhail's letter. She saw the old land-hunger in his eyes—the longing that he had put aside as he went out every day to haul rubbish for the folk of Los Angeles. "We can buy land," he whispered, still holding the letter as if afraid it would dissolve in his fingers. As Nadya's eyes misted, it did look as though it were melting away.

"THE LAST TIME I saw these mountains," Piotr told Ilya Valoff, "Makar and I were going out to dig the Elizabeth Tunnel. Look! From here, or near here, I looked down into this valley, and it seemed impossible. Now . . ."

"God has provided." Ilya leaned toward the train window, and the floss of his beard seemed to draw in the fuzzy mist that settled between the broad, brown-turfed roots of the Tehachapi Mountains. They were traveling to Fresno and from there to the town of Kerman.

Piotr glanced about eagerly. It was the first time he had made the journey across the Tehachapis into the valley that had so lived in his memory. Ilya, however, had been north before. Many Molokan families had scraped up enough cash from their city jobs to buy land in the San Joaquin Valley, and Russian settlements were beginning in the dusty, little towns—Kerman, Shafter, Porterville. Ilya, who had been in California longer than just about anyone, would accompany prospective buyers to help them choose their acreage and deal with the American land agents. "The land is dry but full of sharks," he joked nudging Piotr.

The train followed its slick rails down past Bakersfield. The fog pushed in around the station house and pressed down on the fields, but Piotr and Ilya studied the half-obscured countryside as though they planned to buy up half the state. Sometimes the frail skeletons of railway trestles would rise from the mist, and Ilya would peer down at the water. "Kern—that must be the Kern River. . . . Now that's the Kings River, I'm sure of it."

Piotr could see nothing but milk-white fog. By the time they reached Kerman, the fog was beginning to lift, and they could make out an occasional black-limbed oak tree etched against a shorn field.

"Don't sit under the oaks," Ilya warned. "They drop branches like a moulting hen drops feathers. The Indians of the area claim that the spirits of the dead have taken up residence in the trees and that they throw branches about as a punishment to the living. Restless spirits or not, it's no place for a picnic."

They spent the night with a Molokan family in Kerman. The

next day the farmer harnessed his team and took Piotr and Ilya out to look at properties.

"Now," Ilya confided as they drove several miles west of the town, "this won't look like much. It's been neglected, but it's a great buy." They came to a bare field whose furrows pulled Piotr's eyes right up to the doorstep of a green board bungalow. Toward the north stretched rows of wildly disheveled vines, their whiplike canes lashing at the white blot of the sun. Weeds and curled brown leaves cluttered the spaces between the vines. But Piotr could see that these were strong bearing vines that with care would yield a good crop. His arms ached to lavish that care.

"Sixty acres," Ilya was saying. "And with water. Here's the ditch."

They walked to the edge of the field where the irrigation channel cut through the soil. The astute old man looked sharply at Piotr. "I see your hands are already curled around the plow. No need to talk you into it."

Piotr nodded silently, unable to speak. Ilya spoke for him. "The dry years are over, son." His keen blue eyes above the snowy fanfare of beard swept out across the land, weighing the promise of soil and water. "Yes, praise be to God," he murmured. "'He changes a wilderness into a pool of water, and a dry land into springs of water; and there He makes the hungry to dwell so that they may establish an inhabited city, and sow fields, and plant vineyards, and gather a fruitful harvest.'"

"Tomorrow," Piotr said, "I will send for Fenya, and my sister and brother. And we will begin." The harvest of the next year and all the years after that already sprouted in his mind.

WITHOUT REGRET NADYA STEPPED AWAY from Los Angeles and onto the platform to wait for the train that would take her away. A flickering expectation quivered within her. They shouldered their few bundles and boarded. Fenya held Semyon's furiously waving little form, and waving just as furiously were Ilya Valoff and Aksinia and Ivan and their twins. But Nadya found a seat by a eastward window so that she could watch the curving line of cars in front plunge into the golden mountains. The land folded back in front of her in brown, featureless waves. The dark blot of a tunnel's mouth sprang out from the tawny hills and swallowed the train; then they came out again into the bright fall day.

In the evening they pulled into Bakersfield and were told that they would have to change trains to go farther north. Nadya stood outside the station house. The brisk, erratic wind sometimes smelled of smoke and sometimes of alfalfa. Brass and glass railway lanterns winked at her from passing cabooses. Dark, smothering freights lumbered by; then she would see them again—the winking flicks of light. They stirred up something in her mind—that one last memory she had fought off. She felt it piercing her through and through. Stone walls and a webbed loom and herself struggling within the dark membrane of a dream—and Vaktang with his lanterns . . .

In those days her blood had been black and sluggish with shock, but now she felt the clear, red coursings throughout her body. She was shaken by an unabashed longing for the slender Georgian youth with his open hand and clumsy kindness and swift, intelligent glance.

Fenya called to her, and she was caught up in the press of passengers. They came finally into Fresno where they spent the remainder of the night at the train station. A morning train took them out to Kerman where Piotr waited for them with a wagon. Nadya looked about eagerly as they left the tiny station. Cultivated lands stretched out on either side. Then they came to a bleak landscape of winter-ready vineyards, their pruned stumps looking like amputated limbs.

"These are our own fields," said Piotr.

Part of the land lay fallow, yellow with grasses and dotted with oak trees. The rest was in mature vines, blunt stumps with a few canes splayed against the bare ground. On the south end of the property was the bungalow, fairly new. They went in and set down their bundles. The house had only two rooms and a tiny alcove kitchen, but it was almost twice as big as the shack in Los Angeles.

"We'll build a lean-to shed and use it as an extra bedroom, Nadya." Piotr seemed eager to make her feel that the place was her home, too. "And here," he indicated the blank end wall, "will be our hearth." Semyon came over and peered expectantly at the empty space.

Fenya laughed. "Nothing there now, little berry, but you won't wait long!"

She was right. Within two months Piotr had built the attached shed and constructed a stone fireplace with a zigzag chimney to capture more of the heat—like the ones in the old country. The American who delivered their lumber and stakes for the new vines shook his head. He was sure it was a mistake. Nadya and Fenya were busy setting up house and planting winter vegetables in the kitchen garden. They were glad for the hearth. The winter was not cold, but many days were heavy with dense fog. It was not like the fleeting vapors of the mountains or the straying mists of Tiflis, but a white smother wet enough to remind Nadya that it was, indeed, cloud come to earth.

On one of these days, she and Fenya were harvesting cabbages, working hurriedly because they were soaked to the skin. Semyon was stumping along after his foster mother, clutching an armful of the ice-green heads. Nadya had only to move a pace, and the two of them were swallowed up in fog. She could hear Fenya chiding her son for being out in the cold and Semyon's voice, unusually deep for a child, stubbornly refusing to go in. Still, she felt cut off and alone on her haze-rimmed circle of ground. *A soft, comfortable wadding—like snow or wool. But I don't want it anymore. I am not inert, and I will act!* Suddenly she called out to her sister-in-law. "Fenya!"

"What?"

"I want to ask you. Will you write a letter for me?"

"Of course! But who to?"

"Someone in Georgia—a friend who helped me."

"But, Nadya, I can only write in English. That wouldn't help much. Why don't you ask Piotr?"

Nadya bent her burning face, glad for the concealing fog. "I don't want to trouble him," she muttered.

But later in the kitchen Fenya gave her a searching look. "Better ask him," she said.

Piotr's face stiffened when Nadya asked him about the letter. "A tribesman? Of course, it's good to offer thanks. But why now? It might look odd. He may think things that you don't intend."

"Maybe I do intend them," Nadya said quietly.

Piotr's manner became chilly. "Maybe I've been remiss in thinking of your future, sister. There are many young Molokans here who would be glad for a wife."

"They haven't spoken."

"But it's not for you to speak. Not to an outsider. A *nynash!*" But his own speaking of the word seemed to throw him into a brooding silence. Later he softened toward her, but no further word was spoken of any letter to Transcaucasia.

On another winter day when the little house was swaddled with fog, Piotr came in and swept Semyon up in a big embrace. Fenya's face, pink and wreathed with smiles, appeared behind him. "So, Semyon! You're to have a little brother. Or sister!" Nadya joined them in their joy. This was unexpected good news. The Molokan midwife had told Fenya that she was "ruptured," an evil result of allowing the American doctor to cut her so freely.

"God has given us a place to set down roots, and now the fruit is coming." Fenya laughed gleefully.

Nadya watched as her sister-in-law swelled into lush womanhood and grew more beautiful than she had ever seen her. Her irregular features took on a lilting, generous cast, and her azure eyes gleamed with happiness. *Good*, thought Nadya. *Good*. She felt that something significant had been resolved and that now she was free.

On the sunny days she stood in the fields and looked at the coast ranges blue and indistinct in the distance. On the foggy days she stood in her fuzzy, earth-bound circle, and for some reason she was filled with secret hope. In the evenings she took out stray pieces of linen given her by the Wentworths and embroidered elaborate white-on-white patterns on blouses and aprons. Fenya handled the fine work with one of her rough hands. "It's exquisite. But why always white—the color of mourning?"

"It's what I have," Nadya replied. But on Sunday she wore her embroidered apron to one of the Molokan meetings in Kerman, and the women exclaimed over it and gave her orders for their white burial garments. Nadya spent her evenings stitching snow-white flowers onto the garments of death.

After *Paska*, Fenya was huge with child and unable to go to the town, but Piotr and Nadya planned a trip into Fresno with Semyon. Piotr wanted to get some stakes for the new vines he was setting out in the eastern ten acres, plus he was buying some linoleum for the tiny kitchen as a surprise for his wife.

"Get me some *halva*," Fenya begged as she waved them off. "I've been longing for some."

The vines that had looked so dead and hopeless only a month ago were now covered with brilliant green leaves, big as hands and with a sunny, translucent look to them.

In Fresno they made their purchases, and Nadya bought a length of brown cotton figured with peach-colored roses and green foliage.

"Don't forget Fenya's *halva*," she reminded her brother. There were plenty of Armenians in Fresno, and she guessed that it shouldn't be hard to find the Turkish treat of sesame seeds and honey. They found a shop under a sagging yellow awning that threw shade on two Armenian farmers sitting outside sipping Turkish coffee.

"Makes me think of Tiflis." Piotr smiled. But Nadya saw his face go rigid when they went into the shop. She looked around to see why, but the shop seemed ordinary enough. In fact, it seemed more like a shop from their native village than anything she had seen so far. Two walls were hung with vivid rugs from Azerbaijan; the shelves were stocked with rounds of *lavash*, a tray of *baklava*, tins of tea from Sochi, and small packets of rich coffee. A glass display case held a small collection of Armenian items—a silver cross, some filigreed demitasses. A dark-haired woman presided over this. But her face, too, changed when she caught sight of Piotr.

"Piotr Voloshin!"

Nadya turned to stare at the woman. She was dressed like an American with a pleated shirtwaist tucked into a burgundy skirt that hugged her slim hips. Piotr moved toward her, choking on whatever he had in mind to say. He was interrupted when a burly man came in from the back room. Sirakan Abajarian! Nadya was stunned. Piotr looked like he had been stung; then his face broke into a huge smile; his curly brown beard bristled with it.

"So, friend," Sirakan said calmly. "I hardly recognized you in that thicket of a beard. So you're a married man."

"Yes! Yes!" Piotr was laughing with joy. "To Fenya Kostrikin! And our child is on its way!"

Nadya began laughing, too. Sirakan was leaning over his counter with his swarthy arms and bristling his mustache just as he had done in the village store. She felt that she was a plump little girl again, slipping in to buy gingerbread. And, in fact, Sirakan bent over to grin at Semyon and offer him a piece of marzipan. "So," he said straightening up, "you're not the only one to settle down and marry! You know my wife, Irina?" Nadya saw that Piotr recognized this Irina, and he was obviously baffled.

"Yes," said the beauty behind the counter, "Piotr and I have been through much together!"

"Well, our road has taken some strange turnings." The Armenian looked at his wife, and Nadya saw that his usual businesslike expression was gone. How Sirakan had changed! His thick eyebrows still swept in the same dark arc, and he still had that weighty, deliberate way of stroking his lavish mustache. But the dark eyes with all their light and depth showed that they had known joy as well as sadness, and a smile kept tugging at his mouth.

"I see that the change has done you good, Sirakan," Piotr was saying. "But how? How did this all come about? I can't hide the fact that I'm dazed with it!"

Irina's gaze caressed her husband. "You explain," she joked. "It's too much for me!"

Sirakan sighed in his old morose way, but his expression was so far from morose that they all laughed again. "Well, this will be a long meeting. Better heat up the samovar."

Listening, Nadya was stuck by the fact that a single strand threaded through each of their stories. Each one had wanted something, willed it for themselves, lost it, and then with a broken spirit had reached out to receive something completely different, something much greater.

Sirakan saw it, too. "There's an old folk saying: 'Don't wish for something too strongly, or the weight of it may turn and crush you.'"

Nadya said little, but she felt herself swept up into Piotr's long journey, Irina's inner contest with her unreasoning heart, Sirakan's confrontation with the barrenness in his own soul. In every case there was an agonizing relinquishment, then an unforeseen gift. *What will mine be?* Nadya felt that Piotr's jagged descriptions, Irina's hoarse confessions, Sirakan's rumbling tale had scoured her to a raw sensitivity of body and soul.

"The afternoon is far gone," Piotr said noticing with a jerk. "Fenya will be beside herself with worry."

"You know the road back," Sirakan reminded them. "One more thing, Nadya. You should know that you had a visitor after you left the village. A young Svanetian came looking for you. He was bitterly disappointed to find you gone."

Nadya could hear the blood roaring in her ears, and she could hear the calmness in Piotr's voice. "Is this the young man who helped Nadya and Semyon after the uprisings?"

"Yes. That's the one. Vaktang Rukhadze, it was. He was not someone easy to forget." Sirakan was smiling at the memory. "But you, Nadya, maybe you'll get a reminder soon enough. I think he was going to work in Kutaisi, but his intention was to find his way here. He seemed determined. As cockily determined as anyone I've ever seen!" Then he turned his dark eyes on Piotr. "And you, friend, don't forget what you've been taught!"

Piotr was quiet and thoughtful on the way home; occasionally, he'd snap the reins and mutter to himself. When they came to the outskirts of Kerman, he turned to her. "This will be news to Fenya! But, listen, maybe we should write that letter. To Kutaisi, he said?"

"He may be gone from there."

"We'll try anyway."

They mailed the letter the next time they came to town, but Sirakan was pessimistic. "These letters go astray more often than not. When I stopped at a village along the Mamison Road, I had gone to the starosta's house, and he proudly showed me his 'archives'—piles of letters, mostly written in Russian, that he'd saved for years! He thought he was doing his duty by hoarding them year after year."

But as they were leaving, he said to Nadya, "This Rukhadze is one young man who doesn't need a letter. If there's a way, he'll find it."

If . . . Nadya reminded herself as the hot summer days drew out.

In August Fenya's baby was born—a tiny girl who quickly threw off the wizened newborn look and turned into a healthy little creature with red and white coloring and a whitish fuzz all over her round head. From the first, Semyon, now almost six, was wildly protective of her. He would stand over her bassinet admonishing her in Russian and with a smattering of the English he had picked up in school. And, strangely, Nadya noticed that a few stray Georgian words crept into his cradle-side monologues. They must have stuck in his memory from those days in Svanetia. The little girl, Natasha, would stare back at him with the wondering look she gave everybody. This look always seemed to fill Semyon with a chagrined gentleness, and he would softly stroke her rosy cheeks or the backs of her plump hands.

The weather, always a matter of great concern in the valley, held beautifully with long, hot days that sweetened the grapes and gave no sign of the rain that could destroy a crop. When harvest time came, the whole valley filled with the unforgettable, syrupy smell of drying raisins.

About this time bands of migrant laborers appeared in the valley—hard-bitten vagabonds who would hire themselves out by the day. Most of these men were also immigrants—Germans, Swedes, and Irish—but the Molokans would have none of them. Most of the Kerman farmers relied on family members who would travel from Los Angeles to help with the crops.

The Voloshins already had their crop spread out on the ground to dry. Fenya and Nadya were turning over the drying grapes with rakes while Piotr went off to town to rent horses and a trailer to pick up the sweat boxes. Semyon stalked among the drooping vine leaves, and baby Natasha lay in the wheelbarrow inspecting a grape with cross-eyed diligence. Fenya was working quickly, with occasional nervous glances at her baby. She moved her shoulders uncomfortably; Nadya knew that her engorged breasts were painful and that she was hurrying to do as much as she could before Natasha began squealing for her lunch.

"*Chesshi yeddish, dalili bodish,*" Nadya chided her sister-in-law. "Go a little slower; you'll go farther. Don't tire yourself; take a rest. I can finish." And she emptied a last paper of raisins into one of the sweat boxes and dragged it to the edge of the field.

Fenya shook her head. "You're so strong, Nadya. I couldn't budge that! You know what?" She shaded her eyes with a hand and looked at her sister-in-law intently. "You remind me of *spacitilniya repka*. You somehow survive and stay strong in spite of—in spite of everything."

Spacitilniya repka! Savior turnip. Nadya remembered the wild turnip so valued by the peasants because it would grow in times of drought and famine, providing strength and sustenance when there was nothing else. *Well, I've come through. God be praised,* Nadya thought.

Then she saw her sister-in-law's blue eyes cloud with concern.

Semyon, always vigilant, crawled out from under a vine branch and stood beside them. His suspicious, far-sighted eyes were fixed on a group of men coming down the road. "Bad guys," he exclaimed in English. "Blam, blam!"

Fenya laughed. "What are they teaching him?" But Nadya heard the nervousness in her voice, for these men were vagabonds, of ill-repute, and they were two women alone.

Every inch of Semyon's sturdy frame wound up to a fierce watchfulness. Then he muttered something in Georgian. His voice was so deep and rough for a little boy! But Nadya knew she had heard those words before, endearing words whispered to a lonely toddler by a Svanetian woman—all fire and smoke—Esma! But why?

Nadya dropped to the sand beside her little brother, searching his face. The sun was beating on her like a brazen drummer, and the sweat crawled along her temples and between her breasts. The air was heavy with a sweet, fruity aroma. She tasted the salt of her labor on her lips. Then she saw Semyon's face flame with recognition. She followed his gaze. There among the trudging migrants was one whose back was not bent. Road dust and heat-haze couldn't disguise that cocky, swaggering step, the slim elasticity of his whole body.

Semyon tore away from her and started running, his shadow bobbing behind him in the heat-baked furrows. But Nadya quickly overtook him, with the wind of her running laving a coolness on her drenched face and smock. The dark, slender figure had broken away from the stooping group of laborers. On either side of her stacked boxes of raisins exhaled their pungent fruitfulness. The fruitfulness of the valley and the latent power of the dry years pushed her from behind, and she ran until her eyes told her what her heart had already guessed. It was Vaktang!

Glossary

bashlik—A hooded headdress.

basturma—Air-dried beef served in thin slices.

chaikana—Tea house.

chakhokbili—Pheasant or chicken stewed with tomato, vegetables, onion, and coriander.

churchkhela—A sweet made from boiled grape skins and walnuts.

droshky—Low, open four-wheeled Russian carriage with a long, narrow bench that passengers straddle.

druzhko—Best man in a Molokan wedding.

dzedha—Grandfather.

halva—Turkish sweet made of a paste of ground sesame seeds and nuts mixed with honey.

izba—Traditional Russian peasant house; usually constructed of wood, it consisted of one main room with a clay stove in the corner opposite the front door.

kasha—Porridge of cracked buckwheat, wheat, or barley, sometimes served with meat.

kasinka—Women's kerchief, usually trimmed with lace.

khachapuri—Goat cheese pie.

kintos—Petty tradesmen of Georgia.

kizyak—Animal dung used for fuel.

kosovorotka—A side-opening peasant shirt with an upright collar. It was usually worn long over trousers and tied with a rope or sash.

kvas—A mildly fermented, often fruit-flavored beverage made from rye or barley.

lapsha—Noodles, usually served in soup.

lavash—Georgian or Armenian flatbread.

mir—Literally means "world"; in tsarist Russia, the village community of peasant farmers.

muzhik—a peasant in tsarist Russia.

nabadi—Traditional mountain woolen cape.

nachinki—Fruit-filled pastry.

nash—Literally means "ours"; one of our own people.

nynash—Literally means "not ours"; not one of our own people.

papachka—Tall Georgian cap made of lamb's wool.

Paska—Passover; the week before Easter.

penovani—Type of goat cheese pie made of many thin layers of dough.

pilaw—Rice pilaf, usually prepared with mutton and seasonings.

piroshka—Bread pastry stuffed with meat or cabbage. Plural, piroshkiya.

pridanoe—A bride's marriage portion consisting largely of clothes, bedding, and draperies.

smetana—Sour cream.

tcherkeska—Skirted Georgian coat, fitted at the waist and with special breast pockets designed to hold rifle cartridges.

verst—.66 mile (approximately one kilometer).

zemstvo—Prerevolutionary government council responsible for educational, medical, and farm advisory needs.